P.S

A Lover

by

Patricia

Lucas White

LionHearted Publishing, Inc.
Zephyr Cove, NV, USA

This book is a work of fiction. Names, characters, places and incidents are products of the author's imagination or are used fictitiously. Any resemblance to actual events or locales or persons, living or dead, is entirely coincidental.

LionHearted Publishing, Inc.
P.O. Box 618
Zephyr Cove, NV 89448-0618
888-546-6478 Phone/Fax

admin@LionHearted.com
http://www.LionHearted.com

Copyright © 2000 by Patricia Lucas White

All rights reserved. No part of this book may be reproduced or transmitted in any form or by any means, electronic or mechanical, including photocopying, recording, or by any information storage and retrieval system, without permission in writing from the publisher. For information contact LionHearted Publishing, Inc.

ISBN 1-57343-004-8

Printed in the U.S.A.

For Mary Jo Hannah,
who is not Mary Alice Cassidy Bates
but is a Forever Friend

Prologue

♥   ♥   ♥

"Zounds! Gadzooks! And a wicker basket scupper-full of scummy balderdash!"

Silly as they sound, archaic oaths, a melodramatic scream or two, or even a bit of hair-tearing and woe-is-me-ing seem singularly appropriate right now. Far more appropriate than the rattle of typewriter keys—a manual, of course: madwomen aren't allowed to have electrical cords, or belts, or shoelaces. Almost too appropriate now that I'm embroiled, up to my naked earlobes, in what has to be the ultimate in clichés.

It still doesn't seem quite possible.

But, nevertheless, here I am. Me, Elizabeth Gilmartin, ersatz writer, cast in the role of hapless-heroine-waiting-to-be-ravished; a role straight out of Poe, or perhaps one of the other more erotic and terribly decadent Romantics. Incarcerated in a madhouse, at her husband's behest, her protests of sanity ignored; the heroine, chained and weeping, is totally at the mercy of her cruel and sex-mad attendants.

And then, just when she thinks she has plumbed the depths, she is forced, by her mild-mannered but sadistic doctor, to submit (horror of horrors) mind, memory, and slim white fingers, to participate in a hackneyed plot device.

And so it is that I, darling of the talkshow circuits, critically acclaimed author of sophisticated sexual romps, have fallen to this. Now I am that empty-eyed lunatic, crouching at my poorly lit table, authoring this sad tale of my plunge into murky madness.

A tale to be embellished, or so I'd guess, with lurid accounts of lecherous orderlies, incestuous fantasies, and bed-crawling fellow inmates. And, in the end, if this tale follows the formula, will be my complete cure by my devoted doctor and a heart-rending reunion with my estranged, but still adoring, husband.

I have just been chided, in warm-honey tones, but chided nevertheless, for my unseemly lapse into levity. My keeper, Nurse Chatsworth, smelling of dawn-picked rectitude and eternal morality, slipped up behind me and read what I had typed.

She was not amused.

It seems I have approached the writing of my "Life-Notes" with not only what she termed "an improper attitude," but also with a universe of misinformation oozing from the tips of my fingers. However, Miss Chatsworth, armored against the vileness of recalcitrant patients by a full suit of shining humorlessness, decorated here and there with swaths of doctor-worship, was sure I could not only mend my ways, but would, just as soon as she pointed out my flaws and fallacies.

"Harmony House," she said, looking at me with eyes of deep, reproachful blue, "was established by Dr. Abernathy to be a haven for you poor unfortunate creatures who are troubled in mind and spirit and need a helping hand. Doctor is a very sensitive man, and I can assure you he would be terribly hurt if he heard you call this beautiful facility a *madhouse*.

"And, as for your other nonsense, you have to know Doctor is very progressive in his treatment of the mentally ill. You won't find any bars or chains. Mrs. Gilmartin, our orderlies are under strict orders. They do not fraternize, in any way, with our patients. Indeed not!"

She glanced at the double-spaced sheet in the typewriter, and compressed her lips. "I'll have you know, Dr. Abernathy is a highly respected man. He utilizes every mode and method of modern diagnostic testing and evaluation, and that, my dear Mrs. Gilmartin, includes patient-written 'Life-Notes.' That particular evaluation tool is Doctor's contribution to the scientific community. 'Life-Notes' have been read and commented on at a multitude of prestigious symposiums. All I can tell you is, you should be honored to have even a small part in a such a great man's work." She smiled then, but not at me.

She glanced at the typewriter again. Her smile faded and her sweetness hardened, just a little. "And, as for you, Mrs. Gilmartin, Doctor wants us to remind you, as often as is necessary, that you are not a writer, ersatz or otherwise. You would be very wise if you try to remember that."

Nurse Chatsworth paused, waiting for me to perjure myself, to admit to duplicity. But all I could say was, "I am Lolly Horn."

"Mrs. Gilmartin, Doctor Abernathy has, to my certain knowledge, told you, at least seven times, that your belief that you are Lolly Horn is a delusion. And I would also add, from seeing her on TV and looking at you, that the idea is totally preposterous."

I squirmed in the chair, trying to ease myself back and away from her. But she reached out, took my hand in hers, and patted it while she said, "Now, dear, I want you to remember that you are Mrs. Edgar Gilmartin of Cragshome. You, Elizabeth Gilmartin, have never been a guest on a national TV talkshow, have never held an autograph party, have never, and I repeat, *never,* written a book of any kind, especially the kind Lolly Horn writes.

"You are a nice person. The mother of two grown, married sons. You are a dedicated home-maker, an occasional volunteer at the Cragshome Historical Society and at the Cragshome Library, and nothing more."

I tried to protest, to straighten out some of her misconceptions, but she waved me back into silence.

"You are here, Mrs. Gilmartin, because your husband signed you in for thirty days of observa-tion and evaluation. He had to get a court order to do that, but no one, absolutely no one, has said you are a lunatic. Delusional, yes, but...."

I snorted.

"Please, Mrs. Gilmartin, try to understand that we are not your enemies. We want only the best for you. Dr. Abernathy says the delusional-writer-you is nothing more than a leftover dream from your childhood."

She glanced around to see if anyone were close enough to overhear and lowered her voice, and her eyelids, as if she were speaking of some incredibly delicate, or else some incredibly filthy, condition. "My dear, you are at that age when... ah... when your life seems over... ah... your body has... well, it is at that stage of your life when all of the bright dreams and wishes of your productive womanhood come back to fill all the empty spaces in your barren...."

I was still convulsed with laughter when Nurse Chatsworth came storming back, handed me two yellow pills and a small paper cup of tepid water. "Here," she snapped. "Take this medication immediately. It will enable you to regain your self-control."

Her rubber-soled shoe tapped the polished floor and blue eyes were narrowed, gun-fighter mean. She reached across my shoulder, grabbed the top of the typed page, jerked it out of the type-writer, and squeezed it into a tight, wrinkled ball.

"And, Mrs. Gilmartin," she said coldly, "you were told how these should be written. Even an ersatz writer should be able to put her 'Life-Notes' in the proper form, the form Doctor has told you he prefers."

It came out as a gusting giggle, but I found enough breath to ask, "Which is?"

"Third person, past tense," she said, and then she clamped her mouth shut, either because she had forgotten the rest, or because she was waiting for me to betray my ignorance by asking unwriterly questions.

Laughter bubbles exploded in my throat, but my voice sounded suspiciously meek, even to me, when I asked, "Is limited omniscient the doctor's choice also? In this case, do I get to be God, telling the whole thing from my...?"

Her fingers closed around my wrist, thumb pressed against the pulse point. She nodded. "That's right. Use your point of view and you can begin right after your nap. And, Mrs. Gilmartin, please start at the beginning. Doctor does, on occasion, publish some of the more interesting 'Life-Notes' in book form. It saves him time and trouble if the notes are in proper sequence—no flashbacks—and as complete as you can make them."

My tongue felt slightly prickly and it was hard to push the words past the laughter that still hid within me. "Oh, I see. From the moment I was born."

"No, dear," she said as she pulled me up from the chair and led me like a mother leads a wobbly-legged child, across the dayroom and into my cell. "Just from the time you started having your delusions. You know, when you began to believe you were a writer. That, I'm sure, will suit Doctor's purpose admirably."

"Okay," I mumbled through a mighty yawn. "It isn't a delusion, but I know when I... I know exactly when it all began. It was a sunny, warm morning in early September."

I chuckled as I added, "It was just over a year ago, and summer. The day when I was still *just* Mrs. Edgar Gilmartin. Mrs. Edgar Gilmartin, Edgar's trainee house mouse."

Chapter One

♥   ♥   ♥

If I, Elizabeth Gilmartin, an incarcerated mad-woman afflicted with a terminal case of whimsical hyperbole, can be believed, it all began thusly:

"It sounds wonderful, but I…. Oh, Cass, you know I can't go. You know how Edgar feels about me going anywhere without…."

The caller interrupted forcefully.

The white telephone vibrated in Elizabeth Gilmartin's hand. She held it away from her ear, trying to protect herself from the ear-blasting sound of Cass' unrestrained response; but even as she winced, Elizabeth smiled.

Cass—Mary Alice Cassidy Bates—had been Elizabeth's dearest friend in grammar school, and their friendship hadn't lessened through the years. Cass knew, or thought she knew, what was best for Elizabeth in any and all instances, and she wasn't adverse to saying so.

But Cass knew where Elizabeth's dreams were

buried also, and had shared Elizabeth's unvoiced grief at each small, silent funeral. Perhaps, in one case, at least, the burial had been a tad premature. Even as the slim, nondescript woman listened, with Cass' eager plans overriding her own feeble denying noises, Elizabeth could feel something like excitement, for a dream that still lived, stirring in her stomach, moving like the quickening pangs of an unborn child. Small, prenatal still, the dream was real.

"It isn't too late, Elizabeth," the dream wheedled, using Cass' hoarse, breathy voice. "You're only fifty. Lots of women start new careers when.... Oh, Elizabeth, listen to me. You don't actually have to write anything, just come with me. We could have such fun. It would be like.... Honey, if Edgar won't give you the money, I'll pay for the..." The voice went on and on, outlining the plan, tempting, pleading.

And when there was a moment of silence on the other end of the telephone line, Elizabeth heard her own voice whisper, "I'll ask Edgar."

Before Elizabeth could waffle or hedge, Cass asked, "Promise?"

"Promise." Elizabeth's echoing response was a vow given to a friend, the ritual of years renewed and perpetuated. It was a promise Elizabeth had to keep, could never weasel out of. She knew that, and a tingle of unease joined the excitement that hiccoughed and kicked inside her flat stomach.

Cass' victory chuckle and breathy farewell were almost lost in the chime of the microwave oven. Elizabeth held the receiver for a fleeting moment before she dropped it back into its cradle and exchanged a shimmer of dreamscape for the task at hand. Edgar's oat bran muffins were hot, and Edgar Allen Gilmartin, successful investment counselor and husband of thirty-three years, waited.

The woman knew just exactly how he waited. The morning paper, still neatly folded, was at his left elbow. A cut-glass bowl of whole-grain cereal, topped with five slices of banana and a quarter of a cup of skimmed milk, was setting squarely in front of him. A bone china cup of steaming decaffeinated coffee, still untouched, sat within easy reach of his right hand. His breakfast was four minutes late, because she had forgotten to heat the muffins, and Edgar was waiting, probably not even tapping his forefinger on the edge of the table, with well-concealed, well-mannered impatience.

Elizabeth picked up the designer muffin basket, a gift from Edgar's secretary, Karoline Marshall, the previous Christmas, and took a shallow breath.

She wasn't afraid of her husband, but he always made her feel so... so.... She refused to entertain the rest of the thought, but was too late to block it out completely.

The nip and surge of her excitement turned to a sour taste in her mouth. Old, unshed tears, like furry mice, with sharp, hot claws, scrabbled up from her stomach, filling her throat too full. Her hand had a slight tremor as she brushed back a straying wisp of her blunt-cut hair, hair that was neither glossy with youth nor shimmering silver.

As she turned, Elizabeth caught a single glimpse of a distorted reflection in the gleaming black glass of the oven door. Her own bland, colorless face peered back at her. Her lips twisted into a wry smile. "Elizabeth Gilmartin," she whispered, "resident rug."

The smile was gone when she slipped quietly, and with no apparent grace, into the long, narrow dining room. Edgar's polished and perfect dining room, with its wall of east-facing windows, limed-oak furniture, and grass-papered walls. Or, rather, Edgar's decorator's polished and perfect dining room—glossy-magazine perfect and expected to stay that way.

Setting the basket of napkin-wrapped muffins three inches to the right of his ice-nested glass of fresh orange juice, Elizabeth saw the back of Edgar's neck and felt an emotion she thought was stone-dead which made her want to reach out and caress him. Instead, she pushed absently, with a gesture Edgar deplored, at the nosepiece of her gray-rimmed glasses, and looked away. She didn't see anything but her own need, a need that made her feel selfish and obscurely ashamed.

The wiggling worm of guilt attached itself to

the underside of her promise to Cass, went chrysalis, and fluttered out as a gilt-hued butterfly. It swooped through her thoughts, her fraying resolve, coloring everything guilt gray, ugly.

Edgar worked hard, worked long hours. Maybe he was right, maybe she should be happy to stay home and take care of his house. It truly was a beautiful house. The house he had dreamed of owning all their married life. Everything in it was perfect; just the way Edgar wanted it. It was the realization of his dream, and he was certain no one could maintain its perfection like she could.

She wanted to be able to give him this small thing, this gift of service, freely, lovingly. But why did she have to feel…? Why did she have to need more, need…?

"Elizabeth, I asked you a question."

The exasperation in his deep, rather precise tones cut through her interior monologue, a monologue that had replayed too many times in the past year, the year since James's wedding, since.…

Hurriedly, she pushed that thought away, tried to concentrate on what Edgar was saying, but the meaning of his words still wandered aimlessly, and unrecognized, through the haze of guilt and growing remorse that filled her. Guilt for her disloyalty, her discontent in Edgar's house, remorse for a promise made in haste, a promise she felt honor-bound to keep—just as she had kept all her promises to Cass through the years.

With pale eyes, almost colorless and oddly blank within their fringe of stubby lashes, she looked at him. She saw the deeply tanned face (from every Wednesday afternoon, five to six, spent in a tanning booth) the eyes of sparkling blue, the almost black hair with its distinguished frosting of silver.

The guilts she had nurtured and tended over the years struck again, wounding her. *Edgar Allen Gilmartin was still a lean and handsome man, a successful man, a man who had too much to do. He didn't have time to worry about her needs, her wants, her frustrated desires....* She pushed that line of thought away, and turned, almost too quickly, to other, less hurting, guilts.

People looked up to Edgar, sought him out, took from him, and begged for more. He came home from the office so worn, so weary he could scarcely.... Maybe he was right, maybe she should be there when he came home, waiting for him in his spotless house, a hot meal ready to go on the table. Maybe. Could he be expected, on top of everything else he had to do, to worry about her unimportant little angers, her need to.... He had always given her....

And he had always taken away.... The last thought crept in unbidden.

"Elizabeth, have you been taking your estrogen?"

Shame, and a tiny flare of resentment, set up a crimson clamor on her high cheekbones and the tip of her slim nose. She smothered the resentment with a practiced hand, and then, more like a chastised child than a grown woman, she nodded mutely.

"Well, in that case, perhaps you should make another appointment with Dr. Swart. Your present dosage is obviously too weak." His thin lips smiled, but not his eyes. "You're still wandering around like you're in your dotage. It seems to me like you should be more careful, especially considering what happened before. I do not want you getting ill again, particularly now."

"I'm sorry," she said, but she wasn't, not really. The placating response was automatic, a habitual apology, soft words intended to soothe his ire, to fend off criticism of her many flaws. Flaws that seemed more manifest since he had found her hot flashes and night sweats so distasteful and moved out of their shared bedroom. And completely out of her bed.

Sighing heavily, Edgar said, "Elizabeth, I asked you who was on the phone. Surely you can answer a simple question like that."

Her tongue flicked palely across her bare lips. She felt rather than heard the sting of his carefully controlled irritation at this new example of her total incompetence. Her own resentment combined with her guilt made her almost inarticulate. Her voice was reduced to a sliver of sound. "It was only Cass," she said.

Elizabeth saw the little moue that twisted his lips. She bowed her head, refusing to see the disapproval in his eyes, of her continuing friendship with Cass.

"What did she want?"

Elizabeth could only shake her head in reply.

"She must have wanted something, Elizabeth. Not even *Cass* would be rude enough to call at this hour of the morning unless it was for something that *she,* at least, considered to be of some importance." Edgar picked up his glass of orange juice, held it midway between the table and his mouth, and waited, looking at her expectantly.

"She… one of Cass' ladies when she.…" The words stumbled across Elizabeth's tongue and died of oxygen deprivation on her lips.

Sounding as phony-tolerant as a long-suffering but liberal parent, Edgar said, "Oh, for God's sake, Elizabeth, speak up. I'm not going to spank you or send you to your room. Just tell me what your rich friend…" his voice coarsened, took on the rasp-tones of a sneer, "the Widow Bates, wanted at this time of the morning." His hand jerked on his last word and droplets of yellow juice splashed up and out of the glass, flashing like pure gold in the sunlight that lay aslant the gleaming tabletop.

Fingers pressed to her mouth, Elizabeth watched the drops of juice fall, splatter, and although she didn't really want to look at him, she saw the annoyance that darkened the blue of her husband's eyes, deepened the furrow between his brows. "I'll get a cloth and clean it up," she said hurriedly.

"Not yet, Elizabeth. Tell me what Cass wanted," he said tightly. A little muscle jumped at the corner of his mouth, but his voice was under rigid control, each syllable weighed, measured, and chilled for the most effective decibel content.

"She wants me to go to a writers' conference with her." The words came out in a single strand, stark and ugly as cheap plastic beads molded together on a plastic string. And then, without waiting to hear his response, Elizabeth turned and scurried out of the room.

Edgar followed her into the kitchen, put his hand on her wrist as she reached for a tea towel. "My dear," he said, sounding a good deal like a saint about to be martyred, "I cannot believe that after all these years you are bringing up that silliness again. You are my wife, *Mrs*. Edgar Gilmartin, that should be enough. There's no need for you to go out and grub, to degrade yourself, and *me*, by...."

She had to stop him. "I know. I know. It's just.... Cass asked me to go, I didn't tell her I... Edgar, she thought I might enjoy meeting some famous writers. She thinks I should get out more and.... She wants me to stop moping.... Now that I'm staying home.... I did not tell her I would go with her. I just promised to ask you if I could go. That's all."

"And that's enough. It seems to me that we agreed, last year when you.... Right after James got married, that you would...." Smiling ruefully, Edgar shook his head. "My dear, I thought it would be enough for you to be my wife. I truly did."

"Edgar, I..." Elizabeth started, but Edgar seemed not to hear her and went on, "I've worked day and night to give you everything any woman could possibly want, but it's not enough. You have this fine house, one of the most beautiful homes in Cragshome. You have credit cards, as many clothes as you want. Not only that, but you get to stay home, surrounded by the finest artwork, furniture, with nothing to do but a little housework and.... I truly don't know what more I can give you, Elizabeth. What do you want from me?"

He was singing the theme song of their marriage, a love song turned to dry and bitter ash. Elizabeth's chin came up, and there was only the faintest of quivers in her voice when she said, "I don't know what I want now, Edgar. I did once, but.... At this moment, all I know is: Cass' friend invited Cass and me to keep Cass company, to that big conference they have every year at Seaview on the Oregon Coast. The woman is a writer and she used to be one of Cass' hairdressing customers when Cass worked at the beauty shop."

"I'm truly sorry, Elizabeth, but it is absolutely

out of the question. And, what's more, Cass knew it before she even asked you. The woman's a home wrecker. She gets her kicks out of upsetting me, making my life miserable."

Elizabeth couldn't argue; it was partly true. But neither could she tell him that Cass thought he was a "selfish bastard" who hadn't a thought for anyone but himself.

"You aren't a rich widow like the estimable *Mrs*. Bates. You can't just drop everything and go rushing off like a goose. You have certain obligations and duties, as most responsible people do. After all, you are a volunteer at the library, and they're counting on you. And what about this house, would you trust anyone else to care for it in the proper manner?"

He paused for a moment, smiled down at her, and asked, almost coyly, "And me, Elizabeth? Who will take care of me if you go off with Cass?"

His unexpected cuteness jangled her nerves, set up a disharmony in her mind. Elizabeth wanted to jerk loose from his hand, scream like a fishwife, "What about me, Edgar? Do I even exist?"

But she didn't. She couldn't stop her muscles from stiffening, but her voice was completely calm when she said, "Excuse me, Edgar. I have to clean the table before the juice spots the wood."

Her husband was less than two steps behind her when she reentered the dining room, and still talking. "But it's true, Elizabeth. Whether you want to admit it or not, you do have obligations. It isn't like it was when you and Cass were girls and could run off and.... Elizabeth, do you still want to be a writer?"

The abrupt question surprised her, touched the small channel of love that still ran somewhere deep within her. She wanted to comfort him, to hold him in her arms and take away the undertone of hurt in his voice. Her hands came up, reached out, slowly, involuntarily, but she couldn't, in all truth, answer his question. Neither could she actually touch him.

She didn't know if she still wanted to write, or even if she could. Not now. Not after all the years of pushing the dream aside, letting everything and everyone come first. Nor could she tell him, or anyone else, including Cass, of the pages written since her younger son's wedding. Written and hidden away. Pages written in secret to relieve the pain of loneliness, of depression, of feeling so tired, so useless.

No, she couldn't explain the black despair that wracked her, made her yearn desperately for something more than what she had, something that had no name, yet. She couldn't tell him, couldn't expose her fragile need to the killing cold of his lack of understanding. Could not abort the unborn dream.

She just shook her head, and it could have meant anything.

It was the only answer he needed. Edgar's smile was warm, like his voice when he said, "That's my good girl."

He took a quick sip of cool coffee, set the cup back onto the saucer with a decisive click. "Elizabeth, you really do understand why I thought it best that you stopped writing, don't you? Your working was the only way I could get my degree and we both wanted that. Now, if I thought you had any talent, even the smallest amount, I would insist you go out to the university and sign up for some writing classes. But, my dear, I see no reason why you should embarrass yourself, embarrass us both, by pursuing...."

He chuckled softly, inviting her to join his mirth. "But going to this writers' conference would be pure craziness."

He shook his head and his voice was still jovial when he said, "Well, Elizabeth, when you make that appointment with your gynecologist, you'd better make one for the Widow Bates at the same time. I honestly can't believe she's taking any estrogen at all. Sometimes I think she's gone over the edge, is as mad as a hatter."

Anger, sudden but impotent, spread like acid in her chest, burned in her throat. Elizabeth bent her head, scrubbed at the drops of juice that marred the lustrous perfection of the tabletop, holding back the bitter words that wanted to be said, sharp words she wanted to hurl at his head like knives, words that she swallowed adding to the iron weight in her stomach.

Realizing he had gone too far, he tried to make amends. "I'm sorry, my dear. I shouldn't have made fun of your friend like that, it wasn't kind."

Edgar's voice got lower. "I realize you are sensitive right now, that The Change is.... But, my dear, I ask that you remember that I'm only trying to take care of you, to insure that you do not fall ill again."

After a moment of silence, he said, "You should thank me. Women do go mad, you know. I've heard... it's the hormones or something. I.... Elizabeth, look at me." The last was an order.

Heat surged, boiled through her veins, oozed through her pores, turned to sweat on her brow. Red mottled the pale skin of her face and neck. Tears of anger threatened to spill from her eyes, but her voice was rock steady and totally without inflection when she said, "You'd better hurry. You're going to be late for your first appointment."

He glanced at the futuristic clock that opened like a golden fan against the papered wall, stifled an exclamation of dismay, and looked back at her. "We'll discuss this later," he said quickly, but not quickly enough to hide the relief in his eyes, the easing of tension in his jaw.

"There's really nothing more to discuss, is there?"

Ever the proper wife, Elizabeth walked before

him to the tiled entry, opened the spacious guest closet, took out his lizard attaché case, and, when he was standing in the open doorway, handed it to him without a word.

When he tried to kiss her, she turned her head. Edgar's ritual kiss, an empty rite no longer holding either love or meaning, landed somewhere in the neighborhood of her left ear.

"Elizabeth," he snapped, ire raising his voice, "you make me so.... You're acting like a spoiled child."

"Am I?" she asked evenly.

"You know damned well you are. This conference can't mean a single, blasted thing to you. *You* aren't a writer. You don't even know any writers, so why are you making it so important, blowing it out of all reason? You always do this. Every time you disagree with what I decide, you...."

"Good-by, Edgar," she said as she gently closed the door, forcing him to step back, cutting off his recriminations. Holding her breath for a long count of three, Elizabeth waited for him to pound on the door, to demand she hear him out. But there was no sound from without.

Her pent breath came out softly, almost a sigh. Elizabeth turned and walked away, turning left instead of right, going toward the bedroom wing, a faraway look in her eyes. The look made her blind to dirty dishes and the other duties assigned to the day, Monday's duties.

Anger was still driving her, goading her forward with jabbing prods of memory, memory of other anger, other pain. She grabbed the brass knob of her white-painted bedroom door, jerking the door open with a wide, sweeping gesture and letting it bang shut behind her with a muffled crash.

She stood for a moment, a slim shaft of cornflower blue in a smothering dazzle of pinks and white. White carpet. Pink draperies. White satin spread on a white bed. Pink pillows, like a clutch of satin eggs, in shades of pink and froths of lace. The pinks and white echoed and re-echoed in the mirrored wardrobe, the cheval glass, the lighted makeup mirror over the white dressing table. Pink, white, ruffles, and lace. A little girl's room.

Taking another deep breath, Elizabeth held it for an instant and then expelled it through her nose as she dragged a white satin chair to the far end of the room-length closet. Sliding the mirrored door aside, she climbed up on the chair, carelessly disregarding the marks her slippers were making on the cushion.

Her touch was gentle, reassuring as her fingers brushed the thin sheaf of papers that rested at the back of the shelf. Forty-three pages that pretended to be the first two chapters of a novel, her novel.

She couldn't make her fingers close around the pages, couldn't drag them out into the light. "Damn! Damn and blast!" she muttered. "Damn! Damn! Damn!"

Heat and fury raced through her again, fury that couldn't be expressed, fury that had no roots in today's minor upset. "Edgar hasn't changed," she said. "He's still the same: pompous, conceited, thinking only of…. It's me that's at fault. I let him…. It's all me. I can't… I can't go on like this. I can't pretend…. Dear God, what am I going to do?"

The chair teetered, fell backward with a hushed thud. She jumped down. She didn't even look at it. Tearing off the dressing gown, two buttons flying loose, skittering across the thick rug, the silk ripping under her vicious fingers, she let it drop to the floor. Clad only in a lacy bra and bikini panties, Elizabeth stood for a moment, but she had no time to look at her reflected body, no wish to admire the tight, smooth muscles of her hips, thighs, and waist, the generous length of her legs, the full curve of her well-shaped breasts.

Pulling on a long, full, gray and tan shirt, loose-legged tan pants, canvas walking shoes, and adding a large hat for shade, Elizabeth walked out of the bedroom the decorator had said was "truly her" and out of her husband's house, leaving obligations and unmade beds behind her without a single twinge of guilt.

The telephone rang just as she opened the front door. "Shut up," she snarled. "I don't want to talk to you or anybody else." The heavy door whispered closed behind her and she walked away, taking only her blind rage as a companion. The rage, as it had done so often in the past year, made her step out like a marathon walker—a walker who would win the race or die.

The telephone was still ringing, or ringing again, two hours later when she returned from her walk in the sun. The anger was hidden deep, out of sight, out of mind, and calmness hung around her like a sweet-scented cloud.

She walked to the den, a tiny room tucked in between the guest powder room and Edgar's imposing library-office suite. It was the only one in the house that had, thus far, escaped the decorator's hand, surrounding her with the familiar, the comfortable. It was her room, her haven in Edgar's sleek house. Her calmness deepened as she reached for the phone, an old black rotary phone, sitting amidst the papers and books on top of her scarred maple desk.

Elizabeth thought she knew who was calling, who had been calling when she left, and now she was ready to refuse Cass' hoarse-voiced demands that she tell Edgar she was going to the conference with or without his permission.

She was smiling when she said, "Hello, Cass."

It wasn't Cass' familiar voice that answered.

Her eyes wide, Elizabeth's voice was almost as husky as Cass' when she said, "What did you say? What are you...? There has to be some mistake. Who...?"

Chapter Two

♥   ♥   ♥

"No. No, I don't understand what you're saying.
I can't.…" Elizabeth pressed the receiver a little
closer to her ear, trying to hear words through the
buzz and whir of electronic noise that almost
drowned out the polite, but firm, voice of a total
stranger, whose disquieting words were dissipating
Elizabeth's hard-won calmness.

Frowning with concentration, she listened for a
moment longer and then said, "Yes, I am Mrs.
Gilmartin. Yes, that's my address and telephone
number, but I didn't.…"

The voice interrupted, patiently explained the
reason for the call, and then at Elizabeth's insis-
tence, explained it once again.

Elizabeth's free hand reached behind her,
fumbled for the chair that should have been there,
patted empty air until her groping fingers found
and seized a rounded expanse of nubby material.
Without being consciously aware of the act, she
recognized the contour of the chair arm and

tugged hard, sliding the chair forward until it touched the backs of her legs.

The phone gripped in her right hand, Elizabeth forced her tense body down, perched, like a frightened bird too weary for further flight, on the front three inches of the chair.

"Yes, I'll write them down, but...." She fumbled through the desk drawer for a pencil and a pad, found them both, pressed too hard on the pencil, snapped the point off the lead, and finally wrote down the numbers she heard.

"I still think you've made a mistake," she said when she was done, but the polite voice laughed in her ear and assured her no mistake had been made. Elizabeth was still unconvinced as she returned the phone to the hook and stared at the numbers, flight numbers for a trip to Seaview, Oregon.

"Who would do...? It has to be a mistake. Edgar said I couldn't go; he wouldn't do something like this. He just wouldn't," she told the empty room. "And Cass wouldn't. Not without...."

Even as she said the words, realization swooped through her and Elizabeth knew she was wrong. Cass would, and probably had. Cass would do almost anything to get her own way, anything to force Elizabeth down the path Cass thought she should follow. Any path that would lead Elizabeth away from Edgar.

Anger, mixed with a touch of throat-aching

love, pushed up inside her, made her grab the phone, dial Cass' number with sharp, jabbing strokes. Anger was in her mouth when she held the phone to her ear, listened to the distant ringing. When it rang for the nineteenth time, Elizabeth slammed the phone down.

But the anger was still hot within her when she stalked down the hall, stormed into her pink and white bedroom, and went to the closet. Righting the fallen chair, she climbed up, reached into the back of the closet. There was no gentleness in her now, no love. Her fingers were savage, destroying, when they closed around the cherished sheets, crumpling the crisp paper like so many soiled dinner napkins as she pulled them out of their hiding place on the high shelf.

Elizabeth didn't even look at the typewritten pages she held in her fist, but a mist of tears blinded her and a wave of bitter grief made her cling to the back of the chair for a moment before she climbed down with slow, careful steps.

The tears were a passing thing, soon dried by her anger. Anger at them both, her husband and her friend, but mostly anger at herself for daring to dream again.

"Edgar's right," she said. "It is all nonsense. All of it. I couldn't do it. I couldn't do...." The papers seemed alive in her fingers, twisting and turning, trying to escape the cruel hand that squeezed them. Perhaps trying to tell her she could if she'd only try, the dream could be real if she cared enough to reach out and take it and make it come true with her own labor.

"No," she said. Setting her jaw, stiffening her spine, she strode determinedly down the hall to the kitchen. She stopped in front of the trash compactor, pulled it open. Hesitating only the barest of instants, Elizabeth tore each sheet in half lengthwise before she dropped it into the waiting maw. Her finger trembled, but it jabbed the button forcefully, turning the mutilated dream into a hard-packed memory.

The machine growled like a feral beast, rending the flesh, grinding the bones of her poor murdered dream. The woman shuddered. Her hand went to her chest, pressed against the ache of loss that had taken up lodging in her heart. She turned away.

The perfection of the house didn't intimidate her today, didn't make her want to tiptoe from room to room, slink about like a timid beggar in a king's palace. With the broad-brimmed hat on her head forgotten, Elizabeth stomped through the house, slamming doors, opening draperies that were supposed to be closed, jerking bedding straight and smooth, washing, dusting, waxing, completing the chores assigned to Monday (by one of the decorator's hirelings) in record time.

But even the rapidity of her anger-fueled labor had taken time. The afternoon was far advanced when she folded the last of the fresh-scented, static-free laundry and returned towels, linens, and garments to their designated shelf or drawer.

Stretching the kinks out of her muscles, she walked out into the back garden to cut some flowers. They were in one of the laundry trays when Elizabeth allowed herself to sigh.

"Time to start dinner," she said to the flowers. "A cozy dinner for two, replete with candles, you, and Edgar's tirade."

Salad crisping, wine breathing, the table carefully laid, silver-banded china, heavy sterling, and ruby stemware ranked on place mats that matched the shaggy white chrysanthemums, Elizabeth was pouring mountain spring water into the coffee maker when the doorbell rang.

"Cass," Elizabeth said, feeling a small blaze of anger, willing it to grow strong enough to help her say what had to be said.

But her anger had already been spent on household tasks and wasteful sighs. It was only strong enough to send Elizabeth to the door with its dying embers in her eyes and acrid ashes bitter on her tongue. She had no flaming words to hurl at Cass when the opened door revealed her friend's face, smiling brightly over a mountain of gaily packaged purchases.

"Oh, Liz, just wait until you see what I got for you," Cass almost shouted, excitement in her hoarse voice. "You won't dare get mad at me when you see how great you look in spangles and beads."

She took a quick step forward, and thrust the toppling mound toward Elizabeth. "Quick, take some of these before I drop the whole...."

Elizabeth caught a shower of rainbow-hued bags and moved to one side, allowing Cass room to come into the entry. She looked at her smiling friend, but there was no welcoming smile on her own lips, and her voice was soft, sorrowful, when she asked, "Why, Cass? Why did you do it?"

"Oh, damn! I didn't mean to make you cry, Lizzie. I just wanted you to have something spiffy. I know what kind of clothes you buy for yourself and.... Well, you need something with sparkle and dash." She dropped the rest of her packages on the gleaming teak table that flanked the door and looked at Elizabeth quizzically. "Are you going somewhere?"

"Of course I'm not. Don't change the subject," Elizabeth snapped.

"I'm not." Cass looked at her again, tried to keep a straight face and tittered. "It was a natural mistake. Take a look." She pulled Elizabeth two steps to the left, turned her so she faced the gilt-framed mirror over the dark table.

Elizabeth's frown vanished. She felt a giggle start at the base of her throat, bubble up like an Italian fountain, turning the thin, smudged-faced apparition in the glass into a laughing woman, an absurd woman, dirty-faced and young-looking beneath the wide-brim of a floppy, pink straw hat.

Dropping the bags she held in a heap on the table, she reached up and removed the hat, looked at it for an instant as if she didn't quite recognize it. Then she tossed it on top of Cass' packages.

"Maybe Edgar is right, Cass," she said slowly. "Maybe menopause really has made me nuttier than your black walnut tree."

Cass hooted, her loud, uninhibited amusement swelled, filled the shadowy emptiness of the large house with a flood of honest laughter. It gave lie to Elizabeth's words. When the flood ebbed and died to a trickle, Cass tried to compose herself, wiped the laughter-tears from her brown eyes, smearing mascara and eyeliner, and chuckled again.

"If anybody's nuts, it's got to be Edgar," she said, and then she added, in a voice devoid of everything except total seriousness, "Elizabeth, I don't know what's going on between you and Edgar, and I don't want to know. But I do know if you go on letting him boss you around, getting you in states like this, it won't be long until you really are crazy."

It was then that Elizabeth remembered her anger, searched out the remaining bits and pieces, tried to make it whole and strong. It was damaged beyond repair. Nonetheless, she had to try and make Cass see that Edgar had his rights and privileges and that she, Elizabeth Gilmartin, wife and friend, had obligations and loyalties to them both. That between them they were tearing her apart.

She was choosing the words she had to say, readying her defenses for Cass' retaliation when Cass asked plaintively, "Elizabeth, have you heard a single word I've said?"

Guilt making her smile lopsided and tentative, Elizabeth shook her head and said, with more bare truth than she had intended, "No, I was trying to figure out how to tell you you're every bit as bad as Edgar. Cass, you shouldn't have...."

Cass misunderstood and dismissed her objection with an airy, "Oh, don't be such a spoil sport. What's the good of being a rich widow if you can't buy a few things for your best friend?"

Then, before Elizabeth could correct the misunderstanding, Cass added, "I asked you if you didn't just about drop your cookies when Edgar said you could go with me to the conference?"

"He didn't, Cass."

"Now, stop acting silly. Of course he did. But forget Edgar, we have lots to do before we leave on Wednesday morning. Now, if you will just grab a few of these sacks, we can go to...."

"Cass," Elizabeth said with a sigh, "I don't have the faintest idea what's going on in that mind of yours, but Edgar didn't say.... I'm not going to the conference, and you know it."

"Do I?" Cass made a mournful face. "Poor baby."

"Stop it, Cass."

"Okay, but if you know so much about it, Lizzie, why did Edgar, or rather that sexy secretary of his, the marvelous Karoline.... But you know all about that. Come on now, help me with these packages. You'll have to try some of the things on. If they don't fit, we can exchange them in the morning while we shop for the rest of what we need."

Memory of Edgar's morning rage made Elizabeth strong enough to say, "Cass, listen to me. I'm not going with you."

"Of course you are. It's all arranged. Now, look at what I bought." Cass rummaged through the sliding stack, knocking some of the bags off the table, tearing others open, talking huskily and breathlessly the whole time.

"We'll have so much fun. The ocean and all the famous writers and.... Oh, Elizabeth, just imagine. Maybe the next conference we go to you'll be the famous writer everyone is going to see. Wouldn't that be something?"

Holding back the tears that rose up from the grief locked in her heart, Elizabeth put her hand on Cass' shoulder, felt the warm flesh beneath her palm, the smooth padding of fat that gave Cass the look of plump lushness. "Please, Cass," she said quietly. "Don't say anything more. I'm not a writer, not now, not ever, and you know perfectly well I can't go with you. Edgar was.... He hates the idea of me even thinking about.... He was furious when he left this morning and he's going to...."

"Well, all I can say is: He changed his mind pretty damned quick."

"No, I don't think he did, and when he finds out about the plane reservations you made in my name, he's going to have a fit. Oh, Cass, I told you I'd ask. Couldn't you wait that long? Couldn't you talk to me first?"

"Wow! Reservations? I never even thought of.... I'd better call the airline right away and...."

"Don't Cass. The airline clerk called me, confirmed my reservation to Seaview on Wednesday —that was two reservations, Cass. I have the flight numbers, the layover times, everything all written down, so don't try to...."

Cass laughed again. "Why that sneaky son-of-a..." she grinned at Elizabeth and finished, "gun." Her voice almost admiring, she added, "Boy, when old Edgar gets his... in gear, he dusts up the whole damned track."

"Edgar? You think he did.... No, Cass, you really can't expect me to believe that."

The plump woman turned, faced Elizabeth squarely, and there was no laughter in her voice when she said, "Elizabeth, we both know I go off half-cocked some of the time, lots of the time, and I know I've managed to get you in trouble more times than I can count, but I've never deliberately lied to you. Have I?"

Feeling the red creep up to dye her cheeks, Elizabeth looked down, away from Cass' face, but only after she had shaken her head, affirming the truth in Cass' statement. "But Edgar was furious when he left," she said slowly. "He wouldn't...."

"Well, it was probably the marvelous Karoline who actually did the dastardly deed, but she wouldn't have dialed a digit if old Edgar hadn't given her the nod. You can bet your wisdom teeth on that."

Confusion bound Elizabeth's tongue.

Cass was under no such restraint. She continued, "That's why I thought it was all settled, that your great lord and master had patted you on the head and given his kind permission for you to go out and mingle with the lesser folk."

"You're rambling, Cass."

Her good nature restored, Cass wrinkled her nose and winked at Elizabeth. "I guess I am," she said, "but the marvelous Karoline wasn't when she called me this morning, before I was even up, and asked a thousand and three questions about my friend, Caress Love, the conference, time, location, costs, you name it."

"Karoline called you? Cass, are you sure?"

"Yes, Elizabeth, I'm sure. And very brisk and businesslike she was, too."

"She always is," Elizabeth said absently. "But that doesn't mean Edgar changed his mind. Why would he?"

She started to say, "He hates you, and the whole idea of me even thinking about writing, why would he send me off with a whole pack of them?" But all she said aloud was, "Why?"

"Lordy, Liz, how would I know? Edgar is your husband." It wasn't an envious statement. But then the jeering, cynical tones dropped out of her voice, leaving it soft, almost gentle, when she asked, "Elizabeth, you aren't getting sick again, are you? I've been worrying about you for months. Are you really okay now? I know I don't have the right to pry, but I... I mean, is he.... Is it worse now, since the wedding and... and everything? Have I made it worse?"

"Oh, no, Cass," Elizabeth whispered, giving her friend a quick hug. "You could never.... I need you, Cass. Sometimes I couldn't go on without...."

Elizabeth was on the verge, as she had been several times before, of confessing her confusion, her depression, her loneliness, her frustration. She wanted to tell Cass she had not been intimate with her own husband for over two years, but she couldn't. Loyalty to her marriage, and her growing sense that it was all her own fault, that she was so unattractive and worthless no man would want her, kept her silent. Instead, because she felt the need to say something, and because, as far as it went, it was absolutely true, she said, "It's this house. Edgar's house. I hate it. I don't know how much longer I...."

Cass' arms reached out to hold her, to give her comfort, but Elizabeth stepped back, withdrew behind her wall of social smiles and surface chat. "I'm sorry, Cass. Forget I said that. It seems that lately all I've done is complain about nothing."

Cass' dark eyes looked grave with worry, but she smiled as she brushed Elizabeth's thin cheek with chubby fingers. "Think nothing of it. Everybody's got the need to bitch sometime," she said in a singsong. "Even the skinny Mrs. Gilmartin. Skinny? My God, you really are skinny. Oh, my bald Aunt Tilly, I'll bet you three dimes the clothes I bought for you are all eight sizes too big."

Elizabeth didn't say anything, and Cass turned away from whatever she saw, and probably pitied, in Elizabeth's colorless face and grabbed one of the packages. "Come on, Liz," she said, her voice straining for animation, the rebirth of its former lilting joy. "You'll have to try some of...."

"I can't take...." The almost inaudible protest broke, fell away when she saw the pointing hands on Cass' oversized wristwatch and exclaimed, half in panic, "Oh, no! It's time for Edgar to come home and.... After what happened this morning, he'll be.... Oh, hurry, Cass, we have to get this stuff back in your car before he...."

"Take it easy. He's not going to give a care. I told you, Edgar changed his mind. He wants you to go." Cass spoke soothingly, but even as she spoke, she imitated Elizabeth's actions and began piling her day's purchases like cordwood on her crooked arm.

Cass tried again, looking at Elizabeth's frenzied movements with real worry written in broad strokes across her face. "Liz, this is really silly. Why don't we wait and show Edgar everything. He would enjoy...."

The nondescript woman shook her head with almost sullen stubbornness and continued to add slippery, plastic-bagged bangles, beads, and other shimmering fripperies to the growing stack on her own arm.

Nothing but one shiny yellow bag and the pink straw hat remained on the table when Edgar's key entered the lock and he pushed open the door in almost the same instant, catching the two women in frozen postures of guilty departure, waiting silently for his scathing disapproval.

They waited in vain.

Smiling affably, Edgar glanced at them both, his eyes narrowing only a trifle when he saw his wife's stained, rumpled garments, the dusty smudges on her face. "Been shopping for the conference?" he asked as he placed his attaché case and a large, gold-colored box on the closet floor.

Cass looked at Elizabeth, grinned an I-told-you-so smile, and answered his question. "Just me. Elizabeth's been cleaning house, I think. I caught her before she could make herself decent."

She started to say something more, but
Elizabeth shook her head in warning. Taking the
hint, Cass said brightly, "Well, I'd like to stay and
visit, but I do have a lot...."

Edgar didn't try to detain her, but he did say,
"Here, let me help you with those bundles."
Suiting his action to his offer, he took Elizabeth's
packages and followed Cass to the open doorway.
There, he paused, went back to the table, picked
up the pink hat with the barest tips of his well-
manicured fingers. "I'm sure you wouldn't want
to forget this... ah... this," he said with a grimace
of distaste.

Elizabeth added the last yellow bag to his
load, but neither woman corrected his mistaken
assumption that the offensive headgear belonged
to Cass. Instead, Cass flung a breezy, "See you
tomorrow," to the silent Elizabeth and rushed
Edgar out to her car.

Tears lurking just behind her pale eyes,
Elizabeth only nodded before she turned and crept
away to the kitchen. She stood, hands hanging
limply at her sides, shoulders bowed, staring at the
trash compactor. She was still there when Edgar,
a drink in one hand, a gold box only partially
concealed behind his back, found her.

Her hand came up, brushed ineffectually at the
smudges on her shirt, but she didn't apologize for
not being freshly attired for his homecoming, or
for anything else. When she finally spoke, all she

said was, "Dinner will be a few minutes late."

"No rush," Edgar said with a wave of his gin-and-tonic and a convivial smile. He took another deep swallow, set the glass in the sink, and looked at her searchingly before he slid the box onto the counter in front of her. Slightly flushed, sounding boyish and shy, he said, "I.... This is for.... I'm truly sorry, Elizabeth."

So much had occurred that day, Elizabeth had no idea which one thing he was sorry for, sorry enough to bring her a gift from the most expensive boutique in Cragshome, a shop so over-priced it didn't even use a logo on its golden boxes. Afraid something new was afoot, something that was bound to be painful, she stood, stiff as a department store dummy, and waited for him to provide the clues, bludgeon her with the whatever. She was afraid, but she didn't want to guess, dreaded knowing what new torture he had planned.

"Aren't you even going to open it?" Edgar asked with a hurt little smile.

She tried to do what he wanted, but her hands were lumps of ice, too numb to do more than fumble with the lid. He shook his head, but Edgar was still smiling when he came to her rescue, flinging the lid aside, lifting out a long, wide-shouldered jacket of golden tweed, turning it this way and that, so she could admire the butter-colored leather elbow patches that covered half the sleeves.

Still not knowing what he wanted from her, Elizabeth looked at the jacket, the calf-length A-line skirt of matching tweed, and the shimmering blouse of golden silk, with its double row of tiny pearl buttons and an enormous bow centered on the high collar, and then she nodded slowly.

"You'll need it for the writers' conference," he said.

"But...."

"Karoline... ah... Miss Marshall picked it out for you. She said they told her at SHRADER'S— that's where it's from, you know—anyway, the clerk told her it was perfect for where you're going. It's the kind of thing all writers wear. And I... Elizabeth, you know how I feel about you dressing appropriately."

"The writers' conference," she whispered, and there might have been a sob in her voice as she remembered the treasured pages, the novel that had died in her hands, the dream that was still too battered to even stir.

Staring at his golden gift, Elizabeth felt her numb indifference lift. She didn't say gold made her look jaundiced and old, she just looked at the heavy material and felt love, sweet love, gentle love, forgiving love. It closed her throat, hurt in her chest, dazzled her eyes with moisture. Her grief for the dream merged with the love-ache in her heart and was gone. The dream didn't seem to matter much, not now.

"Did you say something?" Edgar asked.

"Only foolishness," she said.

"Not about the conference," he asked quickly, too quickly. "I mean, you still want to go, don't you?" Before she could answer, he said, "You have to go. I have gone to considerable trouble to.... The arrangements are all made. I must insist you go."

Almost oblivious to his sudden anxiety, his agitation, she asked, "What about the house? Who will take care of it, and of you? Fix your meals? Do the laundry?" She raised her hands, palms up, stared down at them with sightless eyes. "Edgar, the conference doesn't mean anything to me. I don't want to go off somewhere and leave you alone for five days."

"You're being silly, Elizabeth. I am perfectly capable of taking care of myself," he said hurriedly, trying to forestall any more argument.

Watching her warily, he rubbed his left forefinger down the side of his nose nervously before he felt inside the golden box, pushing aside silk and tweed to pull out a large, leather-bound notebook. He showed it to her, proudly demonstrating its many clever features, all, according to him, perfectly suited to the needs of a professional writer. "There wasn't time for Karoline to get your name put on it," he said, "but when you get back, you can have it done."

A doubt too nebulous to be given credence

shadowed her love, but only for an instant, only long enough to make her ask, "Why, Edgar? Why are you so eager for me to go to the conference?"

He looked down, ran his finger across the edge of the notebook, but he didn't answer.

Elizabeth's voice was soft, gentle, but it held something far stronger than steel when she asked again, asked her husband, "Why, Edgar? Are you trying to get rid of me?"

Chapter Three

♥   ♥   ♥

Her question seemed to hang in the air, separating them like a wall of ice, thick ice that pushed them back and back, farther and farther apart, destroying any common ground they had left—if indeed there were any.

Elizabeth, caught in the enormity of what she had done, wanted to snatch the words back, cram them deep into some hidden place, slam down the lid, make them unthought, unsaid. But wishing and wanting changed nothing. The words had been said. They had cast a tall, dark shadow of doubt, an ugly stain on the purity of her trust. Suddenly, she was afraid her husband would tell her the truth, would confess to some horror too great to forgive. And the heart-puckering fear was as shadowy and as large as her doubt.

Perhaps he felt her fear, or perhaps Edgar, too, had doubts, a taste of his own fear. "I can't tell... Elizabeth, I wouldn't want to do anything that would...." He spoke slowly, haltingly, choosing each word with care. "You've been.... Things haven't been good between us for a long time. I tried, but you.... The Change has made you.... There have been times when I thought you were actually crazy. Maybe I haven't been.... I want you to be like you used to be. Years ago, when we first got married, you were happy being my wife, the mistress of my house. I want that again. I deserve it again."

"Edgar, I...."

"I want us both to be happy," he said, ignoring her attempt to speak. "Except at the very beginning, those years when I was finishing college and getting started, you've never *had* to work, and you don't have to now. This writing thing is only a.... You should know it isn't an easy thing. Your education isn't.... Well, I decided I wanted you to go to this conference, listen to the real writers talk, and get all this nonsense out of your system once and for all."

"I didn't say I wanted to—"

He held up his hand for silence and continued, "Please, Elizabeth, trust me in this. I want you to go. I want you to have a good time with Mrs. Bates and her friend and not give me a single thought. Can't you do that for me?"

"Oh, Edgar, I...." Trust rushed back, almost choked her. Guilt, for all her own shortcomings, for the fading moment of doubt, for the morning's anger, for all petty resentments that demeaned him in her mind, was a heavy weight on her breastbone. Confused feelings tangled her thoughts. She wanted, more than anything in the world, for him to hold her, to let her weep out her love and guilt in the shelter of his arms.

His hands reached out, but they didn't pull her into a warm embrace. Rather, they fastened on her shoulders and turned her around until she faced the door.

"Now! Now!" he said gruffly. "Just run and wash your face. That's my good girl."

"Edgar," she whispered, "I love...."

"My dear," he said quickly, perhaps too quickly, "I realize you're happy about this, but there's no need to get maudlin." His deep voice was firm, but it held an undertone of sadness; sadness and something else she couldn't quite identify, but it sounded very much like guilt.

"No, I suppose not. Thank you, Edgar."

"There's nothing to thank me for."

Her smile was soft, misty with love, with gratitude, and, at that particular moment, she loved him more than life itself. If he had pointed and told her to jump, she would have thrown herself into a blazing funeral pyre. "I think there is something to thank you for," she said as she walked through the door. "A lot."

"Elizabeth!"

Her name, on his lips, was sharp, and clearly a reprimand. She stopped instantly, whirled around.

Fearful she had committed some new sin, she looked at him pleadingly, wanting nothing more than to bring the gentleness back to his voice, the smile to his face.

He did smile; smiled and shook his head in mild reproof. "My dear Elizabeth," he said, "maybe I was wrong. Maybe I should reconsider letting you go wandering off into the wilds of Oregon."

Her dry mouth opened. Her lips framed a question, but all that came out was a whimper of sound.

"It's your memory again. What if I let you go and you forget to come back. It might not be safe." He shook his head again, but he didn't mention menopause or estrogen. He just bowed, every so slightly, and handed her his golden gift and the notebook. "You'll want to pack these, I think."

Red flooded her face, stood out in ugly blotches on her neck. "I'm sorry, Edgar. I.... It's a lovely suit. I.... Thank you."

And then she fled. Her heart was drumming rapidly, but the woman thought she heard him say, "I'm doing this for your own good, Elizabeth."

She spun her love and gratitude well, wrapped it around herself in an intricate weave, made a strong glue of her guilt, and hid inside the resulting cocoon, letting it blind her to the world. The cocoon stayed with her through the next thirty-nine hours, making her clean house frantically, shop for all Edgar's favorite foods, cook sumptuous meals, freeze them in microwave dishes, printing careful instructions for heating and serving each one.

And with each task, her guilt mounted, rode her with spurs and whip, took all the joyful anticipation away from the forthcoming trip. It prodded her with her selfishness, her insensitivity to his needs, made her see herself as an uncaring woman, going off to have a good time while her poor husband was at home, alone, lonely, having to fend for himself after working all day.

The chores filled the day, left no time for Elizabeth to get her hair done or go shopping with Cass. Reluctantly, Cass agreed to return the clothes and things she had purchased for Elizabeth, but as she was leaving Edgar's house, she asked, "Liz, did Edgar tell you why he changed his mind and decided to let you go with me?"

"I know you think he's a…. But he…. Cass, Edgar really wants me to be happy, it's just that sometimes he gets so busy he…."

"Hog puddles!" Cass said with a snort of disbelief. "He doesn't give a feather in a… in a fireplace for anything but Edgar Gilmartin. And he never will." She looked at Elizabeth consideringly and added, "He's got you right where he wants you and he's planning on—" her tone became carefully neutral, "I know you're pretty trusting and I don't want to.... Ah... Liz, that secretary of his, the marvelous Miss Marshall, is.... They might be...."

"Don't say it, Cass. Don't even think it. Edgar isn't having an affair with Miss Marshall, or with anyone else," Elizabeth said, and there wasn't a whisper of uncertainty in her voice or on her face.

"How can you be so sure?"

Without giving away her own secret, Elizabeth couldn't tell her friend how she knew Edgar was faithful—that Edgar was too fastidious, too power-driven to need casual sex, or even married sex. All she could say was, "I just am, that's all."

"Well, maybe you're right, for now at least, but remember I said this. The sexy Karoline has got the hots for Edgar, and she'll do a roll-over quicker than a mink. She'll try every twitchy trick in her book to get him to give her lessons in body-language."

"What an awful thing to say!"

"Open your eyes, Lizzie. Watch her. She hangs on his every word like a limpet on a.... What's a limpet?"

Elizabeth laughed. "I don't know." She pushed Cass gently but firmly toward the front door. "Go do your shopping."

"I suppose it's going to be like this all the time when you're a famous writer," Cass said mournfully. She tried to pull the corners of her mouth down, but the laugh lines pulled them back up. She grinned impishly. "I'll see you in the morning."

When Elizabeth didn't answer, Cass sobered and asked quietly, "You are going, aren't you?"

"I don't know. Edgar insists but...."

"But nothing! You've been hanging around this house for the past year. I'll pick you up at nine, and you'd better be wide-eyed and kicking. You hear me?"

The slim woman laughed. "Yes, Cass."

"Lizzie, I don't know what happened to make you like this, but even if you've forgotten, you're still a person, too. You have needs. Do you still want to be a writer?"

"I don't know, Cass. I don't know much of anything any more."

"Liz, you don't have to worry about it right now." Cass gave Elizabeth's elbow a quick squeeze. "See you in the morning?"

Elizabeth nodded, but when the door closed behind Cass' ample back, Elizabeth leaned her face against the cool wood. "What do I want?" she asked the emptiness around her. "I used to know, but now I just...."

A faint mental whispering, a weak stirring told her a part of the truth, told her the dream, her childhood dream of being a novelist, was still alive. Alive and growing.

The knowledge added new girth and bulk to her self-imposed burden of guilt. She backed away from the mahogany door, fled back into Edgar's house, flung herself into body-wearying labor, but it quieted neither guilt nor dream. They clamored at her, and she knew she could not live with them both. One would have to die.

Pale eyes bruised by sleeplessness and feeling like a well-used rag doll, Elizabeth sank into the passenger seat of Cass' blue Fiat, let Edgar kiss her cheek before he closed the door beside her, and then she sat, huddled into her own indecision.

"Have a good time, my dear. I'll see you Sunday afternoon," Edgar said as he stepped back and stood watching as Cass roared out of the circular drive.

Elizabeth nodded then looked back and saw him standing alone, straight back slumped a little, his handsome face shadowed by sadness. Her heart felt withered and thumped painfully, sending up hot, salty tears she could neither swallow nor shed. She looked at him, felt his loneliness like a knife in her own chest. Her lips opened to tell Cass to stop, to take her back to Edgar, but her tongue was too dry and her mouth was empty of words.

Cass glanced at her several times, but said nothing. Elizabeth endured the pain, tried to banish the guilt, but no matter what she did, Edgar's tired, lonely face haunted her. It even invaded her dreams when she fell into a fitful slumber on the plane to Portland, Oregon.

Muzzy-headed from the airsickness medication Cass had insisted she take, Elizabeth followed her friend out of the plane and through the crowded terminal.

"Three hours," Cass said.

"What?"

"We have a three hour layover here. The plane for Seaview doesn't leave...." Cass smiled at Elizabeth. "Boy, you're really out of it. Come on. Let's go get a drink. That'll make you feel better, and besides, I promised Emma we'd meet her in the lounge."

Elizabeth wrinkled her brow, tried to follow thoughts that vanished into the fog that beclouded her brain. "Emma?"

"You know. Emma Lawler. My friend. The writer."

"Oh. I thought her name was Desire or Caress or something like that."

"It is. I mean, they are." Cass took Elizabeth's arm and steered her into the bar. "She writes romances and uses—"

"A *nom de plume*," said a laughter-filled voice from behind them. "Or maybe, considering how

I've been getting on with my editor, *nom de guerre* is better."

Cass shrieked, turned and threw her arms around a woman as well-endowed as herself. She interrupted the embrace to introduce Elizabeth, and then, even before Elizabeth could murmur, "Hello," whisked them into a large booth, and ordered drinks around, all the time talking like an auctioneer, fast and loud. Emma Lawler, beige hair topping her round face like toasted coconut on a custard pie, talked every bit as fast, and almost as loud.

The buzz of talk stumbled and crawled through Elizabeth's haze. Time seemed distorted. She sipped at her foamy pink drink, and then at another without fully realizing the first had been emptied and removed.

Two middle-aged women, writers heading for the conference, crowded into the booth with them. Elizabeth slid to the outside edge of the seat, giving the chattering, laughing group as much room as possible. Someone pulled the adjoining table up to the booth. Four more writers, three men and one woman, sat down. Another round of drinks appeared. The noise level was almost unbearable.

Elizabeth rubbed her temples with her fingertips, trying to push out the dull nothingness that lingered inside her skull. But she couldn't force herself to join the carefree laughter that exploded around her, couldn't feel less than totally alone.

Edgar's face floated before her. His sad eyes begged her to come home. Guilt pushed her up and away from the crowded table. As she rose and walked away, placing her feet with exaggerated care, Elizabeth heard Cass call something about the restroom and nodded a reply.

But as soon as she was out of her friend's sight, Elizabeth hurried to the rank of telephone booths she had seen on the concourse earlier. A smile of love softened the lines of her face as she dialed the operator, reversed the charges, and waited for Edgar's receptionist to answer.

Humming a wee tune, she tried to imagine Edgar's surprise when she told him she was coming home on the next plane, told him she no longer wanted to be a writer, that she would be home in time to cook his dinner.

Lost in her daydream of Edgar's joy, their happy reunion, she jumped when a voice in her ear said, "Gilmartin and Associates. May I help you?" But the woman could hardly wait for the girl to accept the charges before she said, "Thank you, Betsy. May I speak to my husband, please?"

"Oh, Mrs. Gilmartin, I'm sorry. You just missed them. They left for Las Vegas not more than twenty minutes ago. You might call the airport," the girl said doubtfully.

Elizabeth heard the girl's words, mundane, information-giving words, but her sudden foreboding turned the words into clods of dirt thudding on the closed lid of a coffin, her own coffin. Although she was smothering, almost gasping for air, Elizabeth tried to say good-by graciously and hang up the phone before she screamed, or fainted, or swore viciously, but she was horrified to hear herself ask, "They?"

Surprise was in the girl's tinny-sounding voice when she said, "Miss Marshall and Mr. Gilmartin." And then pity was added to the faraway voice when it asked, "Mrs. Gilmartin, you haven't forgotten, have you? I mean this is that big financial symposium, the one where Mr. Gilmartin is going to sit on a panel. It's a real honor, and it's been on our calendar for over two months."

Had she forgotten? Was she really going mad? How else could she account for forgetting something that was so important in Edgar's life?

Holding the receiver against her ear, Elizabeth sat, trying to remember, and then knew with a pain that pierced her like a crooked ice pick, knew for absolute certain sure she had never been told of the symposium. Edgar had deliberately lied to her, had made her feel dirty, guilty, worthless, all for nothing. Edgar had lied to her. Had lied. Lied.

The word echoed in her mind, sickened her, but, somehow, she forced her voice to sound calm, unconcerned as she uttered her own lie. "Oh, no," she said with a little laugh. "I haven't forgotten. I just thought I could catch him before he left and…. Oh, well, it wasn't important. I

forgot to wish him luck before I left this morning
and…. Well, you know."

She exchanged a few more social noises with
the girl, laughed a little tinkly laugh, and said her
farewell with an unconcern that would have
fooled a lie detector. But when she tried to slip the
phone back on the hook, her hand shook wildly,
just like the rest of her body. Resting her head
against the back of the booth, she fought back the
shock waves that battered her, threatened to
destroy her, bury her in grief for a marriage that
had died. Died after a very long and lingering
illness.

"I never thought it would come to this," she said
wonderingly. "I never thought he would actually
kill it. Not like this. Not like some worn-out useless thing." She sighed.

Elizabeth didn't know how long she sat in the
booth, never remembered finding her way to the
blue-tiled restroom. But she was there, her glasses
sitting on the shelf beneath the mirror, cold water
gushing into the sink, hands splashing water onto
her flushed face, a face that held no trace of tears
(if any tears had been shed) when Cass found her,
caught her by the gray-clad shoulders and turned
her around.

"You look like hell," Cass said. Her voice was

hoarse, rasping, but there was real concern in her eyes and tenderness in her hands when she guided Elizabeth to the sofa and forced her to lie down.

"You've been gone a long time. I looked everywhere. Are you sick?"

Voicing another lie, because she couldn't yet expose the truth to her friend's eyes, couldn't tell Cass how little Edgar cared for his wife, their marriage, she said, and it was almost the truth, "No, I just can't seem to wake up. My head feels like it's full of oatmeal—the kind you used to make, slimy and full of lumps."

"It's those damned motion sickness pills. I should have had better sense. They do make some people feel like that." She stood, looking down at Elizabeth for a long silent moment and then she stooped, brushed back her friend's hair and placed her palm flat on Elizabeth's forehead.

"Liz," she said slowly, "look, if you want to go back home now, I'll understand."

"No!" Elizabeth wiggled away from Cass' hand and sat up. "No," she said again. "I do *not* want to go home."

"There's no need to get huffy. I just thought.... Liz, you looked so sad when we left, I just thought you might be missing Edgar."

"Edgar," Elizabeth said bitterly, and then she laughed, a harsh, savage sound. "Who the bloody hell is Edgar?"

Cass laughed, too, a little belatedly, but the

laughter didn't reach her eyes, didn't dislodge the worry line on her forehead that stayed during the short flight to Seaview.

Elizabeth saw the worry, but she was entangled in her own bed of thorns and couldn't make Cass' way any easier. The scotch and water seemed even less potent than its prior foamy pink partner. Her legs were steady, her voice unslurred, her brain rerunning Edgar's misdeeds, when Cass told her their luggage had been lost in flight. It was the crowning irony. The final straw.

Laughing with good, honest mirth, Elizabeth said, referring to Edgar's lost gift, "Fool's gold. Only I didn't know I was the fool."

"What?"

"Private joke," Elizabeth said. "Anyway, I'm glad. Gold isn't my color. It makes me look as yellow as... as... as yuk."

"Maybe you'd feel better if you had some coffee," Cass said. "I've never seen you—"

"Mary Alice Cassidy Bates, I'm ashamed of you. You think I'm drunk! Me, Elizabeth Gilmartin, Edgar's tame rug? Drunk? Impossible! Edgar would never allow...." She turned away, quickly, before Cass could see the naked grief in her eyes, grief that was undiluted by tears.

"Honey, I don't know what's wrong, but if you need me, I'm here. If you need to talk or...."

Perhaps Elizabeth would have told her then, but there was no time. Emma hustled them into the Seaview Inn's crowded courtesy car—a van, actually. Talk swirled over and around them. Writer talk. Gossip about markets, other writers, editors, agents, about themselves, their newest project, the critics, books. Writer talk.

When she walked into the inn, Elizabeth's mood had shifted from grieving to reckless uncaring. "You register for us," she told Cass. "I'm going to spend money, lots of money." Without waiting for an answer, Elizabeth strolled across the lobby and into a small, beautifully appointed shop.

The clerk smiled and looked at her expectantly.

"The airline lost my luggage," Elizabeth said as she dropped a handful of credit cards onto the counter. "All my luggage."

The clerk's smile grew wider. "Size nine?" she asked.

"Size nine," Elizabeth agreed.

Her metamorphosis had begun.

When Cass and Emma followed her into the shop, Elizabeth Gilmartin was already slightly more than one person.

Buying almost wildly, she had stepped beyond mouse-gray and housewife drab, had bought a deep-rose chiffon dress with a low neckline and sequins aglitter on bodice and skirt; matching thigh-high nylons and high-heeled sandals; several filmy teddies; French bras; lace panties; a flannel gown in Day-glo red, with a robe to match; white silk pants and a pink velour tunic; a sweet-scented hodge-podge of other garments and sundries, including a Garfield pencil tablet and two Bic pens.

"For a writer?" Cass asked quietly.

"For me," Elizabeth answered, just as quietly, "whoever I am."

But there was no time for soul searching, identity crises, or tearing grief for a dead marriage. There was only time to grab her purchases and credit cards and follow Cass, Emma, and the inn manager as he led them out a side door and down a covered path to the VIP annex and into a very large, bright, filled-with-flowers living room.

"A suite?" Emma asked, looking like a bewildered grandmother lost in a stranger's flower garden.

"Oh, yes," he said. "Nothing but the best for Caress Love, America's Queen of Romance." He smiled, pointed to the wet bar, and said, "Champagne's chilling. There's wine from most of the Oregon wineries."

He turned slightly, indicated a wall of drapery-covered glass. "The deck is through there and the beach is just beyond." Turning back, he said, "Your bedroom suite is on the fireplace wall, Miss Love, and there are two smaller bedrooms on the opposite walls for your guests."

"I had no idea," Emma said. "I'm sure we don't need...."

"Oh, but you do. It was planned early on.

There's an open house for all the writers tonight. You are the hostess, so naturally it will be held here. Tomorrow there are the television interviews, several small gatherings for fans, a reception for local dignitaries and so on. I'm sure you understand."

Emma obviously didn't, but she shrugged. "Why not," she said. She was still talking to the man when Elizabeth and Cass went to their adjoining bedrooms—each with its own private bath.

Cass inspected her room and then came into Elizabeth's. She was admiring Elizabeth's purchases when Elizabeth realized Cass had lost her luggage too and the small shop had had nothing in Cass' size. "Oh, Cass," she said contritely, "I'm sorry. What are you going to wear?"

She sounded so much like the old Elizabeth, Cass' face brightened with relief. "Oh, don't worry about that," she said airily. "The famous Caress Love travels heavy. She's got enough clothes, all from New York, too, to outfit me and three other economy-sized orphans of the airways."

Perhaps she sounded like the old Elizabeth, but the woman, painted and curled by Cass' expert hand, who slipped out of the bedroom two hours later didn't look like the old Elizabeth. But she was still only a single step away, only just beginning to twin.

The rose dress clung to her breasts and waist, floated around her long legs. Her hair was streaked with glitter and had been pulled back and up with a rhinestone clip; foundation and blush gave her face a healthy glow. Elizabeth Gilmartin left her glasses in her room and wandered out into the world. Her shadowed eyes large and bright, and somehow innocent without their shield of glass, showed no sign of grief.

She laughed and nodded as she sipped wine, listened to the babble of party voices, but she made no effort to separate the shifting blur into individual people, didn't try to see or feel. Edging through the crowd, she heard bits and parts of conversations. Someone pushed a card into her hand, explained how to fill it out if she were planning on entering the contest for new writers, a contest with a ten thousand-dollar prize and publication by a major publishing house.

She smiled, listened, agreed to enter, and, only a moment later, laid the card on the mantle of the fireplace and forgot it even existed. Then she accepted another glass of wine.

After her fourth, or maybe fifth drink, memory tried to drag out the evidence of Edgar's sin, but she fought it away and stepped out onto the deck. It was crowded, too crowded, too many strangers, too much noise. Elizabeth had to get away.

In an agony of haste, she pushed between talking groups, heard someone say, "What did she expect?

All she did was lollygag around the house...."
And then from a different group, "Oh, she's one of
those women who wait at home, hoping her husband will come home horny and say a few nice...."

She didn't know whom either group was talking about, but the words hit home. The pain came
roaring back as a black, ravening beast, ripping
and tearing at her, clawing, killing, ugly as sin—
Edgar's sin.

Tears started in her eyes. Her hand groped for
support, brushed down the smooth, chilled side of
a wine bottle. She hefted it, knew it was nearly
full before she stepped off the redwood deck and
walked into the night. She headed toward the sea.
It was only a blur, a dark-sheened blur that moved
restlessly under a bank of white that trailed long
streamers as it moved slowly toward the shore.

Elizabeth couldn't see the fog, didn't know the
menace in the changing tide. She pulled off the
high-heeled sandals, let them lay where they fell,
and walked down the hard-packed sand at the
edge of the water. Walked. And walked. Walked
and drank from the cool bottle. Drank wine and
cried for yesterday, all the yesterdays. The yesterdays that were gone beyond recall; gone, taking
love with them.

When the bottle was empty and the tears only
salt marks on her cheeks, she turned her back on
the crashing tide that crawled farther and farther
up the shore.

"Damn you, Edgar," she said hoarsely. "Damn you! Damn you!"

She stumbled, fell to her knees. A wave roared in, ran cold across her rose-nyloned feet. Gasping, Elizabeth scrambled up, took four running steps and ran solidly into something—something warm, something male.

His arms closed around her, held her.

Wine had lowered her defenses. Her starved body betrayed her, lusted mightily. She snuggled against the stranger's chest. But only for an instant.

And then, horrified, ashamed of her own reaction, she jerked free, took a stumbling step back, looked up at the looming shadow, a dark, faceless shadow whose arms still reached for her.

The back of her hand against her mouth, she took another step away from him.

He came toward her.

"No," she moaned deep in her throat. "Oh, please, no."

Chapter Four

♥   ♥   ♥

The fog swirled, drifted. The quarter moon touched his face with silver, hid his eyes in dark pits. Silent as the fog, he moved toward her, reached out with shadowy arms to hold her.

Elizabeth took another faltering step backward. Her mouth was open, her teeth pressed into the back of her hand.

He laughed softly. "I bet I can guess."

She didn't answer, just stood, poised for flight, fear yammering in her chest.

"It has to be," he said musingly. "Her hair caught back in a net of diamond dew, she backed away." He chuckled. "Of course. A Gothic heroine. Right?"

"What?" Elizabeth edged back, away from his looming shape, black fear against the featureless night.

"Nothing important," he said. "But I was wondering if...? You know, I really do need help with my lust scenes. I thought you were just the...."

Fear pushed her back. Her icy foot snagged a long hunk of kelp. She shuddered and tried to escape from it, too. An incoming wave built higher than its fellows, and then higher again, towering over her. It broke with a roar. The man shouted. The wall of brine rolled over her, tumbling her over the wet, cold sand.

Elizabeth sputtered, gasped. Sand rasped across her back, her knees, her elbows. She fought the yielding water, rolled hither and yon at its whim. She swallowed, gagged, and went limp. Too limp to struggle when something clutched her wrists, slid her, face down, across water-bubbled sand.

Finally, she knew it was the man who held her arms, but she didn't fear him now, and was too weak, too soggy, to thank him—if, in fact, he deserved thanks.

"Can you get up?" he panted. "The tide's coming in pretty fast. You.... I can't drag you any further."

She got to her hands and knees. The night air wrapped her wet body in icy sheets. Elizabeth started to shiver. "Sorry," she said through chattering teeth. "Can't... can't."

"Horse pucky!" he said, his laughter making the mild oath sing. "You're drunk. That's all. Just plain old falling-down drunk."

Anger gave her a little strength, enough to pull her legs under her and stand up. "I'm not!" she said. "I'm not drunk. I...."

She started to slump back to the sand. He

caught her by the arm. "Come on," he said. "Let's get you warm and dry and then we'll argue about your sobriety or lack thereof."

His arm around her, they staggered up through the loose sand, around the end of a jack-strawed pile of driftwood, and into a shallow cave hollowed out of the smooth wall of stone by a millennium of winter seas. It was warmed and dimly lit by the dying embers of a campfire just outside its wide mouth.

"Hurry," he said as he eased her down on the soft wool blanket that lay like a rug on the sandy floor. "Take your wet clothes off while I build up the fire."

Half-blind without her glasses, the cave was a jumble of leaping darks and shifting lights and her body was almost numb with cold. The cold had invaded her to the very bone, shaking her so violently she was unable to undo the zipper and hooks that held the sodden dress around her. Beneath the chill something else made her shiver. Something that was akin to fear, of herself as much as of the unknown, unseen man.

She tried, but all she could manage to do was pull off the ruined nylons. She heard him grunt as he heaved something onto the fire, saw the flickering light grow red-gold and bright; a haze of red against the shadows that veered and moved like dancing snakes. One shadow detached itself from the rest, came toward her, stood over her.

"I was right, wasn't I? You are a Gothic heroine. Too pure to undress in front of the hero. Or maybe I'm the villain." He talked on, nonsensically, as his hands, impersonal as a grave robber's, opened zippers and hooks, pulled the pink dress over her head, followed it with her satin slip, then tossed her lace bra onto the discarded heap.

Chilled air slid silkily across the curves of her suddenly bare body. She sucked in a quick, involuntary breath, sat a bit straighter, and then she shivered, not entirely from the cold, and bent her head forward, hiding her flushed face behind the tangle of her sea-dank hair.

The fire flared skyward. Rosy light flickered and gleamed on the swell of her right hip, up the smooth length of her bent leg, and across the high arch of her narrow foot. She knew he was looking at her; knew it and didn't try to hide. For an instant, neither man nor woman moved, spoke, or breathed. But only for an instant.

Then he reached into the shadows beside him, dragged out a folded blanket, shook it out, wrapped the fleecy folds around her, making her feel like Cleopatra in the rug. For added warmth, he tucked the blanket she was lying on up and around her feet and legs, after he had propped her against the cave's back wall, two king-sized pillows probably stolen from his own bed protected her from the hard, cold stone.

He knelt in the sand, a dark shape against the

golden rose of the fire, and she thought he pulled off his sweater or sweatshirt and used it to towel his fog-damp hair. The firelight curled around his head, glinting off his tousled hair—wet hair that was either streaked with blond or frosty silver.

For a brief, improbable, breath-holding morsel of time, her cold fingers itched to run down the strong bones of his face. A face she still couldn't focus. Edgar Gilmartin's wife shivered.

The man moved away from her and blended with the shifting blur of fog and shadow, but Elizabeth knew he was still there, she could hear the sand crunch beneath his feet as he moved around. Clearing her throat, she said softly, "I have to go back. They'll be worried. Back at the hotel, I mean. I didn't tell anyone I was leaving the party. I really have.…" She wiggled her bound body, trying to free herself from the blanket's enfolding wings.

"Not until you're warm and dry," he said from somewhere near the fire. A moment later, he chuckled and added, "And sober."

"I'm not drunk," Elizabeth said. It was true. She wasn't drunk, only distant from herself, not fully connected to the Elizabeth she had been; the lonely, heartsick Elizabeth who mourned a marriage that should have lived, should have been filled with love and meaning. She knew all that, but there were no words that could explain it. So she could only repeat, "I'm not drunk."

"Of course not," he said agreeably. "How stupid of me to forget. Gothic heroines aren't permitted to get drunk. They just wander around in the fog, hoping the hero will arrive in time to...."

"I'm not much of a heroine either," Elizabeth said, and then she added, almost accusingly, "You're a writer."

"Not much of one," he said somberly. He came back to the blanket, stood looking down at her for a moment before he dropped down at her side, draping still another blanket over them both and pulled her shivering body close to his warmth. "I won't be a writer at all," he said, "unless I can get those damned.... Are you sure you can't help me with my lust scenes?"

The heat of the roaring fire, of the man so close to her, was trapped in the blankets, encircling her in comfort, well-being, making her relax in the stranger's embrace. She knew his words were half-joke, half-plea for aid and knew she should answer lightly, but the words that came were from Elizabeth's pain, Elizabeth's degradation. The bitter words of a rejected, unloved woman were puffs of steam in the cold air before she could close her mouth, banish them and send them back into their place of darkness and shame.

"How would I know anything about lust," she said. "My husband hasn't..." her voice shook like her body, steadied, went on, "my husband hasn't even tried to make love to me for years."

Ice crept into her voice, made it cold, distant. "Not even the one time I went to his room and... and begged him to hold me and....."

She lifted her head, stared out at the unseen night, her chin high, her tense body daring him to offer her pity. Yet, in some strange way, she wanted his pity, his understanding; wanted to give him all the secrets that were cankering her soul, and all the small, fragile dreams.

"Could be a mid-life crisis. Or perhaps he's having an affair," the man said, and it sounded as if he were discussing the plot of a book, as yet unwritten.

"No," Elizabeth said slowly.

"Too trite, huh?" he asked, and she felt rather than saw him nod in answer to his own question. "You're probably right. How about impotence? Men are ashamed of that."

"No, I don't think he's.... It's something else, it has to be."

"It's his loss. They say, or if they don't, they should: A little fornication is the staff of life."

She laughed, a warm, husky laugh that carried away any lingering guilt, or sense of duty undone —and the woman who wasn't exactly Elizabeth felt freer than she had ever felt. She settled deeper into the warm nest of blankets. "Not Edgar," she said, "he would never even think such a thing, let alone say it."

"That's your answer then. The man has to be a

fool, a blind fool, or dead."

The implied compliment that said he had looked and found her desirable lit a fire that spread through her body, turned her bones to over-cooked noodles and tied little knots in her breath. But free as she was, Elizabeth was not yet free enough to admit her need.

Instead, she told him a secret, a precious secret tossed out like so much fluff. "When I was young, I wanted to be a writer."

"And now?" He twisted his body, getting more comfortable in their shared bed.

"I think it's too late. Maybe it was always too late. I married Edgar when I was seventeen, the week after I graduated from high school. That's when dreams are the brightest. I guess I...." She shook her head, not wanting to remember the young Elizabeth, the girl who had been so eager to sacrifice her dreams, her hopes and her future.

"Lots of things die on love's altar," he said quietly. "Probably too many things."

"Edgar needed me then."

"Does he need you now?"

She read the other question behind his actual words and knew he was trying to tell her to do what she had to do, but she just said, "He says he does. But it just.... He needs me to clean his house and cook for his clients."

The man didn't say anything.

Elizabeth tried again. "The dream is dead.

Reincarnated dreams are worse than ghosts. They lead you on and.... They're not real either."

"Oh," he said, politely as a matron at a tea party. "I see. You're afraid of the work. I agree, it is much easier to talk writing than it is to write. Perhaps you could write a few sweet little poems and show them to your friends. That should make them oooooh and aaaah and give your ego—"

"I.... Edgar doesn't want me to...."

"So? Don't tell him."

"But he.... I owe...."

"What do you owe yourself?"

"But I.... Maybe I can't do it. Maybe I...."

He yawned. "Excuses."

After the briefest of pauses, she agreed, "Excuses."

"Why are you so afraid?" he asked gently.

"Because...." Anger whipped through her. How dare he question, make her dig so deep, expose more than her body. And then the anger was gone. She answered his question honestly. "Because I might fail," she said, "and then the dream would be truly dead." Then, faint as a dying echo, she added, "Or I might succeed."

The fire died down to a bed of coals. Night drew in close around them, but Elizabeth didn't care. The whole thing—the man, the cave, the closeness—seemed a waking dream, a fantasy. Languor cradled her, laved her with warmth and trust.

Her head sank into the softness of the big pillows. Perhaps she dozed, but she awoke to hear him say, with laughter hiding in the nooks and crannies of his drawl, "Gothic heroines aren't afraid of anything."

"I told you, I'm not...."

"You could practice," he said innocently. "You're probably better than you think. You fooled me, you know. You really did that hand-to-your-mouth, eyes-dark-with-terror bit good."

"No," she said slowly. "Once I was.... I'm not good for anything now except being Edgar's rug."

"What color?" he asked.

"What color what?"

"Rug," he answered. "If you're going to be a writer, you're going to have to describe things better than that."

"Am I?" She turned her head on the pillow, tried to see the face so close to her own. She could feel his breath feathering across her cheek, could smell his spicy aftershave, slightly tainted by the sea's salt-fish tang, but she couldn't see his face, couldn't judge the truth in his voice when he said, "Oh, yes, you'll write. What's the use of hurting so much if you don't use it in a book?"

"But...."

"No excuses."

"Yes, sir," she said softly.

His fingers trailed down the line of her jaw, brushed her lips, set them a-tingle. "No one can order your life, beautiful lady from the sea. No one but you."

"Can I?"

"I don't know," he said slowly. "I know only this. Birds are born to fly and dreams have to be followed. Fly free, love, and leave fear behind. But if you can't, that's not the end."

"No," she said, but there was no firmness in her voice. Doubt crept in, gnawed at her self-content, made her remember who she was, what she was, and what she wasn't. Made her know she was still Edgar's wife, she had never truly walked free, couldn't fly.

But the new self, the one that was part of the dream, that struggled to be born, pushed the doubt away and asked, "Is that from one of your books?"

"No," he said. "Perhaps it will be in…. No, not mine. Yours. You will put it in your book."

"My book," she whispered, tasting the words in her mouth, but it wasn't quite a question, nor was it a statement of fact.

He leaned over, kissed her on the forehead. "Your book," he said, and it was a benediction.

Before the silence could lengthen and erect a wall between them, the man asked, "Are you hungry? Soul-searching always makes my stomach whimper for food."

"Famished," she said, laughter warming her voice, making it rich and free.

They shared his hoard. Talking as they ate ham

sandwiches and munched crunchy apples. They covered many subjects, if scantily, but none of them personal. She was an awed listener as he talked of the craft of writing, giving her snippets of information, jumping from finishing manuscripts to agents, from tense agreement to rewrites; telling her how to appear professional, and warning her of the shoals and sharks along the way.

She understood, if dimly, most of what he was saying. But when the man at her side told her to use how-to sex books for her sex scenes, baby-naming books for her character names, and books of astrology for their distinguishing characteristics, Elizabeth laughed.

"You'll find out," he said. "Just wait until your first lust... ahem... I mean, love scene is staring back at you while you're trying to arrange all those arms and legs and lips and sighs and panting breaths into something that will make other people do a little panting of their own. Then, my lady, you'll be really sorry you laughed."

Chuckling at the scene he had conjured in her mind, Elizabeth agreed he was probably right, but she didn't want to agree when he said, regretfully, "I think your fairy godmother is calling you, Cinderella. I think it's time to go home."

Salt-stiffened and chilled, the skirts of the ruined rose chiffon slapped at her legs. The sand was cold beneath her bare feet, but one of the wool blankets was snug and warm around her body—the blanket and the man's arm as they walked back through the swirling fog, silently and as close as lovers, beside the dark, mourning sea.

When they reached the redwood deck outside her door, he put his hands on her shoulders and turned her to face him. "Don't be sad, Wanda. After all, it is a happy ending. The Gothic heroine is still a virgin."

She knew he wanted her to laugh, but Elizabeth couldn't, not then, not when parting with a stranger was such a hurting thing. She asked, more to hold him there than because she wanted to know, "Who is Wanda?"

"You, love."

"No, I...."

His finger touched her lips, silencing her protest. "It's only a dream," he said. "I created you out of the night. I called on all the old gods, demanded a maiden for.... Anyway, you are my creation. I have the right to name you."

His hand slid across her cheek, down her neck to her shoulder, around her back, pulling her close. His other hand joined the first. He held her against his heart as if she were precious beyond pearls.

Her face chilled by the fog, Elizabeth lifted her head. Their lips met, clung. His arms tightened. Her arms ached to return his embrace, to slip around his neck and pull him closer—but they were held fast inside the imprisoning blanket. She couldn't reach out and draw him back when he finally released her and stood for a moment looking down at her upturned face.

She had no breath to speak, and his voice was husky when he said, "You're beautiful, Wanda."

She struggled to say something, but all that came out was, "I.... Oh, Barry, I...."

"Who is Barry?" he asked, mock anger bringing the teasing quality back to his drawling voice.

"I.... Maybe I created you," Elizabeth said. "Maybe the old gods answered my...."

He kissed the tip of her nose. "Perhaps they did, love," he said. "Or perhaps this is only the first chapter of your novel."

Elizabeth looked up at him, straining her myopic eyes, trying to see his face. He bent his head, kissed her gently. "Good-night, love," he said. And then he stepped away from her, stepped back into that blur that was the foggy night.

She didn't try to call him back. The thin, not-quite-so-nondescript woman, Edgar's obedient wife, with a stranger's kiss still warm and sweet on her lips, walked quietly across the sandy deck and into the living room of the VIP suite.

A small lamp burned behind the bar, another cast a circle of light on a table. They didn't help much. Elizabeth threaded her way blindly through the shadowy maze of furniture, pausing at the fireplace to scramble across the mantle with her fingers, searching for the entry card for the writing contest she had tossed there earlier.

She found it. A smile made her pale eyes large, her lips soft, her face young and somehow innocent. And it didn't fade entirely when she fumbled her way into her dimly lit bedroom and saw a shape siting up on her bed. She heard Cass' voice say, "Where on earth have you been?"

It wasn't possible to tell Cass all that had happened, not without explaining about Edgar, and the middle of the night wasn't the time for that. Elizabeth took a little breath and said, "Walking."

"In this fog? Without your glasses? Bosh! You can't see six inches without them. You'd have been lost in...."

"I was," Elizabeth said dreamily. "But a man found me and we...."

"Hog flanders!" Cass snapped. "You had too much wine at the party, wandered off somewhere, and fell asleep. I sure hope you didn't ruin that blanket. They look expensive and I'm sure the inn doesn't want its guests taking them down to...." She stood up, came over to Elizabeth.

Pulling the blanket a little tighter around her shoulders, Elizabeth said, "It's not their blanket."

"God deliver me! Elizabeth," Cass said tiredly, "their name and crest is right here." Her pointing finger touched the midnight-blue blanket somewhere near Elizabeth's belly button.

She couldn't see it, but Elizabeth traced the white embroidery with her fingertip and understood. Her smile deepened and was as innocently joyful as her thoughts. He was a guest at the inn. He had to be. Probably in Oregon for the conference.

Her heartbeat speeded up. They were staying at the same hotel. *I'll get to see him again!* Giddy with the thought, she laughed aloud, and the laughter was only partially at her own silliness.

She couldn't see the man again. She hadn't seen him at all yet. No, she thought, still breathless, she hadn't seen him. Only kissed him. Then another thought came, unbidden but true, terribly true. *I wanted him. Dear God, how I wanted....*

"Stop standing there, grinning like a cross-eyed ninny," Cass said shortly. "Go to bed. The good Lord knows you're going to feel like hell tomorrow, but maybe some sleep will help." She turned away from Elizabeth, walked heavily to the queen-sized bed, and flipped back the covers.

"Soon, Cass, soon," Elizabeth said softly. "There's something I have to do first. Something important."

"What could be important at this time of night?" Cass asked. "Why don't you just put on your night clothes and get into bed? Whatever it is will keep until....

"Elizabeth, please, don't get your sick-mule look. Nobody knew where you were and I've been worried sick."

"I'm sorry, Cass," Elizabeth said. "I didn't

mean to worry you. It just happened. I mean...
I'll go to bed in just a little while." And then,
because it seemed proper to the time and place,
she invoked their private ritual. "I promise."

Chapter Five

♥   ♥   ♥

Elizabeth's soft promise seemed to touch Cass as she swallowed hard before she said, "Forget what I said. I'm nothing but a mother hen. Look, do what you have to do. I'll see you in the morning."

She turned away from the bed, came to Elizabeth and brushed the backs of her fingers down her cheek. "Sometimes I forget we're both grown up now. I used to have to take care.... You were so damned dumb, for a smart person, when we were kids I just got into the habit of looking after you. I'll try to.... Good night, Elizabeth." She moved away, out of the hazy limits of Elizabeth's vision.

Elizabeth stood quietly until she heard the door shut behind her dearest friend, the friend she couldn't tell her secrets to.

Smiling again, Elizabeth released the blanket, let it fall at her feet, pulled off the ruined dress, dropped it on top of the blanket, and suddenly realized she had left her bra and slip in the cave.

Dismissing the memory lapse with an airy laugh, and clad only in her lacy panties, she stood in the warm, unfamiliar room and tried to remember where she had left her glasses.

During the course of her fumbling, shin-cracking search, she found the robe and slippers she had bought earlier, slid her cold feet into the scuffs and belted the robe tightly around her as she patted tabletops and pawed through sacks and dresser drawers. She found the Bic pens first, dropped one into her robe pocket, to keep company with the card she had put there for safekeeping.

She kept feeling through scarcely seen, unrecognized objects until her toes collided with her large purse, which was setting just under the edge of the bed. Then she remembered the grieving, long-ago Elizabeth putting her glasses away so carefully, almost fearfully; wanting to wear them, to hide behind them as she had always done.

But now she didn't need to hide, she just needed to see. The gray-rimmed glasses perched on the bridge of her slim nose, Elizabeth tapped the end of the pen against her front teeth, considering the card that lay, almost white and only slightly wrinkled, on the desk before her. She read and thought, and then, giggles crowding in her throat, she began to write.

Elizabeth Gilmartin was Edgar's wife. She would never be allowed to write, but the slim woman in the Day-glo robe was more than just

Elizabeth. She remembered the fragments of conversation she had overheard at the open house, the same conversation that had struck the old Elizabeth like a blow and sent her weeping into the night.

"That's right," she mused. "That was me. I was the woman who lollygagged around the house, waiting for my husband to come home horny." Eyes sparkling, she wrote "Lolly Horn" on the line that asked for the author's name.

And so, Lolly Horn, child of party gossip, foggy midnight, a stranger's kiss, and a woman's dream, was born alive and kicking.

It was Lolly who printed Elizabeth's address and telephone number into the proper blanks on the card. It was Lolly who giggled softly as she wrote *A Touch of Fornication* as the title of her novel.

Although she walked on Elizabeth's narrow, high-arched feet, it was Lolly who went boldly through the night to the inn's deserted lobby and deposited the filled-out card in the slotted box she had noticed earlier; a medium-sized box, wrapped in white butcher paper, and marked, "Writing Contest Entries."

But it was Elizabeth, wet hair wrapped in a towel, memory making her voice shy, who said, "Wait, Cass," the next morning when her friend came back from answering a knock on the door.

Cass was carrying a package, wrapped in plain

brown paper, and muttering, "I tried to tell him it was a mistake, but he wouldn't listen. Now, I'm going to have to take this to the front desk and let them take care of it. Wanda, whoever she is, is probably expecting it."

"No, don't, Cass. I'm Wanda."

Elizabeth's quiet claim stopped Cass in her tracks. "But…" she started, and then she closed her mouth, swallowing back whatever it was she was going to say. Cass could stop her words, but she couldn't stop the worry that rushed up to fill her eyes.

Her lips a narrow slash of scarlet, Cass said nothing more as she handed the heavy package to Elizabeth, who hugged it to her breast before she sat down on a bar stool, setting the package on the bar before her, then tearing the wrapping with eager fingers.

Eyes bright as a child's on Christmas morn, breath caught and held in her lungs, Elizabeth pulled loose the final, crackling fold of paper. She found a stack of books, lifted them one by one, looking for a note from the giver; a note from the unseen stranger.

But there was nothing, except for Cass' shocked whisper, "What in God's Sweet Name have you done, Elizabeth?"

"What?" Bewilderment creasing her forehead, Elizabeth turned her head, looked at Cass.

"First, last night. Now, these books. I should

have realized something.... I know you don't want to talk about...."

"The books? What's wrong with...?" The slim woman glanced down at the double stack of books, read the titles of the top two, both highly touted, very explicit sex books, and then blushed as she tried to convince Cass of her own innocence in the face of the very incriminating evidence.

"It isn't what you think. It's just.... Well, he said sex books would help.... That I could learn how to...." The words stumbled across her tongue and fell into a deep, silent pool of misunderstanding that vanished without a single ripple.

"Who, Elizabeth?"

"I tried to tell you. Last night, when I.... The man who found me in the fog. He.... I ran from him and... the ocean rolled me over. He pulled me out and...." The words of explanation floundered, tried to find firmer footing. "I was all wet and freezing. He had to undress me and...."

"Oh, yes, I know the rest. This shining knight of yours took advantage of a drunk."

"I wasn't drunk."

"Be that as it may, the man is still a pervert," Cass said bitterly. "Sending books like that to.... Elizabeth, you've never said a word, but I know things aren't good between you and Edgar. There's no need to... to...." Her voice softened. "Sometimes women do things when they get older, things to prove they are still beautiful and… but this isn't the right way. If you're not happy with Edgar, get a divorce, but please, I beg you, stay away from this man."

"Oh, Cass, I…. You don't understand."

"Don't I?" Cass asked. "You're wrong, Elizabeth. I understand only too well." She turned away, walked to the door to the deck, stood there, straight-backed, pain in every line of her ample body.

"I always thought I did, but I guess I really don't know you very well, Elizabeth. I never thought you would…. It isn't right, not for you. Some women can sleep around but not you. You're too…."

"Nothing like that happened," Elizabeth said.

"Not yet, maybe," Cass answered, and then she faced Elizabeth. "Who is he?"

"I…." Elizabeth couldn't tell Cass she didn't know the man's name or anything about him.

"Dear God, you don't know, do you? Oh, Elizabeth, can't you see this is wrong? Don't you know someone has always taken care of you? You don't know the first thing about the real world? We've all protected you, let you live in your world of books. You're a *nice* person and you're as innocent as they come. Too damned innocent."

"Innocent?" Elizabeth asked. "And nice? That's all I am?"

"That's the best. You don't know what it's like to be so damned lonely, so starved for love you'd….

You have a husband. You don't have to go out looking for...."

Before Elizabeth could ask, "Don't I?" Emma breezed into the room. "Aren't you two ready yet? It's less than thirty minutes until the big breakfast in the ballroom. You'd better get going or we'll miss my speech."

"I'll hurry," Elizabeth said. "I'm all ready except for my hair." She picked up the four sex books, the baby name book, and the two astrology books and started to go to her bedroom. Pausing for an instant, she looked at Cass and said, "Cass, I *do* know. And sometimes nice is terminal, as terminal as any other social disease. But I hope to God it's not too late for me. I hope mine is still curable."

Emma laughed. "That's great, Elizabeth. You sound just like a writer."

"Well, she isn't," Cass said, the bitterness back in her voice, "and she never will be if she keeps on the way she's going. She won't be anything but... but sorry."

Elizabeth walked out of the room without replying, but Lolly smiled and hugged the books a little tighter, anticipating the first day of her life. It was a day that would bring her face to face with the stranger, and with the magical world of writers and writing. And at that moment, she couldn't have said which of the two, the man or the dream, was the more important.

The conference was food for her starving spirit, solid nourishment for the unfledged dream; a banquet so rich and varied it left Elizabeth breathless with wonder. Edgar's new perfidy was pushed to the back of her mind by the flood of new savors—leaving her hurt only enough space to creep out at odd and infrequent intervals to torment her with her own inadequacies.

Too greedy to pick and choose, Elizabeth, pink-cheeked and smiling in the midst of a flock of other would-be writers, moved from panel discussions to workshops, from seminars to book signings, filling her Garfield tablet with almost unreadable scribbles. She filled a large shopping bag with autographed books for Edgar, as her mind toppled with a mass of undigested information.

Silent as a mouse, she stayed on the edges, not yet daring to enter into the rowdy give and take of mealtimes and the noisy debates late at night. She was always there, listening avidly; her pale eyes alight, begging for more writer talk, but she didn't ask questions.

And she didn't find the stranger. Her excitement faded a little and the foggy night-wanderings seemed remote—the sad fantasy of a lonely woman —a woman who no longer existed. Elizabeth tried to deny it, but she felt a haunting loss for something that never was, would never be.

However, Lolly Horn, in some fey, unknowable way, was glad the stranger hadn't made himself known. She neither wanted nor needed him, nor anyone else. Not when she was the dream and growing stronger by the hour.

Lolly was glad. But somewhere deep within her, Elizabeth was afraid of Lolly, the dream, and, most of all, herself. She knew, when she allowed herself to think about it, what she had to do when she went home. Her marriage was dead. She knew she had to forget that and go on playing the strumpet, being Edgar's colorless wife. Or she had to bury the marriage and take whatever consequences that entailed—not a divorce, though, Edgar had already refused that when....

That was another path she couldn't take, but it led her back to the same place in her thoughts. She was afraid that either course would kill the dream; the dream that was Lolly and still a child, too young to ruthlessly defend itself.

And the fear was a black weight on her heart on Sunday afternoon when she waved goodbye to Cass and carried the bag of books and the new suitcase into the silent, vacant-feeling house. Tense as an intruder, she almost crept down the hall to the small den, the room most nearly her own.

Sitting down at the desk, Elizabeth bowed her head, tangled her fingers in her hair. The pink velour tunic she had bought at the inn blurred into a haze of hot, shifting color when tears misted her eyes. "I can't leave him. He swore he would.... I can't. Where would I go? What would I do?"

Her fingers, almost as if they had a mind of their own, left her hair, floated down, touched the two topmost books in the oversized canvas tote; the books the stranger had sent her. One by one, she pulled the books out, laid them on the desktop.

At the inn there had only been time to riffle through the pages, shake each book to see if it concealed a note, but no time to read them.

Slowly, she opened one of the sex books and read a passage. Her eyes widened, red rushed up to her cheeks. She gasped a loud sound in the absolute stillness of the house, and turned a page with a rapidity that denied the maidenly blush.

"Is that you, Elizabeth?"

Edgar's voice shocked her. Elizabeth closed the book, pushed it and its fellows into the back of the bottom desk drawer, pulled some loose paper over them, and slid the drawer shut—just in time.

"Elizabeth?" Edgar stood in the doorway to the den, glanced around the room with distaste curling his lip. He didn't say, "I'm going to get the decorator back and do something about this room," as he usually did, instead he asked, "What are you doing in here?"

She straightened in the chair, stared up at him. Heat dyed her face. Her voice came out in a croak of guilt, but it held a hard core of anger. "I didn't think you'd be home yet," she said.

"Home from where?" he asked. His eyes were

intent on her face, but there was a hint of some-thing in his deep voice, something that might have been guilt. "Where else would I be?"

"I...." She shook her head. The flame in her face burned hotter, dried her throat. She waited for him to say more, to admit to his lie. He didn't and the fear rose up around her in a cloud.

And when she said, "I had to buy some new clothes, the airline lost my luggage," she knew she had made her choice, knew she would stay on without asking him any questions.

"You look nice in pink," he said with a smile. "You should wear it more often."

"I will," Elizabeth said submissively. Then she pointed at the tote bag of books, pushed them toward him with her foot. "I thought...." She swallowed the bitter taste of defeat and started anew. "They're all signed. I thought you might like to have them for your library."

"That was nice of you," Edgar said as he stepped into the small room, knelt on one knee beside the books. "Very nice, indeed. It's been a while since I had any new books and...." He glanced at her quickly and then looked away as he went on, "I'll take some of them with me to the office tomorrow. Clients are impressed if they think you know some.... They get a big kick out of things like this."

He took out several of the books, glanced at the spines. "Lots of big-name writers there, I see."

Nodding, Elizabeth stood up, picked up her suitcase, and edged around him, starting toward the door. His next question stopped her.

"Well, did you talk to enough people to find out I was right? That you've been fooling yourself? I mean, after all, when you meet people like this and find out how *real* writers think." He tapped the books he held. "It has to make you know you have absolutely no talent and none of the skills required of writers." He stood.

"Edgar, I...." The nondescript woman, without even trying to save herself, jumped feet-first back into her mire of worthlessness and wallowed in self-contempt. "I'll go change," she said, "and start dinner."

"It's a hard thing to acknowledge, my dear, but I know you'll feel better soon," Edgar said gently, and then he leaned forward and kissed her on the forehead. "I've missed you, my dear, and I've missed those wonderful meals of yours." He smiled at her and added, with just the proper touch of humility, "Somehow microwave heat-and-eat, even if you did prepare it, just isn't the same."

Elizabeth's hand went up to her throat. She looked at him, saw his smile, his blandly innocent eyes, and doubt swooped in and began to plague her. *Had his receptionist made a mistake? Had Edgar really been at home alone the whole time?*

Suddenly, the woman didn't know what was true or what was false; didn't know if she had wronged him, had almost been unfaithful to a man who was still her husband in thought, word, and deed. She just didn't know, and her doubts increased a hundred-fold when she went into the kitchen and found the sink filled with dirty dishes, microwave dishes she had filled and frozen just before she left for the conference.

Sloshing in guilt, like a pig in a mud hole, she started to scrub and rinse the white crockery prior to stacking it in the dishwasher. She cleaned four pieces before the evidence presented by her eyes and fingers reached her sluggish brain. Something wasn't as it should be. The clinging bits of food adhering to the dishes were all the same, all fresh, very fresh; far too fresh to have set more than a couple of hours.

Her doubts dissolved with the food. This was part and parcel of his lie and this new realization didn't hurt. It touched off a spark of anger, made her mutter, more because he had wasted her carefully prepared food than because he had added to his lie, "You bastard. You'll be sorry for this, too."

She didn't confront him, afraid that if she did, she would have to leave and she wasn't ready for that yet. No, she had to stay, had to go on being a rug, a nice obedient rug for a time longer, had to stay until....

There was a shine of mischief deep in her eyes, but a sigh whispered out of her mouth that carried no real despair, only a fleck of anger.

"I have to stay," she said, moaning the melo-dramatic words she had read in a book. "I just have to. I don't have any place else to go."

Cass, a tiny voice seemed to say inside her head. *You can go to Cass' house.* But even as the voice tried to tempt her, Elizabeth knew she couldn't go; just give up her own life and run to Cass like a child runs to its mother. She knew, too, that going to Cass would be no real improvement; that Cass, in her way, was just as demanding, and just as selfish as Edgar.

"But can I stay here?" she asked herself. "Can I go on until…? Can I pretend to be Edgar's good little housewife until…?"

Her words trailed off into silence, but the conflict that made her almost blind and deaf to her sur-roundings was no nearer resolution two weeks later when she reached into the mailbox and drew out a thick stack of envelopes. Following Edgar's oft-repeated instructions, Elizabeth sorted the mail, dropping the household bills, unopened, into the lidded, copper box on the hall table, pitching the boxholders and other advertising material into the pierced copper wastebasket.

When she was through, she held only a single envelope in her hand, an envelope Edgar hadn't anticipated or ordered, a thick envelope addressed to Lolly Horn.

The hot, sweet memories of sand and sea and a hidden cave, a dark and foggy night, a man and a woman, rushed at her like a wild sea storm. Hands flat on the polished surface, holding her erect, Elizabeth glanced around quickly, almost furtively, and then she slipped into the small den and pulled the door tightly shut behind her.

Heart fluttering, Elizabeth Gilmartin opened Lolly Horn's letter. As she unfolded the paper, she felt a pang of bitter disappointment. The disappointment was illogical, without basis, but it was there, all because the letter was from the publisher sponsoring the writing contest she had entered, and almost forgotten, that long ago night.

Slowly, she read the computer-generated letter thanking her for entering the contest and expressing the usual good wishes for success. Then she glanced through the accompanying rules and regulations. For an instant she allowed herself to dream the old dream, heard it chuckle in exaltation. But only for an instant. Then she squashed it, heard its plaintive little whimper as she crumpled the glossy pages and started to drop the wad of paper into her plastic wastepaper basket.

The dream's whimper couldn't stay her hand, but caution could, and did. Edgar emptied the trash, all the trash—his one chore around the house— and he might see the letter, demand to know who Lolly Horn was and why Elizabeth had opened someone else's mail. It was a baseless fear, but she didn't dare take a chance. She couldn't... No, wouldn't tell him the truth. She smoothed the pages, running her fingers carefully over the sharp creases, squared the pages, held them.

"I can't," she told the letter. "I can't write a book. It was just because I... I'm not really Lolly Horn. I'm somebody else. Somebody who... I don't know. I just don't know." The last words came out in a soft moan.

She folded the pages gently, opened the bottom desk drawer, slid Lolly's letter in on top of the stack of hidden books. Her fingertips brushed the bindings, page edges, and lingered, like the hands of a lover, to caress the covers. She remembered the books were the gift of a faceless stranger whose kiss still haunted her lips.

Her yearning fingers caught the corner of a slim volume, pulled it out of the deep drawer. Sighing, eyes wide and blind with memories, Elizabeth held the book to her bosom, pressing it against her like a sleeping babe.

Anguish was in her soft voice when she said, "I'm sorry, Barry. So very sorry. I wanted to.... I'm sorry."

As if it had grown stiff and old with her acknowledgment of defeat, Elizabeth eased her body down into the desk chair. Then she placed the book, *Baby Names from Around the World,* on the desktop and cupped her hands protectively around it.

She sat, staring down at the cover for a long time and then she smiled. "Wanda," she said, changing the smile to a laugh, the throaty laugh of a woman. Opening the book with eager fingers, she found the listings of female names and their meanings, paged through them to the "W's."

She laughed again before she read the entry aloud, the entry for Wanda.

Chapter Six

♥   ♥   ♥

"Wanda," Elizabeth read. "A dream-led wanderer, roaming the earth, seeking violets in the snow."

Rose burnished her cheekbones, dreams and memories intermingled, sparking fire in the depths of her pale eyes, Edgar's wife reread the words. She slid her index finger from word to word, speaking each one slowly, making them real in her mouth and in her spirit.

There was something hand-written in the margin, something she wouldn't allow herself to read, but something she had to approach obliquely, lest it disappear and return to the foggy unreality of a single night spent on an Oregon beach.

She had no need to hurry. Elizabeth was lost in the dream and the memories. So lost that when the telephone on the desk screamed for attention, she reached for it absently, brought it to her face, and said, "Violets in the snow," in a soft wondering voice.

"Mrs. Gilmartin? Is that you?"

Coming only part way back from the distant place the dream memories had transported her, Elizabeth said, "Yes, this is Mrs. Gilmartin."

"Are you ill? I mean, do you...? Are you all right, Mrs. Gilmartin? I mean, should I send somebody or something?"

The worry in her husband's receptionist's voice erased the dream and the memories in a single, cold antiseptic swipe. "No, don't send anyone. I'm perfectly fine." Elizabeth spoke far more forcefully than she intended.

"Well," Betsy said doubtfully, "if you're sure?"

"Very sure."

The silence stretched fine. Betsy's young voice broke it. "I wanted to.... That is, Miss Marshall asked me to call and remind you that Mr. Gilmartin is entertaining six clients at home tomorrow night. That means dinner at 7:00 and time for them to talk business afterwards. Miss Marshall wanted to be sure you had put it on your calendar."

Elizabeth pulled her appointment calendar toward her, flipped the page to the next day's date. It was virgin white. She felt a surge of panic. It was followed by an absolute, unshakable certainty she had not been informed of the impending dinner until that moment—it was the perfect Karoline who had erred. *If it were an error and not deliberate.*

Playing the cards she was dealt, Elizabeth did the only thing she could do: bluffed. "Repeat what you have on your calendar," she said. "Let me double check to make sure this is correct."

As the girl listed names and dietary restrictions, Elizabeth wrote frantically, filling the white space with slashing black marks. And before she was finished comparing calendars, Elizabeth had added two more dinner parties, for the following week—parties Miss Marshall had also failed to mention.

Chatting calmly, Elizabeth thought she had kept every trace of her growing anger out of her voice, but at the end of their conversation, the girl asked again, "Mrs. Gilmartin, are you sure you're all right?"

The book of baby names, warm under her fingertips, Elizabeth smiled. "Far better than you could possibly know," she said softly. She thought she heard Betsy say, "Mrs. Gilmartin," as she took the receiver away from her ear, but Elizabeth didn't answer.

She just set the instrument in its cradle, breaking the connection, and looked down at the book. It was then that she read what the stranger, the man she had called "Barry," had written.

"Dreams *are* for following, love." She whispered his words, and then she smiled again.

"Of course," she said. "Of course they are. Everyone knows that but me. Edgar followed his dream, no matter what it cost others, no matter what it cost me. He's still following it. And Cass. She follows hers, whatever it is at the moment."

Elizabeth's smile broadened, took on a hint of malice. "Even the fantastic Ms. Marshall," she said. "Or maybe Cass is right. Maybe Karoline is chasing hers, wagging her tail and panting every time Edgar tosses a biscuit." She chuckled. "That'll probably be all he'll toss her. Edgar doesn't know anything about the staff of life."

Giggling at her own wit, Elizabeth took Lolly's letter out of the drawer and reread the rules, skipping the fine print, looking for the contest closing date and a minimum word count for the work.

"December 31?" she muttered as she read. "Good Lord, that's only a little over three months from now. Nobody could write a book that quickly." Her shoulders drooped a bit, and she sighed before she said, speaking as if to someone who lived only in her memory, "It's not just an excuse. I just don't think I can...."

Her head bent forward, letting her hair swing down to hide her face. Her hand reached out blindly, sought the book of names like a shipwreck victim seeks the shore. Barry's message seemed to tingle against her fingers, ran up her arm, until she swore she could hear him laugh. Elizabeth squared her shoulders, raised her head and sat taller in the chair.

"I can do it," she said aloud, then she laughed.

"And if I can't, I'll jolly well give it a damned good try."

The dream sang.

Lolly Horn pulled a yellow legal pad and a pencil from the top drawer, uncovered the typewriter, inserted a sheet of paper, and began *A Touch of Fornication* that same afternoon—began the first chapter of the wild, sexual tale of Barry, the Druid who had mastered the art of eroticism, the man who drove women mad with his educated lips and all-knowing fingers—and of Wanda, his only true love.

She began the first paragraph with their meeting one dark and foggy night beside the wide and mourning sea, and went to their parting and their long search for love and meaning in a young and wonderful world bright with magic and innocent love.

She wrote rapidly, x-ed out words, sentences, paragraphs and rewrote. She threw wads of crushed paper at the wall, on the floor. Tugged her hair into elf-locks around her face and scowled at nothing, twisting her mouth into grotesque and unnatural shapes. Stalked like a hunting lioness around the confines of the small room. Jerked open and slammed shut drawers, mumbled dialogue, and cursed, using oaths both creative and common, and various unlikely combinations of the two. Searched through the dictionary for elusive spellings, muttered, moaned, and swore some more.

And started the first chapter over again, and again, and again.

Through it all, excitement ran up and down her spine like a swarm of tiny, iridescent lizards, adding giggle after giggle to the already unruly horde playing in her throat.

Five hours later, she had three full pages written and typed; three beautiful pages she considered good enough to keep. And every sign of her clandestine assignation with Barry was gone.

The den had returned to its usual guise of shabby drab. The mountain of wadded paper was hidden until she could safely destroy it. The book of names was back in the desk drawer, snuggling close to its sexier companions. And her writer's cramp was just a pleasant ache in Elizabeth's fingers. Her first day's work was done.

But scene after intriguing scene were still unreeling behind her eyes and laughter still lurked in her mouth, when Edgar, sour-faced and irritated, came home.

As she always did, Elizabeth, her hair smooth and tidy, fresh, dull clothes hiding the curves of her body, met her lord and master at the front door, took his attaché case from his hand, and asked rote questions about his day.

Edgar stopped just inside the front door and glowered at her, but his anger didn't seem to matter, at least, not then, not when she had just been touched by creativity's fey finger—had taken her first tottery step toward tomorrow. She dropped his case with a thump, pushing it deep into the closet with her foot, trying to control the joy that tingled on her skin, loosened the bonds on her tongue.

Elizabeth stepped away from the closet and let it swing shut behind her. She moved toward him, her slim fingers caught his and squeezed. "Oh, Edgar," she said breathlessly, "I'm so...."

His entire body stiffened. He pulled back, almost jerking his hand away from her grasp. "For God's sake," he said coldly, "haven't you already acted the fool enough for one day?"

Still dream-dazzled, insulated from reality by her sheltering web of euphoria, she reached out again. "Oh, Edgar, I *can* do it," she said. "You were wrong. I still have talent. I can...."

Perhaps his fury stopped his ears, or perhaps he put her words down to menopausal maunderings and dismissed them, or perhaps nothing she said was important enough to be heeded. He said, ignoring both her smile and her outstretched hand, "You made a fool of yourself today, and in the process you humiliated me. I don't understand how you could do such a thing, Elizabeth. I really don't. I swear, sometimes I believe you have lost your mind."

His anger pierced her joy, made it shrivel, wrinkle away like a ruptured balloon. "What did I do?" she asked. Fear became an icy flame in her breast, spreading out to flush her face, burn her neck and shoulders. Fear that she had forgotten something important again.

"What did you do?" His voice rose, almost shrill, then he controlled his anger and spoke with sweet reasonableness. "Elizabeth, you don't honestly expect me to believe you've forgotten that, too?"

"I...." she started.

He ignored her protest, or declaration of innocence, or whatever it was going to be, and said, "I try, very hard I might add, to be patient with you. But you won't even try to...." He sighed and shook his head.

Watching him with wary eyes, Elizabeth licked her lips and swallowed, but she didn't try to speak.

"I know," Edgar continued, "The Change is... has.... But this cannot go on. I cannot allow you to.... Your lack of consideration has.... My whole staff is whispering about.... Laughing at...." His frown deepened, and his next words seemed to be torn from him.

"Good God, Elizabeth, do you realize what you have done? Karoline had to disrupt our working day, call the staff together and explain, very nicely, of course, that you were going through a very difficult period in your life and.... My God!" His well-manicured fingers raked through his carefully arranged hair, setting it on end, then came down to jerk at his blue silk tie. "Violets in the snow! My God!"

She felt a surge of anger, held it back. "I don't think that was enough to.…"

Misunderstanding, perhaps on purpose, Edgar snapped, "I don't care in the slightest what it was or wasn't. I just will not allow it to happen again. After this you are not to talk to anyone in my office except Karoline or me. Do you understand?"

"Yes, Edgar," Elizabeth answered. Her voice was meek and her face was smooth, bland even, but a giggle began to dance across her tongue. She knew she was about to fall prey to a mirth he would never understand or condone. She knew, too, that she had to hold it back, keep it out of his sight and hearing.

Her hand came up, pressed, palm out, against her quivering lips. Her teeth caught the skin on the back of her hand, nipped it hard enough to make herself gasp and swallow the bevy of wiggling, squirming giggles.

He didn't notice her Gothic-heroine stance, just said, slowly, pontifically, "If anything like this happens again, I'll be forced to insist you be examined by a different doctor. Miss Marshall tells me they have made enormous strides in treating… ah… female complaints. Perhaps your present doctor isn't up on the latest studies and medications. Whatever the reason, I'm sure you'll agree your present estrogen dosage isn't doing all it should."

Rebellion, and more than a speck of anger,

overwhelmed her usual reticence, made her say, almost mockingly, "Ah, yes, of course, the marvelous Ms. Marshall. What does she know about my... ah... female complaint? Or anything else for that matter?"

Edgar bristled. "Karoline is an excellent secretary, the best I've ever had. There's absolutely no reason for you to take that tone, to malign her just because you're ashamed."

"Ashamed?" Elizabeth asked wonderingly. "What exactly am I supposed to be ashamed of, Edgar?"

"That your body is... Karoline said.... Because you can no longer function as.... That you are...."

"Old?" she asked softly.

Edgar was over three years older than Elizabeth, and very aware of the fact. "No," he snapped, "not old. Age has nothing to do with it. You are just no longer...." He had the grace to pause, look at her quickly, and lower both his eyes and his voice before he said, "useful, productive."

Elizabeth chuckled.

Red turned his tan to ruddy copper. A small muscle jumped in his rigid jaw. "Karoline went to a good deal of trouble to find out.... She knows, if you don't, how much I worry about your mental state. I do not need that extra stress right now and she is wise enough to know it."

His eyes darkened. "Miss Marshall has read all the latest information about women in your condition. She has explained the symptoms, the prognosis, what can be expected, everything. I have bent over backward trying to make allowances for you. Karoline says it's the best thing to do, but I just don't know. It doesn't seem to be helping."

She waited in silence, knowing he wouldn't relish an interruption at this point in his tirade.

"Elizabeth," he said, "I honestly believe that if you wanted to, if you really cared about me, you would try to understand how difficult this is for me. If you were just half as understanding and considerate as Karoline, I would have a lot less to worry about. Especially right now."

She didn't ask, "Why is *now* different?" Elizabeth just said, "Yes, Edgar." It sounded like the proper reply for a good and obedient wife, but she was only mouthing sounds that no longer had any real meaning to her—if they ever did.

Edgar said something more, but she didn't hear him. She had physically left the entry and mentally returned to the land of the book, early Britain, and was running and refining scenes that would, in time, fill page after exciting page. As the shadow images took on form and color, acting and interacting, Elizabeth smiled a blank-eyed absent-minded smile.

The next day the smile had faded, taking with it her sense of euphoria, allowing the *can* and the *can't* of her real life to fire the first salvos in what was to be a very long and tedious battle, one she had to refight every day.

She battled with her doubts, but her absent-mindedness didn't fade, it grew faster than the stack of hidden manuscript pages that were its parents. It grew and grew as the leaves turned red and gold. The frosts came, the days shortened and sped by at an alarming rate, dragging the bedeviled Elizabeth, and the ever-diligent Lolly, closer and closer to the holiday season and the moment of truth.

Lolly was industrious in the performance of her task, working at the typewriter or the desk from the time Edgar left until shortly before he came home—taking real delight from the fact that he was often late, very late.

Elizabeth, giving Lolly the largest share of her day, grew lax, more absent every day. Edgar's house demanded too much and the woman was tired of giving. She refused to give in, to sacrifice the living dream to the house's petulant whine for constant attention, couldn't steal the time away from the growing book to polish away the miasma of disuse that was hazing its shining perfection.

Edgar's wife knew, with a stomach-churning stab of guilt, partially relieved by a good healthy dab of whimsy, that the dust bunnies under beds, chairs, and couches had mated, littered, parted, and filed for child support since last she routed them with broom, duster, and vacuum. She knew, too, that spiders had spun yards of fragile lace, held a successful arachnid craft fair, and spun anew since she had taken a single destroying swipe at ceiling corners and light fixtures.

"Spray paint them gold," Cass said one day in late November when Elizabeth had given the webs as her excuse not to go shopping, "and tell Edgar they're the latest thing in Christmas decoration."

But Elizabeth felt no such levity. She knew that soon, probably too soon, Edgar would pull himself away from the new activity at the office, would notice the wholesale neglect, and would back the house's demand for a human sacrifice. Then, probably, she would have to kill the dream, banish Lolly, and go back to being just a housewife.

But Elizabeth had walked too far. She didn't know if she could go back again, retreat into the yesterdays of being nothing. And she was afraid. Sometimes she would wake in the night, sweating and afraid the next day would be her undoing, that she would have to give up writing.

The fear was real, but Lolly and the dream had become one, and a silent nondescript Elizabeth had to bow to their dictates—and she bowed smiling. Lolly didn't walk in fear shadows or let fear twist and hurt her in the night. Lolly walked tall and proud and she was ruthless.

Obsessed with the book, scornful of Elizabeth's gasps and blushes, she underlined in red, starred in purple and green, and wrote pithy comments beside numerous passages in the sex books, after she had dog-eared three-quarters of the pages. She used the information in her own fashion, or rather refashioned the sex information for the lust scenes, and the love scenes, in *A Touch of Fornication*.

It seemed to Elizabeth there was never a moment when she was entirely free from Lolly's besetting passion. It went with her to the supermarket, forcing her to jot down words and phrases on the backs of envelopes and the sides of brown paper bags. It rode on her shoulder during her brisk walks, working kinks out of the plot line; stretching and reshaping knotty problems, leaping over Elizabeth's inhibitions, disdaining the hastily built writer's blocks she tried to throw in its way.

The obsession joined her in the kitchen, making her write, either physically or mentally, while Elizabeth prepared the dainties and delicacies that Edgar ordered for his dinners and parties; parties that seemed to multiply as Thanksgiving passed and Christmas quickly approached.

The dream accompanied Elizabeth to the dinner table, tickling her fancy, adding giggles to her quiet voice and otherwise showing Elizabeth's most manic face. It was a face that blushed at things her husband and his guests couldn't hear, smiled at things they couldn't see, deafened her ears to their words, and made her mouth utter things beyond their immediate comprehension.

She was almost totally caught up in the book, but Elizabeth knew, at some level, she was moving toward the inevitable; soon, one way or another, it would have to end. She went on, following the path of least resistance, but perhaps that was her decision. Perhaps the inaction was her way of forcing the action.

If so, it seemed to work. Edgar tried, repeatedly, to talk to her about her mental problems. Her apparent indifference made him wild and he would order her to make an appointment with her doctor. Her smile, nod of agreement, and absent, "Yes, dear," made him shout she was mad, totally mad.

Wandering in her other land, Elizabeth scarcely heard him most of the time, but in early December, Edgar forced her to listen. Putting his hand on her shoulders, he looked her full in the face and said, "Elizabeth, this has gone on long enough. Your actions are interfering with my work, making me the butt of jokes. I realize you aren't well, but I cannot tolerate such behavior any longer. Miss Marshall has made an appointment for you with a Dr. Bonder. He is new in town and has the reputation of being an expert at… you know."

"No, I don't know. I.…"

"Don't interrupt. Your appointment is at three tomorrow afternoon. Miss Marshall will pick you up at 2:30."

Elizabeth shoved Lolly and Lolly's book back, concentrated on what he was saying, and finally understood. Resentment swelled hot within her, flushed her face, made her voice sound clipped, harsh-edged with anger. "What gives you the right? Edgar, I am a fully grown woman, and in this, if nothing else, I am perfectly capable of knowing when and if I need.…"

His hands tightened on her shoulders. He shook her hard, if only for an instant. Then, the muscle in his jaw jumping and quivering, he almost leaped back, away from her. "Damn it, Elizabeth," he said, his hands clenching and unclenching at his sides. "Can't you see you're driving me mad! God, if this keeps up, I'll be as crazy as you are." He took a deep breath, expelled it slowly. "I am worried about you. We are all worried about you. Miss Marshall did some calling yesterday. You haven't been doing any of your volunteer work. Haven't been seeing your friend, Cass. Haven't been writing to your sons. Haven't been.… Elizabeth, I ask you, is that normal?"

Lolly snickered and said, "You betcha it is, if you're writing a book and are racing to beat a contest deadline. It's normal if you're really Lolly Horn." But the words didn't pass Elizabeth's lips. She looked at her husband and said, "Possibly not."

"Then you'll go to this Dr. Bonder and see if your.… If it's just your.…"

"Saying menopause isn't one of the seven deadly sins," Lolly snapped, evading Elizabeth's censorship. Laughter twinkled in the depths of her eyes, either her secret laughter, or Elizabeth's.

Edgar was not amused. He folded his arms, glared at her. "Are you going?"

"Yes, Edgar," Elizabeth said, "but I neither want nor need an escort."

"Elizabeth, I have to have proof.... That is, given the present state of your condition. Karoline goes," Edgar said. "I have to know exactly what the doctor says. If there is no *physical* cause for your.... I just need a totally reliable witness. Karoline is completely loyal to my interests."

"Oh, of course," Elizabeth said softly, and then, before Elizabeth could gag her, Lolly asked sweetly, "And just what brand of dog biscuits do you feed your little pet?"

Edgar's scowl pulled new lines across his tanned forehead, between his dark brows. "What are you babbling about now?" he asked "You know perfectly well I don't have a pet."

Suspicion narrowed his blue eyes, made him look snake-mean and a lot less handsome. He stared at her for a long moment before he shook his head as if finding her innocent of malicious intent, giving her absolution. For that small space in time, he looked his full age and more, much more. "Elizabeth," he said, "I'm not trying to hurt you. It's just that, well, you've changed since...

since.... You used to be so nice, so damned sweet that I...." His voice hoarsened, "Just be ready when Miss Marshall comes for you," he finished gruffly.

She saw his worry, knew it was real, and for a split second, Elizabeth felt an uprush of warmth so strong it almost took her breath. Melting through her, it became a curious mixture of old love and new pity. She wanted to reassure him, to make his world the safe and familiar place he needed, to be the wife she had been before....

That thought was forbidden. She erased it and a full confession of her misdeeds lined up in her mouth, waiting for their cue to march forth in full panoply.

Elizabeth reached out a long-fingered hand toward him in invitation. "If you'll come with me," she said slowly. "I'll try to explain why I.... Edgar, I'm sorry. I didn't mean to cause you any problems, it was just that.... In the den. Let me show you."

Words failed her. She stood, a tall, slim woman in a gray cotton dress, hand outstretched, eyes pleading for understanding, and she waited, wanting him to take her hand, to help her resolve their differences and breathe life back into their dead marriage.

Chapter Seven

♥   ♥   ♥

Eyes bright with love, Elizabeth took a tiny gliding step toward him, then a larger one and was almost close enough to touch him with her reaching hand. "Please, Edgar," she said, "come with me to the den. Let me show you what I've been...."

Edgar edged back, away from her. His body held too stiff, too erect, he moved slowly, like a man who fears the madness he sees before him; madness he doesn't understand or thinks may be dangerous. Or contagious. His too-soothing tones were ample indication of that very real fear.

"Elizabeth, my dear," he said quietly, "now is not the best time for us to talk. We are both very tired. We need to rest. Why don't you go take a nice warm bath and go to bed. We will have plenty of time to talk later. Tomorrow. Yes, tomorrow, after you've seen this new doctor."

Her hand came slowly down, clutched the folds of her skirt. In an almost dizzying rush she understood, and then she fought the pain that assailed her. Pain for the loss of a love that had never really existed or would never exist. She had made a mistake in marrying him; it had been her fault as much as his. Their marriage was dead, and her love for him was only a fading illusion she had fostered and fed because she couldn't bear to face the truth.

There was no meeting place for them now. Elizabeth swallowed the urge to confess her sins, almost relishing the bitter taste it left in her mouth. It was the taste of endings, the dregs of yesterday's blindness. The bitterness twisted her lips, made her voice brittle when she asked, "You think I'm crazy, don't you, Edgar? Really crazy?"

"Well..." he equivocated. Turning the signet ring on his left ring finger round and round, he looked at the floor, beyond her left shoulder, at the floor again, and his voice was harsh when he said, "Well, I suppose it *could* be something physical, something to do with your time of life, but I honestly...."

"And if it's not something physical?" Her question was soft, almost gentle, but it demanded an answer.

Edgar looked at her and away in the same instant, his gaze faltering, as if shamed by the quietness in her eyes. His tongue made short, flickering jabs at his lower lip. "We.... That is, I think you are seriously disturbed. Karoline says it's not unusual for women of your age." He wiped his cheek with the flat of his hand, let the hand drop down to tug at his tie. "We'll know more about what we have to do after tomorrow."

"We? You and who? Me? Miss Marshall? Will the two of you get together and decide my fate? Decide which loony bin is best for older women?"

Her husband didn't answer. Edgar Gilmartin had already turned away from her, had walked, with assumed jauntiness out of the room. Elizabeth watched him go and she thought she heard him sigh a heart-felt sigh of pure relief as he gained the safety of the hall.

The warmth she felt for him earlier had cooled. Love and pity congealed into an ugly lump in the pit of her flat stomach. The moment of caring was gone. Elizabeth laughed, the oddly disappointed laugh of a woman who had been fooled again by her own need into making an offering where it wasn't wanted—leaving her open to the scorn of the man she had always believed she loved.

But, strangely enough, there was no real pain. There was only a faint wonder that he, who had known her so long, so intimately, hadn't the vision to see her as she was: sane.

She stood there a long time. Stood absolutely still until Lolly ventured out of hiding, looked around, and said, "Look, lady, you don't have time for grand discoveries and interior monologues right now. It's only a couple of weeks or so until we have to get that damned book in the mail. So, get with it, will you?"

Elizabeth smiled. "I can write in the bathtub. Edgar would die before he came in there. Good heavens, he might catch a glimpse of my aging body and go mad." Lolly laughed the low musical laugh of a woman who might find it in herself to pity the man—and then again, might not.

The laughter was gone from Elizabeth's face, but it still lurked in her throat and in the backs of her eyes the next afternoon when Edgar's beautiful young secretary came to pick her up. She was whisked off, willy-nilly and against her will, like a recalcitrant and somewhat backward child, to an unknown doctor to have her body poked, prodded, and invaded by cold instruments and alien hands, hands in the employ of her husband and his Ms. Marshall. Hands Elizabeth had no reason to trust.

Like a deadly viper, anger curled in the heart of her hidden laughter, deep and abiding anger at Edgar, anger she didn't dare show. Not yet. Not until she was ready. Not until she could make him pay for....

The thought had ventured too near the forbidden section of her mind. Elizabeth swallowed hard as she put it hastily away, put it so completely away she forgot its threat.

Nothing, not anger, not laughter, showed on Elizabeth's pale face, unrelieved by lipstick or blush, when she walked, in flat-heeled sensible shoes, buttoning a gray wool coat, out the front door and mutely surrendered herself to the ministrations of Edgar's secretary.

Writing, urgent and demanding, had used up the time, leaving her only moments to groom herself, wash her hands, jerk a comb through her hair and slap on moisturizer. There was no time to apply even the token makeup she usually wore. She was totally nondescript, and Elizabeth didn't really care.

She was aware of Ms. Marshall's appraising glance as it catalogued, with arrogant superiority, her overwhelming flaws. Elizabeth's face was expressionless, and her voice was just as carefully neutral when she replied, ever so politely, to Ms. Marshall's social remarks.

The younger woman, chic and trim in a long, brown suede coat and a Russian-style hat that looked like ranch mink, kept up a bright facade of friendliness. She smiled her shiny red smile relentlessly as she commented on the lowering sky, the patches of dirty snow, the sodden earth and the chill winds of winter.

Elizabeth let the inane chatter float across the surface of her mind, barely heeding its content until Karoline said, perhaps just a little too smugly, "I know you're upset. But honestly, Mrs. Gilmartin, this won't really be as bad as you expect. I took the liberty of giving the nurse all the pertinent medical information. You won't have to do a thing."

"Oh?" Elizabeth said softly and for a wild moment, she thought Karoline was going to reach over, pat her on the knee, and say, ever so reassuringly, "Now. Now. Don't fret, dear."

Perhaps that had been her intention, but Karoline stopped the motion in mid-reach, returned her gloved hand to the steering wheel, and said, "I know you must think I have overstepped myself, Mrs. Gilmartin, but truly I did it for you. Mr. Gilmartin has told me all about your condition. The rest of the information is in Edgar's personal file. So you mustn't feel I'm trying to take over your life or anything. Indeed not. It's just that I know how difficult things have been for you. Why, my mother is also having a trying time with her menopause—not mentally, of course, but she is very depressed."

Laughter strained at its leash, but Elizabeth held it firmly in check. She moved, just a little, squirming in the bucket seat, but she kept her air of disinterest, and her silence.

Her booted foot firm on the pedal, Karoline braked for a red light, smoothed back a tendril of blonde hair, and sat, the picture of a successful, desirable young woman, waiting for the green to flash. When it did, she zipped ahead, whipped into the other lane, cutting off a slower driver, and said, "Mr. Gilmartin has been very worried. He had to talk to someone who cared. He confided in me. I would really like to help you both. Edgar is so.... He needs so much and...."

Her voice lost some of its glittering confidence, trailed off into hollowness. She glanced, a quick sideways glance that held a full measure of slyness at Elizabeth's impassive face, took a deep breath, and tried, once again, to break through the older woman's wall of calm.

"Edgar is.... I can't honestly believe you realize how important he is to the financial community. He works so hard and, Mrs. Gilmartin, he needs someone to take care of him." Then Karoline's full red lips tightened to become a straight line when she looked at Elizabeth and shook her head—a gesture that was a clone of Edgar's own reaction to his wife.

Elizabeth recognized the gesture, just as she recognized the jealous possessiveness in the young woman's voice, but the recognition aroused no emotional or verbal response.

Thick, almost cold, silence filled the car, but it lasted less than a block before Karoline's voice, heated now instead of bright and assured, said, "He is a great man and he's going to be even more important very soon, a lot more important. As soon as this new project is fully launched, millions of people will recognize his financial genius. That's why it's so important you.... He needs a stable, respectable background. You...."

Edgar's wife knew nothing of any new project and Ms. Marshall, in flush of consternation, knew it. Fury sparked hot in her eyes, pulled her jaw tight. But she didn't acknowledge her fall from grace. Her mouth thinned even more, making her face look gaunt. She snapped, "Edgar would confide in you if you weren't so damned crazy."

Elizabeth didn't answer.

Karoline stared straight ahead, but there was real anger in her now, anger enough to take away her caution, make her show a bit too much of her real self. "Do you care? Hell, no! Not you. You just sit in that beautiful mansion and.... You can't even treat him like a human being, can you? You know you're safe. He can't divorce you, the publicity would be.... God, you make me sick.

"Whimpering and whining, doing stupid things, hurting him just because he sold your.... Well, let me tell you something, Mrs. Gilmartin. You don't deserve him. And he damned well doesn't deserve to be treated the way he is."

"Oh?" Elizabeth asked with polite disinterest.

"You think I'm stupid, don't you? Well, I'm not. I know what you're trying to pull, and it won't work. I'll make sure of that." Karoline's well-modulated voice rose a little, hinted at past experience in fishwifery.

Elizabeth didn't answer, but she allowed a faint smile to twinkle in the depths of her pale eyes, uptilt the corners of her generous mouth. It was a Lolly smile, enigmatic, unreadable, and vaguely frightening.

"Dear God, I see what you're doing to that dear man and I'd like to...." Karoline stopped abruptly, took a deep breath, shot a stabbing glare in Elizabeth's general direction.

Her brown eyes were narrow, angry, but the shrillness in her voice was almost hidden beneath a heavy coating of sweetness when she said, "I beg your pardon, Mrs. Gilmartin. I had no right to talk to you like that. It's just that I spend so much time with Edgar and see him worrying about your... the state of your health so much, it is making him ill. I admire Mr. Gilmartin more than you can possibly imagine, and I'd do anything to keep him from a single moment's worry. I guess you know that."

"Yes," Elizabeth said, willing to give this particular devil her due, "I do know that."

"And I know if it weren't for your present mental unrest, you'd want to...." The young woman's speech limped to a halt and she chewed on her lower lip for a second before she went on. "Mrs. Gilmartin, Elizabeth, please don't take what I'm about to say the wrong way, but don't you think it would be better for all of us if you voluntarily signed yourself into a private hospital and underwent some form of treatment?"

"A private hospital?" Elizabeth asked. "Or a private nut house, a holding pond for troublesome wives, keeping them out of the way until they can be, very quietly, of course, legally dispossessed of their share of the community property?"

"Oh, no. No! Nothing like that. It's just that one of our clients has a place called Harmony House. It's a beautiful place, out in the country, very exclusive. Dr. Abernathy is one of the finest doctors in his field. Elizabeth, dear, please think about it. It's very apparent that everyone in the office, the staff, even some of the clients have.... We all know you aren't well."

Elizabeth tensed, but she held back the words of angry denial, forced Ms. Marshall to say whatever else it was she intended to say.

"I know you don't think so right now," Karoline said gently, "but everyone else.... Dear, we all know you are disturbed, terribly disturbed. And all we want is for you to get better. If you'd just go to Dr. Abernathy's hospital and stay until he says you're cured, I'd be more than glad to...."

"Take my place?" Elizabeth asked quietly.

"Well, no, not exactly. I mean, yes, in some ways. I could act as Edgar's hostess, do all the things you do for those business dinners. I know they can't mean anything to you, but they are very important to Edgar's business right now. And there's going to be more and more of them as this new project progresses."

"Oh, how very kind of you to offer, but I didn't know you cooked and cleaned," Elizabeth said as the smile grew brighter in her eyes, tugged harder at the corners of her mouth.

"That's servants' work," Ms. Marshall said hotly, indignation and insult painting twin patches of scarlet on her cheeks.

"Oh, really? That's what I do to make those dinner parties so marvelous," Elizabeth answered, not quite truthfully, and then she added, mentally, *That's what Edgar wants from a wife. Work, submission, sanity; the ideal combination for a house slave.*

Sputtering over Elizabeth's declaration of servitude, Karoline said, "Well, that certainly isn't what I meant. When you go to Harmony House, Edgar will just have to hire someone to do all that. I'll do the planning and...."

"Ms. Marshall," Elizabeth asked, "have you and Edgar discussed this plan for my cure?"

"Not yet. I didn't want him to worry about details; but as soon as this doctor tells us you need professional help, I'll tell Edgar. He will, of course, expect me to make all the arrangements, so if there's any special wishes you have, I'll be more than happy to see they are carried out."

"Very commendable."

"Elizabeth, I really didn't expect you to take this so calmly. I was afraid you would.... But there's no disgrace in being mentally ill, is there?"

"No, I'm sure there isn't, but there is one small item you haven't considered."

"What's that?"

"What if *your* doctor finds me sound, in mind as well as body?"

It was, beyond the whispering echo of a doubt, a new thought to the younger woman, a disquieting thought, one that could possibly destroy Ms. Marshall's carefully laid scheme to rid Edgar's world of Elizabeth and replace her with a younger model—and it was a thought Karoline didn't seem to care for.

"He won't," she snapped. Her voice was hard with arrogance, but a little of her confidence had ebbed, leaving her shaken—if only a bit. The tendons in her wrists stood out, her gloved hands gripped the wheel a little tighter. Her straight white teeth almost gritted together when her mouth clamped shut. She stared, with eyes as hard as marbles, remote as the arctic wastes, at something that lay beyond the storm beginnings, the light misty mixture of rain and snow that streaked the windshield. But Ms. Marshall, Edgar's super secretary, said nothing more until she stalked into the glass-walled, painfully new waiting room and tossed Elizabeth's name to the smiling receptionist.

Her nose faintly itchy from the tang of fresh paint, perfumed room-deodorizer, and recycled air, Elizabeth paused just inside the door, returned the girl's smile, and nodded agreeably when she said the doctor would see Elizabeth in just a few minutes.

Shrugging out of her wool coat, Edgar's wife hung it on the chrome rack beside the reception-ist's window and moved on into the light-filled room, walking its full length before she sat in a green plastic chair slightly removed from all its neighbors.

Feet together, back straight, hands clasped almost primly on top of her leather handbag, Elizabeth didn't even glance in Karoline's direc-tion. The other woman wasn't even in Elizabeth's thoughts as she waited quietly, running scenes and rewrites behind the apparent serenity of her quiet eyes. Waited until her name was called.

She wasn't really nervous, but Elizabeth took a deep breath, held it for a heartbeat, and let it out in dribbles and puffs as she walked, two steps behind a white-clad nurse, to a small examination room. There, she followed the nurse's instructions without a word.

When Dr. Bonder strode into the room, Elizabeth was jerked out of her calm. A tall, lanky, almost ugly man with a fringe of faded hair, he looked at her with hooded eyes that had seen too many women, knew too much about them—to their detriment. She lifted her chin and stared back, silently vowing to give no quarter.

Bonder questioned her sharply, snorting at some of her answers, and, although he was at least ten years her junior, he managed to make Elizabeth feel awkwardly young, exceedingly stupid, and very angry. And her anger grew as he questioned her again and again, repeating the same intimate questions over and over as he examined her body with hands as gentle as his questions were harsh.

Sounding more serious than the situation warranted, Dr. Bonder said, "Regardless of what other foolish ideas you may be harboring, Mrs. Gilmartin, menopause is a perfectly normal condition for a woman of your age. It is not an illness. There is absolutely no reason, especially in your case, to abstain from intercourse."

Her knees high, legs spread, Elizabeth, flat on her back and staring at the ceiling, was every bit as furious, and maybe more so, as the doctor sounded. Her voice was just as terse, just as hostile when she asked, "Doctor, are you suggesting I take a lover?"

He stood up, glared down at her. "I see no reason to...."

She pushed herself up on her elbows, glared back. "I don't give a damn what you see," she said coldly. "And I don't give a damn what you think. If my husband declines to go to bed with me, then as far as I can see, taking a lover is the only way I can stop abstaining."

His deep-set eyes were considering, his voice had softened, but only a trifle, when he asked, "Why were you so anxious for this appointment?"

"I wasn't."

"Of course you were. You called yesterday afternoon and demanded an appointment immediately. You said it was an emergency, you thought you were losing your mind."

Elizabeth took her bare feet out of the stirrups and sat up. "No, I didn't. I didn't call. I didn't want to come. There's nothing wrong with me, absolutely nothing. I feel wonderful. My husband doesn't agree."

Dr. Bonder's face relaxed, a smile made him handsome. "I see," he said, and she knew he, at least, believed her.

He looked at her for a moment longer. "Go ahead and get dressed. I'll talk to you and your daughter in my office."

Unbound by common restraints, Lolly peeked out long enough to give Elizabeth a fleeting vision of Karoline as Elizabeth's daughter and to wonder why the young woman was so intent on incest. Laughter lit Elizabeth's face, warmed her demure voice as she said, "Dr. Bonder, I hesitate to tell you, but I don't have a daughter either."

His gaze sharpened. Then he nodded as if satisfied about something and said, "Elizabeth, it's fairly obvious to me that even if you take that lover I prescribed, in very large doses, you are extremely unlikely to have a daughter now, so who is that woman in the waiting room, the one that said she was your daughter and needed to hear my diagnosis first hand?"

"Ms. Karoline Marshall. My husband's personal secretary."

"Oh," he said thoughtfully, "I see."

Elizabeth held out her hands, palm up, and shrugged. "Maybe you do," she said slowly, "but I don't think it has come to that."

He turned away, stripped off his gloves, and leaned over the wash basin. "Would it hurt so much? I mean, you are obviously a very bright woman, you must have considered the possibility your husband is sexually involved with her."

"I've considered lots of things," she said, "and I don't think Edgar and the beautiful Ms. Marshall are having an affair. Sometimes I almost wish they were."

"Why?"

She made an effort to answer what she thought was his question. "Edgar," she said slowly, "likes power more than anything in the world. He likes to have power over people, to control people and things, make deals, bask in admiration at his astuteness with money and its management. That's what excites him. I don't honestly think he cares much about sex, having it, I mean."

Water gushed from the faucet. Dr. Bonder stuck his hand under the flow, splattering the wall and floor. "And you?" he asked, raising his voice to be heard over the roar of the water.

"Me?"

"You? What has this rejection done to you?"

His voice sounded too loud, almost brusque, but when he faced her there was real concern in his eyes.

Easing off the end of the examination table, she stood. The paper gown slid from one of her shoulders, gapped open on both sides, ended at mid-thigh, but dignity clothed her from head to foot, gave her a gallantry, a grace. "At first," she said, "it almost killed me."

"But it didn't."

It wasn't a question, but she knew he was asking why. She looked deep within herself, far deeper than she had dared to look before, and there was nothing but truth in her voice when she said, "No, because I don't love my husband. I'm not sure now I even like him. I know I have to make some decisions soon, but there's something I have to do first, something important."

He came to her, put his wet hand on her arm. "Perhaps that's best. Take a little more time. Talk to your husband. It well may be that this is a temporary condition, one that can be changed. If you both work at it, in time...."

"Isn't two years enough?"

"The impotence has lasted that long?"

"With me it has," Elizabeth said. "But slightly over a year ago, something happened that made me fully aware of just how little I matter in his...." She changed directions swiftly, rushed away from the forbidden thought, the painful knowledge hidden in the shadowy recesses of her mind. "I'm more or less an unpaid servant in Edgar's house now, someone he's ashamed of more often than not. I'm quite sure he thinks I'm crazy."

"Well, as to that, I'd say not. There's nothing physically wrong with you. The blood and urine tests might show something, but I honestly doubt it. I'd say you're in wonderful shape, inside and out."

"Tell Edgar," she said, and then she smiled up at him, an impish teasing smile that was completely Lolly's. "See if he thinks your diagnosis is anywhere near as good as his secretary's."

Dr. Bonder chuckled. "I'll make sure he knows it's better, a whole hell of a lot better. Want to listen?"

She shook her head. "No, what I really want is a cab and a back door to slip out of. Alone."

"Done," he said, chuckling again. He took her hand, raised it, brushed it with his lips. "Good fortune, Elizabeth."

"Thank you," she answered gravely.

Edgar didn't work late that night. He arrived at the front door at exactly 5:15, but Elizabeth wasn't waiting to take his case, his kiss, and ask rote questions about his wearying day.

The fire in the white stone fireplace, kindled

primarily to consume wads of paper, rejects from several days of writing, had burned down to embers, but Elizabeth, curled in the corner of the white velvet loveseat, stared into its rosy heart, remembering, trying to find the original flaw, the weak spot, the breaking place in her marriage.

She didn't look up when Edgar stomped into the living room and said pettishly, "Your doctor called me. That wasn't at all necessary, you know. It was pure spite on your part. There was no need to humiliate me like that, to put me in the position of.... He could have told Karoline, that's why she was there."

He stepped between her and the fire. "You should be ashamed. Sneaking off and leaving Karoline, worrying her sick. She was in tears when she got back to the office. After all, Elizabeth, she was only doing what I had ordered her to do. I want you to call her immediately and apologize for...."

Elizabeth dismissed his fault-finding and demands with a shooing motion of her right hand and asked, because at that moment in her marriage pondering she needed to know, "Why did you marry me, Edgar?"

Edgar cleared his throat. "I...." Then he stopped, looked down at her for a heart-achingly long moment.

For that brief, breath-holding time, she thought he was going to come to her, reach out, take her in his arms, hold her close. And she stiffened, drew back further into the corner of the love seat.

Her husband turned away.

Chapter Eight

♥   ♥   ♥

Edgar picked up the poker, balanced it on his
palm for a long moment before he opened the
glass doors on the fireplace and began to poke,
haphazardly and ineffectively, at the dying fire.
An ember exploded at his touch, fountained up in
a rich dazzle of fiery sparks. They showered
down, some returning to their glowing bed, others
falling on the hearth, and a few buried their
smoking bodies in the champagne carpet.

Moving rapidly, Edgar pounced on each tiny
spark, extinguishing them in turn, with the toe of
his highly polished shoe while mumbling epithets
under his breath. When each bit of fire had been
ground to nothing, he closed the fireplace doors
and returned the poker to its brass stand.

Elizabeth watched the man's intricate fire
dance, but she followed the path her pondering
had blazed without swerving. "Why me?" she
asked. "Why, Edgar? There were other girls you
could have had, some richer, most prettier. Why

did you bypass them for me?" Her tone was cour-
teous, but it sounded curiously disinterested,
rather like that of a political poll-taker at the end
of a long hot day.

His finger tracing the mortar between the
fireplace stones, Edgar asked, "What can all that
matter now, Elizabeth?"

"I need to know."

He didn't ask why, but Edgar turned from his
study of the white stone and faced her. The large
living room was almost dark, filled with thick
shadows, with the only light coming from the
dying fire and the entryway. The light struck one
side of his tanned face, giving him a sinister,
almost evil look, but his voice was soft, gentle
with a warm undernote of remembering. "I loved
you," he said. "You were so nice, so sweet, so
terribly innocent. I loved you."

"And I loved you," she said, and then, expressing
only polite intellectual interest, she asked, "But
why didn't it last?"

"Elizabeth," he said warningly, "don't start in
with your nonsense. You know perfectly well...."

Seemingly oblivious to both his interruption
and warning, the woman continued, "Love is supposed to be immortal, or else die in a blaze of
glory, like a nova star, burn so hot and bright it
consumes everything, leaving only cinders."

She paused for a second, looked at him reflec-
tively, and said, "It's not supposed to trickle away

drop by drop, and leak away until there's nothing left. Nothing, not even the fabric."

"Elizabeth, I haven't the faintest idea what you are talking about, and I doubt you do either."

"Oh, yes," she said softly. "You know. You're the expert on marriages. You know all about shams and sounding brass."

"I don't care what that damned doctor said, I still think you're...." He stopped, looked at her warily, and then, as if the words were being torn from his own flesh, he asked the question closest to his own heart, "What did you tell him? About our... about us... about me, I mean."

She laughed, and whether the low throaty laugh was hers or Lolly's, Elizabeth couldn't have said. But she did know who said, "I told him everything," and knew she was speaking for herself.

"Everything? My God, Elizabeth, some things are private. Have you no shame? *Your* doctor had the gall to suggest that I see a doctor. Elizabeth, he thinks I can't.... He thinks there's something wrong with me."

"Isn't there?" she asked as she got to her feet.

"No!" he shouted. "There's not a damned thing wrong with me, and you know it. I explained.... Just because I have enough consideration to leave you alone, you.... Damn it, Elizabeth, most women your age would be overjoyed if their husbands would leave them alone. Don't you have any idea how lucky you are?"

The telephone's urgent ring cut through his almost inarticulate ire. He whirled and stalked toward the door. "That's for me," he said. "I'll be in my library. Call me when you have dinner on the table."

"Oh, I shall. The sane servant shall only serve in silence," she said, making a little bow in his direction.

The telephone called again, but Edgar stopped, looked over his shoulder at his nondescript wife. "If that was supposed to be a joke, it wasn't funny," he said. "And the doctor did say you were physically well, but Elizabeth, you would do well to remember..." he waited until the phone was silent once again before saying, "he isn't a psychiatrist."

"No, he isn't," she agreed, and then she added, "but then neither is the beautiful Ms. Marshall."

Edgar snorted through his nose and plunged out of the room. Elizabeth was sure that if doors could slam in Edgar's perfect house, the door to the library would have sounded like a dynamite explosion.

But Lolly wouldn't allow her any more time to probe the past, or search for yesterday's mistakes. The woman was, at the very least, as demanding as Edgar's house, and there was very little time before the manuscript of *A Touch of Fornication* had to be mailed to the contest sponsors. It was time Lolly demanded as her own.

Edgar was very busy, too, preoccupied with his mysterious new project, and that was all that saved Elizabeth's precarious hold on sanity. She stretched each moment, scurried through a bare minimum of surface-only house cleaning, ordered from the bakery and caterer all the goodies for Edgar's almost nightly dinners and parties, and gave the rest of her days, and most of her sleeping time, to Lolly, who wrote like a madwoman.

The book, or rather a photocopy of the book was in the mail four days before Christmas. Her palms sweating, her eyes moist, Lolly handed the well-taped mailing box across the counter in the post office. She smiled at the postal clerk, paid the mailing cost, and responded to his brief questions. But somewhere deep inside, the woman wanted to snatch the manuscript back and run; take the poor thing to the safety of her room, put it on the closet shelf with its parent pages, and keep them both from being viewed by critical eyes or touched by defiling hands. But it was Elizabeth who wanted to hide the work away, Lolly wouldn't allow it.

Lolly did, however, allow Elizabeth the dubious pleasure of a wild orgy of cleaning, shopping, candy making and decorating with plastic mistletoe and trees of fake fur—they didn't shed leaves or needles—wrapping gifts for Edgar and Cass (gifts for her two sons and their wives had been ordered by Karoline Marshall and sent long before).

When Christmas had come and gone, was packed away for another year, in dust-proof boxes with the New Year's surplus whistles and hats, Elizabeth felt nerves crawling like wiggly worms in her stomach and fear touched her deep enough to rouse the sleeping Lolly. They worried, together and alone, waking and sleeping, that the manuscript, Lolly's labor of love, was the object of ridicule; that they had been fools, or worse, to send it off to New York and expose its fragile being to an uncaring world.

For the next three weeks, Elizabeth submerged her worry in frenzied work that left her exhausted, far too exhausted to say anything when Edgar, smiling benignly, came into the kitchen where she was putting the last touches on a meal for two. It was their first meal alone in a month, and he said, "I'm very pleased with you, my dear."

She didn't look up from the sauce she was whisking.

"I was right, wasn't I?"

"About what?"

"That all you had to do was get yourself in hand. You have done just that. The house looks wonderful and everyone has been commenting on how well you've been lately."

She didn't ask, "Does everyone mean the marvelous Ms. Marshall?" she only said, "Thank you, Edgar."

"Now that you're back to your old self," he

said, "why don't you start going to the library and the historical society? It really looks well in my profession to have an interest in history and culture."

She nodded her acquiescence and poured the smooth sauce over the tender spears of asparagus.

"You've never gone, of course, but.... You do remember, don't you, that I signed you up, or rather had Karoline sign up you as a volunteer at both places?"

"Of course," Elizabeth said meekly.

"Then you'll go?"

"Yes," she said, "but first I need to...." She stopped because she couldn't tell him she had to stay home in case she got a letter from the writing contest sponsor, and she was too tired to make up a lie.

"But my dear," he said, "now is an excellent time. A most excellent time. Elizabeth, soon, very soon, I'll be able to tell you.... Sorry, I can't talk about that yet. But believe me, this is a good time, a wonderful time for you, and for me. You are all over your little problem. And me? I am a happy man, my dear, a very happy man. The happiest man in the world, the universe, the...."

Elizabeth turned slightly, resting her hip against the counter, and glanced at him. It became a sharp unbelieving glance when she saw and assessed the ruddy copper patches on his cheeks and the almost feverish brightness of his eyes. The deduction surprised her.

It was almost a certainty that she was mistaken, but before she could stop herself, she asked what had to be a silly question, one that could only lead to recriminations and renewed sanity questions, "Edgar, have you been drinking?"

He laughed—if not immoderately, then as close to immoderate as Edgar Gilmartin could come. "Oh, my dear," he said, swallowing back guffaws and wiping his eyes with his hand, "if I could tell you what this day has brought. If only I could!" His voice dropped, became just a little deeper, and he stepped closer to her, so that she could feel the heat of his body against her back and side.

"Does champagne count as drinking?" he asked softly, his breath caressing her neck with whispery touches of tickly warmth.

Edgar seemed so boyishly happy, like the young man she had loved and married, that her weariness and the years of discord fell away, were lost to the moment. "I don't know," she said almost breathlessly. Turning a bit more, she smiled up at him. "Does it?"

Chuckling, he leaned even closer, reached around and beyond her, his chest against her shoulder, bending her slightly back over the counter as he poured wine from the carafe on the tray behind her.

"I want to propose a toast," he said in her ear, chuckling as she shivered. "I want to drink to you, to me, to us, to my day, and to… to tomorrow."

"Yes," she said. Elizabeth took the glass he put in her hand and sipped at the cold, dry wine, but she didn't taste it, or feel it slide down her throat; didn't know if the wine were what was causing heat to spread through her body. She was still holding her glass when he finished his and the refill he gave himself.

Acutely aware of him, confusion and a sudden shyness made her start to speak, "Edgar, I...."

"Elizabeth," he said. He set his glass on the counter, took hers and placed it with his, and his hand came back to touch, lingeringly, the velour tunic. "Pink," he said softly, his mouth almost touching her ear. "You look pretty in pink."

She held her breath, waiting for his next move, wanting him to go on, wanting him to.... She shivered again when his lips touched the skin behind her ear, his fingers brushed her neck and fumbled with the zipper at the back of the pink velour tunic. Her breath came out in a wondering sound when the zipper slid down to its base, letting the air touch her back, and his fingers grasped the back of her lacy bra.

"Do you remember," he asked softly as he, one-handedly and with amazing dexterity, undid the hooks and eyes, freeing her full breasts in less than an instant.

She did remember. She remembered with a young girl's virgin body, a body that begged his hands to fondle and explore, his mouth to taste and savor, a seventeen-year-old body that had waited a lifetime to be roused. She remembered with her body and her soul that first time Edgar had freed her breasts with his agile fingers.

"I remember," she said, but the words blended together, came out as a single sound; the soft, muted sound of wanting.

The sharp edge of the white countertop dug into the flesh of her hip, but she didn't feel it. All Elizabeth could feel was her husband's lips as they nibbled, in slow time, down her neck, and his hand as it pushed the tunic down, down, down until it hung at her waist. The bra followed and was lost in a slither of lace across the polished floor tiles.

Wanting to touch him, Elizabeth tried to turn, but his hands, one around her body, one undoing the button and zipper of her pants, held her, arched her back over the counter as his lips greedily took possession of her neck and bare breasts.

"Oh, Edgar," she whispered as his hand pushed the pink tunic and white linen pants out of the way and followed the planes of her body down inside her bikini panties.

But her words were lost to the melodious chiming of the doorbell activated again and again by the impatient jab of a finger.

Muttering something against her skin, Edgar straightened slowly, reluctantly, released her, and stepped back.

"No," she whispered, "don't go."

"I'll get rid of whoever it is," he said hoarsely. "Wait for me, I'll be right back."

A smile soft on her lips, her eyes dark and luminous behind her glasses, she waited—a very long time, and when he returned, he had a suitcase in his hand. "I have to go, Elizabeth. The whole deal is falling to pieces. We're going to try to save it. We'll fly to Chicago tonight and then on to New York tomorrow or the next day. I don't know for sure when we'll be back."

Her smile was gone, but she didn't ask, "Who is *we?*" She just stood, white linen pants pooled at her feet, bared to the waist by a man's passion, and looked at him.

"I'm... I never should have... I'm sorry, Elizabeth."

"Good-by, Edgar," she said, and again she remembered the first time he had freed her breasts for his pleasure and her own; remembered beyond the panting and fevered touching. Remembered the young man who had set her girl's body afire and then pulled away, telling her they'd better wait. They *had* waited—until the ring was on her finger and his name was hers.

And when she heard the front door sigh shut, silencing the soft murmur of voices that belonged to a man and a woman, Elizabeth stepped out of the linen pants, pulled the tunic over her head, wadded them together and dropped them in the trash compactor. It was humming its song of togetherness when she walked down the hall, the lacy bra dangling from her fingers, wearing only high-heeled sandals and white bikini panties.

♥   ♥   ♥

It was nearly three weeks before Edgar's receptionist called in the late afternoon telling Elizabeth to prepare for house guests. Edgar was on his way from London and was bringing three business associates with him.

They chatted a bit longer as Elizabeth asked questions, took notes, and then the girl said, "Ms. Marshall tried to call you yesterday and again earlier today, but she said no one was home. Ms. Marshall was worried that you.... She was afraid you might...." The girl's words came out in a gulp of sound, "She thinks you're sick again."

"Oh, no," Elizabeth said pleasantly. "Nothing like that. I was at the library. Mr. Gilmartin wanted me to go."

Lolly snickered silently at Elizabeth's words and whispered, "Liar," as Elizabeth returned the telephone to its cradle. Elizabeth almost nodded in agreement, but it wasn't quite a lie. She *had* been at the library, every single day for the past eight days, but she had been there as a patron, not as Mrs. Edgar Gilmartin, volunteer.

Her intentions had been good the first day, as

good as the rest of the paving stones leading to the nether regions, but Lolly had led her astray, taking Elizabeth on a pencil-and-notebook tour of microfilm land. It was a land rich in history, as much as pictures of old newspapers could make it, and that was rich enough to make Lolly prospect for an idea still nebulous and needing background for another novel. It was already beginning to flame in Lolly's fertile mind, but now it would have to wait until Edgar's house guests came and went.

But Lolly wasn't content with that. She jibed and taunted Elizabeth, calling her a worm and worse, as Edgar's obedient wife readied guest rooms, wrote menus, and ordered a wide variety of supplies.

"Lollygagging!" Lolly said spitefully. "And it won't do you one bit of good. *He* won't come home horny. Not this time."

And he didn't. He came home worn and weary, looking ten years older, worry painting darkness under his eyes, but he made an effort to reassure Elizabeth by following her into the kitchen after his guests had been shown to their rooms.

"I still can't tell you what it's all about," he said. "But we caught it before it fell completely apart. We managed to salvage some, but it's going to take eight months to a year to get it back where it was." He shook his head, took a sip of his gin and tonic, and said, "Thank goodness you're feeling better. I'm going to have to be gone a good deal of time between now and summer."

Elizabeth nodded understandingly, but she heard a note in his deep voice, something that made him look hastily away from her compassionate gaze; something that acted suspiciously like guilt.

She didn't ask questions. Elizabeth just smiled politely, served an elegant dinner, restored the kitchen and dining room to shiny perfection and went to bed alone, leaving Ms. Marshall, Edgar, and the three business associates to discuss their secrets far into the night. The next three days were the same.

On the fourth day everything changed. Elizabeth's world spun wildly around a strange, rainbowed sun, and Lolly chortled with unholy glee. The morning gave no hint of coming events and Elizabeth was too fully occupied with mundane things to feel even a faint tingle of joyful anticipation. Even Lolly, although she denied it, was taken completely by surprise. Elizabeth was rinsing the lunch dishes, readying them for the dishwasher, when the telephone rang. She reached over, took it off the hook, and held it to her ear with a dripping hand.

After her greeting, a pleasant male voice said, "Lolly Horn, please."

Struck dumb by shock, Elizabeth gurgled and sputtered, "Uh. Uh. Ga."

The voice asked, "Miss Horn, is that you?"

"Uh… no… I mean… she's… yes."

"Miss Horn," the voice said, "will you please hold for Benjamin Sessions of Sessions Publications?"

She knew who the call was from, and Elizabeth hissed, sputtered, and finally managed to whisper, "Yes," just as the canned waiting-for-someone-important-to-come-to-the-phone music played in her ear.

Afraid to breathe, to swallow the throbbing lump that filled her throat, Elizabeth sank down on a tall kitchen stool and stared at the microwave oven. She stared sightlessly at the pale reflection of a woman who was afraid to hope, afraid to believe Lolly's triumphant victory tune, afraid, afraid, afraid—and under the fear was the beginnings of joy, total, mindless joy.

"Miss Horn, are you there?"

"Y-y-y-y-yes."

"Here's Mr. Sessions."

"Well, hello, Lolly," a great booming voice said just before it laughed a great earthshaking laugh. "How's my newest author?"

"F-f-f-f-f-fine," Elizabeth stammered, and then realization made her squeak, "Author?"

"Yes," he answered. *"A Touch of Fornication* is, while not our contest winner, a rather remarkable book, one we want for our list."

"List?" Elizabeth repeated, unable to stop her

mouth from speaking random words, unable to stop her heart from pounding like a wild drum in her chest, her ears, her brain.

"Yes," he answered with a chuckle. "We have a brand-new imprint at Sessions and, for a variety of reasons, are a little short on titles. However, we believe your book will fill one vacancy very nicely. You should know, though, that we are going to rush publication on it. We intend to bring it out as soon as possible, probably within the next three months."

Her mouth opening and closing like a goldfish, Elizabeth fought back a wave of giddiness that tumbled over her, leaned her elbow on the counter, took a deep breath, and somehow managed to say, "Yes," when Mr. Sessions asked if she was still there.

"You do understand what I'm saying, don't you?" he asked.

"Oh, yes," she answered without having the slightest notion of his meaning.

"Other than the advance, which is two-thousand dollars, everything else is the same as it was written in the contest rules. You were sent a copy, weren't you? You do know that entering the contest meant you had to comply with all the rules?"

"Oh, yes," she said vaguely, and then she asked, "You are going to publish my book? You really are?"

"Yes, I am, Lolly," he said, laughter lurking in

every word. "I am going to do exactly that." He was silent for a moment and then said, "I have just spoken to my secretary. She will mail your contract today. We'll send your advance just as soon as we receive signed copies of the contract."

"A contract," she said. "In the mail. I sign, send it back. A contract. For my book." Elizabeth knew she was babbling, but she couldn't stop, couldn't push back the excitement that filled her like helium fills a balloon, lifting her higher and higher.

He said something she didn't quite hear.

Elizabeth laughed and asked, "You *are* buying my book?"

"We are indeed, Lolly, and very soon your editor will be in touch, to answer questions and discuss revisions."

She laughed, babbled, and couldn't let him go, not even after he said, "Good-by, Lolly."

"Wait," she said. "I don't.... This is all.... You'll write to me and.... Is this real?"

"It's very real, and I'll write you a letter today, confirming what I've told you." He laughed his big, happy, join-me-in-joy laugh. "I envy you your day, my dear."

She heard the connection break, but Elizabeth couldn't hang up the telephone. She sat, leaning on her elbow, the receiver pressed against her ear, staring at her dark reflection in the oven and smiling foolishly.

Unaware of anything but her own wild elation, she didn't hear Edgar come into the kitchen and ask for a pot of coffee, didn't feel his hand fasten on her shoulder or shake her. Lolly was in control, and Lolly didn't move until Edgar pulled the phone from her fingers, returned it to its perch on the wall, and said, very loudly, "Elizabeth!"

She smiled, wider and even more foolishly. "Oh, Edgar."

"What is it? What's the matter with you?"

"He said…. They're going to…. The book. The book. Oh, the book."

"What are you talking about? What book? Who was that on the telephone?" he asked impatiently.

"My book. They're going to buy…. Oh, Edgar, they're actually going to buy my book!" She slid off the stool, hugged herself with both arms, whirled around twice and reached out to him, wanting someone to cling to, to dance with; someone to believe her words and make them true.

Edgar caught her hands before they could encircle him, held her away, tried to throw ice water on her blazing joy. "My God, Elizabeth," he said coldly. "What's wrong with you? Go to your room immediately. I can't allow this in front of my business associates. Dear God."

Karoline Marshall had followed him into the bright kitchen, and her voice held only plastic concern when she glanced at Elizabeth and asked, "Edgar, what is it?"

"It's Elizabeth," he said bleakly. "She's sick again."

Lolly laughed.

Chapter Nine

♥   ♥   ♥

Iridescent as a hummingbird in flight, Lolly's laugh seemed to hang, shimmering in the air, and mock the man and the younger woman.

Edgar refused to be mocked. "Stop it," he snarled.

His grip on Elizabeth's wrists tightened painfully as he jerked her a half a step forward. "Do you want to destroy everything I've worked to build? Is that what you're trying to do? Damn it, Elizabeth, if I thought that were true, I'd...."

Taking a shuddering breath, he released her. The anger was gone from his voice and only long-suffering patience remained when he said, "Why don't you go to your bedroom and lie down for a while? Karoline will go with you, stay until you can manage to control yourself."

It wasn't at all funny, but laughter bubbled, like a fresh, sweet spring in the desert. She was powerless to stop it, couldn't contain the vast shining joy that filled her. She couldn't look at

Edgar's anger-flushed face. Couldn't answer the front door when the chimes sounded in Cass' particular ring. Couldn't even nod her agreement when Karoline said, "I'll go see who it is."

Elizabeth could only laugh, helplessly, wondrously.

"Please do," Edgar said to Karoline, "and send whoever it is away." He lowered his voice when he added, "And, Karoline, use the phone in the den to call Dr. Abernathy. Elizabeth needs to.... Ask him to.... Oh, God, why now? Keep it as quiet as possible, maybe we can keep it from them until the papers are signed. If they..." he glanced, significantly, toward the living room where his guests waited, "find out, it will ruin me."

"Yes, Edgar, I know," Ms. Marshall said quietly, watching the laughing Elizabeth with what had to be called "Triumph" peeking slyly from her brown eyes. "Don't worry about a thing. I'll take care of everything."

"You'll take care of what?" a hoarse voice asked from the doorway. "If it has anything to do with Liz, I'll do...." Cass let the words die, looking from Karoline to Edgar.

"One of your house guests let me in. He said to come on back, he thought you might be having a party, that someone was really laughing," she said as she walked forward, came to where Edgar and Elizabeth stood, facing each other, and smiled at her friend.

But it wasn't Elizabeth who greeted Mary Alice Cassidy Bates, it was Edgar. He said, almost eagerly, "Cass, thank God you're here to help. Elizabeth is sick again, and this time I'm going to make sure she gets well. Will you take her to her bedroom and stay with her until Karoline can get the doctor? Then, we'll see that she...."

Cass looked from him to the laughing Elizabeth and back again. "Are you sure she's sick?" she asked doubtfully.

Alarm, screaming like all the banshees in Ireland, finally penetrated Elizabeth's bubble of euphoria and deflated it to controllable size. She took a deep breath and said, with scarcely a tremble of joy in her voice, "No, I'm fine." Thus laying the first stone in what would be a towering edifice of lies and evasions.

"We have guests," she said slowly, groping her way toward what had to be a reasonable explanation. "There was an awful lot of work to do and Edgar wanted everything to be perfect. This was so important to his business.

"I was doing fine, and then the butcher called. He..." she improvised creatively, "he can't deliver the crown roast I ordered. Then I... I guess I just laughed because I didn't want to...."

"If that's all it was, why were you talking about a book?" Edgar asked, suspicion making his voice hard and cold.

"My... my cookbook," Elizabeth said, sternly

pushing back the joy that threatened to betray her, to send her, laughing wildly, to the madhouse of Ms. Marshall's choice. "He, the butcher, said.... Oh, Edgar, I was so upset, I yelled at him. He said I could buy a new cookbook. One that told rich people how to... to... to cook hamburger."

Swallowing back an errant giggle while pulling injured innocence across her face like a mask, she added in languishing tones, "Edgar, Ms. Marshall suggested some time before Christmas, that cooking and cleaning were best left to servants. Perhaps she's right. Perhaps we should hire someone, or perhaps a couple, to help me. I'm awfully tired." Elizabeth bent her head, let the final words drift out wearily, but Lolly couldn't resist a quick glance at the silently fuming Karoline.

Cass obviously didn't know what was going on, but somehow sensed Elizabeth needed her support, so she jumped into the fray with all banners flying. "That's absolutely right," she said. "Elizabeth shouldn't have to work like a slave taking care of your clients. Edgar, you are an important man now, and it just doesn't look right for Elizabeth to spend all of her time working." A jab of slyness entered her voice when she added, "That *is* what you told Liz when you sold her...."

Elizabeth, sinking for the third time in her frothy sea of incredible bliss, let Cass' words pass unheard.

But Edgar interrupted before she could finish.

"That's all well and good, but it doesn't help us right now. I have a meeting going on, a very important meeting. What are we going to do now?"

"I don't know what you are going to do," Cass said, "but I'm going to take Elizabeth shopping. Spending some of your money should make her feel a whole lot better. And then I'm going to take her to my house for dinner."

She put her hands on her ample hips, smiled at Ms. Marshall, and continued, "Edgar, I suggest that you, or the remarkable Ms. Marshall, finish these dishes and clean up in here before you make some sort of arrangements for your own dinner."

"No, Elizabeth isn't well enough to..." Karoline began hotly, then visibly took herself in hand and changed her tone to a meeker one. "I really think Mrs. Gilmartin should see Dr. Abernathy at once, perhaps even spend a few days at Harmony House and let the doctor decide how serious her problem...."

"Sigmund Abernathy? The shrink?" Cass almost shouted. "Edgar, you're the one who needs a doctor. You work Liz almost to death, and then, when she's too tired to work, you want to put her away. What kind of a man are you?"

Afraid to look at either Edgar or Karoline, afraid the giggles would explode like fireworks, Elizabeth, swallowed hard and looked down at the floor, "Shopping sounds wonderful, Cass. I do need to get away from here for a little while.

Perhaps if Ms. Marshall would just put the dishes in the dishwasher, wipe everything off, dry the sinks, and polish the counters, when I come back I will feel well enough to cook something simple for dinner."

"No. That won't be necessary," Edgar said firmly. "You just run along with Cass and have a good time. Stay out as late as you want, and don't worry about a thing here. We'll manage just fine."

"Well, if you're sure," she said softly, forcing her shoulders to droop forlornly, her voice to imitate a dying calf's—whatever that sounds like.

"Yes. Yes. Go and change. Karoline will be happy to finish up in here."

"Thank you, Edgar," Elizabeth whispered before she walked across the kitchen. "I usually run a damp mop over the tiles," she said to Karoline. "It keeps them looking nice. You wouldn't mind doing that, too, would you, dear?"

"No," Karoline said tightly, "I wouldn't mind at all."

"How sweet," Lolly said softly, patting Karoline's stiffly held shoulder as Elizabeth walked slowly past the young woman.

Holding her guise of extreme weariness until she was through the door and out of their sight, Elizabeth was barely able to tame the gale of exaltation that shook her. "They bought my book! They bought my book! Sessions Publications bought my book!"

New laughter filled her as she flew down the hall to her detested pink-and-white bedroom. She had enough reason left to close the door behind her. It was closed, muffling all sound, before she threw herself across the wide bed, buried her face in the nest of pillows, and whooped with unrestrained delight.

Drunk with joy of acknowledged authorship, she pounded her fists against the yielding satin. Elizabeth didn't know Cass was in the room until the bed sagged under additional weight and Cass asked softly, "What is it, Lizzy? What has the bastard done to you now?"

Pulling her body upright, she sat cross-legged with a careless disregard of the marks her shoes were making on the spread. Like a child in the center of the bed, Elizabeth said, through her laughter, "Not Edgar."

"Her then? That bitch made you cry?"

"Not crying!" Elizabeth held both hands, one over the other, to her mouth, trying to stop the laughter. She swallowed, hiccoughed, and then giggled.

"You're laughing!" Cass said accusingly. "Damn it, Elizabeth, I thought you were...."

"Shhhhhhhhhh!" Elizabeth whispered, hiccoughing again in the middle of her shushing, and then starting a new giggle. "Shhhhhhh! Edgar will hear. Put me in...." Elizabeth took one hand away from her mouth and swiped at the laugh-tears that ran, in glittering streams, down her face.

Cass sniffed, got up, walked away from the laughing woman with a muttered, "God."

Elizabeth heard the gush and splash of water running in the adjoining bath room and closed her eyes trying to stifle the mirth that held her. She gasped, almost strangled on a hiccough, and gasped again as Cass returned with a cold, wet washcloth and began to wipe away the tears, pushing aside Elizabeth's hands with no pretense at gentleness.

"Tell me what's going on," she demanded fiercely. "Tell me right now, or I swear to you, I'll call Dr. Abernathy myself and haul you out there before you can... can say boo to a goose."

Elizabeth reached out, squeezed Cass' arm, and said softly, because she was almost afraid to say the words aloud, "They bought my book."

Bouncing up and down on the bed, she said the words a little louder, slowly, carefully, wonderingly, "Sessions bought my book."

"Honey," Cass said, "you're just upset. Maybe you'd better lie down for a little while. Or take a nap. That would be good, wouldn't it? A nice long nap?"

"No, Cass, I'm not.... You aren't listening," Elizabeth said, laughing again. "Sessions bought my book."

"Liz, honey, just.... I'll go and.... I can have the doctor here in no time. You'd like that, wouldn't you? He'd make you.... Why don't you just put your head on the pillow and...?"

Cass coaxed soothingly, but Elizabeth tightened her grip on the woman's arm, refusing to let her go as she scrambled to her knees in front of her friend.

"Cass," she said earnestly, although the earnestness was somewhat flawed by a mixture of bubbling joy. "Remember at the writers' conference in Seaview, when they were talking about a contest for new writers? The Sessions Contest?"

A little of the worry faded from Cass' eyes and she nodded slightly, but it was obvious she was still withholding judgement on the matter of Elizabeth's sanity.

"I entered it, Cass. I came home, wrote a book, and I...."

"You won?" Cass asked incredulously.

"No! No, I didn't win. But they called me. Mr. Sessions called me today, less than an hour ago, and they are...."

"Are you telling me the absolute truth?"

"Nothing but." Elizabeth's solemn heart-crossing was interrupted by a loud hiccough and a shimmering giggle, a naughty-little-girl giggle that belonged more to Lolly than Elizabeth.

"But how? Why didn't you tell me? I thought you were.... Liz, you should have told me."

"I know, but I.... Oh, Cass, I couldn't tell anybody. I was afraid I wouldn't... that I couldn't do it. And you were so upset about those sex books and... Cass, I wanted to, but I just couldn't."

"My sweet Aunt Jenny! You wrote a book?" Cass asked, but it wasn't really a question, it was an exclamation, an affirmation of her own long-held belief in Elizabeth's talent. A belief that had spanned the years of their friendship and never faltered. "And this Sessions place bought it?"

Elizabeth nodded.

"Hot willies," Cass shouted. "I knew it. I knew you could do it!" She jerked free from Elizabeth's hand, threw both arms around her, and hugged her hugely. Elizabeth tried to stay upright, wavered, toppled backward, pulling Cass with her. They tumbled to the bed like happy children and lay in a tangle, giggling wildly, shushing each other, and laughing still harder in their efforts to be quiet.

And then, when they were giggled out, limp with spent mirth, they composed themselves, somewhat, and sat side-by-side, legs dangling from Elizabeth's size-nine cloud.

"Oh, Elizabeth Jane," Cass said. "I am so proud of you I don't know—probably for the first time in my life—what to say. But Liz, I can't wait until it's.... I have to read it. Please. Right now?"

"Well, I don't know," Elizabeth said teasingly, and then before the glow on Cass' face could lose wattage, she added, "Of course you can, but not here. Edgar or Ms. Marshall might decide to come and see if I'm sick enough to send to the home."

"At my house then? We can sneak it out and...."

"Cass, I ought to warn you. I used those sex books a lot. My book is.... Well, it's pretty... uh... it's...."

"Sexy? Hot?"

Elizabeth blushed, if only a trace, but Lolly said, "As a forest fire in July."

Cass laughed. "Lizzy, you wrote a.... Wow! I never thought you'd write something like that. Wow!" She snickered. "Wait until it comes out. Edgar will.... Oh, God, Liz, after he fills his shorts, he's going to kill you."

"He'll never know," Elizabeth said. "Unless I tell him."

"Of course he will. The man's selfish, but he's not entirely stupid. He can read. And your name is going to be right there, in plain sight, on the cover of... of what, Liz? What's its name?"

Lips twitching, Lolly said, *A Touch of Fornication.*

"*A Touch of....* Oh, my grapes and gussets, that title will make him turn baby-poop yellow. You.... Oh, my sainted Aunt Tilly, Liz, are you sure you did the right thing. I know he's a bastard, but this.... He really might kill you if.... He might."

Torn between laughter and honest concern, Cass stared at Elizabeth, who hastened to reassure her. "He really won't know, Cass. His precious reputation is safe. I wrote the book under a different name. The book's author, as far as anybody but you knows, is Lolly Horn."

"Why that?" Cass asked. "It doesn't sound anything like a writer's name?" Cass' brown eyes were perplexed and confusion pulled new little lines across her forehead. "My friend Emma, Caress Love, said you should chose a name right for what you were writing."

"Lolly Horn is certainly that."

"I don't see..." Cass started, but Elizabeth interrupted with the story of Lolly's genesis. By the time she finished, Cass was rocking back and forth, clutching her stomach, and roaring.

"Lollygag!" she gasped as she wiped her eyes. "Lollygag and horny. I can't believe it! You.... You... lollygag!"

But she was completely sober when they were in her car, the boxed manuscript resting in a large shopping bag on the backseat. There was only worry in her voice when she asked, "Liz, are you going to tell Edgar?"

"I tried. When Mr. Sessions called, I tried to tell Edgar about the book," Elizabeth said as Cass turned the key in the ignition, started the car and drove out of the driveway. "You saw what happened. He thought I was.... If you hadn't come in, I swear to you, they were ready to put me away. Right then and there."

"Liz, I know that, but sooner or later Edgar will have to know. You just can't keep something like this a secret from your husband."

"Why not?"

"Well, what if it's a best seller or something. What will you do then?"

Elizabeth felt her joy surge high, build to a crest, wash over her, taking worry, care, and responsibility, and she surrendered to it without even token resistance. "Why Miz Cassie," she drawled, "I reckon we'll just have to do like Scarlett and worry about it tomorrow."

Cass braked at a stop sign. "Liz, you really should tell him now, today, before it goes any farther."

"No, ma'am, Miss Cassie, I ain't gonna do that. I ain't gonna tell that damn Yankee nothing, and I ain't gonna listen to no more of your talk. Not today." Elizabeth grinned. "Today I want champagne, expensive champagne, and then I want...." An imp took possession of her tongue, gave her phony drawl a dash and a dab of added innocence. "I want to know something only you can tell me, Miz Cassie."

Cass eased the car into low gear. "What's that?"

"Why would little old me want to say boo to a goose?"

"What on earth are you...?" Cass began, and then she remembered what she had said earlier. Her foot slid off the clutch. The car bucked, coughed, and died a natural death. Cass threw her head back and shouted with laughter before she said, "Liz, you're the goose, and you're going to be cooked if you don't tell Edgar about this book."

But Elizabeth didn't tell her husband she had written a very sexy book that was going to be published. She made Cass invoke the ritual, made her promise she wouldn't tell him either.

Edgar's business associates left the next morning. He worked at his office, leaving very, very early and coming home very, very late, so late Elizabeth wondered why he even bothered coming home at all for the two days following the men's departure. On the third day, Edgar, once again in the company of Ms. Marshall, flew away from Cragshome to quest for fame and fortune in the lofty, rarified heights of the financial kingdom.

But before he left, Elizabeth Gilmartin's lean and handsome husband came into the kitchen and said, "My dear, I'm afraid this is only the first of what will be a large number of business trips I will have to take in the coming months. If you feel you'd be more... ah... happier at the Bates house, I assure you I will not take it at all amiss if you want to spend your time with Cass."

"I'll be perfectly happy here. The house shouldn't be left empty for any length of time—isn't that what you told me?"

"Well, yes, but...."

"There's nothing wrong with me, Edgar," Elizabeth said, and then some devil, probably one Lolly summoned, made her say, "If you feel the house can be safely left alone, why don't I go to New York with you and do some shopping."

Red—dull and almost invisible under his tan— touched his face. He looked down at the counter top, fussed with his tie, cleared his throat, and finally said, "Not this time, my dear. I'm afraid you'd be very bored. After all, it is just a business trip."

"Is it?" she asked.

"Yes, yes, of course," he said, far too quickly. "Why? What else would it be?"

Before she could answer, the telephone rang. Edgar had the receiver off the hook before it could complete its initial ring. "Hello," he said, and after listening a moment, he said, "No, I'm sorry. There is no one by that name here. You must have.... Madam, may I suggest you hang up, check the number, and dial again."

He slammed the telephone down and said, with far more irritation than the incident warranted, "Wouldn't you think someone could make a simple telephone call—long distance at that—without bothering people who have better things to do with their time than answer wrong numbers." He glanced at her and shook his head.

The wild elation had calmed with the passing days, but it was still there, nestled cozily in

Elizabeth's soul, waiting for a magic word, a gesture to bring it back to singing life. Edgar's chance reference to "long distance" triggered a response.

"Who were they trying to reach?" she asked. Now there was a swarm of buzzing bees in her stomach and a tremor in her hands and voice.

Edgar looked at her again, and just as rapidly as before, he looked away. "I don't know," he said. "Some ridiculous name like Polly Thorn, or Molly Dorn, or something like that." He dismissed the whole thing with a gesture of his hand and glanced, furtively, at his watch.

"Elizabeth," he said softly, his deep voice gentle, almost pleading. "I'll bring you something from New York. Something nice. You'd like a present, wouldn't you?"

At that moment, Elizabeth could think of nothing, could want nothing more than for him to get out of the kitchen, to leave for New York before the phone rang again and someone from Sessions Publications asked for Lolly Horn, insisting she was at that number.

"Yes, bring me a present," she said, willing to agree to anything that would make him go. "Bring.... Surprise me. But you'd better hurry, hadn't you? You don't want to keep Ms. Marshall waiting, do you?"

"There's plenty of time," he said, looking at his watch again. "Elizabeth, I had Karoline call Cass. I wanted the Widow.... That is, I wanted

Cass to keep an eye on you while I'm gone. Just in case...."

"In case I run outside and start howling at the moon?" Lolly asked brightly. "Is this your idea or Ms. Marshall's. Probably hers, she knows more about moon baying, doesn't she?"

Anxiety flaying her skin from her flesh, Elizabeth wanted to strangle both Lolly and Edgar, strangle them and let their bodies rot where they fell. Failing that, she wanted to scream at them like a harpy in full flight, order them out of the kitchen.

Beneath the anxiety, the need to get rid of Edgar, ran the fear, the black gibber of fear that whispered the secret she had harbored through the writing, the elation, "It's all a mistake. They've changed their minds. They aren't going to publish the book. They never were. It was all a mistake. You're mad, Elizabeth, totally and completely mad."

The horrible fear pulling and tugging at her, the anxiety making her tremble, Elizabeth knew she had to get him out and quick. She tried, but her quick wasn't quick enough.

He was still there when the phone rang.

He reached for it.

Desperate, Elizabeth stepped forward, took it out of his hand, and said, with far more assurance than she felt, "You go on to the airport, Edgar, I'll take care of this."

"Elizabeth, we need to talk. I.…"

"Good-by, Edgar. Have a good trip." She held the instrument to her ear and said, "Hello," and the tall, thin woman didn't so much as quiver when a female voice said, "Lolly Horn, please."

"Speaking," Elizabeth said, and then because she couldn't allow him to see her weep when the voice told her it was all an illusion, Elizabeth said, "Can you hold for just a moment?"

She turned to Edgar and laid another stone in her building of lies. "It's the library," she said, "and it's going to take a little while."

"But I need to talk to.…"

"Edgar, *you* signed me up as a volunteer. Have you changed your mind?"

Chapter Ten

♥   ♥   ♥

Fear made her strong enough to turn her back on her husband, hold the telephone a little closer to her flushed face, and say, very softly, "I'm back."

Behind her Edgar sighed, just once, before he said, "Good-by, Elizabeth."

She couldn't answer; she was totally Lolly at the moment. And Lolly was too intent, too absorbed in listening to the female voice that spoke of wondrous things, writer things, in her ears. A female voice that had introduced its owner as Lannie Giles, Lolly's editor at Sessions.

Lannie explained, in great detail and with several small apologies, that Lolly's book, *A Touch of Fornication,* would not, despite Mr. Sessions' over-optimistic expectations, be in the bookstores until July or August. Exotica was Sessions' new imprint, and Lolly's book would be the third issued under the Exotica label. It would benefit from the rather extensive advertising campaign that Sessions was mounting to launch the new imprint.

Lolly listened avidly, mumbled "yes" or "no" where indicated by the almost one-sided conversation and tried to understand everything Lannie told her. Some of the information was easily processed, but not all.

"*A Touch of Fornication*—marvelous title, by the way—was chosen because, not only is it quite good, it fits the format we decided on for Exotica. It is short, innocently erotic, and set in an exotic time. Also," Lannie Giles added, "it's pretty clean. That means it won't take a whole lot of rewrites and editing. We were really short on manuscripts, too."

She paused for a moment, obviously waiting for Lolly to make some sort of reply, but all Lolly could do was gulp out a squeaky, "Thank you."

Ms. Giles laughed. "You're perfectly welcome. And now, we need some information about you personally."

The squeak intensified, made Lolly sound like a terrified mouse when she asked, "Me?"

"Yes, you," Lannie said. "It's rather important, too. We are going to publish a short bio of each of our authors. Not more than a paragraph or so, but interesting. I'll get most of the information now and give it to our advertising department. They will do the actual...."

Sheer terror pushed Lolly into the background, made Elizabeth whimper, "I... I can't.

No, I... I can't."

"Well, I do realize it's rather sudden. Maybe it would be okay if you write something down and send it to me. Of course, we do need it very soon, so please try to get it in the mail tomorrow at the very latest."

"I...."

"This isn't one of my whims, Ms. Horn. We need that information," Ms. Giles said: a hint of coolness made her voice clipped and businesslike. "Rest assured we won't print anything confidential, such as your home address or telephone number —we keep to generalities there. We just want some information: writing background, age, martial status, children, hobbies, pets, etc."

Elizabeth, for a single instant, knew all was lost, either Sessions would send the manuscript back and forget the whole thing, or she would have to tell the unknown young woman of her duplicity in entering under another name. She almost laughed and said, "The jig's up. I confess." Instead, she added a new course of lies to her growing edifice.

"I'm afraid I'm not a very interesting person," she said. "But if it will help any, I'm forty-five," she lied, "have no pets, except a turtle, and my hobbies are... uh... I... uh... I collect things."

"What sort of things?"

Her mind working at a runaway pace, Elizabeth Gilmartin, tame rug, tried to give Lolly

Horn, author, a background totally unlike her own, while still being mundane and unexciting, but for a millisecond her mental processes went awry and she said, "Sex books. I collect sex books."

There was dead silence on the other end of the line, and sounding loud in the silence, Elizabeth heard Edgar open the front door and close it behind him. Relief, that he was gone at last, flooded though her. "Mostly just how-to sex books."

"Oh," Lannie Giles said, and then she stammered out, "Well, I expect your husband... your husband... he must enjoy that."

"No," Lolly said. "I don't have a husband. I am now, and always have been, a maiden lady."

"Oh," Ms. Giles said again, sounding nonplussed and then she added, rather hastily, "Well, if you think of anything else of interest, write it down and send it in with the black-and-white glossy."

"A picture?" The squeak was back in Elizabeth's voice and it was a squeak of pure, unadulterated terror that stabbed her with its own frantic thoughts. *Picture. They wanted a picture. A picture of her. She couldn't. Edgar would.... He would die. Kill her. No. No. No picture.* And she said the last frantic thought aloud. "No picture."

"Miss Horn," Lannie asked sternly, "did you read the rules for the contest?"

"Y-y-y-y-yes," Elizabeth stammered, and then honesty made her add, "No, not entirely."

"I suggest you do so at once."

"Yes, I will. I'm sorry, I...."

"By entering the contest, you have given Sessions permission to use your name and likeness in their advertising, in their book catalog, and in various other ways in order to promote the work. In as much as *A Touch of Fornication* is to be published in hardcover, we will need a picture of you for the back of the dust jacket. We will also use the same pose in a number of other aspects of the campaign. Do you understand your obligation now?"

"Yes," Elizabeth whispered, "but I don't have...."

"Get one taken and send it to me within the next month."

Swallowing back the fear that was screaming, "Doom!" at the top of its voice, Elizabeth said, "Yes, I'll do that. I'll send one as soon as possible."

"Good, and I want to say congratulations again, Miss Horn, and welcome you to our growing family of authors. I hope it will be a long and happy association for us both."

"Yes," Elizabeth answered, "I hope so, too."

"Oh, that reminds me. There is one more thing I need from you."

Fear felt like a claw gashing the inside of Elizabeth's stomach. She sucked in a breath and held it while Lannie Giles asked, "What's the title of the book you're working on now?"

Expelling her pent breath with the word, Elizabeth asked, "Book?"

Her good humor restored, Lannie Giles laughed. "I swear, you authors are all alike. I know you're working on some new project. After all, writers write, don't they? Now, all I need is the working title."

Elizabeth's mind was blank, but Lolly rose to the occasion. *"P.S. I've Taken a Lover,"* she said.

"Super title. What's it about?"

"I don't talk about works in progress," Lolly said primly.

And then she retreated, leaving Elizabeth to say their farewells, and to hang up the phone before she took off her gray-rimmed glasses, rubbed her eyes, and whispered, "Dear God, a picture. What am I going to do?"

She didn't have time to brood. The door chimes sounded, ringing in Cass' distinctive pattern, and an angry Cass stomped into the entry before Elizabeth could even smile, however wanly, and say, "Hello."

"Where is he?" Cass shouted. "I'm going to give the son-of-a-bitch two ears full, just after I pin them to the wall."

She stormed past Elizabeth, pounded on the door to Edgar's office complex, and yelled, "Damn you, Edgar, come out!"

Cass had been angry before, but never like this. Elizabeth touched her friend's arm. "Cass," she said softly, "he's not.... He's gone."

"The slimy bastard. I ought to... to...."

"What is it? What on earth did he do to you?" Elizabeth asked, worry darkening her eyes. Cass had been mad at Edgar before, many times, but never to this extent. Never so mad she looked like she was ready to explode from her interior heat.

"I'm going to tell him just what I think of him. He has no right, not even if he is your husband, to treat you like this."

"Cassie, come on into the kitchen. Let's have a cup of coffee or...."

"Where is he?"

"The airport, or at least on his way. He's flying to New York today. Ms. Marshall is...."

"That two-faced, mealy-mouthed bitch! They deserve each other." She whirled away from the door, faced Elizabeth. "You can't stay here. They're going to...."

She bit off her words, looked at Elizabeth searchingly. "Lizzie, they're trying to get rid of you. Ms. Marshall is bound and determined to put you in.... That son-of-a-bitch is in on it, too. He told her to.... The bastard!"

She patted Cass' heaving shoulder. "The marvelous Ms. Marshall called you I presume," she said, her voice calm, her face composed. "Edgar said he had asked her to. He's a bit worried about my sanity." She thought about her own particularly perilous predicament and added wryly, "And so am I."

"Don't say that!" Cass said hotly. "Don't even think it! That bitch'll have you in Abernathy's snake pit before you can... can...."

"Say 'boo' to a goose?" Elizabeth asked slyly.

"Don't joke," Cass snapped. "There's nothing funny about it. Damn it, Liz, that woman asked me to help put you away—for your own good, of course."

Elizabeth laughed. "Well, I suppose that might be one answer, maybe the only answer."

"What are you talking about? This is serious, a real problem, and you just babble on like an... an...."

"Idiot?"

"No," Cass said, and then, almost reluctantly, she smiled. "But close. Damned close."

"And true," Elizabeth answered. "Damned true."

"Liz, listen to me. They really could put you away. I've read about men putting their wives in madhouses."

"Hack novels. Besides, divorce is cheaper," Elizabeth said airily. "It's just Karoline. She thinks menopause is the end of life as women know it, and quite probably the end of sanity."

"That's not all she's thinking about, Liz. That bit.... That female is keeping her kennel warm for your husband. And it seems that he's been doing a little sniffing and panting himself."

"Forget about that, it's not true, about Edgar anyway and it's not important," Elizabeth said, just before she looked at Cass and cried, "Oh, Cass, I'm in terrible trouble."

Cass tossed her suspicions and anger over the rainbow, or someplace, and rallied to Elizabeth's need. "What kind of trouble?"

"Lolly Horn trouble," Elizabeth said. "You were right, Cass, I should have told Edgar and let him demand the return of my manuscript, but it's too late for that now. They sent the contract by express mail. I signed it and sent it back yesterday, right after I got it. I suppose I should still tell him, but...."

"You wouldn't dare. That book is a wowser. It's so hot I had to put it in my fireproof safe." She laughed. "Liz, Edgar's clients are not going to like or understand how his wife.... That book is.... I always knew you could write, but not like that. No, sir, not like *that*."

"Well, *that* is the problem," Elizabeth said. "Lolly's editor called a little while ago. The book is coming out in July or August, in hardcover." Elizabeth took a deep breath to quell the trembling in her voice and forced the words out. "Oh, Cass, they told me to send a picture for the back, a picture of Lolly Horn. Me."

Cass didn't laugh. She reached out, took

Elizabeth's chin in her hand, tipping her face back and forth as she studied it intently. Finally, she nodded. "It's been a while, but.... Yeah, I can do it. Come on."

"Where?"

"To get Lolly's picture taken."

"But...."

"Get your coat and purse, Liz. We have places to go and people to see."

"Like this?" Elizabeth gestured at her dull, blunt-cut hair, her pale unadorned face. "I can't. Edgar would know and... I don't want people to laugh at him, Cass. He's done some terrible things, but he doesn't deserve to lose everything he has, does he?"

"The bastard deserves everything he's going to get," Cass muttered. "But don't worry, he'll never know from the pictures."

"Are you sure?" Elizabeth looked at her friend and almost begged for reassurance, for some magic that would take away her problem, give her an honorable way out.

"Very sure," Cass said. "Now, turn off everything that's on, grab some night clothes, and let's get going. It's a long drive to Montcross."

"Montcross? But...."

Cass explained, excitement making her words come out quick and bright. "First, no one knows us over there. Second, they've got a glamour photographer there—I read about him in the paper.

He's pretty good, I guess. Anyway, the article said he was one of those guys that turns plump bumpkins into centerfolds in the click of a shutter."

"I can't put something like that on my credit cards. Edgar would be sure to...."

"Liz, shut up. Just go get your coat and quit arguing. I'm going to give Lolly a present." She grinned. "And Edgar and his tail-wagging female a kick in the... the...."

"Ass?" Lolly asked.

"Yes, he certainly is," Cass said agreeably.

Almost seven hours later, Elizabeth—her hair squashed flat, pinned tight and stuffed under a nylon wig cap—was sitting, feet aching and shoeless, glasses off, eyes closed, and stomach grumbling with hunger, in a hotel chair, suffering in silence. She allowed Cass, who was mumbling like one of the madder scientists, to transform nondescript into stunning; staid into madcap—Elizabeth Jane Gilmartin into Lolly Horn.

Cass touched Elizabeth's cheek with a brush and nibbled on her own lower lip. She then grabbed one of the three wigs standing in a blonde row on the dresser, like faceless watchers in some manic play, and fitted it on Elizabeth's head, tugging and fluffing the platinum tresses.

After a brief, silent inspection, Cass said,

"No," jerked the silvery curls up and away, and began fitting her second choice into place. She fussed with it for a moment, stepped back, critically eyed it and the carefully made-up Elizabeth and said, "Okay, stand up."

Elizabeth, or maybe it was truly Lolly, obeyed without protest. She shivered when Cass began brushing a shimmer of gold dust on Lolly's shoulders and the upper swells of her breasts pushed up and out by a black bra that barely covered her nipples.

"Just keep your eyes shut. Don't look yet," Cass said.

"You know I can't see a blasted thing without my glasses," Elizabeth said as her stomach growled like a bear fresh out of hibernation. "And if you don't hurry, it's not going to matter anyway because I'm going to starve to death. I don't see why we don't just call room service and...."

"I told you," Cass said absently as she added a few swipes of dark foundation to Elizabeth's jawline, contouring the shape of her face. "I want to see you with people. I mean I want to see Lolly with people before her appointment with that photographer. I need to see how you.... I might need to change the makeup or.... You know."

"Do I?"

"Stop complaining. That's all you've done all day—that and argue."

"Cass, it's costing so much that I... I will pay

you back, I promise. The check for the book should... I got myself into this, I can't let you do all of this for nothing."

"Hush, and step into this."

"Which one is it?" Elizabeth asked, trying to remember, by feel, the dress Cass was sliding, ever so carefully, up her body and zipping tight around her.

"The black one. I want to see if it's right. Yes, I think... pearls. Where did I put...?" She wandered off, mumbling, and Elizabeth could hear the rustle of paper and plastic as Cass pawed through the welter of clothes, scarves, hats, costume jewelry, and shoes that were spread on both beds, a portion of the floor, and on the table.

She waited with her back to the mirror, the room a gently shaded myopic blur as Elizabeth tried to put the day in place. She needed to sort out the features and restore order to her world, but it was a useless striving. The day was blurred like the room, filled with shaded pieces; driving to Montcross, calling on the photographer and bribing him to fit her in the next morning. There had been the shopping, trying on exotic and erotic garments, visiting strange shops, and standing like a dummy—department store variety—while Cass explained what she wanted and/or needed for Elizabeth's face, feet, body, and head. She remembered bits and tatters, but she could not remember the black dress. She thought it might be the demure-looking little gown—it cost far too much to be just a dress—that made Cass gasp, just a little, and say, "That's it. That's exactly what I want."

Her search successful, Cass came back, fastened the faux pearls around Elizabeth's neck, poked at the wig again, and said, "There, that's the way I always wanted to...."

The pleasure, satisfaction, and the touch of pride in Cass' hoarse voice set off a tingle of anticipation in Elizabeth. "Can I look now?" she asked, almost like a child asking permission from a stern parent.

"Sure, only I should.... Well, put your shoes on first."

"My feet hurt! You can't possibly expect me to walk around in four-inch heels after what you put me through today."

"Beauty has a price," Cass said with a laugh. "So, go on, pay it. I'll get myself together and then we'll go down and eat."

Moaning with a pain that was only partially pretense, Elizabeth did as she was told before she turned to face the shadowy figure in the mirror. She leaned closer to see a fuzzily unfamiliar face, an inordinate amount of neck, and nothing else. "Cass," she said, "where are my glasses? I can't see."

"No glasses," Cass said firmly.

"But I want to...."

"No," Cass repeated. "And take off your wedding ring."

"But... I...."

Snorting, Cass took Elizabeth's hand, worked the worn gold band down over the knuckle and off. "Put this one on, it'll hide the mark."

Blind and bewildered, Elizabeth slid the large, gaudy dinner ring on her finger, hiding its nakedness with synthetic diamonds and emeralds. "Why, Cass?"

"Lolly's a maiden lady. You told me so yourself," Cass said with another laugh. "Now, come on, Lolly, let's go eat before Elizabeth starves to death."

It *was* Lolly who walked out of the elevator and into the restaurant with Cass. Lolly who nodded and smiled when the hostess said it would be a few minutes before she could seat them and would they like to wait in the bar. It was also Lolly who said, "No, thank you," when a young-sounding, barely seen man asked if he could buy her a drink.

Lolly knew she had caused a stir in the bar, the restaurant, and at the photographers, but she didn't know what she looked like until ten days later. During this time, Cass and Elizabeth arrived safely back in Cragshome, and Edgar arrived home from one business trip and was ready to leave on another. Elizabeth agreed to hide Lolly's clothes, wigs, make-up, and the manuscript at Cass' house, and

Cass agreed to let Elizabeth pay half the cost of their foray into the wilds of Montcross when her book money arrived.

The ten days of waiting ended on a blustery first day of March. The day started tamely enough. Feeling slightly headachy, Elizabeth saw Edgar off and started to pack his suitcase for the upcoming trip. She cleaned with a laxity that would have shocked and saddened her mother, made a pot of coffee, and sat at the kitchen table until the postman came. Sorting through the bills and circulars with apathetic fingers, Elizabeth tossed the letter from Sessions Publications into the copper box with the household bills before she actually saw it.

Her breath knotting in her chest, she picked it up with trembling fingers and ripped it open. Taking out the thick bundle of paper, she glanced at her copy of the contract, the check for two thousand dollars—which made her heart leap and sing—and read the short accompanying note. It expressed Sessions' pleasure at having Lolly Horn on their team, the usual congratulations and small talk. But it was two short lines, near the bottom of the page, that made both Lolly and Elizabeth gulp.

It said: "As per our contractual agreement, we will be expecting a final draft of *P.S. I've Taken a Lover* no later than December first of this year."

"P.S. I've Taken a Lover?" Elizabeth asked

aloud, and the echoes in the empty house seemed to mock her confusion. "What on earth are they talking about?" And then she remembered it faintly as a small part of a hectic conversation and knew it was supposed to be the title of Lolly Horn's new book. It was a book with a contract but no plot, no characters, and no setting.

Staring blankly, Elizabeth returned the papers to the envelope and took several steps toward the den, intending to hide the letter in her desk. A honking horn stopped her. Sticking the envelope in her apron pocket, she opened the front door just in time to see a wind-blown Cass trotting up the front walk. A wide smile on her face, her coat belling out behind her, Cass waved an unopened photo-mailer bearing Lolly Horn's name and Cass' address.

"The proofs are here," she shouted. "Oh, hurry, Elizabeth. I can't wait to see...." She herded Elizabeth back into the house and to the kitchen, but she couldn't make the other woman hurry, couldn't keep her from pouring them each a fresh cup of coffee and piling cookies on a plate.

"What's the matter with you? The way you're acting, anyone would think you're afraid to...." Cass let the words die on her lips, looked at Elizabeth sharply, and said, "Come over here and quit dithering."

"I can't. Oh, what will I do if you can still tell it's me?"

Cass dropped the thick packet of proofs on the tabletop and came to where Elizabeth stood. "I can't answer that. We won't know anything until we look, will we?" she asked quietly.

Red ugly splotches mottled her white face as Elizabeth tried to smile. It was worse than a pitiful grimace—it was a dead-cat rictus, frozen in place by her growing apprehension.

"Quit acting like a goose and sit down," Cass said as she pushed the other woman to the table and practically forced her into a chair.

"Open the damned pictures," she growled. "I want to see them even if you don't. I've got a stake in this too, you know."

Silently Elizabeth bent her head, tore at the end of the envelope with nerveless fingers, pulling off little scraps of manila, until the envelope fell open. She tipped it up. The proofs, sandwiched between cardboard and secured with rubber bands, slid into her hand.

Moving with agonizing slowness and oblivious to Cass' hurrying motions, she rolled the rubber bands from the package, lifted the cardboard, and stared, her mouth quivering like a hurt child's, at the first picture.

Chapter Eleven

♥   ♥   ♥

She stared down at the bulky packet of pictures, seeing only the first one. Her eyes grew soft, filling with tears. The 5x7 black-and-white glossy was lost in a watery haze; but only to her outward sight. Inside, the image remained shining like a dream of enchantment.

Cass touched Elizabeth's wrist. "Liz? Honey, what's the matter? Are the pictures that bad?"

"No," Elizabeth whispered, blinking away her tears, looking again at the slender woman, with the body of an innocent wanton and the face of an impish saint, sitting cross-legged in the middle of a huge bed. Rumpled satin sheets and misty sheer bed curtains floated apart to show the figure of Lolly Horn. Her large silvery eyes and generous mouth smiled faintly. Lolly was holding a sharpened pencil in her right hand, had a scribbled-on note pad on her lap; her blonde head tilted to one side as she looked into the distance, beyond today into some unseen time.

"Liz?" Cass' troubled voice broke through Elizabeth's reverie, but it didn't destroy her sense of discovery and wonder.

"You should have told me," Elizabeth said, her voice soft and shy. "I didn't know. Cass, I swear to you, until I saw this picture, I didn't know that...." Tears slid from beneath the frames of her glasses and ran down her cheeks. She sat, weeping like a child, suddenly made helpless by the awareness of her own beauty, a beauty she hadn't known existed.

Cass looked befuddled. "Is it the pictures? Don't cry over them. We can have them retaken. I can put more paint on your face, get a different wig. We can...." She handed Elizabeth a napkin. "Here. Wipe your face. Let's look. Maybe the rest aren't that bad."

"No, you don't understand. Cass, the picture is.... Lolly is beautiful."

The other woman laughed. "God, you scared me. I thought.... You are beautiful, Liz. The picture is of *you*."

"I know that, but Cass, why didn't you.... I didn't know."

"Liz, you're not making a lick of sense. Know what?"

There was no way she could explain. The knowledge ran too deep, was too closely entwined in the fiber of her being, but she tried. "I was.... I didn't expect to see myself like this. With those clothes and the make-up, I thought Lolly would look just like me, only made-up like...."

"Like what?"

"A tart," Elizabeth said, and then she smiled, a smile as innocent as Lolly's. "I'm sorry, Cass. I just didn't know you saw.... I didn't know.... Lolly is beautiful."

"*You* are beautiful, Liz. My God, you're fifty years old. You must know that. I didn't do anything except add a little paint."

"But I didn't know I could look like that," Elizabeth said slowly. "When I was younger, I used to wish I looked.... That Edgar would look at me and see me like this. I don't suppose you can understand, Cass, you've always been so beautiful and it was like I was just there, just Elizabeth." She smiled. "Thank you, Cass. I'll always remember."

"Silly," Cass said, touching her own eyes with another of the napkins. "All these years? Elizabeth Jane, why on earth didn't you say something?"

"I...." Elizabeth sneezed explosively. The proofs flew out of her hand, scattered in a broad fan across the table top. Elizabeth sneezed again, setting the slippery prints into new motion. They fluttered and fell until the entire table and some of the floor beneath was decorated with Lolly's smiling face and scantily clad body.

The two women, giggling now, began picking

up proofs and showing each other this pose and that.

On her hands and knees under the table, Elizabeth held the last elusive picture by the corner and said "Look at this one Cass. Lolly is.…"

Cass interrupted with, "Uh, Liz, uh, we.…"

Her voice sounded so strange, Elizabeth looked up, saw Edgar and the impossibly perfect Ms. Marshall standing just inside the kitchen door.

The prints were still spread out on the table. Elizabeth's internal alarm system screamed, "Panic attack! Panic attack!" She jumped, banged her head against the underside of the table, and sneezed again, so strongly her head jerked up and slammed into the table again.

"Damn and blast," she said before she could call the expletive back. Then she watched as Edgar, with Karoline following in the proper "heel" position, walked toward the table.

"Get up, Elizabeth," he ordered coldly. "I don't know what you think you are doing, but it doesn't matter in the slightest. Just get up. Right now."

Too worried about the pictures to do anything but obey, Elizabeth crawled forward. A million icy hands squeezed her heart when she felt her knee hit the edge of the Sessions letter, forcing it out of her apron pocket and across the tiles until it came to rest between Edgar's glossy oxfords and Ms. Marshall's trim pumps. Her hands froze and her breath ached in her throat when her husband reached down, picked up the heavy envelope and turned it over so he could glance at the return address.

"Sessions Publications," he said. "Another one of those! Elizabeth, I thought I told you all these sweepstakes letters are bunk. Why didn't you throw it in the trash as I asked?"

Her mouth sand dry, she scuttled like a large and ungainly crab out from under the table and got to her feet. She took a step forward, but before she could reach out and snatch the letter or even answer his question, Edgar stomped over to the trash compactor, opened it, threw the letter in with the orange peels, coffee grounds, egg shells, and the rest of the sloppy remains of their breakfast. Then, after a scowl in her direction, he turned on the machine.

"No," Elizabeth said. "Oh, no." Her hand went to her mouth and she looked at the growling machine with stricken eyes.

"Stop acting like a fool," Edgar snapped, turning back to glare at her. "If you had taken care of the mail properly, this wouldn't have happened. Not that it matters. I have more important things to attend to at the moment. I told you I was flying to Miami today and expressly told you to leave my suitcase in the entry. It isn't there, where is it?"

She made a vague gesture toward the bedroom wing of the house. "I think I...."

"Oh, never mind," he said as he walked out. "I should have known better than to expect you to.... Never mind, I'll take care of it myself."

Anger crept through Elizabeth, freeing her paralyzed body, her frozen tongue. "Yes," she said, "you do just that. Find it, pack it and carry it away." Not satisfied with that, she whirled on Ms. Marshall, grabbed the hand that was reaching toward one of the pictures on the table and jerked it back. "And you, my dear Ms. Marshall, have my permission to trot right along behind him."

Karoline pulled her hand free and wiped it on her skirt. Her eyes looked like glass and tiny frown lines embraced her red lips, but her voice held only compassionate understanding when she said soothingly, "Mrs. Gilmartin, I heard you sneezing. Perhaps you're coming down with something. At your age, these sudden illnesses are difficult to cope with. Why don't you sit down and look at your...."

She glanced down, saw what the subject of the photographs was, and asked, "Are you sure you should...? Does Edgar know you're doing something like this?"

In the trauma of the moment, Elizabeth had forgotten the pictures of herself, rather of Lolly in all their sexy, revealing glory. "Doing what?" she asked, completely aware that fear had made her voice sound sullen.

"That you are... ah... you are...." Karoline's

delicate distaste for Elizabeth's occupation was evident in her every word, and it was equally evident she thought she had found another manifestation of Elizabeth's growing madness even before the young woman said, "Now, you can see what I've been talking about. Mrs. Bates, surely you can't ignore this. May I speak to you out in the hall?"

"Cass is my friend," Elizabeth said, " and she's not going to do as you ask and drag me off, kicking and screaming to Bedlam. So you might as well say what you want to say right here because she's going to tell me anyway."

"Really, Mrs. Bates, I find your lack of discretion appalling. I really thought you'd be more than willing to…. Especially in view of Mrs. Gilmartin's condition. She's your friend, and I thought you'd want to help her."

Cass came over to stand at Elizabeth's side. "I'm afraid you forgot something, Ms. Marshall," she said, her voice amused, her eyes twinkling.

The younger woman took a step back, eyed the two women who stood shoulder to shoulder, facing her with deep distrust. "Oh?" she asked slowly, "what's that?"

"I'm also menopausal."

Elizabeth snickered, but Ms. Marshall was far from amused, so far in fact that she took Cass' words and attached her own value to them. "Oh," she said, "I am really sorry. I should have realized. Mrs. Bates, please forgive me for being so insensitive. I am sorry. I would be more than happy to ask Dr. Abernathy if he will see you, too—perhaps you could have adjoining rooms or something. I can see now that you are as mentally...."

Elizabeth's face contorted as she tried to hold back the laughter crowing inside her. She didn't dare look at Cass, but she could feel the other woman's shoulder shaking against her own. Despite the hidden froth of laughter, Elizabeth was incredibly calm when she said, "My dear Ms. Marshall, I would like to remind you that you are my husband's employee and Mrs. Bates is a guest in my house. It is true that, at times, she acts rather strangely, but I do not believe it is your place to say so—no matter how expert you are in the madness of menopausal women."

"I..." Karoline began uncertainly, looking from Elizabeth to Cass and back again. "Perhaps it isn't, but it is definitely my place to tell Edgar that you—both of you—are looking at pornographic pictures of young women. I'm absolutely sure he will not consider that normal behavior."

Lolly was aghast and ready to defend her honor. "Pornographic pictures?" she asked. "Well, I'm sure Cass' famous-writer friend will be glad to hear you said that. You were only joking, I'm sure. Anyone as intelligent as you would have to know these are proofs. We are choosing one for the back cover of her new book."

And then, before Elizabeth could stop her,

Lolly gathered up a handful of the prints and handed them to Ms. Marshall. "Perhaps you'd like to help?"

Taking the photos, Karoline shuffled through them, stopping now and then to look at one closer. "This is the best, I think," she said finally, holding up the picture that had reduced Elizabeth to tears. "I really shouldn't have called them pornographic and I apologize," she said to Cass. "Your friend is a very attractive young woman and these pictures are elegant."

"Thank you," Cass said. "I'm sure my friend will appreciate your interest and your help." She took the pictures and asked, stopping Elizabeth's heart in the process, "Do you think she looks a little bit like Elizabeth?"

Looking from the black-and-white proof to Elizabeth's drab, colorless face, the young woman shook her head. "Well, I.... It's possible, I suppose, but she's so much younger than Mrs. Gilmartin, younger and prettier and.... Well...."

Elizabeth's heart restarted and kicked into high, then began to slow down to only a few hundred beats a minute. "I'm quite sure you're right," she said. "Cass is just being kind. That woman is far younger and far more attractive than I've ever been. And I'm sure Cass' writer friend wouldn't be at all pleased by the comparison, no matter how flattered I am." She looked at Ms. Marshall and smiled.

Edgar called for immediate assistance, and in the mild flurry of his leave-taking, Cass, left alone in the kitchen, gathered up all the proofs and stuck them in her purse.

When Elizabeth came back, she didn't even look toward the table.

The door was scarcely closed behind Edgar and his sleekly smiling secretary before Elizabeth, without a word to her watching friend, ran to the kitchen, jerked open the trash compactor, and sneezed three more times before she fell to her knees beside the tightly packed mass of smelly garbage. Delving and tearing at the noisome block with frantic fingers, she tried to hold her breath while calling maledictions on Edgar's head, cursing every root and branch of his family tree, declaring his ancestors unwed canines unto the twenty-seventh generation. And all the while, Elizabeth was clawing, poking and jerking at the block of garbage.

Holding a cup of coffee and several cookies, Cass munched and sipped several minutes before she said, "Okay, Liz, I give up. Why are you doing that? Whatever the reason, the results are really disgusting."

Holding up the several scraps of paper she had managed to pry loose from scraps that bore no relation to anything seen in nature, she said, "Damn him! May he rot forever in Dante's frozen fruit cellar."

"I don't understand. Was it the letter?"

"Yes, damn him."

"But Liz, it was just one of those sweepstakes things, wasn't it? I mean you aren't that upset over.... Liz, what on earth is the matter with you?"

"My check!" Elizabeth wailed. "Damn him, he threw it away. My check for *Fornication*. My letter from Sessions. My copy of the contract. Edgar had no right to.... Damn him. Oh, damn him to hell."

She stood up, kicked the trash compactor, and came toward Cass crying, "Oh, Cass, my check. What am I going to do?"

"Wash your hands!" Cass said, backing away. "And then call your editor at Sessions and tell her what happened—well, not exactly what happened. Tell her the check was... was..." she giggled, spewing out a spray of cookie crumbs, and continued, "was compacted, I mean destroyed, accidentally. It happens all the time. They'll just stop payment on this check and send you another."

Sneezing again, Elizabeth went to the sink, ran water on her hands, and turned, holding up her wet hands like she expected a surgical nurse to come rushing up to glove them. "The editor already thinks Lolly is a real nut. I can't ask for.... My contract was in there, too."

"Do you need it? The contract I mean?"

"No, I guess not, but...."

"Well, then, just tell her about the check and

quit worrying."

"But damn it, it was mine. I wanted it. I...." She shook her head, dried her hands on a paper towel, sneezed again and wiped her dripping nose on the wet towel. "Oh, damn."

"You're just upset. Everything will be fine, you'll see. Come on, forget about him. Let's look at the proofs again. I'm dying to get a good look at them, aren't you?"

"Yeah, I guess so."

"Liz, are you sick?"

"No. Yes. I don't know. I suppose we should pick out the one I want to send to Sessions so I can send the photographer an order tomorrow."

She walked to the table, took a sip of cold coffee, grimaced, and said, "I don't know about any of this, Cass. Maybe it would be better if I just forgot the whole thing." She rubbed her temples, trying to ease the headache that had increased to a throb and stab behind her eyes.

"Look, you just need to get away from this damned house. Why don't we drive to Montcross and place the picture order ourselves? Then we could do something. Go to a concert or...."

"I can't, Cass."

"Why not? You don't have anything else to do?"

"Yes, I do," Elizabeth said, another moist sneeze providing punctuation for her words. "Or at least Lolly does. She has to start writing another book." An odd little chill tiptoed up her spine that might have been fear, or the harbinger of a spring cold. "Sessions wants the final draft by the first of December and I'm not going to go through what I did with the last one—I'm not going to rush through, getting it done at the very last minute."

"When did all this happen? Why didn't you tell me they were going to buy another book?"

"I didn't know anything about it until this morning. It was in the letter." She pointed toward the voracious trash compactor. "That letter."

"Gee, Liz, that's really great. What's this one going to be about?"

Elizabeth took another swallow of the cold bitter coffee and sighed. "I haven't the faintest idea."

A faint idea was all she had after two weeks of reading and thinking, a faint idea rapidly becoming a ghost of itself. Pink-nosed and blinking, a canvas bag of overdue library books heavy in her arms, Elizabeth scurried before the March wind and tried to force life back into the expiring idea. "No," she said, unaware she was speaking aloud, "if they do that, then nothing will be right. Absolutely nothing. I could just spit."

"It's a nasty habit to start," the elderly gentleman she had almost run down said as she paused in her monologue.

Elizabeth stopped, her coat billowing around her, looked at him blankly, seeing only the shriveling idea for a nonexistent book called *P.S. I've Taken a Lover*. "It wouldn't work," she said flatly, and it sounded almost as if she were arguing with him, or an invisible someone.

"Certainly not," the stranger agreed. "But then, what would work?"

"Nothing! Not one damned thing. I might as well chuck the...." Elizabeth woke from her blue funk with a start and looked up and down the unfamiliar street. "Where am I?" she asked, trying to remember how she had gotten from Edgar's house to this tree-lined street of modest homes while walking to the Cragshome Public Library. She looked at the silvery-haired man standing before her and asked, not quite rudely, "Who are you?"

He chuckled an old man's twinkly-eyed chuckle. It was a pleasant unhurried sound in the hiss and scurry of traffic and wind. "Well, maybe it's Camelot and I'm Merlin, but likely it's not. Likely it's just East Garfield Street, named after the president not the cat, and as likely I'm just Andrew Merlin, bookkeeper, retired.

"I'm sorry," she said, and then she wasn't sure if she were sorry it wasn't Camelot or if she were sorry for being rude. "I... I was going to the library."

He pointed west. "Back down that way eight or nine blocks and then three or four blocks south, maybe a little more. It's quite a walk. Want me to call you a cab? I mean if you're sick or something, maybe you'd be...."

"I'm not sick. Well, I'm getting over a cold. I like to walk, and I was just thinking of something and.... Somewhere I turned the wrong way and.... I'm really sorry I bothered you."

"No bother at all," he said gallantly. "It's always a pleasure to talk with a handsome woman." And then he smiled, just a bit slyly. "I, only on occasion, mind you, have been known to talk to myself, also—but rarely in public. People look at you oddly and think strange things."

She said, unintentionally blurting out the truth, "I'm not really crazy. I was just trying to find a plot."

"Cemetery or literary?" he asked.

"Maybe both," Elizabeth answered, her grimness only slightly lightened by her smile. "One to use if I can't find the other."

Clouds hurried across the pale sky to some distant rendezvous. The fitful sunlight gleamed on the carved handle of his cane. The stiff breeze lifted his silver mane, giving him a wild, free look that didn't match his thoughtful, cultured voice when he said, "Well, don't just write about Arthur and all that silly rot. There's too much nonsense written about him now. And, as far as that goes, I don't know why anyone would want to read about Merlin anyway. Wizard! Paugh! That man was nothing but an interfering old busybody with a hankering after young women."

Andrew Merlin of Garfield Street continued his impassioned discourse attacking Merlin's reputation of wisdom and magic as so much hog swill, but Elizabeth didn't hear a word he said. The plot—literary—had sprung, fully realized, like Athena from Zeus's forehead, into Lolly's mind, and she began to clothe and groom it. The plot that would send an unhappily married, interfering young busybody back into time; send her to quest and lust in a younger time when magic was possible and knights were real.

"Thank you," Lolly said to the man. "Thank you very much."

He smiled, and the rosy glow of her boundless joy seemed to surround him, turning his cane into a wizard's staff and his coat into a cloak. His smile became a benign acknowledgment of her enchantment.

"I'll call her Merlin," Lolly said, "and when the book comes out, I'll make sure you have a copy."

He bowed before she turned and hurried away, but when Elizabeth, or rather Lolly, stopped at the first intersection and looked back, the tall, thin, bearded old man was gone. He had vanished as if he had never been, disappeared into that tiny portion of time and space reserved for Good Samaritans.

♥   ♥   ♥

Elizabeth and Lolly read March into April, April into May, taking mountains of notes, consulting obscure authorities, and wandering in a daze.

Edgar mentioned her abstraction several times, but he was gone, either to his office in downtown Cragshome or away on business trips, or too involved in his own affairs to notice anything that didn't actually infringe on his own comfort.

On May 11, Elizabeth's birthday, Lolly began writing *P.S. I've Taken a Lover,* and she knew, with a breathless quiver in her stomach, it was going to be good, no, *wonderful!* Merlin was a better, more exciting and lustier heroine than Wanda had ever been.

And Lolly, grown monsterish with creative obsession, adopted Merlin as her shadow. The pair of them were highly possessive of Elizabeth's brain, attention, and time; directing and producing her dreams, exercising her imagination on her daily walks, and banishing from her life even the concept of housework. They allowed her only brief intervals of hectic labor, making her either mentally absent, or harried by the hounds of matrimony—faithful, obedient hounds that howled at spousal neglect and furry things growing in the refrigerator.

But the hounds only panted and wagged their

tails when, in mid-July, United Parcel Service delivered a box of books from Sessions Publications addressed to Lolly Horn containing twenty advance copies of *A Touch of Fornication*. Twenty slick, shiny new books with the beautiful, sexy Lolly, sitting in cross-legged splendor on the back of each dust jacket.

And suddenly it was real.

"Oh," Elizabeth said softly. She touched the books with gentle fingers before she picked up one and held the crisp, sweet-smelling newness against the beat of her rapidly thumping heart.

Enchanted, bemused and with eyes as bright as a new mother's, Elizabeth left the box gaping wide on the entry floor and strolled down the hall to her tiny den. "Cass," she said. "I'll call Cass. She'll want to...."

She couldn't bear to release the book, so holding the receiver in her hand, she dialed awkwardly, held the telephone to her ear, and waited. On the second ring, she heard her name being called, but not on the phone.

Chapter Twelve

♥   ♥   ♥

"Elizabeth!"

The angry call echoed through the large house, and surrounded Elizabeth's creative joy, compressing it into a jump of fear.

"Elizabeth!" The second shout and the hoarse-voiced, "Hello," in Elizabeth's ear were almost simultaneous.

Clutching the copy of *A Touch of Fornication* like a talisman against unseen demons, Elizabeth forced the words out of her dry mouth in a husky whisper, "Cass. It's me. I...."

"Elizabeth!" Edgar thundered.

"I'll call you back, Cass."

"You sound.... Is something wrong? Is it the party?"

"Party?" Elizabeth asked absently, her full attention focused on the door as she waited for Edgar to appear, a ranting and foaming Edgar rabid with rage.

"The dinner party tomorrow night. The one for

Edgar's clients. Liz, you haven't forgotten, have you?"

"No, Cass, I haven't," she said, fibbing only a tad. "I can't talk right now. I'll call you later." Her hand trembled as she replaced the receiver, and panic, like a pack of wild dogs tearing at her vitals, set in. But Elizabeth's soft voice didn't even hint at her fear; fear she had been discovered and unmasked. She walked back to the entry, confronted her irate husband who held, one in either hand, identical copies of Lolly Horn's book.

"Put those down," she said, protectiveness overcoming her fear.

"Just what is the meaning of this?" he demanded as he dropped the books back into the open carton with a decisive thud. "Who is Lolly Horn and what is this doing here?" He glared at his wife and pointed an accusing finger at the large shipping carton.

The lie, or rather the series of lies, slid, smoothly and sedately, from Elizabeth's lips, but it was Lolly who formed the words and spoke them, Lolly who jumped blindly into the conversation, saying the first thing that came into her mind without giving a thought as to where it might lead.

"Now," she said, her mouth a little pouty, "you've spoiled everything. Why did you come home so early? Oh, dear, Karoline isn't with you, is she?" She looked around quickly as if searching for the young woman. "You didn't let her see, too, did you?"

"No, Miss Marshall is still at the.... Elizabeth, what is...?" Anger replaced the baffled expression in his eyes. "Stop trying to change the subject. Who is Lolly Horn?"

"Oh, Edgar," she said, smiling sweetly, "you must remember."

"Elizabeth, you're doing it again. Answer my question."

"I am. Lolly Horn is Cass' friend. The writer."

He stared at her, creases joining ranks on his forehead, disbelief bright in the blue of his eyes. "I thought.... You told me Cass' friend was Caress Love," he said, suspicion making each word a pointing finger.

"Oh, yes, it is. That is, one is," Elizabeth said quietly. "This is a different friend. I met her at the conference at Seaview last fall."

He grunted what might have been a grudging acceptance. "And this?" He kicked the side of the box.

"That's the surprise and you ruined it," she said, or rather wailed.

Edgar, looking terribly uncomfortable, shifted his weight back and forth, cleared his throat, took a step back and away from her. "Elizabeth, you are upset and...."

"That's because I wanted to surprise you," she said, sounding as if she were going to shed a river of tears in the next instant. "And I especially wanted to surprise Karoline. She does so much for you and... and worries about my health.... You won't tell her, will you?"

"Tell her what? Elizabeth, you aren't making any sense," he growled as he took one step back and then another as she made little lost-puppy noises in her throat. "Perhaps you should go lie down. I'll call the delivery company and have them come back and get...."

"No!"

"Elizabeth, are you even listening to what...?"

"I have to.... It's too heavy. Help me." She tugged at the carton, trying to slide it across the tiled floor. "We can hide it in the closet for right now and...."

"Stop being foolish. The box is going to go back to the sender just as soon as...."

"No, it is not!" Elizabeth said, almost angrily. "It's mine."

"I read the label. It's addressed to Lolly Horn." Edgar walked to the box, peered down. "It's been sent to her at this address. Why, Elizabeth?"

"Because of some silly rule. I don't know exactly. It has to be in Miss Horn's name because these are advance copies of her new book, the one that's coming out next month. And, Edgar, send them back if you want to, but you should know these aren't sent to just anyone."

His patience was tattered, hanging in shreds.

"I'm warning you, Elizabeth, if you don't...."

"If you would just listen for once, you wouldn't have to get so irate," Elizabeth, or maybe Lolly, snapped. "Cass and I, and Ms. Marshall, of course, chose the picture for the back cover."

"Why?"

"Miss Horn had to be out of the country—researching another book, I think. Anyway, she had the photographer send the proofs to Cass. Cass brought them over here and...."

"Ah, why didn't you say so in the first place. I remember now. Karoline was very impressed with the woman, I believe."

"Well, this is the book. Miss Horn wanted to do something for us, to thank us, and she called me. I told her.... She had the publisher send these here."

It was a plausible story, but his suspicion wasn't laid to rest so easily. He stared down at the full carton of books and asked, "Why so many?"

"Oh, Edgar, you're going to spoil everything. Couldn't you just wait and...?"

"I would rather know right now, Elizabeth." He spoke quietly, but his manner implied that if she didn't tell him immediately, and make him believe what she said, Abernathy's home-away-from-home was waiting, with welcoming smiles and open arms for its next nut.

"Well," she said softly, almost as if she were embarrassed, "you said, last month when you planned it and gave me the guest list, this dinner party tomorrow night was extremely important to your future, and I wanted to make it.... Well, I guess I wanted to make it special, better than anything I've ever done before. I thought and thought and then I remembered how much you liked the autographed books I got for you at the conference. Miss Horn's book won't be in the stores until some time next month, and I thought it would be so...."

"Party favors? You managed to get advance editions of a book for party favors?" Edgar asked, anger and suspicion disappearing beneath his pleased astonishment. "My dear, you went to all that trouble for.... How nice of you, how very nice indeed. I am truly touched."

"Thank you," she said, accepting his gratitude without a qualm of guilt for her lies. "And, remember, don't tell Cass or Karoline. I'd like for them, at least, to be surprised."

"I won't, but are they signed to each guest?" he asked eagerly as he reached down to pick up the top book.

"Just don't," Elizabeth said sternly. "Push the box into the closet and forget about it. I'll take care of everything else."

Leanly handsome, he smiled as he obeyed. And when he had finished the task, Edgar dusted off his hands and said, "Karoline grew up in a very poor family. She hasn't had many things in her life and... she will be as thrilled as a child over this gift. I can hardly wait until tomorrow night."

He stood, smiling down at his nondescript wife, and said, "My dear, at times, you amaze me."

"Why?" she asked, not because she truly wanted to know, but because she wanted to lure him away from the open closet door and the books she would have to sign and give to uncaring strangers. A sadness hung, like a leaking cloud, over her; a curious, indefinable sadness that hurt in her chest, ached in the dryness of her eyes.

"Most of the time you act like you aren't aware of me, the house, my needs, or.... But then you.... This is such a thoughtful gesture that I...." He shook his head. "My dear, I do thank you, far more than I am able to say."

Dry tears were in her voice, quivering in her lower lip, but Elizabeth smiled wanly and said, "I'm glad you're happy." And then, for something to say, she asked, "Aren't you home awfully early?"

Red suffused his face, flared hot and dark beneath his tan, and his eyes couldn't meet her steady gaze. Edgar, lord and master of all he surveyed, looked down at the toes of his shoes, his deep voice was hushed when he said, "Yes, and I have to ask your pardon for that, my dear."

He paused, obviously waiting for her to question

him or for her to, perhaps, forgive without question, but Elizabeth did neither. She just stood, a slim, straight woman in a gray cotton dress, and waited in an alert, watchful silence, for him to continue.

"I've told you, of course, how important this dinner is, but not why. If I can get Matt Caspar to sign up for this new project, the rest of the money men will follow like sheep. I need that, Elizabeth. Karoline was afraid that.... Well, you've been fine lately, but for something this important, Karoline was afraid you might have a relapse and... I thought I should come home and see if everything was all right."

Her laugh was like an arctic winter wind, but her words were innocent of malice or pain. "You thought I wasn't to be trusted with something this important? That, at any moment, I might have another attack of..." she shrugged, "an attack that should only be treated by several decades in Harmony House?"

"Something like that," he admitted, and then he looked at her squarely and said, "We were wrong. Your thoughtful kindness puts my suspicions to shame, absolute shame. I am truly sorry."

She wanted to tell him she had lied, there was no kindness involved. But the time for honesty between them was past. She almost wept for the love that was gone, the trust that had failed, but she smiled instead and said, "I have a lot to do to get ready for the party. Why don't you go back to the office and reassure Karoline."

"Yes," Edgar said slowly, "that would probably be the best, unless, of course, you need me."

"No," she said, "I don't need you at all."

And when he had kissed her cheek and gone, Elizabeth Gilmartin stood alone, looking out the front door, watching long after he had driven out of sight. "I wish I did, Edgar. I want to *need* you, to love you, but...." She sighed as she closed the heavy door.

The next evening, Elizabeth's sighs and tears and wanting were locked away, hidden behind a brittle social mask, a gracious but empty smile, and small snips of social chat as she guided her husband's eighteen dinner guests—mostly older couples with the two stray males balanced by Cass in a bright red dress and Karoline lovely in blue—into the beautifully appointed dining room.

The appreciative murmurs were muted as the guests, and Edgar, examined their autographed first editions, but the trembling in Elizabeth's stomach seemed to be a scream of despair that was partially fear and partially excitement. But at the beginning of the "very important dinner" the fear was uppermost. Fear that the guests would toss the books aside, or else read and deride the poor author, or be embarrassed at her lack of skill, or damn her with faint praise. She made herself swallow back the fear and refused to allow Lolly to dwell on a failure that had not yet come. She didn't dare sink into acute depression; there was no time.

No time to do anything but acknowledge Edgar's appreciative smile as he explained the unique literary place cards and lifted his wineglass to Elizabeth in a silent toast. The guests followed suit, and Elizabeth smiled again, modestly, and felt heat burn its way up her neck and across her face.

"How charming," the man on her left said. "It is refreshing to know there are still ladies in the world who blush."

Elizabeth thanked him nicely, but she didn't tell him it was a hot flash brought on by fear; not a gentle ladylike flush. But neither her dinner partner's misplaced admiration nor the tide of fire that dewed her face with a glow could keep Elizabeth from watching Karoline as the younger woman read the inscription in her book. It was a graceful inscription, written by Elizabeth not Lolly, that made the young woman blink back tears and smile mistily.

For just an instant, the smile tugged at Elizabeth, made her want to give the other woman anything and everything Karoline wanted, but the moment of empathy was lost in the subdued clink of sterling against porcelain, the murmur of get-acquainted table talk, and a quickly suppressed gasp followed by a titter of pure delight. Thinking something had gone amiss or that the hired maids were having some sort of difficulty, Elizabeth started to rise.

Fingers touched the gray silk of her wrist-length sleeve as Mr. Caspar, the roly-poly gentleman on her right, looked fondly at a woman seated at the other end of the table, and said quietly, "Please forgive her, Mrs. Gilmartin. My wife usually has excellent manners, but she is a compulsive reader and I'm very much afraid you have lost her for the evening."

Elizabeth glanced across the centerpiece of roses and sweet peas, the tall white candles, the gleaming array of silver and crystal, and saw the older woman seated in the place of honor, and Edgar Gilmartin's pale wife knew dismay on the most intimate of terms. The woman, pink-cheeked, sweetly beautiful in purple chiffon and diamonds, was ignoring both Edgar and her other dinner partner to stare, oblivious to the world around her, at something in her lap.

She couldn't actually see what Mrs. Caspar was looking at, but with joy exploding like rockets, Lolly knew Mrs. Caspar was reading with total and absolute concentration, was completely enthralled by *Fornication*. Lolly's smile was wide, uninhibited, but nothing showed on Elizabeth's composed company face.

Bemusement clouding her eyes, Mrs. Caspar raised her head and gave her husband an impish, beguiling smile that included Elizabeth in its warmth. The older woman asked, "Mrs. Gilmartin, have you had time to read this book?"

Elizabeth wanted to toss decorum to the nearest wind, leap on top of the table, whirl like a dervish, and shout, "I not only read it, I wrote it!" Instead, she smiled her hostess smile and shook her head.

"Read it. Read it just as soon as possible," Edythe Caspar said. "It's wonderful, absolutely wonderful—I am in your debt for introducing me to Miss Lolly Horn. Thank you, I won't forget your kindness."

She bent her silvery head before Elizabeth could do more than nod and smile, and rejoined Wanda, wandering with her in the wilds of Old Briton for the rest of the meal—and several more of the guests, including Karoline Marshall, took surreptitious excursions into the land of woad and wonder between courses.

By the time the deft-handed maids had served flaky apple tartlets and cheese, fully half the guests were either reading openly, calling their neighbor's attention to this or that titillating passage, giggling like school boys and girls, or were so engrossed in the book they were unaware of all that was happening around them.

Lolly was ecstatic, and humble.

Elizabeth was only mouse-gray and mouse-timid, afraid to even look toward Edgar's end of the long dining table. She knew he was puffed up like an adder, fury freezing his face into angles and harsh planes. He glowered at her, silently demanding she do something. But there was nothing she could do, the damage had already been done. Despite her best efforts, the dinner, at least as far as Edgar was concerned, was a flop. The guests were far more interested in *Fornication* than they were in Edgar's grand plans and grander schemes — and Edgar was almost ready to explode.

The evening did not improve.

The freshly brewed coffee, aromatic and steaming, was ready to pour when Elizabeth paid the maids and sent them home before she carried the silver tray into the large living room, announced its presence and set the tray on a low table so Edgar's guests could serve themselves. There was only one taker: Edgar.

The guests were all sitting, some chuckling, some gasping, some silent, as they read in the pools of light cast by the lamps. Only Edgar paced. Only Edgar drank coffee. Only Edgar was having a rotten time.

It was fairly late, as dinner parties go, when Edgar shut the door behind the final guest, let the forced smile fall away from his face, and followed his wife into the kitchen. Angry, a muscle twitched in his jaw as he looked at her with narrow eyes and said, "Well, I... I was a fool to think you could handle anything this important. I should have known you'd find some way to foul it up. That damned book! My God, Elizabeth, you should have had the decency to tell me it was... was a...."

She didn't ask what he meant. Elizabeth just returned things to their proper places, wiped off counters, and smiled as she remembered the evening; smiled Lolly's cat-full-of-cream smile, and didn't hear a word he said.

"Do you realize what you've done? Caspar will never sign now. The whole damn thing is going down the tube and all because you had to.... The man thinks I'm some kind of pervert. Giving out books like that in my house! Elizabeth, that book is... I want it out of my house, right now, before you go to bed.

"And furthermore, you are to stay completely away from that Horn woman. She's not.... No decent woman would write trash like that. Elizabeth, are you listening to me?" When she didn't answer, he raised his voice, shouted at her. "Damn it, Elizabeth, do you understand what I'm saying to you?"

She nodded absently. Elizabeth heard him, understood him, but was too immersed in her warm puddle of euphoria to feel his ire. Her joy kept her safe, untouched, but it also made her foolish. "Wasn't it a perfectly wonderful party?"

Lolly asked dreamily as Elizabeth turned to face her husband.

"Gaaaaa!" he croaked, eyes bugging frogishly, almost choking on his own rage. "Elizabeth, if I thought for a single moment you did this on purpose, I swear I would kill you." His hands knotted into fists, he cocked one as if he intended to hit her just before he whirled and tore out of the room.

Giggles high-kicked up her throat, but Elizabeth, despite Lolly's floaty disregard of the consequences, kept the fey laughter in check until Edgar was far down the hall, almost out of earshot.

Edgar was coldly silent the next morning, refusing to answer her cheery good morning and her equally cheery good-by. But a whole bevy of others who didn't have his gift of anger or silence called to say their thank-yous for the lovely dinner. But these thank-yous were more than merely polite, more than just socially correct. Each of the callers made a final plea, begging Elizabeth to invite Lolly to Cragshome and introduce her around.

Elizabeth listened, made vague promises, thanked each caller, on Lolly's behalf for their kind words about the book, and hung up with a feeling of pride, strongly laced with relief and the need to get back to Lolly's new book—a book that was growing far too slowly.

One caller, the last dinner guest, didn't accept Elizabeth's vague promises. That caller broke Lolly's bubble of successful intrigue and threw her out into the storm with fear as her only companion.

Mrs. Caspar called in the middle of the afternoon, saying she was sorry to be less than prompt with her appreciation of the party, but she couldn't do a thing until she finished the book. Elizabeth murmured all the proper phrases and moved restlessly in her chair, wishing the woman off the phone so she could go back to Lolly's labors.

But if Mrs. Caspar was the final caller, she was also the most astute; although she didn't sound so at first. "I would like to meet Lolly Horn," she said. "So much so, I would gladly give her a reception at Cragshome Park Lodge when her book is officially out. Would that be at all possible?"

Elizabeth looked down at the empty legal pad on her desk, mumbled her usual evasive reply, and started to say, "Good-by. Thank you for calling," when the woman's next words chilled her.

"Miss Horn is your niece or cousin, isn't she?" Edythe Caspar asked.

Jolted by the woman's words, Elizabeth stammered, "W-w-w-w- whatever gave you that idea? Miss Horn is…. I hardly know her. She is a friend of Cass', Cass Bates. I…. That's all I really can say about her. I hardly know her at all."

"Dear, I'm an old woman, but I'm not yet senile. The picture on the back of that book bears a strong resemblance to...."

She stopped. The line hummed emptily for a long moment, and then Mrs. Caspar said, ever so softly, but with satisfied certainty, "How silly of me. It's you. You wrote.... The picture is of you, isn't it?"

All she could think was, *This will kill Edgar, destroy everything he's worked for.* Swallowing the lump of fear that seemed larger than the inside of her throat, Elizabeth chose her path.

She laughed, a rueful empty-headed laugh, and said, one hand pushing tight against the tremor that began in the pit of her stomach, "How nice you are to think so, Mrs. Caspar. What a very charming thing for you to say. You have, indeed, brightened what started out as a very dark day." She pushed a little harder at the burning that had come to join the tremor and tried to laugh again.

"Mrs. Gilmartin, Elizabeth, I realize we are virtual strangers, but..." she hesitated, and then continued, very quietly, "I'm sure you must have a very good reason for what you are doing, and I will respect that. I won't say a word to anyone. It's just that I loved your book so much and I.... You can trust me, my dear. Please. I will never, by word or deed, betray that trust."

The gentle entreaty in the woman's voice

almost overcame Elizabeth's need for secrecy, her need to protect her husband from laughter—but not quite. She held her silence, but Elizabeth felt awful, like she was being deliberately cruel to a sweet, trusting child when she said, with an airy lightness that held not one grain of truth, "I'm sure I could, Mrs. Caspar, if I had anything to trust you with. But I'm not Lolly Horn. I'm just Elizabeth Gilmartin."

The last three words seemed to echo, to twist and writhe like snakes in her mind. Snakes of guilt and shame that crawled and twined in murky pain when Mrs. Caspar said, her voice sounding full of tears, "I *am* sorry. I was so sure that I... I seem to have made a fool of myself. I apologize."

Elizabeth almost told her then, but before she could speak, Mrs. Caspar said, "I will always treasure the book and if Miss Horn is ever in Cragshome, I would be overjoyed to meet her. She is a fine writer, one of the better ones I've ever read."

"Mrs. Caspar, I...."

"Dear, don't let an old woman's fancies give you pain. Good-bye, dear, and thank you. Perhaps sometime in the future I can render you a service."

There was a faint click and then the dial tone sang in Elizabeth's ear. She held the receiver for a moment longer before she slowly replaced it in its cradle. Her hand was still above the handset when it rang again.

Sure it was Mrs. Caspar calling back, Elizabeth made up her mind, snatched up the phone, hoping she could undo some of the harm she had done, could take away some of the sadness, the disappointment she had forced on the other woman.

Breathless with haste, Elizabeth said, "Hello," and before the other person could speak, or she could change her mind, she added, "You were right. I *am* Lolly Horn."

Chapter Thirteen

♥   ♥   ♥

"I *am* Lolly Horn!"

Her confession seemed to struggle within her, like a wounded eagle, before its wings caught the wind and flew free. Suddenly angry at her own weakness, her lack of resolve, she waited for the older woman to acknowledge the gift of trust, to… to…. To what?

Elizabeth didn't know that, or much else except that she had acted on impulse, had been gulled by the imagined need in an old woman's voice, and acted foolishly without regard to the consequences to Edgar. She had put his career in jeopardy and had compromised him on impulse.

A laughingstock, she thought, *that's what he'll be. Edgar Gilmartin, the husband of a wanton, a writer of naughty books.*

She couldn't allow that to happen. She had to beg, had to swear the woman to silence. "Mrs. Caspar, please." The words were in her mouth, uncurling from her tongue, when someone, an unknown someone, chuckled warmly in her ear, and a voice, nearly as deep as Edgar's but filled with gentleness, spiced with humor, and strangely familiar, said, "Well, I certainly hope so. I've been trying to reach you for hours."

"What?" she asked, too disconcerted to feel anything but bewildered, and stupid.

"I meant I'm glad you are," the male voice answered. "Since Lolly Horn is who I've been calling, off and on, most of the day. I am gratified to have at last reached that—"

"What are you talking about? Who are you?" She sputtered out the question, knowing that once again she had acted the fool. And the knowledge made her, if not angry, then at the very least, testy. It burned in her cheeks and crackled in her fingers like electricity as she shoved her glasses back up her nose and waited for him to continue her humiliation.

He laughed softly, and for the most fleeting of instants, Elizabeth Gilmartin, resident fool, was lost in fog and night and breathing in the aroma of a dark and mourning sea. And then the moment was gone, leaving her disoriented, and angry—angry at herself and at the feeling of loss that left her so empty.

"What do you want?" she asked, and the bite of her loss turned the question cold, making it a distant, lonely thing lacking a soul to warm it.

Laughing again, this time with a leaven of sympathy, he asked softly, "Bad day, love?"

Again she felt the haunting familiarity, and perhaps it was that memory of closeness that let her say, "If it gets much worse, Edgar will have me hauled off to Harmony House before the end of the week."

"The local madhouse?" he asked, and the gentle teasing in his voice, the warmth to her ear made her glad she was sitting down, glad her weak-kneed body—that suddenly felt glowingly alive—didn't have to support her.

"Yes." She tried to keep her breathlessness a secret.

"Don't worry, love," he said. "If you drop out of sight, I'll come riding to your rescue."

Completely giddy now, but safe, so terribly safe, she asked, foolishly, "On a white horse?"

"If that be your wish, Miss Lolly," he answered, and she had a vision of a tall, white-clad stranger doffing a plumed hat as he bowed low.

"Wh…?" Her breath caught in her chest, snagged fast on the too rapid beat of her heart.

"But that's for tomorrow, or was it yesterday?" he said, laughing softly, so softly she could almost feel his warm breath on her neck.

"Yes," she said, but she had no real sense of what she was saying, or even what she was trying to say.

"Miss Lolly Horn, I really called to give you a most important message. Your book," he paused, and Elizabeth could hear the amusement in his voice when he said, *"A Touch of Fornication,* has gone into a second printing, a pre-publication second printing."

"Is that good?"

"Very, very good. If you aren't careful, you're going to be bound, gagged, strapped to a wild best-seller, and dragged down Main Street, USA at high noon."

Her mind was working again, or rather it was dashing hither and thither, twirling like a dust devil, and trying, vainly, to make sense of what was happening. "You work at Sessions Publications then?" she asked hesitantly, aware Lolly Horn was, once again, dancing alone by the light of a full moon; lunacy her only garment.

"No, not exactly."

"Then how did you know...? Why are you calling me...? Who are you?"

"Does it matter so much? After all, a rose by...." He chuckled again and said, "Good-by, love. Don't go mad without me."

Elizabeth's eyes were dream-shimmered when she whispered, "No, I won't." She was smiling when she hung up the phone and reached for a pencil and a legal-sized pad of paper.

The long yellow page was soon filled, and after it another and still another. The steamy love scene she wrote that afternoon was her own fantasy, a fantasy that needed no coaching from the ink-marked, dog-eared sex books hidden in the bottom drawer of her battered desk.

But she had a need for something when Edgar, still cold and angry, came home that evening. He glared at her, "Well, I hope you're happy. Caspar didn't sign."

Elizabeth couldn't think of a suitable answer.

It didn't seem to matter. Angry enough to be almost irrational, Edgar went on. "I have instructed Karoline to make an appointment for you with Dr. Abernathy. He is out of town at present, but as soon as possible after his return, you *will* see him."

She had been forced, by his homecoming, to leave the land of knightly romps, but Lolly's creative spark was still aglow. She looked at Elizabeth's husband and, with malice sparking silver in her too-innocent eyes, said sweetly, "Mrs. Caspar called. She loved the book and wants to meet Lolly Horn."

Edgar's face flushed darkly and he shouted, "Damn it, Elizabeth, I told you to keep quiet about that filthy book and the bitch who wrote it."

Her eyes still sheened with silver, Lolly nodded —but not submissively.

Glaring at her again, he said, "My God, if I thought for one minute you did that to me on purpose.... You'll never shame me again; not if I have to lock you away for the rest of your life."

He ranted on, but it was Elizabeth who tuned out his voice, his bitter threats and recriminations, with a small wifely sigh that held only pity.

The next day even the sigh was forgotten when Elizabeth and Lolly returned to Merlin and her lusty adventures in a benighted land—it was a journey Edgar's wife took often.

Edgar, too, was journeying, flying away several times a week, visiting New York, or Boston, or any one of the other major cities in his wide-flung homeland. And his absences were a boon, giving Elizabeth hours and hours to spend on her writing. She built a slender sheaf of papers into a respectable stack, which she hid with the sex books in her old desk.

With Edgar gone, Lolly was busily burnishing breastplates with Merlin, when Cass stormed Gilmartin Manor and carried off one protesting, bewildered prisoner.

One sneaker untied, baggy tan pants sporting a stain on the left knee, hair finger-clawed and wild, Elizabeth tried to resist. "No," she said, "I can't go with you now. I have to.... No, Cass, I...."

"You're going," Cass said firmly, laughter sputtering in her brown eyes, secrets lurking in her wide smile. "Come on. This instant. Right now."

She pushed Elizabeth out the front door, after allowing her just enough time to tie her shoe and grab her purse. The telephone shrilled as Cass jerked the heavy door shut behind them and herded

Elizabeth toward the car.

"The telephone, I have to.... Cass, it might be important. I have...."

"No." Cass' hand between Elizabeth's shoulder blades nudged her forward. Breathing rapidly, Mary Alice Cassidy Bates gasped, "I can hardly wait. Get in. Quick!"

Almost before Elizabeth could obey, Cass started the engine, roared down the drive, and turned, with tires squalling like a barrel of battling cats, into a residential street. "Oh, Lizzie, you'll be so.... Oh, I'm so...."

"Slow down! If you don't, I won't be around to do anything," Elizabeth said, trying to fasten her seat belt while she pressed her feet against the floor in a vain effort to brake the speeding car.

Cass slowed, if only slightly. "I know, but.... Oh, Elizabeth, I guess I'm speechless." She glanced at the pale woman sitting beside her, a crinkle-eyed glance that was the precursor of laughter, making secret telling impossible for the eight blocks between them and the shopping mall.

Once there, Cass pulled Elizabeth across the parking lot, through the Sears store, and into the stream of shoppers that crowded the mall's interior. When they had moved far into the large mall, Cass turned Elizabeth to her right, positioned her in front of a store, and said, excitement making her even hoarser, "Look. Oh, Elizabeth, just look!"

Standing rock-still in the eddying flow of chattering shoppers, Elizabeth looked. Awe-struck, she stared at the featured display, the bright poster, the books, *her books,* filling a round table in the front of the bookstore.

"Thank you," she said softly. "Oh, thank you." And perhaps she was talking to Cass.

"Isn't it wonderful?" Cass asked breathlessly. "I'm going to buy one. No, ten. I'm going to buy twenty and send them to the butcher, the baker, the...."

"I... Oh, Cass, how did you know?" Elizabeth gestured helplessly. "It's all so.... How on earth did you know?"

"Mrs. Caspar called me. She's here, or at least she was. She wanted me to.... Elizabeth, she loved *Fornication.*"

The giggles began at her toes and swooshed up and out. "Doesn't she still? Probably too old for that sort of thing, huh?"

Cass put her hand to her mouth and stared at Elizabeth, "Oh, Liz, don't."

"Mostly I don't," Elizabeth said. "Edgar doesn't approve of f-f-f-forn...." Laughter took the rest of her words, but she didn't need them. Cass understood.

The two reasonably mature women stood in the middle of the mall, clinging to each other, trying, not very successfully, to still the laughter that poured from them in a river of happy sound.

"Liz, straighten up," Cass said at last, trying to control a flood of laughter. "Come on, I'm going to buy a hundred books and give them to the first hundred people I meet."

"Please, let me buy one first. Edgar threw mine in the.... He threw it away." Tears of laughter misted her eyes, but her voice was sure when she said, "Damn him, Cass. I'm going to make him pay. He's going to be damned sorry he ever sold.... I'll make sure he gets exactly what's coming to him."

"Liz, don't do this to yourself, not today. Today is special, too special to waste on a bastard. Come on, I'm going to buy you a present. Something to celebrate this marvelous day. Now, I wonder what you'd like? How about a... hum... how about a book?"

Book was the magic word. It erased the past in a flicker of time. Elizabeth put all worries on hold and was smiling again as they entered the bookstore and walked to the display of *Fornication*.

"Oh, my, Elizabeth, look at this one. Doesn't it look interesting?" Cass asked, picking up a copy of Lolly's novel and riffling through the pages.

"Yes, it certainly does," Elizabeth replied, playing the role of browsing-book-buyer. "You know, I believe I'll buy one."

"No, no, dear. My treat," Cass said loftily. And before Elizabeth could make a move to stop her, Cass picked up another copy, carried both books to the cash register, and asked, only a trifle too loudly, "Is this the book everyone is talking about? The one that's supposed to be the biggest seller of the century?"

"I haven't heard that, madam, but I do know quite a few people in Cragshome are talking about it. People have been buying it like crazy," he said, and then with a bright smile, he asked, "Do you want both copies?"

The smile grew a bit shocked when Cass said, "Oh, yes. These copies and a hundred more please. I understand they are in short supply." She laid the two books on the counter and dropped a charge card on top of them.

"Oh, dear, I would like to... I'm afraid we... that is, we only ordered.... We've sold so many already this morning. People are still coming in and I would... I would really hate to disappoint them," the young clerk stammered. He swallowed hard, looked around for aid, and then said hopefully, "I could order them for you. It would only take three or four days."

"Well, I suppose that's better than nothing, but why did you order so few? I mean, after all, it's going to be on every best-seller list in the country in a very short time and everyone will want one then."

"Lolly Horn is a new author and we probably wouldn't have ordered this many if one of our best customers, a Mrs. Caspar, hadn't told us about it several weeks ago and insisted we increase our order. Now, I'm going to have to re-order for the store at the same time I place your order—that is, you *do* want to order, don't you?"

"Yes," Cass said grandly. "I'm sure that would be the best. However, I do want to take these two with me. You will call when the others arrive—I mean, call immediately?"

"Oh, certainly. I'm sure I could even have them delivered if...."

She winked at Elizabeth while the man made out the order, charged the entire purchase, and bagged the two copies of Lolly's masterpiece. That done, they drifted around the store, pretending to look at other books so Lolly could have the satisfaction of watching other customers buy *A Touch of Fornication*.

After the fifth such purchase by strangers, Elizabeth hugged herself, letting the mounting tide of excitement ravish her senses. Catching her breath, she held it for an impossible time before she let it out in a soft whisper. It was real. Lolly Horn was a real writer. People—real, honest-to-goodness people—were paying real money for Lolly's book. It was almost more happiness than she could stand, but she wanted it all, or rather Lolly wanted it all and more, demanded it, saying it was her just due.

Lolly caught Cass' hand and squeezed it. "Let's go to all the bookstores. The Eastriver Mall, Ye

Olde Books, Carver's, The Book Mart, and...."

"And The Book Nook?" Cass asked softly.

The soft question made Elizabeth tread too close to the forbidden shadows in her mind, the hidden place she dared not go. Lolly, if she even heard Cass' suggestion, ignored it and continued her list of bookstores, a list that did not include the big, blue store on Grant Street.

Cass knew too many secrets, painful, destroying secrets, to mention it again.

When they had visited almost every bookstore, and watched gleefully as buyers bought and browsers gasped and giggled, the book was, at last, a reality to both Lolly and Elizabeth; a reality that made Elizabeth very strong—and very tired. But not too tired to laugh.

Cass stopped her car in front of Edgar's house and waited for Elizabeth and Lolly to get out. But Lolly wanted to drain every ounce of joy from the day, knowing it was a day that would never happen again.

"Come in for a while, Cass," she begged. "Edgar's in... I forget where. Someplace nice that doesn't deserve the punishment, no doubt. We can drink his wine, toast his marshmallows in his white fireplace, and jump on his prissy-white furniture if we want to. We can do anything we want. Please, Cass. Pretty please."

Laughing and groaning at the same time, Cass said, "Well, okay, but only if I can take my shoes off."

Lolly laughed, danced a few steps on the walk. "You can take off anything and everything that is causing you trouble," she said as they walked up to the door. "You can strip to the buff and sprawl in voluptuous abandon like a houri in Paradise, and I will don the magic cloak of author and read the first chapter of Lolly's new book for your delectation."

"Would you really?" Cass asked, wonder softening her voice. "I thought you didn't want anyone to.... Oh, Liz, would you really?"

"Yes, I would. It's sort of hard to explain, but... well, yesterday Lolly was just... I don't know, playing maybe. Today she is a writer and can prove it," Elizabeth said as she pulled open the door. "You go in the living room and get comfortable. I have to put these away." She held up the bagged copies of *Fornication*. "And then I have to zip through that mess in the den. You dragged me out of here in such a hurry I didn't have a chance to.... I left my writing out and I don't want Edgar to...."

As if her words had conjured him up, they heard Edgar's voice say, impatiently rather than loudly, "Elizabeth, is that you?"

The women looked at each other. Elizabeth said, "Well, I guess that tears it. Part of Lolly's new book was lying on my desk. What'll you bet he's found it and is planning my murder?"

Cass started to answer, but was drowned out by Edgar's, "Elizabeth, I want to talk to you."

He stood in the doorway to his office, tapping his toe, slapping something white against the palm of his hand.

They couldn't tell what it actually was, but Elizabeth jumped to the most obvious conclusion and assumed it was folded pages from Lolly's new book he was savaging. It had to be. What else could he have found that would make him so furious? And strangely enough, she didn't really care. She was ready to face him and her lies and stare them both down.

She swallowed back an unseemly giggle as he stepped back into his office and ordered her to attend him, sounding more like a tyrannical principal with a youthful and completely irresponsible miscreant. Trying to hold back the laughter that threatened to engulf her, she stumbled as she walked from the entry slate to the hall carpet, banged into the wall hard, scraped her shoulder on the rough plaster, and swore under her breath. "Well, Cass," she muttered, "now's when the fit hits the shan."

"You don't know that. Maybe it's something else. Go see what he wants," Cass whispered. "I'll let myself out."

"No, not yet. I'm going to rub his nose in the

truth. I might have to go home with you—if I can still go anywhere."

"Elizabeth!" Edgar's anger growled down the hall like the thunder of a rapidly approaching storm, one both fierce and ugly.

"Elizabeth, wait," Cass said urgently. "He's in a foul mood, he might do something…. Why don't you…? I really wish you would wait."

"Why?"

"I don't know. I'm afraid he will.…" She took a breath and tried again. "Today was special. Don't let him ruin it."

"Okay," Elizabeth said, "but I am going to tell him, and as soon as possible. If he doesn't like it, then pfffft." She waved airily and walked, almost jauntily, down the hall. Her voice still harbored the day's joyful mirth as she stopped just inside the open doorway and asked, "Is something wrong, Edgar?"

The broad empty expanse of his gleaming desktop stood like a barrier between them. His arm, rigid with anger as he tossed the white paper toward her. It landed partway across the desk and slid to the front edge before it came to a teetering halt. "*That* is the matter," he said, the fury in his voice sharp enough to cut through nails.

Elizabeth could feel Cass stiffen behind her, could hear the other woman's breath quicken at his angry tone, but Elizabeth didn't react. She just glanced down and then looked at him questioningly.

It was only a letter, nothing to cause so much commotion.

"Look at it."

She smiled as she stepped forward, picked up the envelope, and looked at it. Her face didn't change when she saw the Sessions' logo on the hand-addressed, in purple ink, letter to Miss Lolly Horn. For an aching instant, the joy of the day returned, flaring bright and strong, claiming her completely, and she forgot everything but the stiff white envelope in her hand. Elizabeth's smile deepened and her slim fingers started to tear at the sealed flap.

"Elizabeth, have you taken leave of your senses? Stop that at once!" Edgar growled.

She saw what her hands were doing and almost grinned. "Yes," she said, falling back, with conscious effort, into her old Elizabeth self, "I didn't mean to.... I thought it was for me." Her hand fluttered helplessly as another lie left her mouth. "Why did it come here?"

His anger eased a trifle. "That's what I want to know," he said. "As I remember, I told you I did not want you to have anything more to do with that... that...."

"Oh, you did, Edgar," Elizabeth said softly, and her face was as smooth and bland as her voice when she added, "Cass, will you call those people at Sessions tomorrow and tell them Miss Horn does not receive mail at this address?"

Cass made her own assessment of the situation and told her own lies. "I am so sorry, Edgar," she said, sincerity dripping from each word. "This is entirely my fault. Lizzie told me you didn't approve of Lolly, but Miss Horn is in... ah... in Alaska. She's doing research for another book and it's almost impossible to get in touch with her. I'll call Sessions and have them send all of her mail to my house. I can always forward it to her in...."

"I don't care what you do or how you do it, just as long as it's done," Edgar said coldly. "I want anything and everything having to do with that... that tramp out of my house." He glared at them both, but his final words were for his wife. "You do understand what I am telling you, don't you, Elizabeth?"

"Oh, yes. Yes, indeed," Elizabeth said obediently. She gave Lolly's letter to Cass and turned back to face him, standing head bowed, hands folded, waiting pointedly for his dismissal.

It didn't come. He just stood, like some dark and evil god behind the gleaming desk and glowered, fury mingling in his eyes and in the grim set of his jaw.

"Dinner," she said, swallowing back an impious giggle. "I'll go see...."

"I have had my dinner."

"Cass and I haven't."

"The Widow Bates has my permission to eat at home. As for you, you can...."

For an instant Elizabeth thought he was going to send her to bed without her dinner and laughter swam like a school of silver minnows in the depths of her eyes. Then the laughter turned to anger, steel-bright to match his own.

Cass touched Elizabeth's arm and shook her own head in warning. "Lizzie," she said, "I'm not really hungry, and it's not worth spoiling the day to fight over such a small thing. If I could just make a telephone call...." She let the words hang and glanced toward the slice of dusky dark showing through the den's partially open door.

Anger at his rudeness and his disregard of Cass was like acid on her tongue, but Elizabeth nodded silently and held her peace until Cass had gone into the small room and closed the door firmly behind her. Waiting until the murmur of Cass' telephone voice came faintly down the hall, Elizabeth faced her husband and said, with more than a little venom in her voice, "Cass is my friend. If she isn't welcome in this house, neither am I."

"Now, now, my dear, you mustn't get excited over nothing." He came around the desk to stand beside her. "I commend your loyalty, but find it unwise at this particular time. You are a nice person, perhaps too nice for your own good. You can't possibly understand about women like Lolly Horn. But the Widow... ah... Cass has been around. She...."

"She what, Edgar?" Cass asked from just beyond Elizabeth's shoulder.

Chapter Fourteen

♥   ♥   ♥

"She what?" Cass asked again.

"Don't, Edgar," Elizabeth said, in a hissing whisper of caution.

He was not deterred. "Cass, you've been around lots of common women, you know exactly what kind of... of chippy Lolly Horn is."

"Lolly Horn a chippy? Good Lord, Edgar, you have to be joking," Cass said with gusts of laughter that shook her; genuine laughter filled with amusement and contempt for the man and his arrogant judgements.

"It's something no respectable woman would.... You read the book. Even you must see that nobody but a chippy would think such things, let alone write them down for others to read."

"Lolly a chippy?" Cass laughed again, and she sobered. "Liz, you have my sympathy," she said, and then she looked straight into Edgar's anger-narrowed eyes. "And so does the marvelous Ms. Marshall. If you think Lolly is a chippy, then I'm sure you can't be doing either Liz or Karoline much good in bed."

"How dare you!" Rage purpled his face.

"I'd dare a lot more than that for... for any one of my friends," she said, "and while we're talking, maybe you should be aware Lolly Horn has never been accused of..." she grinned, "fornicating with *her* secretary."

Edgar's lips thinned, a muscle twitched in his eyelid, but he didn't rise to the bait. *"He's* probably the only one," he said frostily. "But that is off the subject, isn't it? Elizabeth is having enough problems without being exposed to that sort of woman. And whatever you may think to the contrary, I am only acting in Elizabeth's best interests."

Cass' chuckle had an evil sound, but all she said was, "Good-by, Lizzie." She patted Elizabeth's arm lightly. "I'll take a raincheck on the dinner. Right now, I've got to run." The Sessions letter sticking out of the top of her purse, she walked down the hall and out the front door without another word.

Elizabeth watched her go, turned slightly, saw the rectangle of light that marked the entrance to the den, a wide-open door leading into a brightly lit room. Smiling inwardly she widened her eyes, placed the back of her hand against her mouth, and assumed her Gothic heroine stance. For an instant, it seemed as if she felt sand beneath her feet and heard a dark and mourning sea; and laughter, bright as sunrise, innocent as yesterday, rose to her lips.

"Edgar," she said, "I have something to tell you." She walked to the door of the den and looked inside at the bare desktop with disbelieving eyes.

Her husband saw nothing amiss. When she tried to continue her confession, or rather her announcement of dual identity, he ignored her and continued with his own abstract conversation—a conversation that did not include her.

"This room is an eyesore, but it could be…" he said from behind her. "It's not good enough for anyone to use now, but as soon as this newsletter deal meshes a little more, I.…" He stepped into the room, looked around, measuring it with his eyes. "It'll do fine. I'll have the… hmmmmmm… yes. It will make an excellent.…" He was still muttering when he came back out into the hall and started toward his office.

Elizabeth caught his arm and said firmly, "Edgar, wait. I have something to talk to you about."

He smiled at her, a benign, fatherly smile, and said soothingly, "I don't think it's good for you to get so excited. Why don't you just run along and take a nice warm bath. It'll make you feel better, and later, after I've taken care of some business, maybe we can have a little chat."

He walked away before Elizabeth had a chance to argue.

"Chat?" she said to his retreating back. "Chat indeed! This is a full confession of dastardly deeds and chippy thinking."

She was talking to the closed door of his office, and it had nothing to say. Smiling ruefully, she said, "Okay, Eddie, if that's the way you want it." The day of days, the publication day of her first book, wove its euphoric net around her, and she strolled to her own room, her purse hanging from her shoulder; Lolly's books swinging from her hand, her mind already returning to Merlin and her latest long knight.

But Merlin couldn't hold her attention. Lolly's letter from Sessions nagged at her, whispered so insistently and so long that Elizabeth climbed out of the tub, wrapped a satin robe around her wet body, and walked, lithe and barefoot, to the kitchen.

Cass' number was punched in and the sound of distant ringing was in Elizabeth's ear when Edgar walked in and stood, like a distinctly uncomfortable statue, just inside the door.

"Hang up," he said softly just as Cass growled, "Hello?"

Smiling an apology, Elizabeth gave her head a quick shake before she turned her back to Edgar and said, "Hi, Cass. It's me. I'm sorry if I interrupted anything but I...."

Edgar took several steps into the room. Elizabeth glanced at him and shook her head again. Cass put her own interpretation on the brief silence. "What's the matter?" she asked tensely. "Has he...? Do you want me to come and get you?"

"Oh, no, it's nothing like that," Elizabeth said hastily. "I was just wondering what was in the letter." She glanced toward Edgar again, hoping he had tired of listening and had left.

It was a dead hope.

He was still there, watching her with a brooding look, one in no way belied by his smile, an unreadable and faintly lecherous smile.

It made her nervous, started an itch in the middle of her back, made her feel crawly. She tried to shrug off the feeling, held the telephone a little closer to her ear, and laughed. It was supposed to be a light, carefree laugh, but it came out a hollow, phony laugh that sounded much like a second-rate witch's laugh.

Somewhere between the first laugh and the second, Elizabeth Gilmartin realized she did not want her husband to know about the letter from Sessions Publications, did not want him to know about her other self, and was not about to tell him of Lolly Horn and the joys of *Fornication*.

So, she lied again with a smile on her face, knowing what she was doing; lied without a pinch of guilt—perhaps it was Lolly who lied, but

Elizabeth didn't think so; she knew Lolly wasn't married.

"Oh, Cass," she said brightly, "I believe you're getting as forgetful as Edgar says I am. Did you look in your purse?"

Elizabeth covered the mouthpiece with spread fingers, knowing every sound would go through, and said, "Edgar, Cass got a letter from a friend of ours, but she forgot where she put it."

"Liz, are you asking me to read you the letter from Sessions."

"Certainly," Elizabeth answered, and then she fought down a sudden attack of panic, afraid to know what horrible news the letter brought.

"Okay. Hang on a minute. I have to go get it."

A loud clatter assaulted Elizabeth's eardrum and she heard a distant, "Horse puddles," and knew Cass had dropped the phone. Elizabeth tried to smile, but it was nearer a grimace as she shifted the receiver to her other hand and wiped her sweaty palm on the damp satin of her robe.

Edgar walked toward her, and Elizabeth knew she had to get him away before Cass came back with the letter. Had to. Cass' voice carried. He would be able to hear every word and.…

"Edgar," Elizabeth said, a little too quickly, "if you would be so kind, I feel a little.… I think some wine might help.…"

He didn't respond to her request. Manic excitement lit his lean face, darkened the blue of his eyes. He was breathing fast, and his fingers were trembling when he brushed them down her cheek to her neck. "Caspar's going to sign," he said. "The newsletter is in the bag. It means millions, Elizabeth. Millions. And I did it. I did...." His hand slid a little lower, touched the swell of her breast, then crawled warmly beneath the clinging fabric of her robe.

Her body didn't betray her this time. She stiffened when his hand delved lower. Frantic thoughts scurried, like a covey of cat-chased quail, through her mind. She licked her lips as she searched wildly for something to say, something that would make him step back, without making him think she was having another of her infamous insanity attacks.

His hand fondled, rather too familiarly. Elizabeth took a deep breath and asked, "Newsletter?" And then she cursed the pointy-tailed demon who had dropped the word into her mouth.

His hands shook with the force of his excitement. His breath quickened. "I've worked.... I wish you could understand how much this means.... Oh, God, Elizabeth, you mustn't say.... Not a word of this must leak out, not until Caspar has actually signed.... Forget everything I've said, I shouldn't have...."

"Edgar," she said, crystals of ice almost visible on each word, "if I am as crazy as you seem to think, rest assured no one will believe a word I say. I can forget anything, including the fact that we are married." She whirled, jerking his caressing hand out of her robe, and stood rigidly, her back to him, the picture of an angry wife.

Sure of his power, he stepped closer, close enough so his warmth mingled with hers. He encircled her body with his arms, unfastened the belt of her robe, and took a breast in either hand as he nuzzled her neck and whispered against her skin, "My dear, don't be angry with me now. Not when I need you so...."

Once it would have melted her anger, turned her body to fire, but not now. She wanted nothing more than to be free from his hands and his hot lips. But before she could pull away, Cass spoke in her ear.

"Liz," she said quietly, "this letter is awfully personal. Are you sure you want me to read it?"

"Personal? How could it be?" The astonishment in Elizabeth's voice was unfeigned, it was so great she forgot Edgar was embracing her, his hands and lips moving possessively on her body. But beneath the astonishment was an intuitive knowledge that made her shiver.

"Honey," Cass said gently, "I know you and I'm sure you wouldn't.... You're much too nice to have an affaire. But this really sounds like a love letter."

"And I'm telling you it can't be," Elizabeth snapped, moving irritably as Edgar's mouth moved down and across and his hands turned her body so his lips could seek anew.

"I don't know how, Liz, but I hate to…. Listen, can Edgar hear what I'm saying?"

"Edgar?" His name, the very thought of his existence was a surprise, and with the surprise came heat. The world swam in a haze of fire. A wet glow popped out on her flushed face, beaded on her upper lip, and Elizabeth pulled away from Edgar's grasping hands and greedy mouth to fan herself with her hand. Fire flooded her entire body. She wanted to tear off the robe, douse her body in ice water. But it wasn't passion that burned her.

"Liz? Liz? Are you still there?" Cass asked. "Is something the matter?"

"Just a hot flash," Lolly answered, darting a small glance at the distaste on Edgar's face before she added, placing another wee lie on the pile she had already built—but in a good cause. "I forgot to…. I haven't taken any estrogen for two or three days. I'll be sweating like a pig all night."

Both Lolly and Elizabeth watched as Edgar stepped back, moved over to stand beside the door, but it was Elizabeth who grinned, a hidden grin that held only a tincture of triumph. Then it faded before the wave of heat that engulfed her and she said, far too softly for her husband to hear, "Read it to me, Cass. Please."

"Well, I suppose I…. Okay. It says:

Fornication is rampant in the land.
Congratulations, love.
Now, you and I can dream
and wander without fear.
Soon the snows will fall and we,
two mad creatures that we are,
will wallow in violets.

         —A rose by any other…"

The faintest of pinks bloomed in Elizabeth's cheeks and a soft smile that made her thin face look young and terribly vulnerable. "Thank you," she said quietly.

"Well, what does it mean? Who wrote it?" Cass asked, crossness mixing with the worry in her hoarse voice.

"I don't know," Elizabeth said honestly. "I think it might be from Barry."

"Lizzie, Barry's the Druid in your book. He's not…." Cass' voice had a hushed quality. "Are you sure you're all right? I mean, I don't mind coming and getting you."

"Oh, no, Cass, that isn't necessary. I'm just fine, better than fine," she said. Her voice was an excellent match for the fond smile that illuminated her face.

"Lizzie, it's been a big day and you must be tired. Why don't you go to bed now? I'll call you first thing in the morning and we'll talk."

"Good-night, Cass, and thanks." Elizabeth returned the phone to its hook on the wall, closed the front of her robe, tied the belt, and she smiled.

Edgar saw the smile, the dreamy-eyed, heavy-lidded smile of desire, and took it as his husbandly due. He embraced her, and said in a voice that was huskily heated, "Elizabeth?"

Lolly looked up at his flushed face, but it was Elizabeth who said, as gently as possible but with absolute finality, "I don't believe sex is the proper treatment for someone in my fragile mental condition. You never know Edgar, the excitement after all this time might push me completely over the edge." And then she looked at him squarely, with nothing but innocent trust in her eyes, a soft smile on her parted lips.

His gaze fell before her steady regard and a moment later his hands fell away from the satin that clung like skin to her firm body.

Whoever she was at that moment, the woman, who was a little more than nondescript and a little less than gorgeous, murmured something and drifted away, down a foggy shore, with a faceless man to a hidden sea cave, and didn't know her husband stood and watched her for a moment before he turned and walked toward the front door.

She didn't hear the heavy door open to his touch or swing shut behind him—and if she had known, she would not have cared.

♥   ♥   ♥

Even the sand and sea were memories the next morning when she stood with Edgar at the door, wanting him gone, and quickly so she could return to Merlin and the stack of manuscript pages that awaited her healing touch.

He wasn't to be rushed. There was no guilt in his deep voice, but there was an odd note of small boy pleading when he said, "I wish you'd forget about what I said. I shouldn't have mentioned it. I was just so excited about Caspar that.... Elizabeth, wouldn't you like to go away for a few weeks? I'm sure Karoline could get you cruise tickets. You and the Widow... ah... you and Cass. Somewhere you could shop and...."

"No," Elizabeth said, fighting off Lolly's attempt to say something rude and obscene. "I can't. Not now."

"That's silly. Of course you can. There's nothing to keep you here."

Lies, as colorful as the frost-nipped leaves of autumn, swirled up in her mind and then settled back with a rustling sigh. She didn't need them. Elizabeth Gilmartin was tired of lies, evasions, and half-truths. She said, "I'm not going anywhere, Edgar. I'm writing my second book and I'm going to stay right here and finish it."

His own need stopped his ears, making her

honesty a waste of breath. He broke in with, "I can't tell you.... This financial advice newsletter to a select group of subscribers will make me a power to be reckoned with. I want...." He paused, caught his lower lip in his strong white teeth and stared at her for a long moment.

"I really shouldn't have told you anything about it. It was premature. If even a hint of scandal touches me at this point, it would.... Please, my dear, I beg you, don't do anything right now that could destroy my career."

All the weapons were in her hands. Lolly chortled gleefully, but for that brief time, Elizabeth was the stronger of the two and she held her silence.

"It's only for a month or two, or possibly until the end of the year. Will you promise to do nothing during that time, Elizabeth?" Edgar asked.

"Exactly how much is a madwoman's promise worth?"

"Elizabeth, I've known you all your adult life, and I've never known you to break a promise."

It wasn't a promise she wanted to make. The pale-eyed woman bowed her head, took a deep breath. "I promise," she said gravely.

"Thank you," he said, "you won't be sorry." He tilted her face up, kissed her forehead, and was gone.

And just as quickly forgotten. Lolly leaped out of her hiding place, took charge of their body and soul, marched the captive Elizabeth to Merlin's land of never-was, and threw her in, laughing as they sank deeper and deeper into steamy prose.

So wound up she jumped when the phone screamed like a wild barbarian. She had to take a deep, trembling breath before she could answer, and even then the forced time-travel made her voice weak and shaken when she said, "Hello?"

"Lolly?" Benjamin Sessions asked, his great booming voice sounding happily in her ear. "Ah, Lolly, my darling dear, you are a hit, a smash, a wonder, a morsel of delectable delight. How soon can you get here?"

"Get where?" Her question sounded whimpery, too whiny to belong to Miss Lolly Horn, but Elizabeth couldn't make it any stronger.

"Here!" he shouted, his explosive laughter making her wince. "New York. Where else is there?"

A foreboding sensation swelled in her chest, smashed against her ribs, and thumped on her heart like it was playing a hollow drum that signaled the burial of a promise, a promise made in good faith, a promise she just had to keep. "I can't," she whispered. "Mr. Sessions, I can't."

"Balderdash," he said heartily. "You're going to have to come sooner or later, and, my dearest dear, sooner is elected—by a landslide vote. *Fornication* is number seven on the *Times* list and climbing fast, faster almost than the printer can

print. At this moment, every bookstore in
America is on back order. You, dear girl, are an
item, a red hot item."

The certainty of her coming defeat and Edgar's
downfall, made her gibber. "That's… ah… that's
wonderful?"

"It's better than wonderful," he said, adding
another ear-shattering bellow of laughter for
punctuation. "And, by all that's warm and furry,
we are going to do everything in our collective
power to keep it just that way. That's why I want
you here no later than week after next wearing
your sexy duds and ready for battle. We have to
keep public interest, and sales, soaring."

"I can't come," she said again, knowing even
though he hadn't said so, that he was going to
make her go on TV, make Elizabeth Gilmartin tell
the whole damned world that Lolly Horn didn't
exist except on paper—and it made her squirm a
little to realize she was going to destroy Edgar's
dream, toss him down as she climbed up. She
wasn't sure she could do it. "Please, Mr. Sessions,
I…."

"If it's money," he said, "don't let that trouble
your pretty head. It's nothing but the very best for
our Lolly. We'll pick up the tab, pay for the whole
ball of wax, rent the largest suite in town and
throw the biggest champagne reception known to
man."

"No. Oh, no."

"Stage fright doesn't cut any butter when you've got a body like yours," he said. "Every male interviewer in town is panting to get you in his clutches.... But Lolly, don't waste a bit of your time on the panting folk. Get your body back to the typewriter and finish my next best seller. We'll be in touch in a day or two to firm up the travel arrangements."

The line hummed emptily for a moment, and then he said, "Until then, my treasure."

"Mr. Sessions, I...."

"No maidenly swooning. You have no choice, my dear, and you have only yourself to blame. Your erotic Druid spelled you with enchantment, and I, for one, think this sort of magic is food for the soul—not to mention our coffers."

Before Elizabeth could gather up her scattered wits, Benjamin Sessions wished her a fond, and rather loud farewell, and hung up.

Cold foreboding cramped the pit of her stomach. Elizabeth stared at the receiver as if it were an unknown artifact; stared at it for a long time before she laid it gingerly on the scarred desktop and went to change into her Nikes and walking clothes.

Lolly chortled once, but Elizabeth was stern when she forced her back and refused to allow her even one gleeful thought about Edgar and his comeuppance—the shadow of the thought was enough to make Elizabeth walk even faster.

"You may be a... a chippy," she muttered, "but I made a promise, and I damn well intend to keep it."

A giggle that had to be Lolly's followed her as she walked, trying to sort out chaos and return order to the jumbled mess cluttering her conscience. But there was no order, there was only unresolved paradox. No matter what she did, there was bound to be publicity—and, according to Edgar, that publicity would crumple his dream into a wad of newsprint and pitch it into the trash.

Elizabeth sighed and struggled with her dilemma, but she didn't give up the quest. She was still walking fast hours later, still trying to unriddle tomorrow when a car pulled up to the curb beside her and a voice called, "Get in. We have to talk and quick."

Chapter Fifteen

♥   ♥   ♥

"Hurry up! Liz, get in the car before Edgar sees you or something. He may not be gone yet."

Buried deep in a blue funk, Elizabeth took several steps before the urgency in Cass' hoarse voice penetrated her concentration and brought her to a reluctant halt.

"Cass," she said, choosing her words with great care because she needed to be alone but didn't want to hurt Cass' feelings by telling her so, "something is bothering me. I need to think it out and walking is… walking helps me."

"Lizzie, you can think all you want, but do it later. Right now we've got to get you off the street. Liz, please, get in the car."

Sighing, Elizabeth turned back, walked the few feet to the car, and paused momentarily before she did as Cass requested. The sun, now a hot ball of red-orange, was far lower in the western sky than it should have been, and it made her feel slightly disoriented, almost faint. Gripping the edge of the open door with tingling fingers, Elizabeth eased her body into the seat with a painful slowness that made Cass rev up the engine to a thundering roar.

She whipped the car into the light traffic almost before the door was completely closed and said something Elizabeth didn't quite hear.

Elizabeth didn't ask the other woman to repeat what she had said, it didn't seem to matter. There was a leaden weariness in her legs that made sitting a pure pleasure. She wanted to wallow mindlessly in the pleasure, but she couldn't. Her mind was still cluttered with bits and pieces of ethical argument, untidy stacks of pros and cons, and a carved-in-granite belief that promises, all promises, written and spoken, had to be kept—and by her definition, promises included contracts.

Cass reached over and pinched her arm; anger making her talk faster and louder than usual, "Damn it, Liz. Will you listen? This is serious."

In all honesty, Elizabeth tried to listen. She squirmed into a more uncomfortable position in the bucket seat and asked, "Is it Edgar?" Then, she closed her eyes and again fell victim to her ruminating.

"Liz!"

Startled by the woman's scream, Elizabeth said what was uppermost in her thoughts. "I guess I could tell him I have contracted a dread disease, something terribly contagious. That it's disfiguring my face, that I have giant purple spots all over my.... No. He'd never believe that. Maybe an allergy, an allergy to city dust."

"Do you have the slightest idea what you're saying?"

Taking a deep breath, Elizabeth sighed heavily and said, "I absotively, posilutely cannot go. It doesn't matter what he does to me, I can't go."

"Are you stark, staring nuts?"

"Yes, of course. That's it. Nuts," Elizabeth said, with the air of someone who had solved the secret of the universe, and then her laughter rang free, madly free. *That's probably the only answer. If Edgar, very quietly, locks me up in Harmony House, I won't have to break my promise, either promise, and, it's a sure thing, Lolly can't possibly go to New York without me.*

"Liz, please."

Cass' alarm jerked Elizabeth back from the edge of her too dangerous solution, made her gather up her laughter-scattered wits. "I'm sorry, Cass," she said, contrition filling the quietness of her voice. "I shouldn't have stayed away for so long. I really am sorry you were worried."

"Never mind that now! Where, in the name of seven dancing ducks, have you been for the last six hours?"

"Walking. I had to.... Why?"

"Edgar has been trying to call you. Finally, the operator told him your phone was off the hook. He rushed home, thinking you had flipped your wig, and found nothing. Well, to put it mildly, the man is pissed."

"I… ah… how did you…?"

"He called me. Not Miss Round Heels but the great man himself, he called me. Liz, I swear I was only trying to help. Really I was. I didn't mean to.…" Cass' voice shrilled to a wail and her foot slammed down on the gas pedal. The car shuddered for a moment then sprang, like an attacking lioness, at the gray Buick in front of them—almost catching it.

Elizabeth screamed.

"I see. Edgar hired you as his hit man," Elizabeth said, the humor in her voice only slightly diluted by her shaky knees and lumped throat.

"Oh, no, not Edgar. I did that in the name of friendship. Those near-accidents.… Oh, God, Liz, I may have done a whole lot worse than that. Liz, when Edgar called, I told him you were probably at the library doing some volunteer work. He must have wanted to talk to you. He called and you weren't there. They told him you.…"

"Weren't there, and as far as anyone knew I had never been there," Elizabeth said grimly, finishing Cass' broken confession.

"Yes. He was.… Well, upset is putting it mildly, so he called me back and.…" She gnawed on her lower lip and stared straight ahead.

"And?"

"Liz, he said he was worried about you, really

worried about what you might do, and he sounded like he really meant it."

"Oh, I'm sure he did," Lolly said lightly. "I'm sure Edgar Gilmartin is as worried as a newsletter can be."

"Now what are you talking about?" She hesitated again, and then words seemed to explode from her mouth. "He could be right. My Aunt Fanny's flapping rooster, sometimes I think you go out of your way to.... I think you're goofy as... just plain goofy."

"Perhaps I am," Elizabeth said.

"Damn it, Liz, you know you're not!" Cass snapped. She glanced at Elizabeth almost furtively and said, "Edgar is gone or will be in a couple of hours or so. He has to fly to Miami and is going to be gone for several days."

Edgar's absences were so commonplace they were hardly worth noting. "So?"

"So he asked me to stay at your house while he's gone and take care of you. I'm supposed to make sure you don't... ah... you don't...."

Both Lolly and Elizabeth grinned. "Well, did you promise to keep me out of trouble until he gets back?"

"Liz, I did what I did for you. I wouldn't promise Edgar anything," Cass said. "That selfish bastard doesn't deserve anyone's promises."

Elizabeth laughed again, but there was no madness in it now. The warm laughter held nothing but the sound of crystal bells in the moonlight.

Hoarser and much more uncertain, Cass' laughter joined Elizabeth's, but only for a moment, only until she slapped the steering wheel with the flat of her hand and said, vehemently, "Damn and blast, I forgot to call Sessions Publications and change Lolly's address for you."

Elizabeth's personal dilemma surfaced again, tossing her back into chaos. "What on earth am I going to do?" she asked.

It was a rhetorical question, one that led to an interior monologue that lasted far into the night.

For the next three days Elizabeth worried, Lolly wrote. Cass did whatever else was done, mundane tasks like dusting, cooking, and answering the phone.

On the morning of the fourth day, Cass, declaring the cupboards were too bare to bear, announced a major shopping expedition, one that required Elizabeth's presence as well as her own. When they returned, bag ladened and tipsy with the small adventure, the phone shrilled, sounding much too loud in the waiting stillness of Edgar's house.

Both women were in the kitchen, but Cass was nearer the noisy instrument. She eased her heavy grocery bags down on the counter, plucked the phone from the wall, and said, in her best imitation-maid voice, "The Gilmartin residence. Mary Alice speaking. May I help you?"

She listened for a moment, laughter fading from her face, and then she handed Elizabeth the phone. "You'd better handle this one," she said softly.

"What...?"

Cass shook her head, pointed at the phone.

"This is Mrs. Gilmartin," Elizabeth said, her eyes still questioning Cass.

"Yes, Mrs. Gilmartin, this is Dr. Abernathy's office. We have good news."

"Oh?"

"Oh, yes. We have an unexpected vacancy."

"Vacancy?" Elizabeth asked. "I'm afraid I don't understand."

"At Harmony House," the woman said, the brightness in her voice turning soothingly sweet. "I know we told your husband it would be at least a month before we could accept you as a patient, but one of the doctor's patients is transferring to another state and we can take you at once."

There was a long silence and then the woman asked, "Mrs. Gilmartin, are you still there?"

"Oh, yes," Elizabeth said, anger glowing like molten silver in her eyes. "I'm still here, but I believe you have made a mistake. I have no intention of entering Harmony House either today or next month or next year."

The line hummed for a moment and then the female voice, much subdued, asked, "Isn't this Mrs. Edgar Gilmartin?"

"For the moment, yes."

"Mrs. Gilmartin, I assure you it isn't a mistake. Your husband, and his secretary, made several calls. Dr. Abernathy is only accepting you as a special favor to your husband. Perhaps you should consult with your husband. We can take you the day after tomorrow. Bring personal items, gowns, robes, and a few casual clothes."

Elizabeth interrupted, "I don't think you understand. I have no need of Dr. Abernathy's skill. None. I am almost completely sane, or would be if my husband would leave me alone. I am not, not now, not in the future, coming to Harmony House. Do I make myself clear?"

"Perfectly clear," the voice said with more than a hint of frost, "but rest assured, we will be in touch with your husband about this matter."

She almost told the woman what she could do to Edgar but decided four-letter words were better unsaid, at least at the moment. "That, of course, is up to you," Elizabeth said kindly. "Have a nice day."

Before the woman could reply, Elizabeth handed the telephone back to Cass. "Hang it up," she said. "I... I...."

"Where are you going?" Cass asked quickly.

"For a walk."

"You're not going to just take this without doing something?"

"Oh, don't worry. I'm going to do something all right, but not until Edgar's damned newsletter has learned how to fly. Damn it, Cass, I promised."

"Lizzie, I...."

"How dare he do this to me? After I promised that.... Damn him. Oh, damn him." She stomped her foot. "I'm going to a lawyer later, but I'm going to tell Edgar about Lolly just as soon as he gets home. Being married to a chippy will give him a good, sharp pain in his worrier."

She stomped her foot again, looked at Cass' astonished face, and giggled. "Mary Alice, I shall be unavailable the rest of the afternoon. If Master Gilmartin calls, tell him I've gone out with Lolly Horn to pick up men and get roaring drunk in the town square."

♥   ♥   ♥

Sometime during the long walk, Elizabeth gained tranquility. She knew that regardless of what Edgar had done, or rather tried to do to her, she would keep her promise. That much, at least, was certain. And when his newsletter was fact, one issue out, she would see her lawyer and begin her divorce. That, too, was certain. Until then, she would have to do whatever she had to do to keep the public unaware of Lolly's identity; but only the public. Edgar had to know and would know just as soon as he came home.

Her decisions made, she returned to her husband's house, entered quietly, and went to find Cass and explain. But no explanations were necessary.

Cass saw the serenity in her eyes and smiled, but the question she asked was totally unexpected. "Is your Mr. Sessions married?"

"I don't know. He's not my anything, he.... Did he call?" A faintness almost banished her tranquility, but she held it at bay and waited for Cass' answer.

"Oh, yes indeedy," Cass said with a smile, or maybe her expression was more aptly described as a smirk. "Quite a fellow, that."

"Cass," Elizabeth said warningly.

"Yes, Liz, he called. Right after Edgar's blonde cutie called to tell me to take care of you while they jetted off to Europe for several weeks." She paused, waiting for Elizabeth to react to her news.

Elizabeth shrugged. "What about Mr. Sessions?"

"Marvelous man. He sounded like a creamy-mouthed cat, so I didn't want to tell him Lolly was out drinking and chasing men."

"Cass!" The pale woman spoke sharply, but laughter was beginning to tickle her throat.

"Lizzie, I didn't want *him* to think I was your maid. So I told him I was your research assistant—I mean, I told him I was Lolly Horn's research assistant.

The giggle bubbled up like coffee perking in a pot. Elizabeth caught in the middle of the eruption was helpless, but she managed to gasp out, "Where do... where do you do... this research? Cat houses?"

"Elizabeth Jane Gilmartin! You stop that right now. It's not that funny."

"Oh, but it is. He'll think you're as crazy as I am. Oh, Cass, research for sexy books. How exactly do you...?"

Golden lights danced in Cass' brown eyes, and she said, with innocence dripping like melting wax down each word, "Well, he must have liked the idea. He asked me to come to New York with Lolly."

"Probably wants to contribute to your research," Elizabeth said wickedly, then fear grabbed her and shook the essence of her being, like a good housewife shaking a rug. "New York?" she asked in a whisper.

Cass nodded, and then a little of her smugness vanished. She asked, "Liz, why didn't you tell me you were going?"

"I'm not."

"You are, too. It's in your contract. Benjamin said so." Her teeth gnawed at the lipstick on her lower lip and she watched Elizabeth with an unreadable expression masking her face.

"Liz, if you don't, they're going to haul you into court and make you swear to tell the truth and nothing but the truth. Is that what you want?"

"Maybe, I don't know. It would certainly solve a lot of problems."

"Yes, and make more, for lots of people."

"Did Mr. Sessions say he would sue me?"

"No, but he did say you were suffering from a touch of stage fright and.... Liz, you're a writer, you can make up a life for Lolly, can't you?"

"And tell the world the truth about her life as an old maid recluse? Never," Elizabeth said dramatically, trying to turn her fear into laughter. It didn't work. "I can't, Cass. I just can't. He wants me to go on TV, I know he does. And I can't. The publicity would end Edgar's career."

"You don't have a lot of choices, do you?"

"No, but...."

"Are you ashamed of Lolly's book? Ashamed you wrote it, I mean?" Cass spoke slowly, picking her words with care. "I wouldn't want you to.... Liz, I'm really proud to know you, proud of what you've done. It's a good book."

"No, I'm not ashamed. I'm proud of it, even happy about getting it published and everything, but I can't destroy someone else's dream just to keep mine intact."

"Edgar would, and destroy you in the bargain."

The slim woman smiled, a soft, gentle smile that lit up her face, gave it an inner radiance. "I'm not Edgar," she said, and it was nothing but the truth. She wasn't Edgar, and suddenly she was free—at least for that moment. "Cass, I'm not Edgar."

"I know that," Cass said gruffly, "and it's a damned good thing you're not, 'cause I don't like him very much."

They were still laughing when Cass said, "Now, about New York. TV cameras aren't a lot different from any other camera. They can only show what they see. All we have to do is...." Pausing, she looked at Elizabeth intently, walked around her, examined her from front and back. "We can do it, Liz. A little paint, a lot of practice, some sexy new clothes, and you are Miss Lolly Horn in the flesh."

"Cass, I don't know if I should."

"If you don't, Edgar will win this one, too."

"Yes, I see that."

"Besides you wouldn't want to do Mr. Sessions out of the chance to meet me, would you?

Elizabeth smiled and shook her head, but already doubt was creeping in, waiting to trip her up, and send her back to being Edgar's colorless wife. It was a role she could no longer play.

Cass walked to the other side of the kitchen, pretended to be looking out the large window. "Liz," she said, far too quietly, "there is something more. Ms. Marshall asked me about your illness. The woman at Harmony House evidently called Edgar's office after calling here and Ms. Marshall talked to me."

"Whatever you're planning on telling me, just

do it. I'm not going to kill you over it," Elizabeth said. She tipped her head to one side, looked at Cass' reddening face, and added, "I might hurt you pretty bad though, if you don't tell me. Now, what?"

"Well, she was all for dragging you off to the funny farm, but I told her that in *your* state, it might be better if I took you away on a quiet vacation and you and Edgar could talk when he gets back from his trip. She agreed it was probably the best for all concerned."

"Was this before or after the creamy-voiced Mr. Sessions called?"

"She called before. I called the office after. They, Edgar and bimbo, are in town for a very short period, just long enough to pick up some papers and then go jetting off in some private jet. Now they don't have to worry about you. You're safe with me in some quiet place, like New York."

"I see," Elizabeth said, and she did see. It was the old Cass, conniving against Edgar to get her own way. For no apparent reason, Elizabeth felt light, almost as if someone had lifted her dark cloud of worry and replaced it with sunshine. She smiled, and Lolly said, "Cass, I know you mean well, but I do have one small concern. You said in my present state; which state is mine?"

"Which one do you want, honey?" Cass asked, her hoarse voice growling in a rough impersonation of a slippery door-to-door salesman. "I got your basic model, and I got your deluxe—you should be able to afford both in a very short while. Benjamin said they had had an offer for the movie rights of *Fornication*."

"Oh, it's unreal. I...." Elizabeth shook her head. Smiling, she poured herself a cup of hot coffee and said, "Okay, Lady McBeth, when are we going to take the Lolly show on the road?"

"Soon," Cass answered. "But only if you want to. Elizabeth, I have to ask you something."

"So ask."

"Edgar's not involved in any shady deals, is he?"

"Edgar? Of course not. Why?"

"Well, all this flying around and secret meetings and making you make promises and.... Well, he could be up to something. You know."

"Cass, I'm not supposed to talk about it. Please, you can't tell anyone, not even Benjamin Sessions, who Lolly really is. If word got out, it would probably destroy Edgar's new venture."

"I think he's conning you."

Making up her mind with a swiftness that amazed herself, Elizabeth said, "Edgar is supposed to be some hotshot investment counselor, and he's starting a financial newsletter—international, I think. Adverse publicity, scandal, anything not ultra-conservative would ruin it. It's his baby. And we both know, full well, he would not consider Lolly a fit mother." She sighed as she slumped onto one of the kitchen stools.

Her head hidden inside the refrigerator, Cass mumbled, "Something the matter?"

"Oh, no, I thrive on being a mad housewife and an up-and-coming young author, but it is a tad frazzling. I feel a bit torn." Her voice shook, perhaps from concealed laughter, perhaps from threatening tears, but she controlled it and continued, "Just like I had run afoul of a chainsaw wielding butcher."

"You'll feel better after you have.... Why don't you go pack a few things while I make us a sandwich. We can drive to Montcross this afternoon and do some Lolly shopping and get in lots of Lolly practice where nobody knows us. That is if Benjamin agrees."

"We've already bought Lolly enough clothes to.... I can't allow you to spend any more money on me."

"All right," Cass agreed, "if that's the way you want it. But our Lolly is going to be an even greater sensation if she goes on TV in those naughty nudies we bought last time."

"If Lolly needs clothes, Edgar can buy them. I believe he owes her something for those terrible names he's called her."

Cass straightened up, gave Elizabeth a quick look, and said, only a little too briskly, "Go pack. I have to make a call to... to New York, and I..." she ducked her head to hide the rose that bloomed in her cheeks. "Please. I'm going to talk to

Benjamin personally and... Liz, this once, I'd rather not have an audience."

She couldn't tell, for once, if Cass was joking, but it didn't matter. Elizabeth was too drained to argue. But beneath the growing weariness was something that might have been elation, anticipation, or only the beginnings of dread. Whatever it was, it remained unknown. Elizabeth didn't do any soul-searching, she just did as she was told, and when she came back into the kitchen, suitcase in hand, Cass was chuckling as she hung up the phone.

Chapter Sixteen

♥   ♥   ♥

"That man," Cass said throatily. She turned to face Elizabeth, chuckled again, and said, "Everything is set. A quick call at the Bates' manse, and then we're on the road to New York. We're off."

"I didn't know that had been in question," Elizabeth said, a smile quirking the corners of her mouth. A curious, misplaced euphoria buoyed her, floating her upward like a balloon. She smiled at her own whimsy and made herself ask, with a nod toward the phone, "Edgar?"

"No, but I agree, he's definitely off," Cass said. "Listen. Liz, don't worry about a thing. Edgar's little newsletter is safe. I won't tell a soul who you are, I mean, who Lolly is, or, for that matter, who I am." She looked at her pale-eyed friend and chuckled again.

"That's good," Elizabeth said lazily, "because I think our Lolly is going to enjoy this little junket into celebrityhood."

"And you, Lizzie? Are you going to enjoy it?"

Still drifting on the updrafts of elation, Elizabeth smiled.

"Please do, Lizzie. I... I think I'm going to." Cass held up crossed fingers. "I hope."

"That being the case, Missy Bates, pray tell, why do we linger?" Elizabeth said, in a not-even-plausible accent, presumably Southern.

"'Cause I'm in charge and we're going to be gone for a long time, so everything has to be in order," Cass muttered, ticking off items in the air, saving what she thought was best for last. "And, Lizzie, we fly out of Montcross next week. The reservations are being made, even as I speak, under our new identities. How does that make you feel?"

"Like I'm in trouble enough being two people, I'm not sure I can deal with being a third."

Cass' eyes lost a dusting of golden lights, but she was still smiling when she said, "It was *that man's* idea. He doesn't want you or me bothered by reporters or anything until he has a chance to talk to us."

A thread of uneasiness invaded Elizabeth's drift of euphoria. She smiled at Cass' unconcealed excitement and waited for Cass to finish her tale. But as she waited, foreboding took up lodging in her chest, crowding into the space beneath her painfully throbbing heart.

"Oh, Elizabeth Jane, you drive me to distraction.

Aren't you even the slightest bit curious? Don't you want to know who we're going to be?"

Not wanting to haze Cass' painfully transparent joy, Elizabeth set her suitcase at her feet, forced a look of expectancy to mask her uneasiness, and obligingly asked, "Who are we?"

"I just hope he's not too disappointed."

"Cass, you're being coy."

There was a smile in her brown eyes, her husky voice, even in the lushness of her body when Cass said, "I am Cassandra Troy. You are my dearest sister."

"Not Helen?" Elizabeth asked.

At Cass' quick nod, Lolly and Elizabeth, and possibly even Helen Troy, groaned at the pun, and then smiled. But as the three of them followed Cass out of Edgar's house, Elizabeth's smile faded and the foreboding feeling ate at her.

It was still there, lurking and leering, during the hectic shopping (for both Lolly and Cass) and the Lolly practice supposed to make Elizabeth feel a little more secure in her role of innocent/wanton/writer-of-some-fame. And it was there at the early morning departure hour Benjamin Sessions had chosen as their departure time from Montcross Airport when the speaker system came alive and droned, "Cassandra Troy. Information desk please. Cassandra Troy. Information desk."

Before the reverberating echoes had faded, Cass was out of her chair and sprinting down the concourse. Elizabeth was too numb to move. She watched as Cass spoke to the woman behind the desk, nodded an answer, and picked up the red telephone at the end of the counter.

Elizabeth knew who was calling and knew it could be only one person, but for some reason, she expected only the worst, felt doom's cold hand fasten on her shoulder. She closed her eyes and waited, breathless, for Cassandra to return and foretell disaster—it would be a prophecy Elizabeth would believe.

She didn't have long to wait.

"Liz," Cass said, dropping into the chair she had so recently vacated, "it's nothing earthshaking, but we do have a speck of trouble."

Stiff and straight in the plastic chair, Elizabeth opened eyes dark with fear, and asked with the cooing cry of a dying dove, "What ?"

"Benjamin Sessions can't wait to meet me. Instead of us calling his office when we get to New York, Benjamin is meeting our plane."

"But I.... We.... Cass, are you sure?"

Cass nodded.

And then, sounding mechanically gleeful, the loud speaker called their flight. It was time to step into the spotlight, and Lolly wasn't ready.

Touching her unpainted Elizabeth-face, her drab Elizabeth-clothes, she said, "Cass, I never thought.... We should have expected something like this."

But they hadn't. Lolly Horn was safely packed in a suitcase or two. Helen Troy was every bit as nondescript as Elizabeth—and just as recognizable as Edgar Gilmartin's pale wife.

Squeezing Elizabeth's hand, a little too tightly to be reassuring, Cass said, "Don't worry, Liz. We'll think of something."

Elizabeth's sense of dire happenings clapped its hands and snickered as the two women walked onto the plane. The snicker had turned to maniacal laughter when Cassandra and Helen, their something still unthought of, deplaned in New York.

"Oh, look. There he is," Cass whispered, pointing unobtrusively toward a very large, balding man holding a full scad of white roses and a placard that read, "The Towers of Ilium."

"Blasted Classicist. You talk to him," Elizabeth said. "Tell him something. Anything. I'll get our luggage and meet you at our hotel."

"Which hotel? I.... He didn't.... Where will I.... What hotel?" Cass asked, catching Elizabeth by the arm and holding her as she tried to sneak away.

"I don't know. You said.... He made all the arrangements. You didn't tell me. Where are the famous Troy sisters supposed to be staying?" Elizabeth asked, panic making her voice sharp. And then she came to herself enough to say, "Oh, Cass, I'm sorry. I know I'm acting like an idiot, but I can't talk to him right now. I just can't."

"Liz, you're as important to him as he is to you. He's not going to take one look at you and jerk all your books out of all the bookstores in.... Never mind. I want first chance at him anyway," Cass said, her grin making her look like a woman bent on the best of mischief.

"Although he does look big enough to share, doesn't he? The Towers of Ilium indeed, that man's big enough to be the entire Trojan Horse." She released Elizabeth's arm and gave her a little push toward the oasis for weary female travelers. "Don't worry. I'll take care of everything."

Elizabeth scuttled off without a backward glance, only remembering to breathe when the ladies room door hissed shut behind her. But even as she dawdled, washing her hands twice, touching her lips with coral lipstick, cleaning her glasses, and fought a losing battle with fear and foreboding, she knew she had to go back, had to pay the music, or face the piper, or some other idiocy, an idiocy of her own making.

"No excuses," she said, and the woman standing next to her edged away. Elizabeth didn't care. Her back was straight and her head was high when she walked to where Cass and the very large man were standing. And there was only amusement in her voice when she said, "Agamemnon, I presume."

He threw back his head. His laughter boomed like breakers in a vast and sunny sea, and all around them strangers turned and smiled. Even Elizabeth, and her fear and foreboding, were not immune to the contagion of joy. They caught the malady in a thrice. Fear and foreboding died of the disease, but the pale woman survived, or perhaps she died, too, and only Lolly and Helen survived.

"Liz, I…. Helen, I mean, I…. He…. That is…." Cass stammered as she stared at her friend with guilty eyes and finally whispered, "Oh, Liz, forgive me. I didn't know what else to do. I told Benjamin about… about Edgar and you and… I told him everything."

"Quite rightly so," he said, quieter than Elizabeth would have believed possible. "Don't worry, Helen, although I should have called you Midas, I'm not about to queer this pitch. Whatever you want, you're going to get. I'm pretty sure we can pull this masquerade off—that is, if our Lolly acts like she writes."

"Mr. Sessions," Elizabeth said, allowing her eyes to widen in shock, "you amaze me. Lolly Horn is a maiden lady, and she does not fool around."

"Oh, I beg your pardon. A maiden lady from where?" he asked, laughter chuckling in his every word.

"Precisely. How on earth did you know? It's a rather small place, in the mountains of one of our western states."

"Where?"

"Of course. And in Where, they believe in a good sex education, but everyone under the age of sixty-seven is completely celibate. There is no birth control, but it doesn't matter because the population growth is less than zero—minus zero, I think. And at home in Where, Lolly Horn is considered to be the ugliest of the whole ugly litter."

He laughed again, and again other travelers smiled. "That's a good start. Will you be able to remember all that without getting it mixed up?"

"How long will I have to remember?"

"A month. We've set up a book tour and...."

"Yes, I can...."

"But she doesn't have to," Cass broke in eagerly. "That's the beauty of it. Lolly is a fiction writer. They make things up. She's going to tell everyone who asks her questions she's lying. Lying is what writers do best, and Lolly will have lies for all occasions."

"Sounds good to me. In fact, it's so zany it might actually work. As for me, all I know is..." he stopped, hit his forehead with the heel of his hand. "I almost forgot. These..." he looked down at Elizabeth for a moment, looked at her as if he wanted to ask her a question that required a truthful answer, but he didn't. Instead, he handed her the abundance of white roses and said, like it was a cipher to which she had the key, "I have been instructed to say, 'These *Blanches* are for you.'"

She took them, buried her face in the roses for an instant. "Naturally," she said. "A rose by any other...." The breathlessness in her voice might have been from a fear of new complications, or rose fever, but it probably wasn't.

She loved the roses, and her fear was dead—anticipation is a far brighter lass than her gloomy cousin, foreboding, and much better company. But whatever it was that flamed her cheeks and added quicksilver to her eyes, it didn't make her feel out of place or uncomfortable.

Cass' face clouded for a second, questions rose large in her eyes, but she was too enthralled by the man before her to voice them.

Teasing and laughing as they went, Benjamin Sessions hustled them into a limo and whisked them to their hotel suite in a very short time. And then they were involved in other concerns, concerns that required Cass' steady hand and expert knowledge and left no time for question and answer games.

Sessions Publications was hosting a large champagne reception in just two hours, and Miss Lolly Horn, the guest of honor, hadn't put in an appearance yet.

Benjamin Sessions watched, amazement written large on his face, and exclaimed again and again as Lolly emerged from her hiding places in bottles, brushes, and bags until Elizabeth/Helen was/were replaced entirely by Lolly Horn, the gorgeous writer, the notorious virgin from Where.

"Well, Ben, what do you think? Will she pass inspection?" Cass asked as Lolly, silver-eyed Lolly, wearing a clinging jumpsuit of silver-shimmered black, four-inch heels, no jewelry except a large emerald dinner ring on her left hand, walked, with a slouchy, long-limbed stride, out of the bedroom and said, in a voice that could only be described as smoldering velvet, "It's very nice to meet you, Mr. Sessions."

Arms out, blonde head tipped to one side, full red lips at half-pout, she turned this way and that, giving him the full view of Lolly's firm breasts, narrow waist, rounded hips. She glided forward, ran into a chair, hopped on one foot, and swore in blistering, dire-sounding, archaic oaths.

"Marvelous," Sessions said, filling the room with his roaring laugh. "That's right in character. Marvelous."

"Right in character for Elizabeth," Cass snorted. "She's as blind as a bat without her glasses, and when riled, she swears like a Roman soldier."

"Blind, hmmmmmmm," he said thoughtfully. "That certainly explains a lot."

"Not to me, it doesn't," Cass said.

"Ah, Cassandra, my dearest dear, you can have anything I own, but it's not a tale that belongs to me." he said quietly. "Someday, perhaps, the world will know the whole story, but not now. No, sweet maid, not now."

The huge man and the lush woman were only blurs that moved toward each other and were lost in the greater shadows. Lolly didn't know what they did. She only knew she was almost as blind as Homer and knew almost nothing of heroic epics. But she, too, was destined to travel from place to place and tell her tales of Lolly Horn, the child of fog and dreams. Her tale would hold laughter, innocence, and the otherness of a rainbow's shimmer, but nothing of truth. Nothing of Elizabeth Gilmartin, and nothing of marriage, or pain, or endings. Nothing real, all fiction.

A fleeting sadness tarnished the silver of her eyes, but Lolly wasn't made for sadness, she pushed it back, hid it in the dark with the rest of Elizabeth's taboo subjects, and readied herself to step into the hectic glitter of a world that belonged, by all rights, to Elizabeth alone.

"Your public is waiting, Miss Lolly," Benjamin Sessions said grandly.

"Waiting," Elizabeth said, echoing his word, not questioning. The time for questioning was gone like love and fear and regret for the might-have-beens. Elizabeth was caught in a void, a place beyond time or space, the epicenter of the universe's waiting moment, the poised instant at the top of the precipice, the fatal instant of inevitability.

Cass touched her arm and said something, but sensation and sound were outside, beyond, unfelt, unheard.

"The climatic moment," Elizabeth whispered, eyes aglow with vast and sudden knowledge, the knowledge of cause and effect, root and branch, seed and plant, beginnings and endings, the very soul of the universe, and its bleached bones.

"What did you say?" Cass asked, fear making her voice sharp.

"It's the climax," Elizabeth said softly, and it sounded as if she were explaining wonder to a child, sharing a love. "That point when everything else that follows is inevitable. The topmost point of a roller coaster ride. "Oh, Cass," Elizabeth reached her hands high, "isn't it wonderful?"

"Yes, of course," Cass said, doubt making her sound soothing rather than understanding. "It's been a long day, if you don't feel well enough...."

"I feel wonderful," Elizabeth said as she stepped, of her own free will, back into time and space, became Lolly Horn, slipped quietly over the brink, and smiled as the tide of inevitability bore her, at full flood, down the other side. "Let's go to my party."

Both Lolly and Elizabeth were smiling when they slid their hand into the crook of Benjamin's arm and let him lead them into the world of best-selling author, a world created for, and by, Lolly Horn, witty, sexy, spinster.

A world of shadows. A world that was far from real.

She drank expensive champagne (re-christened "Lolly Pop" in her honor), answered questions (outrageously, audaciously, and with a total disregard for truth), lunched with dignitaries (unseen), signed, in purple ink, autographs, books, and contracts (two book clubs and one movie), and smiled until her jaws ached as badly as her feet.

In that shadow world, Lolly heard only friendly voices — presumably the unfriendly and the too-friendly were kept at bay by Cass, Benjamin, and the huge bodyguard hired to protect Lolly's body. He waited with her in the greenroom (unseen), fended off the advances of other celebrities (also unseen), and watched silently from the sidelines as Lolly glowed at interviewers, camera persons, and program directors. It was Lolly time, and he made sure nothing marred her pleasure.

But beneath the pleasurable excitement was the feeling of time passing, of words unwritten, of things drawing to a conclusion. Lolly and Elizabeth shivered as they stood, the silent bodyguard at their side, in a crowd of reporters, well-wishers, and PR folks, waiting to board a flight to Boston, beginning a book tour that would zigzag across the nation, hopping from city to city, interviewer to interviewer — all to see a book that was already number three on the *Times* best-seller list and climbing.

Cass felt the slight shudder and asked, quietly, "What's the matter, Liz?"

The words fell into a sudden pool of silence, rippled out. A reporter asked, "Liz?" And even in her blindness, the sleek, blonde woman could see the battery of eyes trained on her, eyes that asked questions that couldn't be answered yet.

Lolly smiled beguilingly. "It's a private joke."

"Come on, don't give us that. It's your real name, isn't it?"

Again silence pooled around them.

Elizabeth wanted to take credit for Lolly's fame, wanted to stand up straight, scream, "Yes," at the top of her voice, but she didn't. "No," she said lightly, "it isn't. It's just.... Well, a few years ago, when I was a very little girl," she smiled again, asking them to share the small joke.

"I decided to be a virgin with a purpose. The mountains around Where are all volcanic. I wanted to be the virgin who stopped the eruption. That was before I knew they threw you in. As soon as I learned that, I decided I'd rather be—when I'm elected, of course—the Virgin Queen, Elizabeth I."

"There's already been an Elizabeth I," someone said, his voice almost lost in the Lolly-provoked laughter.

"Not in Where," she said just before she walked into the plane, which began the next leg in her journey of inevitability.

Lollyisms were spawned and hatched, not all by the woman herself, on the trip, but they couldn't compare with the dazed weariness that blanketed Elizabeth, giving her a feeling of unreality, of lostness. She didn't know where she was most of the time, or what day it was, or where she was supposed to be next. She just followed orders, usually from the Sessions Publications representative in each new city, let the bodyguard guide her from one appointment to the next, buy her clean underwear and pantyhose in all-night drugstores, and see she got to the plane for her next round of cocktail parties, book signings, interviews, and photo sessions. But it was fun to stay in the fanciest hotels, eat in the poshest places, smile at well-known, if unseen, TV and radio hosts, thanking everyone prettily for flowers, drinking "Lolly Pop," and declining all invitations with quips and witticisms.

But in—Elizabeth thought it was Denver—Lolly got another flower, a single pink rose, delivered to her suite in a crystal vase. "Please accept this Queen Elizabeth," the card read, "and my congratulations for being Number One on a timely list."

It was written by an unknown hand, presumably the florist's, and unsigned, but Elizabeth didn't need a signature. She knew who the rose was from, and she smiled as she set the delicate vase on the table beside her bed, very close to her pillow.

She received lots of other congratulations for *Fornication's* position on the best seller list, but none made her smile as real, and none tickled her curiosity or made her yearn to meet the sender, and no other made her dream of walking beside a dark and mourning sea.

In another town, she thought it was Phoenix, late at night, when they were removing Lolly's makeup and readying her for a short night in bed, Cass said, her hoarse voice sounding more surprised than joyful, "Liz, I want to tell you.... Please don't laugh, but I think I'm in love with him."

Elizabeth didn't ask, "Who? Who are you in love with?" There was only one person Cass could mean, a very large person with a great booming voice and a balding head, a gentle person who treated Cass like she should be treated. Treated Mary Alice Cassidy Bates with love, with reverence, and with humor. A thoughtful person who called, repeatedly, and asked to speak to Cassandra Troy, holding long conversations that had nothing to do with Lolly Horn, the trip, or Sessions Publications. Benjamin Sessions.

"Cass," Elizabeth said softly, "I'm so glad for...."

"Wait, Liz," Cass said slowly, speaking as if

the words were too painful to drag out of the darkness into the light. "I want to say something, and I don't know if I can."

Chapter Seventeen

♥   ♥   ♥

Cass bent her head.

"Mary Alice," Elizabeth said quietly, "there are secrets people keep, even from their best friends, but about you loving Benjamin Sessions, there can't be anything that needs saying between us. Just love Ben the way you loved Charlie Bates and Ben will be the luckiest man in the world."

"He's rich, too, Liz. Maybe even richer than Charlie was."

"I know, but what...."

"You didn't think I married Charlie for his money?"

"I know what people, including Edgar, said when you married Charlie, but I didn't believe a single word they said. I didn't have to. I couldn't have even if I had wanted to. I know you, Cass, and I knew, just by looking at you, you loved Charlie with every atom of love in your being. That's a lot of love, Cass, and it shows."

"I didn't know you.... Thank you," Cass

whispered, and for an instant tears sparkled in the warm brown of her eyes. "I thought I would die when he did, Liz," she said. "I never wanted his money. I wanted *him*. I wanted to sleep in his bed every night, cook his breakfast every morning for the rest of my life. And then Charlie Bates was gone. My Charlie was gone. Liz, I didn't know it was possible to hurt so much."

"Don't, Cass. Please." Elizabeth reached out, took the other woman's hand, and squeezed it gently.

"You were there, Lizzie, when I needed you. Just like you've always been since we were.... What? Three?"

"Three," Elizabeth agreed.

The silence lasted a long time, and it seemed too loud, to fill time and space too full. And it was so large, it almost took Cass' voice when she asked, "Elizabeth, do you love Edgar that much?"

Lolly had told so many lies that all that was left for Elizabeth was the truth. "No," she said. "I don't love him at all."

"It isn't any of my business, Liz, except I need to know. Why don't you just walk out and tell Edgar and the world *you* are Lolly Horn? It's not a small thing. In fact, it's pretty special. You've done something very few people do, so why let him treat you like dirt?"

It was Elizabeth's turn to hesitate, to struggle with words. "Cass, I... It's hard to explain. I'm going to leave him, and very soon, but I have to wait until he gets this newsletter established. It means a great deal to him, and I couldn't live with myself if I hurt him like he...."

"Like he hurt you?"

"No," Elizabeth said quickly, far too quickly. Forbidden memories strained at their bounds, but she fought them back. Her lips and her eyes were smiling when she asked, "Does Benjamin love you, too, Cass?"

"So he says."

Impending loss, a sudden realization too great to bear took Elizabeth's voice, glistened in her pale eyes, but Cass didn't notice.

She whispered, "Oh, Liz, help me. I don't know how I feel. It's too quick. I thought only schoolgirls or very young women fell like this, fell tennis shoes over tennis racket for a man. I didn't know it was possible for a woman who...." She blushed, and her smile was dewy soft and rapt with memory.

Again the silence fell and ran long. Cass finally broke it. "Who sent you the pink rose?" she asked.

"Didn't Benjamin tell you?" Elizabeth asked, and the question was carefully neutral, betraying nothing of the pulse quickening warmth that surged through her.

"No way. That man is as bad as you are about keeping promises," Cass said, "or as good. I didn't ask him."

"I don't think I'm crazy."

"Of course you're not."

"I think Barry sent it."

"The guy who wrote the love note?" Cass asked. Frowning, she cast a quick sideways glance at the woman sitting before the triple mirror. "Benjamin brought the white roses to the airport. What does this mysterious Druid have to do with Benjamin or Sessions?"

"I don't know," Elizabeth said. "Maybe nothing." She rubbed her eyes, fought back a yawn. "Cass, to tell you the truth, I don't have any idea who he is."

"Well, we aren't likely to find out tonight. Hurry up and jump into bed. You look like you haven't slept in a week, and Miss Lolly doesn't dare look less than lovely."

"True, and what Lolly wants, Lolly gets," Elizabeth said. "Cass, this tour as been fun, but I wish it were over. I want to get back to Merlin and her myth-in-the-making." It was said lightly and through a yawn, but she was worried. The new book was only half-done, and time was running short, too short.

But the book tour wasn't over. It went on, and she went with it, went tiredly to Los Angeles, San Francisco, and Portland, Oregon. It was, Elizabeth thought, their last day in Portland when Cass said she had called Edgar's office and told the receptionist when Elizabeth would be home from her "quiet little vacation with Cass." Elizabeth listened and nodded. The information wasn't as important as an autographing at a local bookstore. The people at the bookstore cared enough about her and the book to serve tea and cookies. Lolly said so, and even the bodyguard laughed.

The tour took them to Seattle, and as tired and befuddled as Elizabeth was, she still knew Washington State was the last stopping place. Very soon Lolly would go back to Cragshome and take pencil in hand. She was glad.

Elizabeth was still in bed, sipping marvelous coffee and eating fresh peaches, when Cass bounced in, a radiant Cass who said, "Liz, Benjamin just called."

Lolly couldn't resist asking, "Oh, did he want to talk to me?"

Cass blushed. "No," she said, "but he did want me to tell you that you're going to be a day or so late in getting home. Lolly has to go back to New York. She's going to receive some sort of award. Ben said it was pretty important, so I guess congratulations are in order."

"A writing award?"

"Best first novel or something," Cass said, and her voice sounded faraway, dreamy, but somehow fearful and excited. "I know you're awfully tired, but I.... Please, Liz, go to New York."

"If Lolly has to go, you can jolly well bet

Lolly will go," Elizabeth said a little sourly, then she looked at Cass' flushed face and chuckled. "And I'll be golly-wobbled if I'm going to let her go to something like that without me."

"You sound.... Liz, is something the matter?" Cass asked, and even her very real concern couldn't subdue the excitement that throbbed in her husky voice.

"No, or, at least, nothing a doctor could cure," Elizabeth said, and it was true. There was nothing wrong, or rather nothing wrong that could be changed, nothing that need cause Cass one moment of lost happiness. No, everything was in place, the coaster was in motion, and the ride was all down hill. And it was Elizabeth's ride to take.

"Good, I was afraid you'd... if I.... Lizzie, if you need someone, back home, I mean, I know Mrs. Caspar would help you any way she can. Call her, Liz, if you need to."

"And where will you be, Mary Alice?" Elizabeth asked, trying to hide her smile.

"Oh, I.... Well.... Liz, I know you're awfully tired, but would you go shopping with me this afternoon?" Cass asked, breathlessness making her sound young again, and very unsure. "Please, Liz, it's awfully important."

"Wedding gown important?"

"Who told you? Did Ben call you and...? Did he?"

"No, silly. You look like lace and June and

306 Patricia Lucas White

innocence." For an instant, the large bedroom was lost to the blur of her tears, tears that fell soundlessly. Tears ran down her face, but her voice was only glad. "It's about time he made an honest woman of you."

"Liz," Cass said plaintively. "Benjamin wants to get married in New York on the afternoon of the sixteenth, the day of the awards, so you can be there and be my matron of honor. Oh, Liz, that's only two days from now. It's too soon. I don't know if I.... What if we don't...? What if it's wrong?"

"What if you don't marry him, Mary Alice?" Elizabeth asked slowly. "Remember, love doesn't hang around waiting for you to pick it up and dust it off and use it for holidays and special occasions. Love is an everyday thing, a now and forever thing. He loves you, Cass, even someone as blind as Lolly can see that, and I know you love him. So, what's the problem?"

"N-n-n-n-n-n-n-nothing, I guess."

She sank down on the edge of the king-size bed and reached out to Elizabeth. "Oh, Lizzie. You have to help me. You just have to."

The embrace overturned the bedtray, silver coffeepot, and bowl of peaches. The two women rocked back and forth, hugging each other, laughing, laughter that held the tears of farewell. And when they finally composed themselves and Elizabeth, dripping coffee and cream, crawled out of bed, Cass said, "Benjamin said he'd consider giving you an extension on your deadline if you'd get me in some kind of shape and in New York, packed and ready for a long, long honeymoon in Europe.

Elizabeth mopped up coffee and peaches and laughed, "I don't know about that. I've had you around for a very long time and I'm not all that anxious to lose you, but.... How long an extension?"

Cass was too involved with her own worries to see any humor in Elizabeth's small jest. "A month? Two months? However long.... Oh, Liz, I don't know," Cass wailed. "I don't know anything right now except if you don't go to New York with me, I won't get married. You've been with me at every single important time in my whole life, you're the only family I have, and I have to have you with me at this wedding."

"I'll be there."

"I want you, not Lolly," Cass said.

"Cass, Lolly is me, probably more me than Elizabeth is now."

"You."

"Okay. I'll be there, standing right beside you when you promise to love, honor, and cherish Mr. Benjamin Sessions. I'll be there no matter what the cost," Elizabeth said quietly. After a pause, she once again invoked their ritual. "I promise."

But it was one promise Elizabeth Gilmartin couldn't keep.

The wedding was supposed to be a secret, but the news leaked out.

Elizabeth was camera shy (on Sessions' express order), so it was Lolly Horn who stood at Cass' side when she exchanged vows with Benjamin Sessions. It was Lolly who signed the marriage certificate as witness. And it was Lolly who smiled and posed and answered questions when the waiting cameramen and reporters captured them outside the judge's office and taped them for the evening news.

Sessions and his radiant bride were in the audience when Lolly, elegant in narrow, black silk pants and a scoop-necked shell to match, both covered by a calf-length beaded coat of shimmering Nile green, accepted the award for *Fornication* (an event taped for both late night and early morning newscasts), an award she gave, very prettily, to her publisher as a wedding gift.

But it was Elizabeth, suddenly alone, Lolly's blonde hair, beaded coat, and glamour bra stowed in her shoulder bag, who boarded the plane back to Cragshome. And she was still only Elizabeth, and still alone, when she walked into Edgar's dream house at noon on October 17, and found herself in a crowd.

Edgar was there, and the ubiquitous Ms. Marshall, as well as Edgar's decorator and several unnamed, unknown henchmen—either belonging to Edgar or to Ms. Somes, the dowdy decorator, or rather the expensive, pretentious, precious, dowdy decorator.

They were all either standing or milling in the hall between the wide opening into the living room and Elizabeth's tiny writing room. Edgar and the decorator were discussing how the small room should best be redecorated for its new use as Karoline Marshall's office—an office she would be using within the week if Edgar's newsletter was to get out to the subscribers on time.

Elizabeth walked closer, heard what they were saying. "What are you doing?" she asked, shock jolting her to the soles of her tired feet as two of the hulking musclemen carried her battered desk, and the secrets it held in its heart, out of the den.

"That's mine!" she shouted. "Leave it alone!" And suddenly she was cold to the bone, but not with fear, just frozen with the rock-hard ice of inevitability. Now was here, and she wasn't ready.

The men set the desk down in the hall and stepped back and away from it. They watched her, not with bold, staring eyes, but with wary, side-long glances, the careful glances of men who had been primed for a meeting with madness.

She advanced on them. They backed away.

Before she could reach her desk and its hidden treasures, Edgar caught her by the arm and swung her around to face him. "Just where in the bloody hell have you been?" he asked coldly.

"To Cass' wedding," she answered truthfully, or partially truthfully—the wedding had been the last place she had been, or one of the last places.

"Elizabeth," he said, and now his voice was hard as honed steel and just as deadly, "don't you dare lie to me."

"Why should I lie?" she asked absently, wanting only to escape his restraining hand, go to the desk, save the pages that gave Merlin life.

"Damn it, tell me the truth before I shake it out of you."

"The truth about what?"

"You were supposed to be home two days ago. Where have you been?"

"I was at Cass' wedding. She married Benjamin Sessions in New York yesterday afternoon."

"Everyone in Cragshome is aware of the fact the Widow Bates managed to trap another millionaire. It's been on the national news every five minutes. But Elizabeth, you weren't there, and don't try to tell me any different. I know better. We all do."

She looked at him. "I was there."

His voice shrilled, his hand tightened on her arm, and he did a very poor impersonation of a local newswoman. "The wedding party was small. It included only the bride and groom and a single attendant: Sessions Publications' star writer, Miss Lolly Horn." His hand bruised her upper arm and then he shook her hard.

"Where were you? What have you been doing? You were ordered to rest, if you've done anything to embarrass me, I swear to God, I'll take you to the madhouse myself, lock you up, and throw away the key."

Almost as if it were a play she was watching, Elizabeth withdrew and gave Lolly the spotlight. And Lolly jerked her arm free from Edgar's painful grasp and stood tall. "I *was* there," she said, her voice two degrees colder than his. "I *am* Lolly Horn."

"God, she really has flipped," someone whispered. There was a titter of embarrassment. Someone shuffled his feet. No one looked directly at Lolly.

And of them all, only Karoline Marshall smiled, the sweet smile of victory, smiled kindly as she said, "Please, dear, there's no need to act like this. Let me take you to your room. It's quiet there. No one will bother us, and we'll talk while you rest."

Lolly dismissed Edgar's paid companion with a look and spoke only to Elizabeth's irate husband. "I am Lolly Horn," she said, opening her shoulder bag and dragging out the blonde wig and the beaded coat. Using one hand, she put the wig crookedly in place, started to say something more, but a flicker of motion caught her attention. She looked over Edgar's shoulder and saw the men opening drawers of her old maple desk.

"Damn it," she said, only slightly softer than a bellow. "That's my desk. Stay out of it!"

And that, too, was what she had to do.

Karoline glanced swiftly at her employer, and her face adjusted itself into the picture of sympathy and sorrow. She said, oh, so soothingly, "Don't upset yourself more, Mrs. Gilmartin. It will be all right. I'll clean your little keepsakes out myself and save them for you. You'd like that, wouldn't you, dear?"

But there was no sympathy or understanding in Edgar's voice, there was only anger, with, perhaps, a heavy admixture of disgust. "Take off that silly wig," he said. "Right now. Do you hear me, Elizabeth?"

When she made no move to obey, he snatched it from her head, grabbed the sparkling green coat draped over her arm, bundled them together, and thrust the bundle at one of the silent minions. "Burn them," Edgar snarled.

The man obeyed without question or delay, and in less than a moment the wig was melting and the very expensive coat, a gift from Cass and Benjamin, was smoldering in the fireplace, like the anger in Lolly's heart.

Swallowing back bitterness, she turned away

from the wanton destruction just in time to see Karoline approaching. The younger woman was holding a stack of well-used, dog-eared, thoroughly marked and annotated books out and away from her body, holding the how-to sex books as if they might soil her virgin purity or steal her virtue, and her well-modulated tones were filled with horror when she said, "Oh, Mr. Gilmartin, look!"

He looked, without touching, and asked, "Elizabeth, what is the meaning of this... this filth?"

"It's mine, Edgar," Lolly said. "My books. My filth. Chippy filth. Whore...."

"Shut your mouth," he shouted. "I will not have you talking like that under my roof. I will not allow you to talk like a...."

"A what? You said it about me. You called me all the names. I am Lolly Horn. Those are my sex books. I wrote *Fornication*. I displayed myself on TV. I autographed the books."

He leaped forward, caught her by the wrist, tried to drag her down the hall, away from the too interested eyes of the decorator and the silently watching men. Then Karoline whispered an urgent something and he changed immediately.

Aware of the others now, his voice lost its anger, became that of a concerned, loving husband. "Come down to my office and sit down, my dear," he said. "Karoline will call your doctor and warm some milk for you. That would be nice wouldn't it. You can sit at the desk and I'll stay right there with you until Dr. Abernathy can...."

Lolly laughed. "A shrink? For me? No, Edgar," she said, "that won't be at all necessary. Why don't you just take your tame shrink and shrink him until he's small enough to...."

"Elizabeth," Edgar said warningly, "no more. You are clearly not yourself. Just come along and let me take care of you."

"I am myself, and part of that self is Lolly Horn."

The decorator, Ms. Somes, from Somes Ltd, slipped closer, watched the by-play with avid eyes, and Elizabeth almost expected the over-dressed, over-scented "lady" to whip out a dainty notebook, probably in pink and puce, and record the scandalous goings-on at the Gilmartin house, entitling her jottings *The Day Mrs. Gilmartin Went Mad and Told Everyone She Was Lolly Horn*. It was a piece of recording that was bound to be replayed at high teas and other social gathering attended by Ms. Somes' family and friends, or passers-by and strangers.

And the presence of a known gossip seemed somehow just, if not right.

"Come along, Elizabeth," Edgar said, changing his direction, exerting himself a little more, trying to force her into the living room.

"Turn me loose," Lolly said. "I can prove I'm telling the truth."

He released her, reluctantly, and Lolly pushed passed him, walked to where her desk was setting, opened the bottom drawer, took out the partially completed manuscript of Lolly's new book, and walked back to Elizabeth's husband.

Lolly pressed the pages to her heart for a moment, held them as if she were unwilling to let them fall into profaning hands, but her need to prove her identity was so great it made her unwise. "This is the first half of my new book," she said. "It's *P.S. I've Taken a Lover*. See. It has Lolly Horn written at the top of each page. Read a little of it. You'll see it's written in the same style as *Fornication*."

Barely contained, eruptive fury shooting sparks from the blue of his eyes, Edgar reached out, almost tore the stack of paper from Lolly's hands, but he didn't even glance at the manuscript. He handed it, immediately, to the hovering Ms. Marshall and dusted the palms of his hands together, brushing off any infecting particles that might have been transferred during the brief encounter.

Ms. Marshall looked at the papers attentively. Read a portion here. Skipped a few pages. Read some more. Found a panting passage. Gasped. Read some more. Paled. And gasped again—but not until she had reached the end of a seduction scene. Then, she murmured something in a stricken voice, a voice that sounded like the screen version of an insulted Victorian virgin, and pointed a trembling finger at the sizzling words.

Edgar's gaze followed where the finger led. And he read of Merlin and procreation, or rather an athletic attempt at it, and stiffened with outrage. Thundering like a mortally offended god, he said, "Smut! I'll not have filth like that in my house. I'm ashamed of you, Elizabeth." And then, continuing in his godlike role, he said to Karoline, "Burn it."

"You can't!" Lolly screamed. She lunged at Ms. Marshall, trying to take back and protect the still forming child of her imagination.

Edgar caught Lolly by the shoulders, his curled fingers biting into her flesh, and held her away from his secretary.

Gleeful, triumphant eyes belying the stern red mouth, Karoline lifted the embryo novel above her head and stepped quickly out of the way.

"You heard me, Karoline," Edgar said. "Burn it! Burn every filthy page! Burn it right now!"

"No," Lolly whispered. "Oh, please don't. No." But she didn't struggle against the cruel, hurting hands that imprisoned her body, didn't try to grab the precious pages, pages written in labor's sweat and heart's blood.

Lolly Horn, author, stood stiffly and alone until Elizabeth abandoned her pose of watchful aloofness, came to Lolly, and held out her hand. Then, they stood together, statues carved from a single aching stone, and watched, in awful, soul-tearing silence, as Karoline Marshall, obeying her master's barked orders with too much dedication, ripped each typed page from top to bottom and dropped the mutilated bodies into the orange fire in the living room fireplace. The mangled pieces writhed and flared and died, leaving behind only shapeless gray ash and an author's untold anguish.

Lolly and Elizabeth watched the wanton destruction with aching hearts and dry eyes, and they didn't know when Edgar's cramped hands lifted away from Lolly's straight shoulders, didn't know when the man moved back, distancing himself from both her grief and her madness. Keeping their shared deathwatch, Lolly and Elizabeth stood until the last innocent scrap of writing was gone, cremated on the worn altar of Edgar's pride. Only then did Lolly weep, weep for her beautiful heart-child, her murdered heart-child.

Elizabeth knew Lolly's grief in full measure, but there were no tears in her pale eyes, and there was no pain in her quiet voice, no pain, no loss, and no bitterness, there was only truth, a truth realized too late.

"Cass was right," she said to her husband. "You really are a selfish bastard."

And when the sting in her toneless words brought fire to his face, she laughed. It was a

genuine laugh that lilted and sang a final farewell
to Edgar and his perfect house, a silvery laugh
that celebrated freedom without guilt or regret.

Her laughter was still weaving its bright design
in the void between them when Elizabeth, and the
heart-broken Lolly, turned away from Edgar's
cold-eyed condemnation and walked, lithe and
lightly, toward the front door.

"Just where in the hell do you think you're
going?" he snarled.

"That's no longer any of your concern, Edgar,
but I'll tell you anyway. I'm going to the Caspars.
Edythe offered Lolly a home if she ever needed
one. I'm going to accept the offer until I can file
for a divorce and get a place of my own,"
Elizabeth said without slowing or looking back.

She was pulling the door open when Edgar
shouted, speaking more of the truth than he
intended, "Don't let her get away! She'll disgrace
me before the whole town. Stop her."

The door left gaping wide behind her,
Elizabeth was striding down the walk when two
of the burly hirelings grabbed her from behind,
picked her up bodily, and carried her back inside
Edgar Gilmartin's house. She didn't struggle,
didn't try to escape. It would have been a senseless
act. The pack of them were too uncaring, too
strong, and too many. She sat on the velvet loveseat
where they had dropped her, not roughly but like a
sack of wheat, an object to be talked about and

disposed of, in the tidiest manner possible.

So she just sat in Edgar's living room and waited in silence until the doctor rushed in, bag in hand, questions on his lips, questions to others about Elizabeth's madness, and when his questions had all been answered, when all the tales told, he came to Elizabeth, his patient.

He was a short, thin, sandy-haired man with earnest concern in every plane and crease of his old-looking face and his tired eyes of greenish-brown. He sat beside her on the velvet cushions, touched her wrist with counting fingers, and said, very softly, "Elizabeth? Can you hear me?"

"I'm supposed to be mad, not deaf," she answered.

The tartness brought a smile to his mobile mouth. "Edgar called me. He's very worried about you. And there's no reason for you to be afraid of anyone. All I want to do is help you. Will you believe that?"

She turned her head, looked deep into the weariness of his eyes, and smiled. "Yes," she said, "I'll believe that. However, trust works both ways. I *am* Lolly Horn. Will you believe that?"

Chapter Eighteen

♥   ♥   ♥

He had to know the calm-faced woman was asking for more than his belief, but Dr. S.K. Abernathy, Edgar's client and friend, shook his head, and the motion made his sandy hair fluff out like a halo, a rusty-gold nimbus against the light.

"No, Elizabeth," he said, "I can't believe you are Lolly Horn. That is *your* delusion. I know it seems very real to you right now, but it isn't true to the rest of us." He smiled at her and shook his head again.

"It's possible you are wrong, all of you are wrong."

"Yes," he answered, "that is possible, but not really very likely. Will you come with me to Harmony House and let me help you dispel the delusion?"

"Not willingly," she answered. "And not without a fight."

He sighed and patted her hand. "I was afraid you'd feel like that and am prepared to do what has to be done. Please know I do not mean to hurt you."

She watched him silently, saw his gaze shift, move from her face to something beyond her shoulder. "Hold her please," he said to an unknown someone behind her. Hands gripped her, held her motionless while the doctor slid a needle into the muscle of her upper arm and depressed a plunger. "We'll talk again after you've had a little rest, You'll feel better then," he said gently.

The colorless liquid raced through her tissue, her blood, her brain, invaded every inch of her body, and felled it. Elizabeth felt herself fading into nothingness even before the hands that held her vanished and she slumped against the back of the loveseat and wilted, toppling sideways with an easy grace. And somewhere between here and gone, she heard Dr. Abernathy say, in his soft, caring voice, "Call your attorney, Edgar. I'll have to have a court order to keep her longer than forty-eight hours."

When she drifted back, the velvet loveseat was in a different world, and day was night, and she was an inmate in an institution, a madwoman dependent on the doubtful mercy of her keepers. But fear was gone with the world, and she was only dry-mouthed, groggy, disoriented, and hungry, terribly hungry.

Somewhere in her lost time, she had been removed from Edgar's house, stripped of all personal possessions, including clothes and glasses, laid-out on a high, narrow bed in a sterile-smelling room, and abandoned, left to wake in darkness and alone. At the returning moment, she wasn't sure who she was, or if she was. Then she remembered, remembered everything. But it was everything in strange new patterns, was dark and light entwined, was images that twisted, shifted, and fled.

Anger and grief were heavy inside her, too heavy to be endured, and straining mightily, as she had done before, she put them away, locked them in with the other anger, the other grief. She was weak when she was done. Too weak to do more than crawl back into sleep like a maimed beast crawls into safe hiding, and let the healing of Elizabeth Gilmartin begin.

When next she woke, in a later darkness, Elizabeth listened to her growling stomach for less than a moment before she turned and slid, feet first, into the vertical bars that turned the bed into a crib, a prison for madwomen. Still only vaguely coherent, she kicked at the cylinders of metal and said, "Damn and blast. May they bake in Persephone's oven!" Said it loudly enough to bring her wandering mind back to its roof and to let the hidden anger seep through the walls of its container and permeate her entire being, every cell, every gene.

"The bastard," she said, just as loudly as

before. "The selfish, conniving bastard."

"'S'matter," a sleep-filled voice muttered from the shadowy, not quite darkness that filled the echoing room.

"Nothing!" Elizabeth snapped. "Not one bloody thing. Everything is just... just ducky."

"Doesn't matter," the voice said, sounding only a fraction more alert. "Wackos don't need to sleep, right?"

"How the hell should I know," Elizabeth said. "I'm not a wacko."

"Ah, but are you absolutely certain sure? I mean, you are awake, aren't you?"

"That doesn't mean a thing."

The sexless voice asked, with amusement strong in its logical cadences, "Doesn't it?"

"No," Elizabeth answered. "I'm not a wacko. I'm not crazy. I'm not mad."

"Then why are you locked up in your friendly, neighborhood madhouse?"

"Because I'm Lolly Horn."

"Ha! Now you've proved my point," the voice said.

"How?"

"You are Lolly Horn. Lolly Horn is a writer. All writers are wacko."

A giddiness of spirit caught Elizabeth unaware, ticked her, made her mirthful. She giggled and said, "You could be right. I've wondered about a few myself."

"I'm Tricia Gast," the voice said, introducing its owner. "And I'm not crazy, insane, or wacko."

Elizabeth, feeling all too much like Alice at the tea party, only hungrier, asked, "How do you know?"

"Simple. I'm not a writer."

"Oh," Elizabeth said, stifling another impulse toward mad laughter.

"Besides, I'm going home today. Even Dr. Abernathy wouldn't send a madwoman back into the real world, would he?"

"No, I don't suppose he..." Elizabeth said, "so, I guess that proves... proves something or other." And then, belatedly, she said, because even at a hatter's mad party, manners are called for, "I'm Elizabeth Gilmartin."

"Ah, yes, of course. A split personality. Two wackos."

"No, it's not like that. I'm really...."

"Yes. Lolly Horn. Elizabeth Gilmartin. Are there any more of you?" the voice asked politely, far too politely to be real.

Politely enough to make Elizabeth realize the whole thing had to be a dream, not a nightmare, just a ridiculous dream that seemed lumpy and misshapen with oodles of hidden meaning, but was probably innocent of any meaning. With that realization, the woman decided to dream the silly thing through to the end. "Any more whats?" she asked.

"Any more yous? Do you have any more personalities with names?"

Fascinated by the ebb and flow of the dream, if indeed that's what it was, Elizabeth said, "Only Helen Troy, but somebody else decided on her."

"Ahhhhhhhh, to be sure. The good shrinking doctor is going to love this," the voice said, and it sounded closer, so close that if it hadn't been a dream, Elizabeth would have felt the crinkle and creep of a chill racing down her spine. "He's full of sound and compassion, but it signifies nothing. Remember, Lolly-Elizabeth, it signifies nothing. He just keeps taking your checks to his bank."

"I'll try to remember," Lolly-Elizabeth said.

"Oh, you'll remember," the voice said, and now it seemed far away, seemed to be fading into the room's drifts and billows of shadow. "Does anyone know you're here?"

"My husband. His secretary."

"Hijacked! Found mad without a trial by jury." The voice unraveled, was only a thread of sound. "Want me to call?"

Call? Call who? Who would help? The thoughts squiggled through the misty fog drifting back into her mind, blotting out memory and thought with equal ease, obscuring the here and the now, covering past, present, and future with its thick, formless persistence.

"Sessions Publications. New York. Tell them Lolly Horn is in a madhouse alone. Tell...." And even as more words fell from her mouth, Elizabeth grabbed a floating hunk of memory and knew, if only for that dreaming instant, that Benjamin Sessions was gone, honeymooning in Europe with Cass, and no one else knew she was Lolly Horn. No one knew. No one cared. No one.

♥   ♥   ♥

"No," Elizabeth said as she was coaxed and harried out of darkness into light, a curious shifting light filled with movement and voices, white movement and brisk voices. The voices, using varying tones and pitches, said:

"That's her. That's the one who thinks she's Lolly Horn."

"Look at her. Any fool with half an eye could see she's not. Poor soul."

"Come on, Elizabeth."

"Wake up, Elizabeth."

"It's almost noon, Elizabeth."

"Doctor will be here soon. You want to be pretty for Doctor, don't you, sweetie?"

"No, I do not want to be pretty for Doctor or anyone else," Elizabeth growled, pushing away the hands that tugged at her person. "All I want is out of this snake pit."

Someone sputtered, readying herself to defend the honor of Harmony House. Someone else laughed and said, "You and me, both, honey."

Elizabeth Gilmartin, incarcerated madwoman, jerked free of the too familiar hands, sat up in the rumpled bed, and tried to look around, but her eyes, without their gray-rimmed glasses, were as blind as Lolly's. She moved too quickly. The bed seemed to lurch, to spin sickeningly, and she thought she was going to sink into the vortex of nothingness again. Gripping the sides of the bed, she fought back the dizziness, the rise of bile in her throat, gulped in air like a land-stranded fish, and said, "Whew! Strong stuff that doctor gives."

One of the three white-clad shadows standing near the bed stepped forward, supported Elizabeth with a strong arm, held something cold to the slim woman's dry lips. "Drink this, Mrs. Gilmartin," she said. "It will make you feel better."

Edgar Gilmartin's mad and discarded wife swallowed obediently, drank a full glass of something that might have been plain ice water, but seemed to have some magical qualities of rejuvenation and restoration. Within minutes her lightheadedness was gone, her glasses were on her face, and the woman, despite the hunger that growled mightily in her stomach, was ready to confront Doctor and face him down.

She was sane, and if he would listen, she could prove it.

♥   ♥   ♥

But she couldn't prove it, not to Dr. Sigmund Karl Abernathy. He listened gravely to her every word, no matter how inane, looked at her with his incredibly weary eyes, and said, "I'm truly sorry, Elizabeth, but it just isn't true. It's a delusion, only a delusion. You aren't Lolly Horn. You have never been Lolly Horn. You are, as you have always been, Elizabeth Jane Gilmartin."

Remembering pieces of the dream, Elizabeth asked, only a spoonful too sweetly, "Are you sure I don't have a split-personality? Or maybe a multiple-personality?"

Her sarcasm was wasted. He smiled, like a tired Buddha, and shook his head, fluffing up his rusty halo, and said, "No, Elizabeth, nothing so exotic. It's just a delusion. It happens sometimes when...."

"When women become menopausal?" she asked, and the anger within her, anger at him, at her husband, spilled over into her voice, showed sharp-edged and steel-bright, a killing blade, burnished and bare between them.

But it didn't touch him. His smile was a shield and impervious to mortal weapons. "My dear, I understand how strange all this is to you, and how frightening," he said softly. "But, in time, you will learn to trust me, and then you'll know I want nothing but what is best for you. I am your friend, Elizabeth, not your enemy."

She laughed, and it was as brittle as glass and hard as the anger-blade. "You didn't answer my question."

"I didn't, did I," he said, still smiling his saintly smile. "I do not think menopause has any direct causal effect. Delusions are—although there are other theories—in my opinion, caused by happenings in a person's life. Events so traumatic they cannot, at that time, be faced. In effect, delusions, like yours, are a retreat from reality. And some delusions are very complete, almost believable to onlookers. Delusions persist until the reality that caused them is recognized and dealt with.

"So, dear lady, don't worry. We will seek out your troubling reality, deal with it, and your delusion will vanish in an instant."

"No," she said, the anger making her sound sullen, "it isn't a delusion. It's true. I am Lolly Horn."

"Don't upset yourself, Elizabeth. I'm not arguing with you. I know you think it's true. But you are an intelligent person, you should be able to see that what you have told me proves nothing. You say Benjamin and Cass Sessions can attest to your identity, and then you tell me they are in Europe on their honeymoon. But don't you see, that's why you chose them as your witnesses? Cass was your best friend, practically your only friend, but she's gone. And everyone who watches national TV knows about their wedding and protracted honeymoon—you don't have to be Lolly Horn to know that."

She nodded, reluctantly, at the logic in his

words, and he hitched his chair a little closer to her bed, and said, very quietly, "Elizabeth, I know you aren't a vain woman, so I feel I can say this without causing you any real pain."

He waited for her reply, but she just watched him with unreadable eyes until he continued his little speech. "Lolly Horn is almost a TV personality and..." his voice got lower, and he glanced, almost guiltily, around the empty room before he proceeded with his confession. "I find her most attractive and have developed a broad admiration for her as a person as well as a writer. She is fresh, unspoiled, and so very beautiful that I.... Well, as I was saying, I can understand why you would chose someone like that for your other self. And, I must admit, there is a slight resemblance, very slight, only fleeting, momentary, illusive."

"It's probably only a delusion," Elizabeth said.

Dr. Abernathy ignored the acid in her voice and smiled, "I can see you are tiring, so let's leave off our explorations for today. Anyway, I see Nurse Chatsworth waiting to escort you to your room and see you have everything you need." He glanced pointedly at her growling stomach and added, "That includes something to tide you over until dinner."

He stood. "I hope you'll be very comfortable here. Ms. Marshall delivered some of your personal articles and some simple garments earlier today, while you were still sleeping. If you need anything else, you can tell Edgar when he comes to visit you this evening."

"I will not see him," Elizabeth said flatly. She sat up, curled her hands around the bars on her bed, glared at Dr. Abernathy, and repeated, "I will not see Edgar today, tomorrow, or ever. I want that understood right now. I do not want to see him. If you force me to see him, I can assure you that you will regret it."

Elizabeth listened to herself making threats and she almost smiled. But it was true, she didn't want to see her husband. It was over. There was nothing between them now, and nothing in their future but a divorce. And that sounded wonderful.

"Of course, I can't force you to see him, But my dear, Edgar was only...."

"Only getting rid of what he considers to be an embarrassment. He put me in this madhouse, and if what you said about a court order is true, he, and probably you, too, lied about me to keep me here for thirty days. I am not a danger to myself or to the community, and I wouldn't be even if I were mad, which I'm not. I will not see him."

"Elizabeth, I realize it's hard, but try to understand. Edgar put you here for your own good."

"Oh, yes, I know that only too well. Edgar Gilmartin has done entirely too many things for 'my own good.'"

His eyes gleamed. He tensed like a cat sighting an unwary mouse. But his tone was mild, almost disinterested, when he asked, "What kinds of things?"

"Oh, for one, he had that damned house built. That whining, sniveling monster of a house, built just for me, he said. And then he hired that prissy-missish decorator, with her satins and velvets and 'it's yous,' and had her decorate that damned house for me, so I wouldn't have to learn about color matching and fabric texture and all the rest. And when I was right in the midst of planning and organizing our youngest son's wedding, Edgar sold my...."

"Edgar sold your what, Elizabeth?" Dr. Abernathy asked softly.

If Elizabeth heard his question, she ignored it completely and switched the conversation to a new channel. She looked at him with nothing but innocent curiosity showing on her face or in her voice and asked, "You mean I don't stay here? This isn't my room?"

Releasing his breath in an almost unheard sigh, he turned away from her gaze and surveyed the six-bed ward, empty now except for the two of them and the white-clad woman standing beside the door. "No," he said patiently, "this is the dispensary. We do, on occasion, have illnesses and minor accidents that require medical attention. And our new patients usually spend their first night here — their first twenty-four hours actually — and then, if they are calm enough, they are transferred to the living wing on the top floor."

"The living wing?" The words struck her as absurd, ludicrous in describing a part of a crazy house, and she very nearly laughed. But she still had sense enough to keep the impulse sternly in check and say, "Dr. Abernathy, I will stay in your nut house because, at the moment, I have no other choice, but despite your instant diagnosis, I know I am as sane as you are, possibly even saner. I am Lolly Horn. I did write *A Touch of Fornication*. I am not having delusions. And, I absolutely will not see Edgar Gilmartin, his tail-wagging secretary, or anyone else who insists he, or she, is doing something for my own good."

"I will call your husband and explain your stand," he said, and then, sounding far too much like a stern parent to make her believe his pose of wise, compassionate doctor, he said, "Elizabeth, I must tell you that I am disappointed in you. Your attitude is totally unreasonable and will cause your husband a good bit of unnecessary pain. He is very worried about you, very worried indeed. However, the Edgar Gilmartin I know is a big enough man to realize it is your illness that is rejecting his loving care and not his own dear wife."

"Bull pucky!" she snapped, and the mild oath sang of fog and sea, comforting her in the midst of madness not her own, and somehow made her strong.

"Time will prove me right, my dear," he said, and then Dr. S.K. Abernathy, still exuding compassion and understanding, and seemingly unaware of the irony in his remarks, gave Elizabeth Gilmartin, and her alter-ego, Lolly Horn, best-selling author, the task of writing the sad tale of her plunge into the murky depths of madness, a sordid tale, one that was to be called, simply enough, "Life-Notes." The title, including the quotation marks, was Dr. Abernathy's choice, not Lolly's.

Elizabeth listened and nodded, in appropriate places, as he outlined the writing project, but, if only for a bleak instant, Lolly remembered, and mourned, another writing, a heart-child conceived in gladness and aborted at Edgar Gilmartin's murderous command. When the instant was gone, she folded her grief and put it away, tucked it in beside her carefully preserved anger. Then she sighed, a sigh of things and people and time that had to be endured, and not of sadness.

But he heard her expel the breath and interpreted it according to his beliefs and said, with another of his ever-so-sincere smiles, "Elizabeth, I realize it seems as if I am setting you to an impossible task, a frightening task for one of your inexperience in writing, but most of my patients, after an initial resistance, write their 'Life-Notes' without too much difficulty.

"You furnish your life experience, and we

furnish everything else: resource books, typing paper, pencils, notepads, typewriters, and a copy machine. I have found it to be excellent therapy, as I'm sure you'll grow to appreciate it as we progress with the writings.

"Now, Miss Chatsworth," he pointed toward the woman at the door, "will be your personal mentor. She has had a number of creative writing classes and is our best instructor in that particular area. That's why I chose her especially for you."

A demon took possession of her tongue, or maybe it was Lolly who said, "Oh, yes, I see. A writing teacher for poor, deluded Ms. Gilmartin, to show her the inconsistencies, errors, and leaks in her story."

"It is a delusion, Elizabeth. And it is my job to help rid you of it," he answered. "As I was saying, Miss Chatsworth will be able to help you with the actual writing—you know, sentence structure, paragraphing, and all that."

"I believe I can handle it alone," Lolly said, and there was more than a hint of malice in her smile, "after all, I have written one novel already."

He smiled back at her, a sweet, saintly smile that only increased the weariness in his eyes, a chiding smile that should have made her grovel with guilt and beg his immediate forgiveness—but it didn't.

She laughed. Elizabeth had allied herself with Lolly Horn, and they were fighting for their very lives, fighting with every weapon they could scrounge or commandeer. Their battle for survival in a madhouse had just begun.

Recognizing her continuing animosity, Dr. Abernathy said gently, calmly, and with much forbearance, "Elizabeth, dear lady, you aren't trying. I want you to remember this at all times, and everyone on staff will be instructed to remind you: *You* are not Lolly Horn. She is a beautiful young woman. *You* are not. She wrote a best-selling book. *You* have written nothing."

Lolly, or maybe it was Elizabeth, laughed, a rich full laugh, the laugh of a woman who was only amused at his petty posturing and pretensions to omniscience.

"It is a delusion," he said defensively, and some of his gentle compassion had curdled, soured into huffy inflexibility, when he continued, "It is nothing more than a false reality your mind has fashioned to allow you to escape from some awful truth, probably some terrible guilt or betrayal you can't face."

"Maybe like taking a lover to escape from Edgar's overpowering and everlasting love, kindness, and caring?" she asked, laughter still lurking in the pale depths of her eyes.

"Exactly," he snapped.

"Damn," she muttered. "Having a lover must have been fun, I sure wish I could remember that."

He stiffened, fought an invisible battle, and

said, with all the old compassionate gentleness back in his voice, "Nurse Chatsworth will see to your orientation. When you are settled in, understand our routine, and feel a little more comfortable, I want you to begin writing your 'Life-Notes.' Within them, we will find all the clues to what is causing you to have delusions. We will pick out the clues together, solve your mystery, and your delusions will be gone in the twinkling of an eye."

"Or in the twinkling of a cliché," she muttered.

A muscle twitched at the corner of his mouth and a spark of something lightened the weariness in his eyes, but he only gave her a brief bow and turned and walked away, stopping at the door to say something, quite a lengthy something to Miss Chatsworth, the lady in white.

When he had disappeared from sight, his delegated champion rushed into the fray. Bristling and stiff-legged, if not in fact, then in attitude, she approached Elizabeth, looked her up and down, and then assumed her self-appointed role as keeper, a morally just keeper who would keep her keepee on the straight and narrow path that led back to cured, obedient Edgar-wifery.

Although she wasn't a nurse, she said, "Doctor prefers you address me as Nurse Chatsworth," as she hustled Elizabeth out of the bed and into the beltless robe and scuffs she had brought with her.

The woman clearly wasn't worthy of her steel, but Lolly couldn't resist twitting her. Lapping the fronts of the robe, she pretended to fumble for the non-existent belt and then said, in mock girlish dismay, "Oh, dear, how will I ever protect my.... Madwomen aren't allowed belts, Nurse Chatsworth?" She rubbed her hands down the front of the open robe and said, "I think I'll enjoy it here. Every one of us is a flasher—how quaint."

"Mrs. Gilmartin, I realize this is very sudden, but I must insist you act..." the pseudo-nurse paused, gave Elizabeth a very significant, woman-to-woman look, and said quietly, "Never mind, dear, I have talked to Ms. Marshall, I do understand. However, that... with your age and all, should never be a problem here. Doctor is very good with hormones and female.... He will take care of you, don't worry."

"Bull pucky," Elizabeth said, for the second time that day.

Chapter Nineteen

♥   ♥   ♥

"Bull pucky? Mrs. Gilmartin, I really must insist you be more careful...." Nurse, as-she-preferred-to-be-called, Chatsworth bit off the rest of her admonition like a sharp-toothed seamstress bites off a hank of thread and let silent outrage darken her face, glower in her eyes, knot her mouth.

Elizabeth, her own pale eyes lively with interest, smiled at her, and Lolly, ever the writer, said, "Pursed? Of course. Pursed."

"Mrs. Gilmartin, what are you...?"

"Your mouth. With all those little wrinkles radiating out from your lips when you do that. It looks just like a purse with a drawstring top. Of course, it would probably be more useful if it had real strings to tie and keep it shut." Lolly's left eyebrow arched up, giving Elizabeth's pallid face a devil-may-care look. The look matched her new manners, manners foisted on her by circumstance—not that she had balked at the taking. In some curious way, the new look suited her, if not her starched-white keeper.

"That's enough!" Nurse Chatsworth said tightly, anger turning the lines around her pursed mouth into a mottle of red and white. "I am amazed at your actions. A woman of your age and position. Have you no shame? This is a respectable house, and we will not tolerate...."

"No," Lolly said decisively, "I really don't believe that's possible. This is a madhouse, a loony bin, and I'm one of the loonies. Somehow, that doesn't seem too respectable to me."

"You're not...."

"Not what, Nurse Chatsworth? Not crazy? Not locked up in a madhouse? If I'm not crazy, why am I here? Why has your wonderful, dedicated doctor conspired with my husband to keep me here, against my will, for a month or more? Why, Nurse Chatsworth? Just tell me why?" As Lolly spoke, both Elizabeth and Lolly, for in that they were of a single mind, advanced on the white-uniformed woman. To her credit as a keeper of two mad madwomen, Nurse Chatsworth stood her ground and tried to soothe her patients, or rather her patient—because she didn't believe in Lolly's existence in Harmony House.

She reached out a hand, palm up, and it had only the slightest of quivers, and said, "Elizabeth, I realize you are terribly upset, and that, later, you will be very ashamed of how you treated me. Rest assured, I will ask Doctor why you are here, and then I will be very happy to explain it to you in simple terms even a layman can understand."

Elizabeth laughed and asked, perhaps perversely, "And a laywoman?"

"Yes, of course," the other woman said somewhat less tensely. "Now that that's settled, come along. I want to show you the general layout of Harmony House and explain a few simple rules before I show you your room."

Walking sedately at her guide's side, Elizabeth listened, with both ears but only half attention, as the woman glowingly introduced her to the wonders of Harmony House, a yellow brick mansion in the style of the Old South—complete with tall white pillars in the front and a flagstone veranda. It sat, settled and stately, on the brow of a gentle hill. Some twenty miles north of Cragshome, the expensive hideaway for rich crazies was beautiful, and so were its extensive, landscaped grounds encompassing rose gardens, sunken gardens, water gardens, oriental gardens, fountains, brooks, duck ponds, rolling hills, groves of trees, and miles of winding, black-topped walks. The estate was girded by a four-foot wall of yellow brick, compete with white-painted iron gates— which sounded formidable, but was, in all truth, only ornamental.

Elizabeth Gilmartin, novice madwoman, was whisked from dispensary to lobby, a spacious, area-lighted, antique-furnished room, totally in keeping with the private mansion concept being fostered by the establishment. They halted at the foot of the sweeping staircase and Elizabeth was informed, with appropriate pointing-finger air-jabs by Nurse Chatsworth's rigid forefinger, that the patients, while it wasn't exactly off-limits, usually only came to the first floor when summoned by Doctor or one of the staff. "Unless," she added as an after-thought, "that patient has Doctor's personal permission to use one of the smaller offices for a particular project."

"Such as?" Elizabeth asked, not because she was particularly interested, but because she felt the need to accumulate as much information as possible about her new prison.

"Well, I don't really.... Doctor makes those decisions, and it's really none of your business. It can't really matter to you. You aren't likely to be...." The non-nurse had a tad of tartness in her voice, but it was replaced by breathlessness when they reached the bottom of the stair that led down to the daylight basement.

Opening out onto a flagstoned courtyard and overlooking a vista that included a slope of lawn and a tree-lined pond of sparkling water, the large basement was, according to Miss Chatsworth's commentary, for the patients' use— or at least the sauna, showers, recreation room, crafts room, gift shop, and cafeteria were; the

kitchen, laundries, and storage facilities were
forbidden territory, except to authorized personnel
only and were labeled as such in bright-red letters.

A peek in at each of the patient-permitted
rooms and three introductions—to staff, not fel-
low-inmates—later, Elizabeth was again in the
stairwell, following impatiently in the wake of
Nurse Chatsworth, who was ascending the stair
like one of Lolly's imagined virgin-sacrifices
climbing to the top of an erupting volcano.

Hunger grumbling and growling in her stomach,
not unlike the mutter of said volcano, the slow
climb not enough exercise to warm her muscles or
quicken her breath, Elizabeth's thoughts reverted
to her own needs, and she said, "I walk every day.
Is that allowed here?"

"Oh, yes. Doctor encourages all our people to
exercise. But, of course, you can't go.... I'll have
to accompany you," Nurse Chatsworth said,
panting a little from the exertion as they reached
the top floor and turned into the left-hand corridor.

"Ladies to the left," the nurse said, "and gentlemen to the right. However, the dayroom is also
on the right, so the ladies do have to go to the
right to get there. That's because we have fewer
gentlemen staying with us at Harmony House."

"Naturally," Elizabeth said.

The other woman gave her a quick, suspicious
glance, but didn't ask what she meant. In fact,
probably because the climb had taken all her

breath, Nurse Chatsworth said nothing more until she pulled open a door at the very end of the hall and ushered Elizabeth into a large, tastefully decorated room, a corner room with a private bath and a view.

"This is yours," she said, rather too proudly. "It is one of our most beautiful guestrooms, and I will expect you to treat it with the respect it deserves."

Elizabeth wasn't intimidated. "After I've had something to eat," she said, "I'll be happy to bow down and worship it, if that is what you want. But right now I...."

There was no need to say more. A girl, dressed in blue, wearing a band of freckles like a banner across her nose, came smiling and chatting through the open doorway and set a tray on the table in the window alcove. "Chicken soup," she said. "It'll cure anything."

And it almost did.

But there was no chicken soup available the next afternoon when Elizabeth Gilmartin, substitute-writer, sat down at the manual typewriter in the dayroom and began, reluctantly and somewhat angrily, her "Life-Notes," with archaic oaths and hyperbole.

And was chided, quite severely, by Nurse

Chatsworth for levity unbecoming a madwoman. Nurse Chatsworth had, indeed, visited with Dr. Abernathy, and had, indeed, put her own interpretation on his diagnosis and treatment of Elizabeth's delusions—seeing the delusions as suitable and apt to Elizabeth's age and state—and plied the laughing Elizabeth with a sedative and sent her to nappytime in the madhouse.

When she awoke, Elizabeth stood, in sleep-crumpled, beltless garments, looking out the window, looking at naked trees, a low, gray sky, and acres of grounds. Her pale eyes saw nothing but the swish and churn of her inner thoughts. She watched them for a long time, and then she saw things the way they should be, the way she could make them be. "Of course," she said, "it's the perfect solution."

"What is?" asked a gentle, male voice from the doorway.

"I'll write the 'Life-Notes,'" she said, without turning away from the window, "or at least Lolly will."

"Elizabeth," the doctor said, "may I remind you that you are not...."

"Who or what I'm not doesn't matter now," she answered. "You see, Edgar's marvelous secretary burned Lolly's manuscript for her new book. She has to have another one done, and very soon, if she is to fulfill the terms of her contract with Sessions Publications."

"Elizabeth, dear lady, you must understand. You are not Lolly Horn."

She laughed, a warm, caressing, Lolly laugh. "We'll see who is right about that, won't we?" Her laughter died. "But not if your... your whatever she is reads over my shoulder, dislikes what she reads, and forces sleepytime pills down my gullet every time I titter. She has to go."

"No, that's impossible. You have to have someone to...."

"I don't have to have *Nurse* Chatsworth. I don't have to have someone who thinks menopause is a terminal disease," Elizabeth said quietly and firmly, and Lolly, not to be outdone, added, "And not someone you keep around because she's your mistress."

"My what?" he asked, shock making his voice squeak.

"Oh, she isn't?" Lolly asked innocently. "I'm so glad. I thought she was and that being around her all the time was what made you look so tired."

His laughter was a swelling roar, a building wave that broke into a wheezing, gasping froth of sputters and sputs. And when he could, he said, "I take it you don't care for Miss Chatsworth?"

"It isn't that," Elizabeth said. She turned away from the window, faced him, and said, without the slightest hint of a smile, "The woman is trying her very best to drive me sane."

He chuckled. "Oh, Elizabeth, you aren't insane."

"I know that, and you know that, but Nurse Chatsworth has other ideas on the subject. I'm telling you, if this keeps on, I will probably go insane, just to be safe from her."

"She really is a fine woman, Elizabeth, and you do have to have someone with you for the first week or so, in case you...."

"Decide to go over the wall?" she asked. "Dr. Abernathy, I do like to walk, but not twenty miles at a shot."

"Just for a few days?" he asked, the gentleness in his voice making it seem as if she would be doing him a great favor if she agreed.

She wasn't taken in, or if she was, she acquiesced in a devious manner. Elizabeth, acting rather like a bargain hunter at a yard sale, said, "If I can have someplace private to write my 'Life-Notes,' I will allow Nurse Chatsworth to act as my own beloved companion. She can walk with me, talk down to me, and insult my intelligence, and I will do nothing more than cringe inside as I act like a lady."

"You may be doing yourself a disfavor. Miss Chatsworth is experienced in customs and conventions of writing. She is a writer herself and likes nothing more than...."

"Oh, that does make a difference. I'd like to read some of her work. Who is her publisher?" Elizabeth asked brightly.

Shaking his head, Dr. Sigmund Karl Abernathy

smiled his gentle smile and acknowledged defeat. "The office next to mine isn't being used at the moment. But if I allow you to use it, you have to promise to...."

"If I run into any difficulty, I promise to ask Miss Chatsworth's aid," Elizabeth said softly. "But I don't anticipate needing it. I've had a small amount of experience along this line myself."

"No, Elizabeth, you haven't. You are not Lolly Horn, that is only a delusion."

Smiling serenely, Elizabeth said, "I'll have to title the work *P.S. I've Taken a Lover.*"

"You'll title it 'Life-Notes.'"

"Will I?" Her growing smile held guile, mirth, and a bit of anger, but no agreement. It held nothing but pure satisfaction an hour later when she was seated at a desk in the promised office, a desk whose lockable drawers were cleared for her exclusive use. Elizabeth Gilmartin glanced at the closed door, her smile widened into a grin of delight, and she turned on the electric typewriter and began to write—began with page one of Lolly Horn's new book, a book about a character named Elizabeth Gilmartin. It was the story of Elizabeth's fall from grace into the murky mire of madness, and, of course, her cure by a dedicated doctor.

♥　　♥　　♥

The nurses and other staff members at Harmony House treated Elizabeth quite well, laughing and talking with her, and even teasing her on occasion. But Nurse Chatsworth didn't join in the jolly fun, she was miffed, and she sniped at Elizabeth every time she was in range.

Elizabeth and Lolly had won the battle for privacy, and Elizabeth could afford to be gracious, even to the point of slowing her walking pace for the younger woman's benefit, walking slow enough for Nurse Chatsworth to keep her in sight—but in the interest of truth, it should be noted that she walked fast enough to keep the other woman too winded to indulge in chit-chat.

However, they were, of necessity, so often together, as keeper and keepee, they became rather well acquainted, enough so for Elizabeth to realize Nurse Chatsworth might be more than she appeared on the surface, might be a friend and an ally in a strange and sometimes frightening land.

On Elizabeth's fifth day of official madness, she was leading Nurse Chatsworth, at a rapid pace, through the twists and turns of the winter garden when suddenly she slowed, tears burning in her eyes, real tears of loneliness, anger, and frustration.

The wind was swaying and tossing in bare trees and shrubs, giving the two walkers' faces a shiny, apple-red look, and thrusting them toward safe heaven with nudges at their backs and urgent whispers in their ears. Memory, years of it, weighed heavy on Elizabeth, bound her steps, ached in her throat.

"Oh, Cass," she said. "Why aren't you here? I need you, really need you." Her steps grew shorter, slower, so slow that Nurse Chatsworth was soon walking at her side.

"Elizabeth," she asked, her concern holding the essence of verity, "is something the matter?" Her hand reached toward, but didn't quite touch Elizabeth's bent shoulder.

"No, I.... It's just that..." Elizabeth could hear the unshed tears tangled in her words, and tried to regain her facade of cool indifference. But the words that tumbled from her lips spoke only of her pain. "Cass loves this kind of day. A wild wind and storm in the air. It was the only time she would ever walk with...."

The silence held for a long moment, was almost louder than the wind, but Nurse Chatsworth, showing her true worth, found the tone of casual interest and the word to break it painlessly. "Cass?" she asked.

"Mary Alice Cassidy Bates," Elizabeth answered, and then, with a rueful laugh, she corrected herself, "Mary Alice Cassidy Bates Sessions."

Nurse Chatsworth's voice was gentle. "That's another part of your delusion, isn't it?"

"No, it's no delusion. Cass is my dearest

friend. We went to school together. Grade school. High school. No. Cass Sessions is *my* friend, not Lolly's."

"But I thought.... Wasn't Lolly Horn her wedding attendant?" the nurse asked, looking down at the path, doubt digging deep lines between her brows.

"Was she?"

Stronger and colder now, the wind harried them, pinching their noses and earlobes with sharp, icy fingers, tearing at their clothes, elf-locking their hair, moaning around them like an apprentice ghost on Halloween.

The path wandered over a stream, down a steep bank, and sharply to the left. Miss Chatsworth's foot caught on the raised edge of the blacktop. She stumbled, almost went to her knees. Elizabeth grabbed her arm, held her until the woman could regain her balance. And she could feel Nurse Chatsworth trembling.

Mentally berating herself for making the younger woman walk in such stormy weather, she said, "You're cold. We can go back right now."

"No, it isn't that. It's just that it seemed so.... Your friend's new husband.... He...."

"Benjamin Sessions?" Elizabeth said in answer to the mute appeal she saw in the nurse's eyes. She knew the other woman wanted something more, but she didn't know what, so she waited, standing with her back to the wind, looking at

Nurse Chatsworth worriedly.

Finally, the woman said, through chattering teeth and with more uncertainty than Elizabeth would have thought possible, "I... uh... I'm writing a book. Do you think.... I've heard how hard it is to get someone to even look at.... That is, do you think...." She licked her lips, hugged herself with both arms, and lapsed back into silence.

"Do you want me to introduce you to Benjamin?"

"No! Oh, no! I couldn't...." She swallowed hard and then confessed, in a soft, dry whisper, her closely held secret, "I.... You wouldn't understand what it's like. Words come so easy to you. I don't know how to.... No matter what I say, it comes out wrong and people think I'm terrible, but Elizabeth, I can understand your illness, can know how dreams can hurt so much that.... All I've ever wanted to do is write. I've never told anyone else because there's never been anyone to tell."

Rain, chill and wind slashed at them with stinging whips, and forced the two women to run, heads down, hands clasped, to shelter. When Harmony House's basement door had closed at their backs and they had caught their breaths, Elizabeth said, because she had heard an echo of her own lost yearnings in the woman's stammered secret, yearnings a faceless stranger had helped her turn into reality, and because she knew it was time to pay her debt, "Dreams are for following, Nurse Chatsworth. If you really want to be a writer, get your manuscript into shape and when Ben and Cass get back from their honeymoon, write him a letter and ask if he will look at what you've written."

"I can't. I've tried to do it like that before and I... I can't."

"But it's the only way to find out."

Nurse Chatsworth's face was full of longing, her eyes looking into some distant place Elizabeth wasn't privy to, and her voice held only shyness when she asked, softly and humbly, "I'll do it if.... Will you read it first?"

"Me?" Elizabeth asked. "Why me?"

"Because you... you're the only one I.... You want to be a writer, too. I know that, and I think that's what your delusion is all about. I don't really know why. Would you, please?"

Elizabeth turned toward her, tried to see more than the woman's face revealed, and finally said, "Yes, if it means that much to you, I'll read it. But...."

"Just be honest. I'm not afraid of that, or even of the work it will take to make it right. I just.... Thank you, Elizabeth."

"Nurse Chatsworth, I don't know. I'm not...."

"Ellen," the woman said. "Please, call me Ellen."

Still not sure she was doing the right thing,

Elizabeth said, "Ellen, I don't honestly know how good an editor I'll be."

"Maybe just talking about it will be enough," Ellen said quietly. And then, with shyness almost stealing her voice, she said, "If you need someone. If you want to talk about your 'Life- Notes,' I'd be.... As a writer, I mean. I won't be bossy."

"Don't promise miracles," Lolly said.

Elizabeth and Ellen were laughing as they climbed the stairs.

In the space of a half an hour, Ellen Chatsworth had become, if not a real friend, then, at the very least, a friendly ally.

And, in more ways than one, Harmony House was the best of all possible worlds for Lolly Horn. She had complete privacy, time to write when she wanted it, someone, or rather several someones to wait on her, cater to her needs, just as Elizabeth had had to cater to Edgar's needs, and the needs of his very needy house. Here there were only Elizabeth's walks with Ellen, one a day; Dr. Abernathy's talks with Elizabeth, one hour every other day; and Elizabeth's visits to the sauna, her own bow to luxury and sensuous enjoyment — the talks with Ellen, usually during their walks, sometimes in the sauna, seemed an extension of Lolly's writing, not an interruption of it.

And the writing itself was progressing, pouring from her fingertips so rapidly it was almost frightening. Elizabeth Gilmartin, Lolly Horn's ersatz writer, had been in Harmony House six days, and had written over seventy pages of her novel, when she confessed her almost-fear to the good doctor.

He laughed and shook his head. "Oh, Elizabeth," he said, with a mock sigh, "it's supposed to be easy. All you're doing is writing down what you believe has happened in your life."

"Am I?" she asked, handing him the stack of finished pages—actually she handed him one of the photocopies she had made and kept the original for herself, and Lolly's publisher.

"I certainly hope so," he said. "It's what you're supposed to be doing."

"According to my contract with Sessions, I'm supposed to be writing Lolly's second novel," Elizabeth said, with just a hint of tartness in her voice. She met his eyes squarely, and it seemed as if she were daring him to condemn her words as delusion.

He didn't. Dr. S.K. Abernathy just sat, a gentle smile hovering around his mouth, and watched her with his weary eyes that had seen too much, knew too much, and were yet too blind to see truth.

It angered her, made her feel edgy, out of sorts. Elizabeth stood abruptly and moved away from the padded leather chair placed just so in front of his cluttered desk. A feeling she couldn't name possessed her. She paced aimlessly, examined books in his bookcase, read the fine print on his framed diplomas, pulled the heavy gold drapes aside, and glanced out the window.

"It's going to snow," she said, and for some reason beyond rational explanation, the thought of snow made her happy.

"Sit down, Elizabeth," Dr. Abernathy said quietly.

"I can't," she said, and it was nothing but the truth. "I have to go." She leaned her forehead against the cold windowpane, peered at something, peered intently for a long, silent moment, and then she chuckled, a soft, throaty chuckle.

"Elizabeth!" The doctor's voice was sharp, almost cutting, and it held a fine point of panic. "What is it? What do you see?"

"What do you want me to see?" she answered, turning to face him, her pale eyes silvery with inner fire, her face aglow with secret knowledge. "Do you want me to say it's Barry? That he's waiting for me in the rose garden?"

"Barry is only a character in Lolly Horn's novel," he said. "And you know perfectly well he isn't real."

"Do I?" she asked, chuckling again.

Dr. Abernathy stood, came to where she stood, looked over her shoulder, out through the window. "There's no one out there," he said.

"Did I say there was?"

"Elizabeth, you...."

"Read the pages I gave you," she said, "and then we can talk about Barry and other things." She stepped around him and started toward the door to the hall.

"You can't just walk out when...."

Edgar's mad wife pointed to the clock on the wall behind the dedicated doctor's desk. "My time is up, and I have to go," she said, laughter hiding in her voice, peeking like quicksilver from her eyes. "Nurse Chatsworth is waiting in the lobby with my coat and scarf. It's time for our walk."

"Yes, but...."

She paused with one hand on the doorknob, looked back over her shoulder. "But what, Dr. Abernathy? Are you really trying to keep me from going out to meet a character from a novel, a figment of my aberration?"

Chapter Twenty

♥   ♥   ♥

"Elizabeth, I...."

"Yes, Doctor?" Her voice was demure, innocent, but the scarcely concealed laughter in her
eyes waited for him to refuse to allow her to go,
admit he was giving credence to her words, that
he doubted her insanity.

He drew back, stopped his protest before he
allowed her to make a complete fool of him, and
said, rather gruffly and with sparks of anger
burning the weariness from his eyes, "Go on.
Take your walk. We can talk later."

She grinned at him. "I'll bring you a snowball."

"It isn't snowing, Elizabeth."

Elizabeth laughed as she closed his office door.
And she was still laughing softly when she
reached the lobby, looked around, spied Ellen
Chatsworth, and walked across the large room to
where Ellen sat, reading intently, turning the
pages of the manuscript photocopy Elizabeth had
made and given to her. She was oblivious to her

charge, the room, the universe, lost in a land Elizabeth had fashioned of ink and imagination.

Touching the other woman's shoulder, Elizabeth said, "I'm ready."

Ellen mumbled something.

Chuckling, Elizabeth shook the younger woman and said, "Ah, come on, Nurse Chatsworth. It's my walky time."

Marking her place with the tip of her forefinger, Ellen looked at Elizabeth blankly for a moment and then said, "Oh, I guess I was.... Elizabeth, this is good. Very good. Did it really happen?"

"I told you I was writing a novel, a mystery I think," Elizabeth answered as she picked up her calf-length, gray wool coat, pulled it on, tucked a plaid scarf around her throat, and buttoned the front of the coat.

"Be serious."

"I am serious, and the mystery is, of course, whether Elizabeth is mad, or is she just playing a part to...." Suddenly her laughter was gone, buried beneath the restlessness that gripped her again, the urgent need to be somewhere other than where she was, the need to be outside the building, to walk to meet the approaching storm.

"Hurry," she said. "Hurry, Ellen."

The other woman squared the stack of manuscript pages carefully, stood, holding the stack out before her, and walked with Elizabeth to the stairwell and down the steps to the daylight basement, all without saying another word. At the outer door, Ellen hesitated and then said, very quietly, "Elizabeth ought to dump Edgar."

"Oh," Elizabeth said, cocking her head to one side as if in deep thought, "do you really think so? I considered killing him off, but he is her husband. I mean the book has to have a happy ending. How would it look if she…?"

"The man's a card-carrying louse. Get rid of him and give her someone else."

Elizabeth's silvery eyes were luminous and her laugh had a heated breathless sound. "A lover?"

"Yes, that would be a perfect…." Ellen came to herself with a start. "It was so good, I forgot. This is part of your 'Life-Notes.' I'm sorry. I had no right to…. Oh, Elizabeth, I am so sorry."

"Why would you be sorry?" Elizabeth asked. "I thought we were discussing the work, the disposition of a rather unsavory character. I told you these are pages from Lolly's new novel." She pushed open the door and stepped out into the chill of late afternoon.

The cold surged into the building, wrapped around Ellen. She shivered. "You go on," she said slowly, looking at Elizabeth as if she were trying to unravel a puzzling tangle.

"Are you sure?"

"Yes, I… I need time to think about something." She held up the typed pages. "I want to finish reading this."

"Okay." Elizabeth gave her a half-salute and turned to face the wind, breathing deep, smelling snow and violets, and set forth, walking briskly, eagerly, to meet with destiny.

It was more than passing strange, the feeling that held her, that all things were rushing into place, following some preordained path, and she was rushing with the rest, that the future was now, and was immutable, unchangeable. Elizabeth wasn't afraid. She lifted her head, felt the kiss of winter like an omen, as a tiny snowflake, the first to fall, melted on her face. She smiled as her feet found the walk and moved forward, carrying her into what-had-to-be without a qualm, a quiver, or a complaint.

Lured and laved by anticipatory delight, she didn't know how long she had walked, or even where she was, when she first heard the snipping sound. The snowflakes were fat, fluffy, and falling fast, streaking down her glasses, frosting her hair, turning her world into a place of blurs and shadows, falling snow and a man, a faceless, shadow man who waited for her. And snipped as he waited.

"What on earth are you doing?" she asked. Although the question was totally inappropriate, she asked it anyway, and felt not the slightest bit of surprise when a male voice, a deep, familiar male voice answered, "Pruning."

"Snow flowers?"

"What else?"

"This has to be the rose garden," she said, delight adding a lilt to her words. "A rose by any other...."

He laughed and came toward her. "Hello, love," he said when he stood before her. "Have you been waiting long?"

"For what?"

"A partner in madness?"

"Six days," she said aloud, but something deep within her whispered, "Forever."

He was standing very close, so close her heart forgot to beat and then had to leap high and run madly to catch up, so close her breath tied knots in itself and made her giddy.

His hands, shadows to her seeing, reached out, brushed the coating of snow from her hair and replaced it with a knitted wool cap, which he pulled warm and snug from his own head. When it was cozy around her ears, he brushed her cheek with his fingertips. "Hello, love," he said again, softer and huskier than before, and then he opened his arms.

She accepted his unspoken invitation without guilt or regret, stepped into his embrace like a child going home after a long, weary day in the company of a stranger, and said, "Hello, Barry."

"Wrong book, love," he said, his arms enfolding her, holding her safe against his heart.

He was taller than she, her head coming just

past his chin. She tilted her face up, trying to see him, but the falling snow settled thick on her glasses, making her even more blind. "Of course," she said. "Of course this is the wrong book for Barry. I beg your pardon."

"After eight or ten books, you'll get the hang of it."

"True, but if one is planning on indulging in this sort of thing, one should learn to keep one's heroes straight."

"Quite so, love."

"Hello, Harry," she whispered, and his name was almost lost when his lips touched hers, melting the flakes of snow that tried to keep them apart, tried to keep Elizabeth Gilmartin pure, unsullied by love, or partners in madness, or delusions.

When the kiss was done, the man and woman talked of madness and court orders, manuscripts and Cass, Sessions Publications and deadlines. When their plans were made, and her new red cap was white with snow, Harry, holding her close and warm against his side, walked his love back to her yellow brick mansion, kissed the tip of her cold nose, and said, "Write quickly, love."

"And you?"

"I'll be here when you need me," he said, and his laughter, soft and deep, warmed her entire body, a fact that caused her no shame.

"Of course you will," Elizabeth said. "Heroes are always there when they're needed."

Harry laughed again before he stepped back into the shadowy blur of her unseen world and was gone.

Elizabeth's lips were pink and soft and her eyes were starred with wonder when she walked across the flagstones and entered Harmony House, stopping just inside the door to wipe her glasses clean and dry with a tissue.

"Where have you been?"

Dr. Abernathy's harsh question startled her, jarred her out of the dream, jerked her out of the stream of inevitability, left her bewildered. The floor seemed to sway beneath her feet, and red flushed her cold face. Drawing a quick breath, she steadied herself with a hand against the wall. A trembling started somewhere within her, but her voice was calm, and it held nothing but truth, when she said, "Walking."

"In a snow storm for almost two hours? Elizabeth, we are not fools. Where have you been?"

"Walking," she said again, and then she smiled. "I did stop in the rose garden for a short time."

"Elizabeth, what you did was irresponsible. I was gravely concerned."

She looked at him, shifted her gaze, looked beyond him to where Ellen Chatsworth was standing. Ellen's face was white and pinched-looking, but her eyes were fixed on Elizabeth's cap like she had seen a miracle. And her voice was a scared-rabbit squeal when she asked, "Where did you get...?"

The snow on her head was melting, dribbling down her face. Elizabeth reached up, pulled off the knitted cap of cardinal, shook it free of snow, ice, and water. "It's pretty, isn't it? Harry gave it to me," she said, smiling at the doctor and Miss Chatsworth alike.

"Harry who?"

The disbelief in the doctor's voice grated on her wonderment, made her perverse. "You should know, Doctor. He's your gardener, or grounds keeper, or whatever you call him. The man who prunes the roses."

"There is no such person."

She smiled, the forgiving smile of a woman who sees folly.

"No, my dear, no," Dr. Abernathy said gently. "There was no Harry pruning the roses. That, too, is part of your delusion. The roses are frosted and bare of bloom and leaf, and it isn't the proper time to prune them. Furthermore, there is no one in my employ whose name is Harry. No patients by that name. We have had no visitors today. There can't have been a Harry in the rose garden—except in your mind, of course."

"The cap," Ellen Chatsworth said calmly and with great self-possession. "Surely that has to prove something. I'll swear, on anything you hold sacred, that Elizabeth did not have it with her when she left this building earlier."

"Be rational, Miss Chatsworth. That proves absolutely nothing. She could have gotten it anywhere."

His tone was kind, almost patronizingly paternal, but Elizabeth, as she unbuttoned her wet coat and slid out of it, detected an under note of anger directed at Ellen Chatsworth. She had only seconds to wonder at its cause.

"I've tried to tell you," Ellen said, "if you'd just listen to Elizabeth instead of that... Edgar, you'd know she's telling the truth about everything. She wrote *A Touch of Fornication*. Elizabeth Gilmartin is Lolly Horn."

"Nonsense! Complete and total nonsense! It's a delusion. Remarkable in its completeness, but nevertheless, it is only a delusion, and just as soon as I can uncover the triggering cause, Elizabeth Gilmartin will be cured of her absurd belief she is Lolly Horn and can go back to being Edgar's wife." His glare included Elizabeth. "And this Harry business is part of the delusion, too."

"Fortunately, Harry doesn't think so," Elizabeth said through her stifled laughter.

"Neither do I," Ellen snapped. She came over to where Elizabeth was standing, took the wet coat and scarf and hung them on a rack over the hot air register. "If you're ready, we'll go up to the top floor."

"Okay, but I thought you went home earlier

than this," Elizabeth said. The shining river of inevitability was, once again, her captor, and it seemed only right and proper when Ellen Chatsworth said, "I'm spending the night. Your freak snow storm made a mess of the roads—no one can leave."

Elizabeth smiled.

"Come on," Ellen said. "I want to look through your 'Life-Notes' again and see if I can't find some way to prove *Doctor* is wrong."

Snorting, Dr. Abernathy raked a hand through his rusty locks, setting his halo atilt, and said, "Miss Chatsworth, you were hired because you were judged to be competent to give remedial instruction in the writing field, not because you are competent to recognize mental stability. If you wish to continue working here, your conversations with Mrs. Gilmartin will be limited to your area of expertise and other ordinary remarks. If you feel you cannot obey me in this matter, then I shall, with a great deal of regret, be forced to give you notice."

"But Doctor Abernathy, couldn't you just compare her 'Life-Notes' and *Fornication?* The writing style is identical. And then if you'd just follow the clues and listen to Elizabeth instead of that... that...."

"What you say is well and good, Miss Chatsworth, but may I, once again, remind you that Mrs. Gilmartin is a patient here, a patient in a mental institution. You've been with us for several years, in that time you must have learned that our patients are not.... Well, not terribly reliable."

"A madwoman's tale can't be believed nor her words trusted," Elizabeth said.

"Precisely," the doctor said. "And that is one of the reasons they are patients here."

Elizabeth's laughter, musical as leaping cascades of water, spilled and ran, filling the space around them with amusement, total amusement. She was still laughing when she climbed a single flight of stairs, went to the office reserved for her use, and began to write rapidly, covering page after page before she locked her writing safely away and went up to her room to shower and don a heavy robe before she went, late and alone, to the warm, steamy sauna.

The snow melted to slush and patchy white splotches under trees and in shady spots, but the skies stayed dark, and the wind whimpered and slunk around the outside of Harmony House, begging to come in. It snowed again. Melted. Snowed, drifted. Snowed again.

Elizabeth, with Ellen as a friendly watchdog, walked every afternoon, but only for exercise, only to get the writing kinks out of her body and mind, freeing her to write anew, write at a feverish pace.

She photocopied her work at the end of each chapter, giving copies to Dr. Abernathy and Ellen, leaving a single copy in the bookcase outside the sauna door for someone else, someone who might be a delusion, or someone who might be sending the manuscript pages to Lolly's editor at Sessions Publications.

The days passed, slid one into another without ripples or haste. Elizabeth wrote pages and pages of scenes and exposition, including Edgar's first attack of passion in two years. Ellen read the account and muttered, "Damn him, he had no right to treat her like that."

"It's only a story, Ellen," Elizabeth said, and then Lolly, ever the author, asked, "Do you think the lust scene was out of character for Edgar? Do you think I overwrote the lust-in-the-kitchen bit?"

"No," Ellen said after considering a moment. "The man's a rotter, but he does have passions. He was excited about something else, and Elizabeth was just handy, I think." She tapped her thumbnail against her teeth. "He doesn't love her. He's just using her to further himself. Is she going to stay with him?"

"I don't know for sure," Lolly said. "Perhaps a hero will rescue her. Perhaps she is truly and completely mad and will spend the rest of her days in a madhouse. And, perhaps, it really is just a delusion and the dedicated doctor will find a cure and they'll all live...."

"Nonsense!" Ellen snapped.

Elizabeth laughed.

♥   ♥   ♥

She laughed again days later when Dr. Abernathy questioned her about Edgar's impotence and told her the man in the sea cave and the man in the rose garden were both delusions and both represented her own lost sexuality.

"Oh, it isn't lost," she said in the midst of her laughter. "I still have my sexuality. I just don't have anyone to be sexual with... unless, of course, I take a lover. Is that your suggestion?"

He was a learned man and he wasn't angry, but when he looked at her, the weariness in his greenish-brown eyes had grown a little more. He sighed, and his voice was very soft, very gentle, when he said, "You've been here almost four weeks. Don't you think it's time to see your husband?"

"No."

"I realize you are still hurt by his actions, but he.... Elizabeth, couldn't you relent just a little and try to see the situation from his point of view. He was trying to take care of you. He wants to.... He, or his secretary acting in his behalf, has called every single day since you have been a guest here. He loves you."

"No, he loves his image in the eyes of the world.

If he could dump me without anyone knowing, he'd do it in a second. I feel the same about him —and I will dump him just as soon as I can get to an attorney and sign the papers."

"Please, Elizabeth. He's...."

"No," she said again. "I will not see Edgar Gilmartin." Her face was smooth, untroubled, but her voice had the flatness of cold finality.

The dedicated doctor plowed his rusty halo with impatient fingers and sighed as he tried a new tact. "Your 'Life-Notes' are among the most interesting I have ever read, but there's something missing. Something traumatic. Something you are hiding even from yourself. I have to know what it is, Elizabeth. I have to."

Compassion was plain in the paleness of her eyes when she looked at him, but the slender woman neither tried to avoid his begging gaze nor offered any suggestions.

"May I give a copy of your 'Life-Notes' to Edgar?"

"Why?"

"Perhaps he can supply the missing information, and, if not, then he will, at the very least, know how deep-seated and all-inclusive your delusion is."

She shrugged. "Do what you think is best," she said, "but he probably will just give it to Ms. Marshall to burn."

"Don't, Elizabeth."

"Don't what, Dr. Abernathy? Don't be angry because my dear husband destroyed two hundred pages of manuscript and then dumped me in your cozy, little madhouse? Oh, I forgot he had his tame doctor drug me first and then he dumped me. I'm mad, so I've lost the right to feel anger and say bad things about my kind, loving husband and his lovely young secretary? Even though the man who swore to love, honor, and cherish me condemned me without a hearing, refused to even listen to the truth?"

"Edgar cares about you," the doctor said quietly, "and this whole business has upset him very much."

"Oh, poor Edgar," she said, sarcasm dripping like venom from her tongue. "I'm locked up, and he's upset? Oh, my, he does have my deepest sympathy."

"Elizabeth, you know he cares."

"Edgar Gilmartin cares about Edgar Gilmartin, and that's it," she said flatly. "He is, as Cass says, a selfish bastard, and the self he cares about is his own."

The storm was dying, but snow still swirled outside the window, and the wind moaned and wept, but neither the man nor the woman heard or saw. They were caught in the web of predestination and had to play their scene to its end.

The doctor fiddled with the papers on his desk, reducing semi-order to semi-chaos, cleared his throat, tented his fingers, leaned back in his heavy, leather chair, and stared sightlessly into the middle distance for a long time before he said, "I called Mrs. Caspar about you."

Surprise at his almost belief tinted her words, made them sound eager, "Edythe? Why?"

"In your 'Life-Notes' you said she knew you were Lolly Horn."

Elizabeth corrected him. "No. In Lolly's new novel, she said Edythe Caspar accused Elizabeth of being Lolly Horn."

His lips tightened momentarily, but his eyes remained fixed on the distance midway between delusion and truth, but his voice was only tired when he said, "Miss Chatsworth is so convinced you are Lolly Horn I had to.... Elizabeth, I want to believe you, I tried to.... If there is any proof, just the tiniest bit, I'd...." He shook his head. "Mrs. Caspar was very upset to learn Edgar had placed you in my keeping. She refused to believe you are deranged. And, she denied, completely, that you are Lolly Horn."

"She's a good friend," Elizabeth said, pushing the words around the lump of love that had formed in her throat. "A far better friend than I knew."

"No. She could have confirmed your story, set you free, instead she confirmed my diagnosis, made me more certain than ever that it is all a delusion, a delusion that shelters you from some very painful truth."

"Maybe, but don't you see? Edythe is a woman of integrity and she cared enough about me to keep my secret against all odds. That makes her dear, very dear."

Elizabeth stood up. "If that's all for today, I'd like to write some before dinner. The novel is almost finished and...." As she talked, she walked to the door that connected his office with the one she used for writing.

"It isn't all." He swiveled his chair, stood, faced her. "Time is running out, Elizabeth."

There was an urgency in his voice that halted her, made her turn, look back, but her own driving need kept her hand on the doorknob.

"If we don't find the answer... Edgar's second court order will be for ninety days, and the one after that for a year. Please, Elizabeth, look deep, tell me what I need to know. You don't belong here, I know that."

"Where do I belong?"

He didn't answer her question. He said, "Help me cure you, Elizabeth."

"Why? So I can go back to being Edgar's meek, obedient slave?" The bitterness and anger in her voice were very real, real enough to darken her eyes, harshen her voice. "So dear, dear Edgar can take my services as cook and housekeeper like he took my...."

"Took your what, Elizabeth?" The doctor's question was only a thread of sound, a small,

pitiful thing that needed instant care and tending
only she could give.

Without acknowledging its existence, she let it
die in the space between them—let it die untended,
unanswered. She looked at him over the body and
said, with a smile both innocent and real, "Lolly's
book is almost finished and she needs a happy
ending. Since you are the dedicated doctor, a
miracle cure would be nice."

His weariness was as real as her smile. He
stood and watched in silence as she walked into
the adjoining room and pulled the door shut
behind her.

♥   ♥   ♥

Elizabeth, too, knew the pressure of time, and
if, for a completely different reason, knew it better
than the doctor. She, or rather Lolly, had to get the
book finished before time ran out, before.... She
didn't know before what, but it pushed at her,
prodded her, and said, "Hurry. Hurry. Hurry,
before it's too late."

The feeling of endings, of uncharted futures
looming too close, persisted, as she finished
chapter twenty, working at a furious pace through
the dinner hour and on into the evening. And
when it was done, she straightened her back,
twisting from side to side to loosen muscles
cramped by typing and concentration, before she

made copies, putting the original in the drawer and locking it away, placing one copy on Dr. Abernathy's desk, and carrying two copies with her up the stair, one for Ellen, and one for the man who might not exist outside the confines of her own mind.

Showered and perfumed, body swathed in an extra-large towel and wrapped in a heavy, hooded robe, wearing floppy slippers on her feet, she was carrying only one copy when she walked back down the stair to the sauna, walked in shadow and light with eyes unglassed and dreaming.

Pausing at the large window that over-looked the courtyard, she tried to see the snow-covered landscape, a moonlit landscape that was a pewter and silver abstraction to her seeing, and so beautiful it ached in her throat, made her heart beat a little faster.

The ache was still there when she put the pages in their usual hiding place and hung her robe on one of the hooks outside the sauna door. She walked into the warm shadows, climbed to the topmost row of benches and sat down, leaning back against the wall, letting the billows of steam lave her and cuddle her, filling her with languor.

Her eyes closed. The ache of beauty and feeling of endings joined, and out of their joining came, from a place beyond thought, joyful, breathless anticipation. Maiden-shy, woman-wise, Elizabeth Gilmartin waited for what-would-be.

She wasn't disappointed when a deep male voice said, "Hello, love," and strong, tender hands lifted hers and put something cold and round into her cupped palms.

Her fingers recognized the object. Her laughter was chimes in the wind. "And he tempted her with an apple," she said softly.

Chapter Twenty-One

♥ ♥ ♥

The apple was cold and solid in Elizabeth's slim, long-fingered hands, and Harry, if, indeed, he even existed, was there, standing before her, a hero conjured live and whole from a dream of need and wanting. Her dream. But the woman couldn't see him. He was her love, but he was still only a dark, unfocused shape in the sauna's shifting billow of steam.

The shadow grew, loomed, bent over her, tilted her chin up until his lips could touch hers. And when the kiss was done, he said, in a voice warm and gentle with teasing, "And are you tempted, love?"

She turned the apple in her hands, tried to find sweet words to fill the moment of steamy silence, but there were no nice sweet words left, there was only the throb of honesty. "Yes," she said.

"Will you fall?"

"I don't know," she said.

His teasing drawl was just as warm, just as deeply gentle, but there was a hint of something underlining his words, a something she couldn't quite name, a simple something that might have been admiration and respect.

"Perhaps this will help, love." He set a basket at her feet and fumbled within its confines for a moment before he straightened slightly and then sat, his bare shoulder touching hers, on the bench beside her—the topmost bench in the shadowy sauna in the very bowels of a madhouse.

She smiled as she heard the clink of glass against glass, and felt again the sense of rightness and of endings. He took the apple from her fingers and replaced it with a stemmed wineglass. And that, too, was right, was a part of what-would-be. She smiled dreamily, let the heated steam bead on her skin, shield her from sneak attacks of doubt, or shame, or guilt.

Her smiled deepened, changed subtly, became less a dream and more of the moment, a moment to be treasured, when the faceless man, his crisply curling hair dewed by fragments of steamy light, looked down at her, said, "Here, love," and poured chilled liquid into her glass and his own.

Their twin glasses chimed, and he asked, softly, "To us?"

"To us," she agreed, lifting her glass, drinking deep of the nectar there—a love potion brewed of silver moonlight and golden summer days and fields of violets and starshine and laughter. A magical nectar made for love and lovers.

Elizabeth, not Lolly, knew it for what it was and drank freely, drank until the fragile glass was emptied and held it out for more.

She took another sip without speaking, looking up at him with blind silver eyes, and held the liquid in her mouth for an instant, letting it transport her, for that tiny space of time, to a hidden sea cave on the shore of a dark and mourning sea.

He said something she didn't quite hear, but it was enough to return her to the sauna's steam and heat, make her ask, lazily, "What?" before she took another swallow of nectar. Her laugh was breathless, throaty—in one of Lolly's books it would have been described as husky with desire—and her voice was nearly the same when she said, "Mad. Totally mad."

"Perhaps," he said. "Or perhaps we are only two writers caught in the tangling madness of our own words, words that make up the final chapter of a new and unread book." He paused a moment, brushed steamy moisture from her lips with his forefinger, and his voice was very quiet, very deep, but strangely shy, almost fearful when he said, "Or perhaps we are only two people in love."

"You're in love with me? Really in love?" she asked, and surprise gave way to wonder, making her sound unsure, oddly vulnerable.

"Would you have it so?" Rippling like a bright banner in a flower-scented breeze, his question hung in the hot steam and demanded an answer, an honest answer.

Again the feeling of inevitability filled her and she asked her own question, a question that had to be answered before she could answer his. "Who am I?"

"You are you," he said softly, his finger tracing little circles on her shoulder. "You are yesterday and tomorrow. You are raindrops and puppies. You are my heart and my...."

His words sounded beautiful, romantic, the words appropriate to a swain, but they weren't what she wanted, and they weren't enough. "No," she said, "name me."

The laughter was gone from his deep drawl when he answered, "No, love, that book is done, or nearly so. Time is almost gone; this is our final chapter. You must name yourself and, be it madness, revenge, freedom, fame, or a return to slavery, you must choose your own path and be who *you* are."

His words cut deep, released old hurts, old angers, and she met them face to face and knew them all. The silence, twisting and writhing like an imprisoned wild thing, held its breath and waited for her to speak, to proclaim her identity. The slim woman no longer hid in nondescript and pale wifery. She untucked the thick, concealing towel, stood, nude and straight, before the unseen man, and said quietly, "I am Elizabeth Gilmartin."

His *question* was a whisper of sound. "And your path?"

"I am Lolly Horn. I wrote *A Touch of Fornication*. I am writing this book. I am sane — or reasonably so," she said, and her voice was music, and laughter, a truth set free to roam the world — truth a madhouse couldn't contain, couldn't keep from the world. "And what I have written for the good doctor is true, or near enough."

Still faceless, still a shadow to her seeing, he stood, facing her. "And my love?" His question was soft, gentle, but urgent.

There was no hesitation, no coyness in her voice when she asked, "Would you have it so?"

"God, yes," he said, the words tickling across her face as he kissed her.

She pulled away, said, shakily, "I can't do a lust scene."

"Lolly's publisher might want one here," he murmured.

"I can't do this."

"Because you're still married?" he asked. There was real attentiveness in his voice, and real love.

"Because this is real. Because we're not panting lovers in one of Lolly's books, and because..." she laughed, "I have to write this chapter for Dr. Abernathy, and I can't."

"Since this is the first time you have taken a lover," he paused, chuckled, "a certain amount of shyness and decorum should be expected, don't you think?"

"Yes, but...."

"Remember the old movies? A slow fade to black when things became, shall we say, heated?"

Her laughter was soft and quickly silenced. Later, she said, "I want you."

"And I want you, Elizabeth," he said softly. "But not in here, not in the cellar of a madhouse." He kissed her again before he pulled her up.

"Out in the snow?" she asked. "You must be as crazy as I am."

Laughing, the man and the woman, in their aspect of moon deities, walked, long-legged and naked, out into the night. He drew her down in the silvery snow, snow that melted and ran when the god knew, in the biblical sense, his goddess, knew her well and truly.

And it was good.

It was still good the next morning when the steady drip of melting snow pulled her into the day. Nude and alone in her bed, she postponed the moment that would send the warm memories into hiding. She smiled, a woman's secret smile, when she stretched, feeling the tingle of soreness in a body unused to the ways of love.

"Heroes," she said softly, fondly, before time, too swift in its passage, caught her up in its flurry, jerked her out of her nest of memories and pushed her into the cold reality of the day—a day that had to see chapter twenty of the book written; and did.

Time hurried her into the day beyond, one of the final days, with urgency and endings shackling her, impeding her movements, constraining her, forcing her to do what had-to-be. The beginning of chapter twenty-one, the very private love scene was sketched in, and then, feeling curiously incomplete, she waited, poised on the brink, ready to take the final headlong dive into inevitability.

It seemed that she hung, suspended, in some airless place of waiting, the place of answers, of knot tying, explanations, and endings. She couldn't draw air into her lungs, and suddenly she was afraid, terribly afraid. Afraid Edgar was right, she was really and truly mad, afraid she was only Elizabeth Jane Gilmartin, doomed to be a house slave all the rest of her life.

"Mad," drummed her heart. "Mad," screamed the sweat soaking her drab garments. "Mad. Only mad."

"No," Lolly whispered, but her voice was too soft to drown out the manic chorus, too weak to stem the panic, too late to stop Elizabeth's charge out the door and down the stair, too late to make her know that walking now was real folly, too late to do more than whisper, "Denouement. Elizabeth, running won't change it. If you are mad, then so be it. A madhouse is not such a terrible place to be."

The woman listened, stopped in the flagstoned

courtyard, stood for less than a moment, and then turned back to climb the stair.

Ellen awaited her in the main lobby, a flustered, excited Ellen who grabbed Elizabeth and hustled her down the empty corridor toward the doctor's office. "Hurry," she said in a harsh whisper, "he's here."

"Who?" Elizabeth asked, but she answered her own question with another. "Edgar?"

Nodding briefly, Ellen pulled her rapidly toward the end of the hall, halting outside the office set aside for Elizabeth and saying, "I'm supposed to take you out of the building, keep you away until he's gone, but I will not let the two of them railroad you again. I fixed it so you can hear every word they say. Just be quiet." She turned the doorknob with great care and led her into the darkened room.

Pale, almost ghostly, light filtered through the drawn blinds, but it was enough light for Elizabeth to see the finger on Ellen's lips. Her finger moved down to point to the door into Dr. Abernathy's office that stood ever so slightly ajar.

Tense with anticipation, her eyes aglow, Elizabeth, silent as a padding cat, a wild and wonderful beast, not a tame housecat, walked forward until the murmur of male voices resolved itself into words she could understand; words from a man about his wife, his cruel and inconsiderate housewife.

Ellen touched Elizabeth's stiff arm, motioned toward the floor, and, providing a visual aid for her gesture, sank down to sit on the thick carpet, patting a place beside her in invitation.

Elizabeth shook her head without looking down. The sense of endings pressed hot around her, sweated her body, shortened her breath, made her move even closer to the door, close enough to hear Dr. Abernathy ask, "Have you had time to read all of Elizabeth's 'Life-Notes?'"

Her husband's voice answered, but it was a voice that sounded strangely unfamiliar, almost ugly in its harsh anger, anger strongly laced with self-pity. "Yes, Dr. Abernathy, I have, and the woman is far sicker than I thought, probably sicker than any of us thought."

"Oh?" the doctor said, or rather intoned, and the listening madwoman could almost see him leaning back in his big chair, tenting his fingers, looking terribly interested. "What makes you say that?"

"This!"

The woman heard the rustle of paper and assumed Edgar was waving the manuscript of Lolly's new book. "This filthy nonsense she wrote.... It's not true."

"None of it?"

"Well, no. But it's only partly true. Fact and fiction are all jumbled together. It's hard to separate the truth from...."

"Try, Edgar," the doctor said softly. "Anything you can pull out as fact may help me cure your wife."

"Well, for one thing, regardless of what she says here, Elizabeth was never just a housewife. Although I practically begged her for years to stay at home and be my wife. It just wasn't right.... I'm sure you'll agree with me on this. It doesn't look right for a man in my position to have a wife out grubbing in the muck to bring in money. My clients can't help but think I'm not a good financial planner if I can't make enough to support my own wife. It looks bad, I tell you, and she damned well knows it."

Old grievances whined in his voice, and old angers joined the chorus, but they left Elizabeth untouched, roused no guilt, no love, nothing.

Quietly but firmly, the doctor said, "Edgar, you are a valued friend, and of course your feelings are important, but Elizabeth is my patient and my first concern at the moment."

"Well, yes, I suppose she...." Edgar started to agree, but his anger refused to accept anything but its own path. "This whole thing has upset me so much it is even affecting my work. I can't allow a silly woman's problems to...."

"Edgar?"

"My irritation does stem from what I... Sigmund, Elizabeth has always worked—petty little jobs that didn't pay much or require many

skills. Oh, I'd be the first to admit it was necessary in the early years of our marriage—when I
was finishing grad school and getting established
in the financial community. But then it would
have looked much better if she had...."

He hesitated, and the creak of his chair was
loud in the silence before he cleared his throat and
continued. "About ten or eleven years ago, she
was a clerk in the Book Nook, the big bookstore
on Grant Street. The owners decided to sell it, and
Elizabeth, without heeding my advice, or even
asking my permission, borrowed the down payment from her rich-bitch friend, the Widow Bates.
However, the bank, my bank, called me and they
refused to finance the purchase unless the contract
was in my name."

The chair creaked again, and the sound
swelled, becoming the knell of doom to the listening woman. She held her breath, trying to hold
back the words her husband was going to say,
words that would return her to nondescript and
mundane. Wishing and breath-holding wasn't
enough.

"Surprisingly, it was a good investment at first.
The property was rundown and Elizabeth was
forced to do a lot of repair work, pay off her loan
from the widow, and then she did some remodel-
ing. The deductions were wonderful until....
Well, I can't imagine how because she isn't very
bright, but somehow Elizabeth managed to make

the bookstore into a growing concern, one that was making considerable profits. Naturally, in my tax bracket, I couldn't allow that."

He went on, explaining, but Elizabeth didn't hear him, couldn't hear him. An ache swelled in her eyes, roared like the winds of winter in her ears, and almost forced her to her knees. Elizabeth's hands curled into fists, which rose slowly, and pressed hard against the pain that filled her chest. Awful anger, terrible grief she had kept bound until that moment, but they were her own, and she knew them now.

She stood tall, like a woman being burned at the stake, and some force greater than her pain held her in silence, made her listen and wait until all the hidden secrets were unveiled and she could write "finis" to Lolly's book.

"And so?" Dr. Abernathy asked softly, so softly it was scarcely more than an expelled breath, a breath of doctorly dedication.

"I did the wisest thing possible. I sold the Book Nook."

"When was that?"

"Just about a year before she went to that damned writers' conference. I shouldn't have allowed her to attend that. I knew it was probably a mistake, but I...."

Dr. Abernathy interrupted. "What did Elizabeth say about you selling her bookstore?"

"It wasn't hers," Edgar snapped, "it was mine.

Stupid, uneducated women like Elizabeth never understand anything about business. She should never have been allowed to.... I mean, she should have been at home doing the things she does well."

"Which are?"

Elizabeth's leanly handsome husband didn't answer directly. Instead, he said, "I have a beautiful home, one of the handsomest and most expensive in Cragshome. It's the kind of home any normal woman would be proud to live in. I hired the decorator. She is the best there is." There was a trace of defensiveness in his deep voice.

"Did Elizabeth object?"

"Well, no, not exactly. To be honest, it wasn't any of her concern, so I didn't ask her. The house had to be done right and rather quickly — Elizabeth comes from a middle-class background and has no experience. The house, which I had had especially designed, was finished and James, my younger son, was getting married. His future wife, Janet, had no family of any importance, so it was an excellent opportunity to pay off some social obligations and renew business contacts.

"It was a huge wedding, and Elizabeth, some-how, planned and executed the whole affair. She still had the bookstore then and people expressed amazement she could run her business, move into a new house, and still put on a production like that—although she had very competent help from caterers and wedding consultants."

He paused, took an audible breath, and asked, "Do you think the strain of the wedding might have caused this breakdown?"

"Do you?"

"Well, perhaps, but.... She seemed all right until I told her about selling the store. Then, she went dead white and for just a moment, I was afraid of her. I thought she might.... Anyway, she just looked at me, and her eyes, Dr. Abernathy, I swear they looked dead. She said, 'You'll be sorry you did this, Edgar. You'll get a housewife, and you'll be sorry. I promise.' It was like a stranger talking."

The chair creaked again, and she heard his footsteps as he paced the floor and said, haltingly, "Doctor, this is probably a silly question, but I've thought about it a lot and.... Is it possible she did this whole crazy housewife bit to get even with me for selling the store?"

"No."

Edgar sighed. "That's what Karoline said, too. She is very sure Elizabeth is crazy."

"Karoline?"

"My secretary and best friend. I would never have been able to get through this mess without her. She is the only one who knows or cares about what this is doing to me."

"You're having an affair," the doctor said, and it wasn't a question.

"Well, yes, but you know how it is. A man has

certain needs...."

"And a woman doesn't?"

"Elizabeth, regardless of the drivel she has written, is past the age of.... A woman like her just can't satisfy a virile man like me. She should be glad I left her bed. Most women her age...."

"Elizabeth knows about Ms. Marshall."

"No, she doesn't. She keeps denying it in those silly 'Life-Notes.'"

"You said they were a blend of fact and fiction."

"She trusts me."

"No, Edgar, it's just that the affair, coming on top of all the other trauma, is something she can't face."

"Are you telling me this whole thing is my fault?"

"Not exactly, although your actions certainly contributed to her mental chaos. However, we can put that behind us. I know how to treat her now. She'll be her old self, with all delusions dead and buried, in a very short time — if, of course, you are willing to do your part."

"Yes, I.... Yes. I'll start negotiations to buy the bookstore — in her name only — and, as bad as I hate to, I'll tell Karoline good-by tonight. Of course, that means I'll have to hire a new secretary tomorrow."

Ignoring the pain in Edgar's voice, the doctor said, "Wonderful."

It was over.

Elizabeth left the door and walked to her desk as the men began the rites of leave-taking. Her anger slipped away, leaving only the rawness of new grief, and tears choked her voice when Edgar was gone and it was safe to speak.

"It's the happy ending, Ellen. Just what Lolly wanted. The dedicated doctor will come up with a last-moment miracle cure. The madwoman will be pronounced sane." She hesitated. "Should the sane woman then be united with her repentant husband?"

Ellen scrambled up from her seat on the floor, came to Elizabeth with tears streaming down her face. "Don't," she whispered. "Oh, don't."

"I'm only sorry there were no lecherous orderlies. Sessions would have liked that twist."

Elizabeth flipped on the desk light and sat down at the typewriter. She smiled, a soft, somehow innocent smile that hid a world of pain and loss. "It will be a good book, won't it?"

Ellen nodded, and quietly left the room.

Alone with her grief, Elizabeth began typing the ending to Lolly Horn's *Life Notes*.

Late that night, when the lights were out and the final chapter finished, someone knocked softly on Elizabeth's door. The soon-to-be-sane woman awoke in her narrow bed, raised her nude body on one elbow, and called, "Yes?"

"Lechery service, love," a very deep and orderly voice drawled as the door opened. "You placed an order?"

Elizabeth chuckled, perhaps a little madly.

THE END

Dear Reader,

We hope you enjoyed this LionHearted novel. I personally enjoy empowered heroes and heroines who show that integrity, persistence and love will ultimately triumph over adversity.

It takes authors with talent, imagination and a diligent and caring editorial staff to produce entertaining and memorable stories. But it also takes you! Please write and let me know what you like, and don't like, so we may continue to provide quality and entertaining stories. And, don't forget to tell a friend about us.

Thank you for choosing a LionHearted book.

Mary Ann Heathman
President & CEO
LionHearted Publishing, Inc.

About LionHearted

When forming LionHearted we discovered many things about the publishing industry that we felt could be improved. For example, due to excessively large print runs, and less than hoped for sales, over half of the paperbacks printed today are now being dumped into our landfills and oceans as waste. Yet, publishers continue to release more books each month than there is room for on store shelves.

An overabundance of titles and lack of display space has led to a shorter shelf life for most titles. Many books may come and go before the reader has an opportunity to see them. If you only visit a bookstore once a month, you've probably missed seeing hundreds of paperbacks. The result is fewer sales per title and lower author royalties. Also, many books being released today are not new titles but re-prints of old titles avid consumers have already read. There appeared to be a need for an alternative approach to the marketing and distribution of novels.

How often have you recommended a great movie, an excellent restaurant, a good book, or even a brand name you liked? All the time! But has any movie theater, restaurant, or bookstore ever reimbursed you for the highly effective "advertising" you did on their behalf?

LionHearted does! Our customers can earn free books or extra cash as a referral fee for introducing new customers. Now, telling friends about books you love can truly be rewarding. Call, email us, or visit our web site for more information.

We publish many sub-genres of romance including contemporary, historical, time-travel, Regency, comedy, suspense, intrigue, fantasy, futuristic, westerns and more.

Our customers have come to trust the LionHearted logo to offer a quality entertaining read that won't disappoint, and our authors love the creative writing freedom.

LionHearted is a reader and author friendly company, so if you would enjoy some new blending of romance sub-genres, let us know.

We encourage you to support your local and national literacy programs. One out of five adults in this country can't read, and illiteracy has been found to be the biggest link to crime. Unfortunately, many adults won't attend public reading programs because they don't want others to know they can't read. In an effort to solve this dilemma we are working on a literacy video that will teach people how to read in the privacy of their home. Let us know if you would like to participate in or contribute to this project.

Your Opinion Counts

LionHearted will send you a free gift for filling out this questionnaire and sending it to us.

1. Where did you get P.S. I've Taken A Lover?
❑ Bookstore   ❑ Online bookstore _____
❑ LionHearted ❑ Friend
❑ Other _____

2. Tell us what you liked about this book?
❑ Overall story ❑ Easy to read type size
❑ Characters   ❑ Good value for the money
❑ Other _____

3. Would you enjoy similar books? ❑ Yes ❑ No

4. Did you dislike something about this book?

_____

5. Would you buy another LionHearted book?
❑ Yes ❑ No ❑ If _____

6. What other romance genres do you read?
❑ Historical   ❑ Regency   ❑ Medieval
❑ Contemporary ❑ Future/Fantasy/Paranormal

7. Number of books you read per Wk___ Mo___

8. Which magazines do you read?

a. _____

b. _____

c. _____

9. What is your age group?

❏ Under 25   ❏ 25-34   ❏ 35-44   ❏ 45-54   ❏ 55+

10. Have you read other LionHearted books? ❏

11. Do you want info on future releases?   ❏

12. Additional comments/suggestions:

_____

_____

_____

_____

_____

_____

_____

_____

Tell us where to send your free gift
(Limited to the US & Canada, 1 per household)

Name: _____

Addrs: _____

_____

Phone: _____

Email: _____

Copy these pages and mail or fax to:
LionHearted Publishing, Inc.
P.O. Box 618, Zephyr Cove, NV 89448
888-546-6478 Phone/Fax
http://www.LionHearted.com/opinion.htm

A Fun LionHearted Contest

Answer the following questions and you could win a prize. Each month we will draw a winner and send them a gift certificate for four free LionHearted titles of their choice.

In the story you just read, what were the three alias' of Elizabeth Gilmartin?

_____

What is the name and address of your favorite bookstore that carries romance titles:

Name_____

Addrs_____

_____

Phone_____

What is your name and address:

Name_____

Addrs_____

_____

Phone_____

Email_____

Copy and mail or fax this page to:

LionHearted Publishing, Inc.

P.O. Box 618

Zephyr Cove, NV 89448

888-546-6478 Phone/Fax

http://www.LionHearted.com/contest.htm

(This contest may be terminated at any time by publisher)

LionHearted Order Form

Paperbacks:

_____	Undercover Love	$5.99	_____
_____	Destiny's Disguise	$6.99	_____
_____	Forever, My Knight	$6.99	_____
_____	Isn't It Romantic?	$6.99	_____
_____	Oracle	$6.99	_____
_____	P.S. I've Taken A Lover	$7.99	_____

Ebooks come on floppy disk in a CD case, or by email

		Email	Disk	
_____	Something In Common	$4.99	$6.99	_____
_____	Turnagain Love	$4.99	$6.99	_____
_____	Unbridled	$4.99	$6.99	_____
_____	My Captain Jack	$4.99	$6.99	_____
_____	Yesterday Once More	$4.99	$6.99	_____
_____	The Alliance	$4.99	$6.99	_____
_____	Echoes of Love	$4.99	$6.99	_____
_____	Spirit of the Heart	$4.99	$6.99	_____
_____	Outrageous	$4.99	$6.99	_____

Disk format: ❑ DOS ❑ Mac (PDF file)

Shipping is FREE in the US   Sub-Total _____

Sales Tax if purchased in Nevada   6.75% _____

I've enclosed a check, cashiers check or
money order to "LionHearted" for $ _____

_____Please tell me how I can receive referral fees.

PLEASE PRINT CLEARLY

Name _____

Addrs _____

_____

Phone _____

Email _____

Referred by:_____

Other LionHearted Books

ORACLE
Katherine Greyle

Jane Deerfield is having a bad millennia. Sucked forward in time two centuries after a cataclysmic nuclear event obliterated most of the planet, she's soon on a mission to keep the survivors from repeating mankind's mistakes. Trapped in a magical world, she didn't plan on falling in love with the man who would plunge humanity back into war.

King Daken's people are in danger of extinction by the murdering Tarveen. Desperate, he seeks an army from the Elven Lord. Jane's sudden appearance becomes more than a distraction when she gets appointed to his position on the Elven Lord's ruling council, then votes against his army. Now she's in the way, and nothing will stop Daken.

Paperback Books

ISN'T IT ROMANTIC?
Ronda Thompson

They've never met, but Katrine Summerville and Trey Westmoreland are sworn enemies. Katrine is a romance writer who, after being abandoned at the age of five, and widowed and pregnant at eighteen, doesn't believe in happily-ever-after.

Trey is a hard-nosed newspaper literary review columnist who carries the bitter taste of a failed marriage around with him along with a resentment toward romance novels, which he believes give women a warped expectation of love.

A case of mistaken identity, a night of ill-fated attraction, and their steamy moment captured on film catapults them into a nationally publicized Hell.

UNDERCOVER LOVE
Lucy Grijalva

Life in the middle class was just fine with Julia Newman. She'd fought her way out of the slums and never planned to go back. Why did she have to find Rick Peralta, her new low-life neighbor, so irresistible?

The last thing undercover cop Rick Peralta needed was a tempting, but off-limits, school teacher poking around in his business. He broke out in a sweat every time he thought about the complications. Soon Rick was sharing more than secrets with Julia, and worried that eventually she'd find herself in deeper trouble than she—or he—could handle.

FOREVER, MY KNIGHT
Lee Ann Dansby

It is 1067 and Cameron d'Aberon, a Norman knight, is in service to William. He does not need or want another wife, after his first betrayed him and caused the death of his son.

Kaela of Chaldron hates the Normans almost as much as she hates her evil and lustful Saxon cousin, Broderick. Now she is the king's ward. Cameron's duty is to escort her to court where the king will choose a husband for the spirited young heiress.

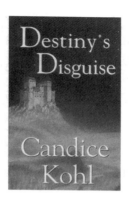

DESTINY'S DISGUISE
Candice Kohl

Lord John, the Earl of Farleigh, never expected
to inherit title or lands. He returns to England
after having fought battles as a mercenary knight,
and arranges to marry the youngest daughter of a
neighboring lord.

Lady Gweneth is the eldest daughter, a widow
bitter toward men. She vows to save her younger
sister from the warrior's hands by impersonating
her sister and marrying him herself. John doesn't
discover her lie until after the wedding.

Expecting nothing but cruelty at her husband's
hand, she is surprised to find herself the recipient
of that which she has so often given but never
received: love.

SOMETHING IN COMMON
Anita Lynn

Beth and Sam barely know each other, but they have something in common. Beth offered to carry a pregnancy for her older sister, Hollie, never expecting her sister to die and leave her pregnant with twins.

Sam thought he'd lost everything, not only his beloved wife, but his hope for a family. Then, seven months after Hollie's death, Beth contacted him asking for his help.

For the sake of the babies, they move in together. Can Sam live with Beth until the twins are born, then let her go? Will Beth fall in love with Sam and replace Hollie in his heart? If not, who gets the babies?

TURNAGAIN LOVE
Nancy Radke

Jennel Foster was stuck on the island and couldn't get off; then she clung to the island and wouldn't get off... not after she discovered that her "rescuer," handsome Zachery Waylan, wanted her to leave immediately.

Both had been hired to remodel the vacant house on Turnagain Island in Washington state, he by the husband, she by the wife. Unable to reach their employers, Zack and Jennel must settle things between themselves.

Jennel panics when she finds there is no water, electricity or telephone on the island. She accepts Zack's offer to stay aboard his sparkling clean cabin cruiser. Each tries to out-maneuver the other while denying their growing attraction. Where are the owners who started all this in the first place? And who invited the raccoons?

UNBRIDLED
Delores Fossen

Texas rancher and socialite, Adi McLaurin, gets more than she bargained for when she travels to her long lost brothers untimely funeral, and discovers she has an orphaned eight-year-old half-breed niece.

Grayson Renaux, the child's half-Choctaw uncle, lied. It was so bold a lie, it surprised him that God hadn't struck him dead. It was for her own good that Adi would never know the whole truth.

To save her family's ranch, Adi had agreed to marry a state politician. Her wedding gown was ready and the guests beginning to arrive for the week long celebration.

Her life is turned upside down when she finds herself unwittingly, but legally, bound to Grayson.

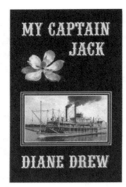

MY CAPTAIN JACK
Diane Drew

Nissa Gedhaul can't support herself and her little sister on a schoolmarm's salary. She sets aside her romantic riverboat fantasies to marry Chase Fortier, but before the wedding, Nissa is blinded by an accident.

Rafe Fortier, Chase's uncle, arrives to escort her to her intended groom, but his attraction to his nephew's blind fiancée sets him at odds with himself. To compensate for the attention he can't bestow on Nissa, he lavishes fatherly attention on her little sister, Katie.

After learning of the accident, Chase changes his mind about the wedding, Rafe is free to pursue her and he wins both their hearts.

YESTERDAY ONCE MORE
Karen Culver

The secret to eternal life is no longer a theory in the year 2188. Time travel has become common, and treacherous in the wrong hands.

Colonel Von Brockman returns from the future on a mission to find a time-traveling

pirate whose greed could be the downfall of all mankind. The key to finding his nemesis is

Alissia Prescott, who may be Lilpout's accomplice.

Alissa, a genetic scientist, is driven to discover a cure to a deadly disease that runs rampant in her family and the only thing keeping her from it is Brock. He must choose between duty and love. Alissa must decide if she can trust this mysterious man from the future, not only with the lives of millions of people, but with her own.

THE ALLIANCE
Patricia Waddell

Lord Reuel Shatar, the handsome governor of Pyrali, and it's three moons, is noble to his galactic core, and duty bound to produce the next ruler of the Alliance. If he does not succeed, then the house of Shatar will fall into disgrace. Unable to father a child with his own species, a rebellious Earthling is found to be a fertile match as his mate.

Christa Kirklan is as stubborn as her earthling heritage and as unpredictable as a cosmic storm. Faced with exile to a frigid asteroid for her treasonous dialogue, or marriage to the man who represents everything she hates, Christa reluctantly chooses marriage. She finds a way to voice her discontentment with the empire's prejudice and archaic social culture by fulfilling Reuel's desire and putting an Earthling on the future throne of the galaxy.

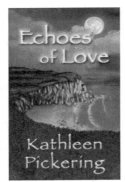

ECHOES OF LOVE
Kathleen Pickering

Melissa Ryan knew her life needed a change. But she didn't expect to inherit half of Carlisle's, New York's most prestigious auction house, along with her cousin, Mark Blaire, who hates her.

Deceit on Mark's part forces her on an ill-timed trip to England to retrieve an ancient sideboard left to her by her mother, and auctioned by Mark to the excruciatingly handsome and mysterious Ian Marshall.

Melissa learns that her sideboard was part of a tragic legend tied to Ian's estate, and that she is part of the legend of Crimson Vale from five hundred years before. But, the murderer who killed the legend's lovers centuries ago, has also returned along with the legend's... Echoes of Love.

SPIRIT OF THE HEART
Barbara Cary

Lindsay Jackson is the bridesmaid and hopelessly in love with her cousin's fiance, Kent Stuart. He is drawn to Sarah's sweet and undemanding love. But, a year earlier Kent was swept off his feet into four days of unforgettable pas-

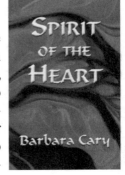

sion with Lindsay. When she didn't pursue the relationship, he moved on.

As the wedding day approaches, Lindsay and Kent realize they still love each other, but their mutual concern for Sarah keep them apart.

Neither is aware that another love, a spirit of the heart stronger than death and infinite as time has a haunting scheme of its own that will forever change destiny for both of them.

OUTRAGEOUS
Norah-Jean Perkin

The new nanny is everything Matt Erickson doesn't want for his three children. Interested only in child care, he feels the woman is too young, too eccentric, much too attractive—and worst of all, likely to take off and leave his children hurt and confused once more. Wanting stability for his kids, Matt makes her an overly generous offer for a long term commitment.

Like armor, Alix St. Germain's outrageous clothing and attitude have seen her through the tough times. She has been an outsider most of her life and hides from her past behind a cocky facade. Affronted that the widowed father thinks her too irresponsible to care for his family, she calls his bluff, and accepts his offer. Just as she realizes love might exist, her past walks in the door.

Patricia Lucas White

Patricia lives with her husband and mentally challenged daughter in the majestic Cascade Mountains of Southern Oregon. The richness and diversity of her surroundings serve as a constant inspiration, tickling her imagination, feeding her creativity, making her want to find the words to express not just what her eyes see, but also the emotional response to the snow-shrouded volcanic cinder cones and the deeply mysterious blue lakes.

She writes full-time now, but after graduating from college in 1972, she taught high school English, was a telephone operator, a grocery store clerk, and a reader for college English instructors, among other short-term jobs. An avid reader, she considers a week lost if she hasn't read at least two books — and her book shelves, where folk tales rub shoulders with histories and philosophies, give ample evidence of her far-ranging interests.

She has won several awards for her best selling novels, poetry and news writing and has been published in a wide assortment of publications but is now concentrating on fiction.

Her husband, Bill, encourages her endeavors — as do her grown sons, John and Greg and her three grandkids, Jennifer, Kelly, and Rylee. Her daughter, Terry, always "does the dishes so Mom can write on the computer." And with three unicorns perched on her monitor and a basket of teddy bears at her elbow, she does just that.